SUPERNATURAL
CRIMES UNIT:
NYPD

SELECTED BOOKS BY KEITH R.A. DeCANDIDO

THE SUPERNATURAL CRIMES UNIT: NYPD SERIES

Supernatural Crimes Unit: NYPD Book 1: *The Thin Blue Ley-Line*

THE PRECINCT SERIES

Dragon Precinct
Unicorn Precinct
Goblin Precinct
Gryphon Precinct
Tales from Dragon Precinct
Mermaid Precinct
Phoenix Precinct
Dragon Precinct Origins
Manticore Precinct (coming soon!)
More Tales from Dragon Precinct (coming soon!)

THE SUPER CITY POLICE DEPARTMENT SERIES

The Case of the Claw
Secret Identities

THE ADVENTURES OF BRAM GOLD SERIES

A Furnace Sealed
Feat of Clay

THE TALES OF CASSIE ZUKAV, WEIRDNESS MAGNET

Ragnarok and Roll
Ragnarok and a Hard Place (coming soon!)

SELECTED OTHER NOVELS

Spider-Man: Down These Mean Streets
Buffy the Vampire Slayer: Blackout
Buffy the Vampire Slayer: The Deathless
CSI: NY: Four Walls
Supernatural: Nevermore
Supernatural: Bone Key
Supernatural: Heart of the Dragon
Sleepy Hollow: Children of the Revolution
Animal (with Munish K. Batra, MD, FACS)
The Inflictors (coming soon!)

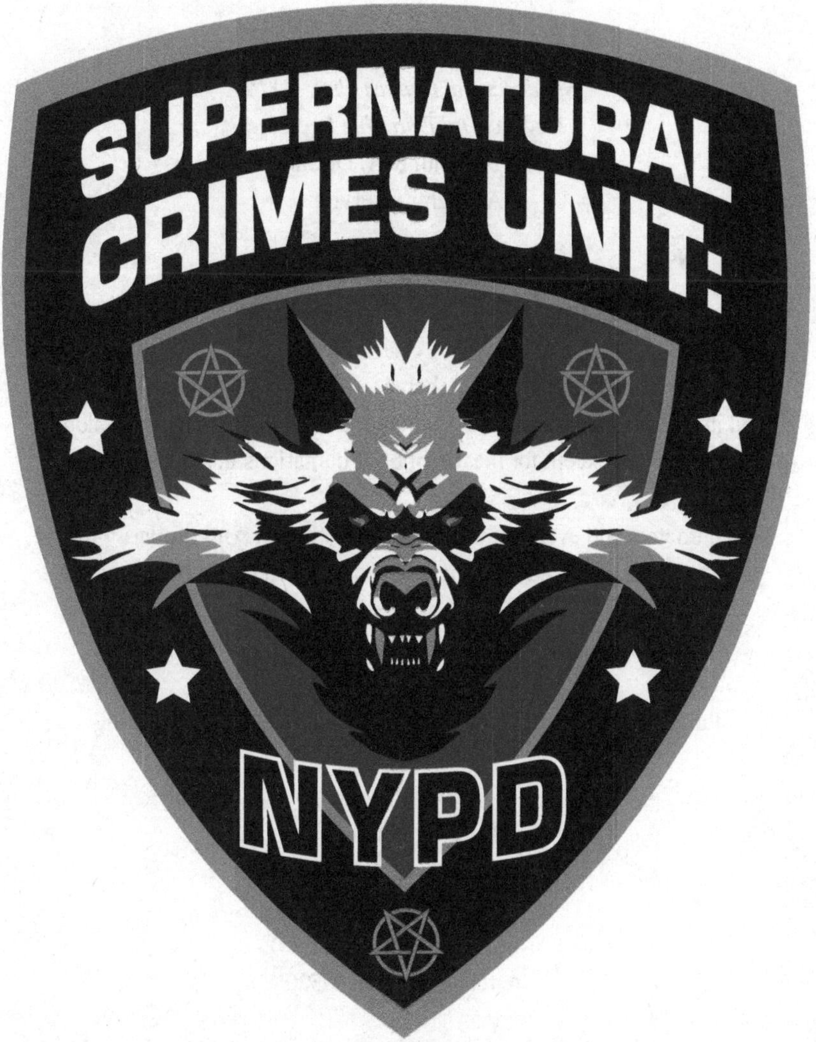

SUPERNATURAL CRIMES UNIT: NYPD

BOOK 1: THE THIN BLUE LEY-LINE

KEITH R.A. DeCANDIDO

Supernatural Crimes Unit: NYPD
Book 1: *The Thin Blue Ley-Line*

Cover illustration/design & interior design by Jeff Wong.

Published by *Weird Tales*® Presents and Blackstone Publishing.

www.WeirdTales.com
www.BlackstonePublishing.com

Blackstone Publishing
31 Mistletoe Road
Ashland, Oregon 97520

ISBN: 979-8-212-91397-3
Fiction/Science Fiction/General

Printed in the United States of America

First Edition: 2025

10 9 8 7 6 5 4 3 2 1

Dedicated to Jonathan Maberry, to whom I owe a significant amount, and who has been confidant, colleague, and collaborator for a decade-and-a-half now. Most importantly, he's a dear friend, and this book wouldn't have happened without him.

NYPD

ONE

As the slavering, hairy beast came charging out of Apartment 2W, Detective First Grade Domenica Kiernan was annoyed to realize that she was going to have to use her last silver bullet.

Her fellow member of the NYPD's Supernatural Crimes Unit, Detective Third Grade Liam Grullon, and three of the four uniformed patrol officers from the 10th Precinct who'd accompanied them on this arrest in the Chelsea neighborhood of Manhattan, moved to tackle the beast.

The hirsute creature tossed the four of them aside like they were twigs. Kiernan had *really* been hoping the shape-changing creature would come quietly. Instead, when confronted with an arrest warrant, he'd altered his appearance from a six-foot-two Russian guy wearing a T-shirt and khakis to a naked, six-foot-two, hairy beast with a snout full of teeth and elongated fingers that ended in sharp talons. He looked like every artist's rendition of a Bigfoot sighting.

The remaining patrol officer unholstered his nine-millimeter.

As she got down on one knee to get at the Sig Sauer P938 with the silver ammo in her ankle holster, Kiernan cried out, "Forget it, Grabowski—regular rounds ain't gonna cut it with a domovoy!"

Unfortunately, the domovoy saw the weapon pointed at him and leapt right at Grabowski.

Cop instincts took over, and the tiny hallway echoed with the report of Grabowski's nine. Kiernan's ears rang, and her nose was assaulted by the gunpowder smell as the PO fired four times.

Every round hit its target at center mass.

The domovoy didn't even flinch. Or slow down. Or show any signs of being wounded. Instead, he tackled Grabowski, pounding at the officer's chest with his muscular arms.

Luckily, Grabowski was wearing a vest, so the damage wasn't as bad as it would have been without it, but the domovoy's superior strength would easily splinter the Kevlar before too long.

Kiernan unholstered her backup weapon—the P938 was nicknamed a "micro-nine," as it was smaller than the usual nine-millimeter—got back on her feet and was about to fire when two of the other officers, Lin and O'Bryan, jumped onto the domovoy, spoiling her shot.

"For fuck's sake, *get outta the way*!" Kiernan yelled as she stood there, weapon gripped in both hands, waiting for the morons to move so she'd have a shot. There was only one bullet in the chamber, the last of the six silvers she'd been issued a year earlier. The department had had hell's own time finding a reliable vendor to supply the bullets in question. The first three they'd contracted didn't work out—one never delivered, one provided silver-plated bullets rather than fully silver ones, and the third had pulled out of their contract right before the delivery date.

Moore Hill, the vendor that had *finally* delivered actual silver ammunition, took forever to provide the goods. Since at last getting her share, Kiernan had had to use one on a vampire that was rampaging through Dyker Heights in Brooklyn, three on a pack of rabid werewolves in the Bronx's Pelham Bay Park, and one on a skoffin that had killed an entire family in Flushing, Queens. Which was a waste, as it turned out that skoffins weren't actually affected by silver, though it still functioned as a bullet and wounded the creature.

Out the corner of her eye, Kiernan saw that Grullon was holding the fourth officer, Maldonado, back. Grullon was relatively new to the SCU, but he'd been with the unit long enough to know what was what.

The same could not be said for the patrol officers of the One-Oh. To be fair, it was a well-honed instinct, to run to the aid of their brother in blue.

Not that she was in a rush to throw the last of her silvers. The paperwork to requisition replacements would be murder; then she'd have to wait who knew how long for Moore Hill to get their shit together.

The domovoy did the job for her, once again tossing the uniforms aside like nothing. Even better, he did it while standing up straight and spreading his long arms wide, presenting a nice big target.

Muttering a quick prayer, she squeezed the Sig's trigger, feeling the recoil through the grip.

This time, the domovoy flinched. His back arched as the silver projectile slammed into his chest, and he let out a howl that sounded like a dog in heat with its paw stepped on.

Then he collapsed onto the linoleum, curling up in a fetal position and whimpering.

"*Madonna mia*," Kiernan muttered, half-collapsing against the stucco wall of the hallway.

"Everyone okay?" Grullon asked.

Wincing in pain as he sat up on the floor, Grabowski said, "Been better." Sweat was beading on his high forehead.

Maldonado radioed in that they had arrested the suspect—even though nobody had read him his rights quite yet.

Lin climbed to his feet and indicated the domovoy with his head while regarding Kiernan with awe. "How'd you *do* that?"

"Domovoys are allergic to silver. Long as that bullet stays in his chest, he can't change shape."

Lin's face contorted into a confused frown. "How's that work, exactly?"

"Hell if I know, Lin, I just know it does."

"Aren't you curious?"

"I don't know how my car engine works either, but I still drive the thing."

Maldonado and Grullon helped Grabowski up; the latter cried out in pain as he was pulled unsteadily to his feet.

"We gotta get him checked out," Maldonado said.

Kiernan nodded. "Go. Now that he's all fetal, the four of us can handle him."

"Thanks, Detective," Maldonado replied as he led Grabowski slowly toward the staircase. Kiernan heard Grabowski raggedly report in that they were heading to Lenox Health, the nearest hospital, and also that he had discharged his weapon and that someone from the Internal Affairs Bureau should meet him there.

Grullon radioed in his and Kiernan's status, including that she had discharged her weapon, then looked at Kiernan, running a hand through his curly red hair. "I'm gonna call for transpo."

Kiernan nodded. The original plan had been for the domovoy to submit to arrest quietly. Now that he was dead weight, they'd need a wagon.

"Remind me," O'Bryan said, "why we couldn't wait for ESU?"

Kiernan sighed. Given the domovoy's shape-changing abilities, having the Emergency Services Unit present to assist in the arrest would've been less stressful, as she had told their liaison with the Special Operations Department.

"Vondelikos over at SOD said they were on another call and wouldn't be available for two more hours," she said. "Your tour ends in forty-five minutes, and I got yelled at the last time we kept uniforms past end-of-tour, since we're still in that damn, stupid overtime freeze, so I decided to go ahead. You got a problem with that?"

O'Bryan held up both hands. "No, I ain't got a problem with it. Grabowski might, but he's off to the ER, so whatever."

"We got a *slight* problem," Grullon said.

Once again, Kiernan sighed. "What now?"

"Wagon won't be available for another two hours."

"*Madonna mia*," Kiernan muttered. "All right, we're gonna have to get this monstrosity downstairs ourselves."

O'Bryan asked, "Shouldn't we read him his rights?"

Grullon shook his head. "Not as long as that silver's in him. He can't think straight right now, so no way he can say he understands his rights, and his lawyer'll use that. Once he's in the Tombs, they can take the bullet out when he's in a cell, and he can be read his rights then."

Kiernan nodded approvingly. For the first couple of months after he joined the unit, Grullon had had a real hard time wrapping his mind around all the weirdness of the SCU, but ever since that awful incident in Van Cortlandt Park, he'd been much more on the ball.

"Wait," Lin said, "we're taking him downtown? Not back to your house?"

Chuckling, Kiernan said, "No, we're full up."

SCU was housed in a five-story tenement building on East 106th Street that NYPD had seized a decade earlier. The place was now equipped with four specially reinforced cells for perps, like the domovoy, that were powerful either physically or magically, or both. The fourth cell had just been occupied this morning, by a kappa that Detective Luis Ortega had arrested on City Island in the Bronx.

Because sometimes, like today, they had more than four perps to put in custody, the city had remodeled a few cells at the Manhattan Detention Complex on White Street—which, like every other detention center there had been in lower Manhattan since 1840, was nicknamed "the Tombs."

Kiernan pulled out her regular handcuffs. SCU detectives were also issued silver and iron handcuffs, which were sometimes needed. But the domovoy wasn't coming back to their house, and it'd take forever to get the special cuffs back from the Tombs. Besides, the bullet was doing the job that the silver cuffs would've done. And regular cuffs were a dime a dozen.

She knelt down next to the domovoy and yanked his arms behind his back. The still-whimpering domovoy didn't resist as Kiernan wrapped the cuffs around his wrists.

Looking up at the others, she said, "Give me your bracelets."

Grullon handed his cuffs over unhesitatingly.

O'Bryan stared at her like she was nuts. "You already cuffed him!"

Lin pulled out his cuffs. "You saw what that thing did to Grabowski. C'mon, Mike, we always *at least* double cuff perps this strong."

Sighing, O'Bryan said, "Yeah, okay." As he handed over his own cuffs, he squinted. "Hey, what happened to his clothes?"

Kiernan smiled as she put the additional sets of cuffs on the domovoy's wrists and forearms. "He wasn't wearing any, he just includes it as part of his shape-changing."

"You mean he's always naked?" Lin asked with revulsion in his voice.

"Yup."

O'Bryan snorted. "You should charge his ass with indecent exposure, too, just for shits and giggles."

Lin shook his head. "I gotta say, detectives, after today, I take back most of the things I said about your unit."

As Kiernan stood, she summoned up the evil stare her grandmother always gave her when she said something stupid and focused it on Lin. Kiernan was only five-foot-two, so she had to rely on the don't-fuck-with-me voice she inherited from her father and the stare of doom she got from her nonna when she wanted to be intimidating. "'Most'?"

Cowering a little bit, which spoke to the stare's efficacy, Lin said, "Fine, *all* the things I said. You ask me, you guys don't get paid enough."

O'Bryan leaned forward conspiratorially. "One'a the things he used to say about SCU is that it's a waste of money."

Lin gently smacked his partner with the back of his hand. "You didn't have to tell her that."

"We've heard it all before, believe me," Kiernan said, saying a silent prayer of thanks to her nonna. "All right, let's get him down to the car. We each take a corner." She crouched down and grabbed one of the domovoy's hairy ankles. Grullon grabbed the other, while Lin and O'Bryan each grabbed a shoulder. "On three. One, two, *three*!"

With very loud grunts, they lifted him. Kiernan felt her shoulders and biceps howl with pain as she tried to maintain her grip on his ankle.

"How much does this motherfucker *weigh*?" O'Bryan asked.

They stumbled down the narrow hallway to the narrower staircase, which went down about ten steps before turning around and continuing the rest of the way to the first floor.

"How do people get furniture up this?" Grullon asked.

Kiernan chuckled. "It's New York. They find a way."

When they got to the first-floor landing, they all, as one, dropped the domovoy onto the dirty floor and caught their breath. Nobody had suggested that, but getting the creature this far was exhausting.

"Jesus, Mary, and goddamn Joseph," O'Bryan muttered as he palmed sweat from his bald head.

The door to 1E swung open with a creak and an older Caucasian woman with a shock of white hair and thick-framed glasses stuck her head into the hallway. She wore a bright orange-and-white housecoat.

"What's all this racket?" She looked down at the handcuffed domovoy curled in a fetal position on the floor. "Is that a dog? We can't have dogs in here. The landlord doesn't allow it!"

Indicating her badge, Kiernan said, "NYPD, ma'am."

"I don't care if you're the Lord Jesus Christ, kindly get that dog out of here!"

A bald man with a thick mustache appeared behind her, wearing an undershirt, boxer shorts, and moccasins. "Oh, for heaven's sake, Jeannie, that's not a dog. He's got thumbs. I bet it's that guy in 2W, the shape-changer. You arresting him?"

"Yes, sir," Kiernan said. "Please go back inside your apartment."

Jeannie frowned. "If I get rabies, I'll sue. Don't think I won't!"

The bald man rolled his eyes. "He's not a dog, Jeannie, he don't got rabies. Sorry to bother you, Officer."

"No problem, sir," Kiernan said.

The woman made a *hmph* noise but allowed the bald man to pull her back into the apartment.

Kiernan turned to Lin. "Go open up your blue-and-white so we can throw his ass into your back seat."

While Lin walked down the hall to the dirty-glass front door, Kiernan undid the Velcro straps on her vest in anticipation of going into the fifty-degree September weather outside. Her blue blouse was stained with sweat underneath, and for a moment, she heard her mother's voice: *"You're gonna catch cold, goin' out in a wet blouse like that, Domenica, what's* wrong *with you?"*

As usual when her mother's voice sounded in her head, she ignored it. Which was also what she often did when her mother's voice sounded in her ears.

Kiernan pulled her department-issue phone out of her pants pocket—once again praising the discount store for having women's slacks that had actual pockets—and took it out of airplane mode. The first thing she did was text Sergeant Hawkins to say that they had the domovoy in custody and that she threw a shot, which the Internal Affairs Bureau would have to be told. Hawk had probably already heard this over the radio, but she wanted to be sure.

Hawkins texted back:

IAB informed.They'll send someone first thing tomorrow.

"*Madonna mia*," she muttered. She then separately texted Simon Delaj, the assistant district attorney who would be handling the domovoy's case, and Catalina Mercado, the woman the domovoy had assaulted, to inform them that he was in custody.

Lin came back, and the four of them hauled the domovoy onto the sidewalk. Both the blue-and-white from the 10th Precinct and the dark blue Chevrolet Malibu that Kiernan had signed out of the motor pool were double-parked in front of the apartment building.

The back door to the blue-and-white was open. The foursome moved toward it with purpose, though Kiernan felt her grip on the domovoy's ankle loosen with each second.

O'Bryan's entire bald head was turning red with the effort. He said, through gritted teeth, "I swear to fuck, whatever don't fit the first time, I'm cuttin' off!"

Mercifully, O'Bryan was spared having to marry that comment to an action, as the domovoy slid into the back seat like a very hairy side of beef.

Once again, Kiernan turned her nonna's look on Lin and O'Bryan. "Remember to tell the duty officer *not* to take the bullet out until he's secured in one of the new cells. *Then* read him his rights."

"Got it," Lin said with a nod.

"We'll take care of it, Detective. Good luck with IAB," O'Bryan added.

"Thanks—you too. And hey," she said, "good work."

"You too," Lin said.

The officers got into their blue-and-white and drove off down 29th Street.

Grullon was staring at his phone in annoyance. "Dammit."

"What's up?" Kiernan asked as she opened the trunk of their Chevy and placed the Kevlar in it.

"More wedding *mishegoss*," Grullon said as he removed his own vest, handed it to her, and got into the driver's seat.

Kiernan chuckled as she tossed his Kevlar into the trunk and closed it. Grullon was Catholic—his Irish mother and Puerto Rican father had met in church. But his fiancée, Rachael Haimovitch, was Jewish and used a lot of Yiddish in regular conversation, which had rubbed off on him.

"What's Rachael's father demanding this time?" Kiernan asked, getting into the passenger seat.

"Oh, it's not Rachael's family this time. It's mine."

Kiernan regarded him with surprise. "I thought you settled that."

"I thought I did, too," Grullon said as he started the engine. "Took two months, but my parents have *finally* accepted that it's gonna be a Jewish ceremony."

"Because Rachael's parents are paying for it," Kiernan said with a grin.

"Exactly. Their money, therefore they get to choose the faith for the incredibly elaborate celebration of their child's marriage to a goy." Grullon pulled the Chevy into traffic, heading toward Eighth Avenue.

Kiernan nodded, recalling that Grullon's father was a construction worker and his mother an admin for the same construction company. They made a good living but were strictly blue-collar. Rachael's parents, who were both chief financial officers of big corporations on Park Avenue, blew them out of the water in terms of tax bracket.

"So what's the problem?"

"Abuela. She's saying she won't come to the wedding because it's, and I quote, 'a heathen ceremony full of heathens.'"

"Try reminding your grandmother that Jesus was Jewish."

Grullon was grinning now. "Actually, I can do one better than that. In the Jewish ceremony, the grandparents are part of it."

Frowning, Kiernan asked, "What do you mean?"

"The procession is the rabbi, the groom, the groom's parents, the wedding party, the *grandparents*, and then finally the bride with her parents. Trust me, as soon as I tell Abuela that she gets to walk down the aisle, she'll be all over it."

"Nice." Kiernan blew out a breath. "Hawk said that IAB'll be by tomorrow morning, first thing. Tour's almost over, so let's just put the car back in the garage, check in with the lieutenant, clock out, and go home."

"Who do you think IAB will send?"

"I hope it's Peña."

"Why?" Grullon asked as he turned north on Eighth.

"Because he's dealt with SCU before. I really don't want to have to explain what we do to *another* Internal Affairs rat."

Grullon smirked. "Thought we weren't supposed to call 'em rats anymore?"

Kiernan blinked and tried to look innocent. "Oops?"

Her phone buzzed again with two more text messages. One was a heartfelt thank you from the victim. The other, ADA Delaj getting back to her:

About time!

"*Madonna mia*, seriously?"

"What?" Grullon asked.

"I just got an 'about time!' from Delaj in the DA's office. It's not *our* fuckin' fault the DNA results took five weeks."

"How the hell does a domovoy's DNA wind up in the system anyhow?"

"Shitty neighbors."

Grullon frowned. "Sorry?"

"Well, one shitty neighbor." Kiernan jerked a thumb behind her. "That building we just left was the site of a rape two years ago. All the men who lived in the building were suspects and were compelled to provide DNA samples to compare to the rape kit. Turned out to be one of the guys in 2E, who's now doing a twenty-five-year bit in Arthur Kill Correctional. But our guy's DNA stayed in the system, and it matched what they found on our assault victim. And then we found out that the identity he's been using, Valery Leybenzon, is one that he stole from someone who died a decade ago. That, plus the DNA, plus the surveillance footage, gave us what we needed for the arrest warrant."

"I still don't see why the surveillance footage wasn't enough by itself."

"The video's how we knew the perp was a shape-changer, but that also means anything visual is functionally useless as evidence. No judge was gonna sign an arrest warrant just on that. Or just on a stolen ID. We needed the DNA."

Grullon shook his head. "Just another day at SCU, huh?"

"Yup."

TWO

Detective First Grade Luis Ortega of the SCU pulled up to the house at the end of Kirby Street and was rather surprised to see a kappa standing in front of it, between two patrol officers. Two kappas lived in that house, but this couldn't have been either of them, as one was in an SCU holding cell and the other was in the morgue, the former having murdered the latter.

He parked his department-issue Chevy Malibu behind the blue-and-white from the Four-Five. When he'd left the scene hours ago, an SUV from the Crime Scene Unit had also been parked there, but it was gone, so the nerd squad was probably done with their work.

Ortega took a deep breath and slowly climbed out of the driver's seat, his knees cracking with the effort. He'd driven to City Island from SCU HQ after being told by the desk sergeant at the 45th Precinct that he needed to haul ass back to the small island off the east coast of the Bronx, as there was a new wrinkle to his murder case.

The house was located right on the water, a one-story structure with a tiny yard in the front and, currently, yellow crime-scene tape across the front door. The two POs flanked a short, squat figure that had green skin coated with a yellow slime, a turtle-like shell on his back, a small snout, instead of a nose, tiny eyes, and webbed hands and feet.

The shorter of the two officers was Black, with a bald head and a goatée. He seemed calm—almost bored. His comrade, a large man who appeared to be Hawai'ian or Samoan, looked completely freaked out.

As Ortega approached, the kappa looked at him and pointed at the house. "Go inside, me?"

Holding up a finger, Ortega said to the kappa, "Wait, you, please?" He turned to the Black officer, whose nameplate read FREDRICKSON, since he seemed to have his shit together. "I'm Detective Ortega from SCU. What's going on, Fredrickson?"

The uniformed officer pointed at the kappa. "We were just finishing up after CSU left when this little guy showed up, sayin' he lives here."

Ortega sighed. The house was owned by a real estate company that was proving annoyingly hard to get in touch with. It was definitely still functioning, paying the property taxes and utilities on time, but its phone number was out of service, and there had, as yet, been no reply to the e-mail Ortega had sent to the listed address. It was certainly possible that another kappa lived with the two who'd gotten into a fight.

"CSU's all done, right?" he asked.

Fredrickson nodded.

"Fine, let's go inside."

The other PO, whose name was Salavea, recoiled. "Do we have to go in there?"

Ortega looked at the larger officer. "What's the problem?"

"You've been in there, right, Detective? It stinks like a motherfucker."

"Yeah, kappas are kinda gassy. So what?"

Salavea started, "I don't—"

Ortega decided not to let him finish. "Look, I need to question this witness. He's only about four-foot-nothing, and if I talk to him out here, I gotta squat down to do it right. I'm sixty years old and I do *not* squat. I want the witness to be comfortable, so it's better to do it in his house."

"You could just take him to your house in your car," Salavea said, referring to SCU's headquarters on 106th Street.

"Fuck no—kappas are gassy. He'll stink up the place."

With that, Ortega went inside, ripping the yellow tape away from the doorframe. The front door led straight into the large living room, which had a small wading pool in the center and plastic milk crates—some black, some red—scattered around. Both the hardwood floor and the milk crates were stained with bits of yellow. There were no decorations on the walls. All the windows were open in a mostly futile attempt to mitigate the methane-like smell.

Salavea's face wrinkled up. "How the fuck do they live like this?"

"This? This is nothing," Ortega said. "Back when I was at the One-Nine, we busted a crack den in an abandoned apartment building on 95th Street. Junkies'd been living there for a year or more, and none'a the showers in the place worked, if you get my meaning. Place smelled like shit—literally, 'cause the toilets didn't work, either. For that matter, my fourth wife, Renata? Worst cook in the world. The kitchen smelled about like this every evening."

The kappa took a seat on one of the milk crates. Ortega did likewise, choosing the one that was the least stained.

"Happened, what?" the kappa said.

"Fought, housemates," Ortega said. "Is dead, one."

"Which?" The kappa's voice went up an octave, and a whistling sound came from its back. The kappa had let loose with one of his epic farts.

Ortega made sure not to inhale for a bit. Salavea and Fredrickson were not so astute, and both nearly gagged.

"You two wanna step outside?" Ortega asked the uniforms.

Waving a hand back and forth, Fredrickson said, "I'm good" in a strained voice.

Salavea, however, practically ran outside, his hand over the lower half of his face.

Ortega thought for a moment about how to answer the kappa's question as to which roommate was deceased. They didn't have names; instead they distinguished themselves by the patterns on their shells. But there was no consistency or standardization to this. The kappa in holding referred to his victim four different ways, all of which applied. Ortega could only remember one of those four, so he said, "Six circles, one line."

"Did deed, ten spots?"

The shell of the kappa in holding did indeed have ten spots, as well as a Z formation of lines. Ortega had come *this close* to referring to him as Zorro in the report.

"Is arrested, him," Ortega said.

The kappa shook his head and looked down at the stained hardwood floor. "Not surprised, me. Did argue, them. Departed, me. Could not endure, me. Swim, me. Journey, me."

"Make statement, you?"

"For what?" As he spoke, the kappa let loose another bit of gas.

Even Ortega was starting to struggle with breathing at this point. But he soldiered on. "Need evidence, us. Get justice, six circles, one line."

"No justice. Dead."

Ortega wanted to argue with that, but after forty years on the job, couldn't do it with a straight face. "Would help, still. Please?"

After a moment, the kappa nodded.

"All right, I'll take him in my car," Ortega said, getting to his feet.

"Go to room, me. Take care, me, things."

"Sure." To Fredrickson, he said, "Go with him, make sure he comes back out to my car."

"You got it, Detective."

Fredrickson followed the kappa to one of the rooms in the back of the house. Ortega, meanwhile, went out front into the pleasant autumn weather—for which he was grateful, as he'd need to drive with all the windows down as long as the kappa was in the Malibu …

Salavea was standing by the blue-and-white. Ortega joined him, shaking his head and saying, "This island always freaks me the fuck out."

"Excuse me?" Salavea stared at the detective as if he were insane.

"I drive over the bridge, and all of a sudden, I'm not in the Bronx anymore. I'm in a fuckin' New England fishing village. It's all sailboats and seafood restaurants and nautical-themed crafts stores. It's just not New York City to me, y'know?"

"You just interviewed a witness that's covered in slime and looks like an otter crossed with a turtle, and *City Island* freaks you out? How the hell'd you even know how to *talk* to the thing?"

"Well, the first time I met a kappa, back three years ago, *that* was a pain in the ass, but you get used to it. Just talk with verb, then subject, then object. Once you get the hang of it, it's pretty simple. You ever try to talk to a junkie coming down off a meth high when you need him to ID the guy who killed his buddy? Compared to that, a kappa's easy."

"If you say so, Detective. I just can't believe this shit's real."

"It really is. And hey, three years ago, it was a lot harder to prosecute a kappa. Laws are constantly being adjusted and rewritten, and the legal precedents are kind of hilarious. Honestly, these creatures all starting to come out has mostly been good for lawyers."

"Am ready, me."

Ortega turned to see the kappa coming closer, alongside Fredrickson. The kappa was now wearing a plain gold medallion around his neck.

To the kappa, he said, while pointing to his Malibu, "Go into back seat, you. Will go, us, soon. Is open, the door."

The kappa nodded and waddled over to the Malibu.

"Don't mind my rookie partner," Fredrickson said. "Until we had a domestic in Co-op City six months ago, he didn't believe there were really trans people in the world."

Defensively, Salavea said, "I hadn't ever met any! I figured it was just some weird shit you saw on TV, like spaceships."

"New York's Finest," Ortega muttered. "Why do you think they created the SCU, Salavea?"

"I've only been on the job nine months, Detective, but I've already come to realize that most of what the bosses do doesn't make any sense."

With a chuckle, Ortega said, "Can't argue with that. But still, there's a lot more going on in the world than you've directly experienced. Take it from an old man who's been on the job *way* longer than you."

"Yes, sir," Salavea muttered

Fredrickson, who was now grinning, said, "Hey, Salavea, remember that dive shop here on the island that had the B&E last week?"

"Yeah."

Turning to Ortega, Fredrickson said, "While we were takin' statements, we found out that divers have their own rules and regs and shit. Completely self-controlled and they're fuckin' fanatical about enforcing it. There's a whole sub-culture of scuba divers. Don't see too many in New York, but we got 'em, and a lot of 'em dive from here." Regarding his partner, he added, "We hadn't *directly experienced* that until then, either."

Ortega nodded. "Can you two stay here until your tour's over? I can clear it with your sergeant—I just want to make sure no *more* roommates show up."

Fredrickson waved him off. "We'll clear it with the sarge. You just get him back to your house before he stinks up your ride too much."

"Yeah." Sergeant Baney in the motor pool had complained about having to get the smell of Zorro—or ten spots, whatever—out of the Malibu Ortega had used this morning to bring their suspect in. Now he was probably going to hear it from Baney again with this car.

As he turned the Malibu around and went back down Kirby Street toward City Island Avenue, the kappa let loose with some more gas.

With a sigh, Ortega gunned the accelerator. He needed to get back to HQ *fast*.

THREE

Farid Anand stood in the back corner of the conference room, staying in the shadows created by the bright lights. Those lights were in use alongside two cameras that were currently pointed at the large table in the room's center. One camera was pointed at Anand's boss, Garth Ohlmeyer, the other at Amira Mireles, a reporter from CNN.

Anand didn't need to be in the room for his client's television interview, but he felt better doing so. The interview wasn't live, so he could cut off any unexpected bits of questioning at the pass.

Not that he expected it. One of the reasons Ohlmeyer had agreed to be interviewed by Mireles was that he knew she wouldn't rock the boat. Generally she kept her questions simple, calling for easy-to-provide answers that wouldn't require any spin-doctoring later.

Of course, there was always a first time …

When Mireles got to her third question, Anand's mouth went dry, and he started nervously stroking his thick beard.

"You're being investigated by the New York County District Attorney for your role in the Hudson Yards development, an investigation that has already resulted in City Comptroller Brandon

Kogan resigning in disgrace and being charged with embezzlement. Can you comment on that?"

Ohlmeyer gave Mireles a rueful smile, showing teeth Anand knew he'd spent thousands to make look perfect. "Your camera can't see it, but one of my lawyers is here in the room with us, and I guarantee that you made him *incredibly* nervous with that question. However, if I've learned nothing else in my years in real estate and venture capital, it's that I should always do what my lawyers tell me to do. So I'm just going to say that I have no comment beyond this: we are cooperating with the DA's investigation, and I'm confident that it will turn out to be nothing."

"What about the rumors that you're involved with organized crime and that the DA's investigation is a prelude to finally confirming those rumors?"

Ohlmeyer chuckled. "You're whipping out all the greatest hits, aren't you, Amira? Look, I'm incredibly rich, and that's made me a target of both the NYPD and the DA. And hey, the Manhattan DA's office successfully prosecuted the president of the United States on criminal charges, so they're probably feeling pretty ballsy. Can I say 'ballsy'? It's cable, right? I can say 'ballsy.'"

Mireles let out a small titter. "I'm sure it'll be fine. I have one more rumor I'd like you to address."

Shaking his head, Ohlmeyer said, "This oughtta be good."

Anand's mouth got even drier and bits of his beard started to come off onto his fingers. Ohlmeyer's answers had been fine so far. He'd skirted the edge but hadn't said anything that would need to be walked back later. However, Anand was genuinely worried that Mireles was going to hit on something that Ohlmeyer had gone to great lengths to keep secret.

"Was that Sara Ramirez you were having dinner with at Sardi's last week?"

Closing his eyes and letting out a slow breath, Anand allowed himself to relax.

"Congratulations, Amira. My cousin will be thrilled to know that she was mistaken for one of her favorite Broadway actors. I actually met Sara at the Tonys a while back, but I promise, I never asked for a date."

The interview went on for a bit longer, talking about Ohlmeyer's family and friends and other harmless topics, before hitting another query that got Anand's attention.

"Last year, you formed an exploratory committee to examine a possible run for mayor. But we haven't heard anything about it since. Why is that?"

"Because it's not happening, Amira. Look, I know it's trendy for New York businessmen to run for office, from Governor Rockefeller to Mayor Bloomberg to President Trump. But I prefer to do a job because *I* want to do it, and I prefer to stop doing it when I'm done. As a politician, I'd be beholden to my constituents and to elections, and that's too much uncertainty for me."

As Mireles moved on to her next question, Anand felt his phone buzz. He removed it from the inner pocket of his suit jacket and saw a text from Ohlmeyer's admin, Jada:

Quinn's here said it's urgent. I put him in GO's office.

Anand's mouth was still dry, making it hard to swallow. Quinn showing up in person for an urgent reason could not possibly be good news.

After Mireles asked her final bland question and Ohlmeyer provided his equally bland answer, she thanked him, he thanked her, and then, after two seconds, the tech standing between the two cameras said, "We're out."

Ohlmeyer immediately got to his feet. The tech removed the Lavalier microphone from the businessman's lapel.

"Amira, thank you," Ohlmeyer said, offering his hand.

Mireles stood and returned the handshake. "No, thank you, Garth. It was fun." She looked over at Anand. "It was fine, right, Farid?"

Pasting a smile on his face, Anand said, "More than fine, Amira, thank you. I'm sorry, but I need to get Garth to an urgent meeting with one of the vice presidents."

Ohlmeyer didn't miss a beat, thankfully. "Like I said, Amira, I do what my lawyer tells me to do. Jada will help you if you need anything."

Once they excused themselves from the conference room and got out into the corridor, Ohlmeyer asked, "What's going on?"

"Quinn's here. Says it's urgent."

"Well, *that* can't be good."

"No, it can't."

As they passed Jada's desk, Ohlmeyer started to speak, but Jada cut him off. "No interruptions while you're in this meeting and I'll help the CNN crew if they need it?"

Raising an eyebrow, Ohlmeyer asked, "You angling for another raise, Jada?"

"Always." She got to her feet and headed toward the conference room to check on Mireles and her crew.

The heavy wooden door, with a dragon's-head design carved into its center and a fire motif carved into the molding, opened smoothly at Ohlmeyer's touch, revealing his corner office, complete with a picture window that looked out over Midtown, with a particularly nice view of Bryant Park.

Standing at parade rest in the middle of the spacious office was a Black man with cornrows that dangled to the bottom of his neck. He wore mirrorshades, an affectation that Anand found tiresome. He was also wearing a button-down shirt and slacks, so he didn't look like a gangster.

Which Quinn most assuredly was. He was in charge of the day-to-day operations of Ohlmeyer's extensive network that distributed illegal narcotics to the drug-taking residents of New York City. The existence of that network was the rumor Anand had feared Mireles would bring up, as it was the reason for several of the NYPD's investigations of Ohlmeyer over the years. But there had never been any evidence of Ohlmeyer's involvement. That was in part due to Anand and the other lawyers Ohlmeyer had on retainer doing their jobs well.

It was also in part due to Quinn doing *his* job very well.

Quinn started to say something as they entered the office, but Ohlmeyer held up a hand. He put two fingers to his temple and closed his eyes.

A second later, he opened his eyes and said, "Okay, the wards are activated. We won't be disturbed, interrupted, or eavesdropped upon. Now then, since I told you never to come here unless it was a major disaster that was too sensitive to discuss over the phone, I assume it's bad."

"Damn right. You know I don't like wearin' these fancy-ass clothes 'less I gotta."

"All right, out with it." Ohlmeyer snapped his fingers and a glass filled with an amber liquid materialized in his hand.

He didn't offer Quinn or Anand a drink. While there were benefits to being one of the lawyers for a powerful magic-user, Ohlmeyer's rudeness to the help in private was not one of them.

Anand had the feeling he was going to need a drink once Quinn explained his presence.

"One of the customers killed Jake the Jake this morning."

Ohlmeyer rolled his eyes. "One of your dealers got killed by an irate customer? For *this,* I activated the wards?"

"Nah, not for *that,*" Quinn said. "It was someone we cut off for non-payment. And we're pretty sure the same customer also killed a dude named Elmore Hertweck."

Anand's mouth got dry again. "Shit."

Now Ohlmeyer sounded confused. "Should I know that name?"

"Corporate lawyer. I've met him a few times. He's squeaky clean, believe it or not. Very well liked." Anand looked at Quinn. "He was murdered?"

Quinn nodded. "The problem is the customer who done the deed. It's one of the fifty who's been takin' the doubly enhanced product."

Again Ohlmeyer rolled his eyes. "For fuck's sake, Quinn, we're in a room protected by the most powerful wards on the planet. We can skip the euphemisms. It's one of the people we need for the ritual this month, who is taking the narcotics that I cast with both the possession spell and the masking spell."

"I like to stick with euphemisms," Quinn said. "Stay in the habit, *you* know."

"Good idea," Anand said, walking over to the water cooler in a corner of the office and pouring some water into a plastic cup. "Better to be safe."

"Farid, we're in the safest place in the—" Ohlmeyer cut himself off. "Fuck it. Never mind. The bodies are at the morgue?"

"Jake's still at the Port Authority. That's where he got his ass killed. Cops still got the scene. But Hertweck's in the morgue, yeah."

Anand swallowed the blessedly cold water, making his mouth almost feel normal again.

"All right," Ohlmeyer started. "I'll get in touch with this customer and—"

Anand interrupted. "Let me handle this, Garth, I—"

"Really, Farid? How're you gonna handle this, exactly? You're going to cast the transmutation spell?"

That brought Anand up short. "Excuse me?"

"We can't let *any* of the fifty be taken in by the police, and we can't send any of them out of town like you'd probably do, because we need them at the new moon."

Completely confused, Anand asked, "Transmutation spell? What are you going to transmute?"

"The corpses. The medical examiner won't have any evidence—hell, they probably won't even be able to say for certain that the deaths are murders. It'll stall any police investigation."

"You sure you want to bring—"

Again Ohlmeyer interrupted his lawyer. "Farid, shut the fuck up. There is nothing—*nothing*—more important than the ritual. Absolutely nothing can go wrong with it, you understand me? All we have to do is stymie the NYPD long enough to get to the new moon. After the new moon, the police won't even matter. Neither will the DA's investigation—hell, neither will that stupid-ass puff piece I just filmed for CNN."

Anand blew out a breath. "All right."

"Damn right, it's all right." Ohlmeyer turned to Quinn. "Get me the name and full contact info. Send it to the encrypted e-mail address."

"You got it." Quinn turned to leave, then stopped at the door. Without turning around, he asked, "You gonna drop the wards?"

"Hm?" Ohlmeyer looked up, seemingly confused. "Oh." He put his fingers to his temples, closed his eyes, opened them, then said, "Go on, leave."

Anand started to speak, but Ohlmeyer said, "You can leave, too, Farid. I got this."

"We need to talk about the next round of subpoenas."

"No, Farid, we don't. What did I just say? Nothing matters but the ritual. Just fulfill all the subpoenas times a thousand. Make sure they get copies of every damn piece of paperwork you can throw at them. We just have to bury them in nonsense for a couple more weeks, and then it won't matter anymore."

Anand had several responses to that but rejected all of them on the grounds that the client was always right—especially when that client had the power to turn him into a newt.

Not that Ohlmeyer was likely to do that, but why take the chance?

Anand left the office and headed to the elevator. His phone buzzed again, and he pulled it out to find a text from another of Ohlmeyer's lawyers, Nick McManus.

Just got word, next round of subpoenas should hit tomorrow.

With a sigh, Anand got on the elevator and typed a reply:

Boss says to bury them in paper again.

Wilco

That was all McManus sent back.

Anand just hoped, for Ohlmeyer's sake, the ritual—whatever it was—worked. Because Ohlmeyer had been careless with Hudson Yards, the DA's case was actually halfway decent for a change. He'd ignored both Anand's and McManus's advice, particularly with regard to that idiot ex-comptroller.

One of his users doing a double murder was going to get undue attention from NYPD, which meant the shit was going to hit the fan hard if he wasn't careful.

But supposedly, if this new-moon ritual thing worked, it wouldn't matter. Anand held onto that hope.

FOUR

The early-morning sun rose over the East River and blazed at Detective Third Grade Sofia Umali, her sunglasses doing damn little to mitigate the glare. She was approaching the bottom of the small stoop that led to the front entrance to the building on East 106th Street, a moving box cradled in her arms. The detective was trying very hard to keep her heart rate from spiking.

I'm finally here. She hadn't been this excited—or this nervous—since her last black-belt promotion. *Hope this goes as well ...*

From the outside, it looked like so many other tenement buildings in the city: three slightly uneven marble steps leading up to a front door. Two separate ground-floor entrances on either side of the short stoop, which, in any normal apartment building, would each be rented out by a business. In fact, an identical-looking building across the street had a Chinese takeout place on one side and a hair salon on the other. Here, though, those doors were opaque and locked.

Like most small apartment buildings, it was five stories, due to the city ordinance that required any building six stories or higher to have an elevator.

Umali walked up the three steps to the glass center door, which was also opaque. Next to it, a large metal box had been attached to the brick, about shoulder high. In the center of the box was a grate that looked like a speaker. Above that was a white sticker with the NYPD logo on it; "S.C.U." was written in a neat hand, with a Sharpie, under the logo. Beneath the speaker was a white button and a keypad.

For a unit as new and well-funded as the Supernatural Crimes Unit, the entry system was surprisingly shabby looking.

Tucking the moving box awkwardly under her left arm, she pressed the button with her right hand. To Umali's surprise, it made no noise whatsoever.

A distorted voice came over the speaker. "Yes?"

"Detective Umali, reporting in?"

A light buzz emitted from the door, and Umali yanked it open.

She walked in, blinking the spots out of her eyes as she adjusted to no longer being in the sun's blinding glare.

Before her was a large metal reception desk, the same NYPD logo painted on the wall behind it, along with the words SUPERNATURAL CRIMES UNIT. A Black woman in uniform whose nameplate read HALL sat behind the desk, holding a copy of today's *Daily News.* As she put it down on the desk, Umali saw the front page. The headline was, DA PROBE INTO OHLMEYER CONTINUES. Below that sat a picture of Garth Ohlmeyer, as well as a shot of Ohlmeyer's real-estate development in Hudson Yards.

Looking around after taking her sunglasses off and setting them in her shirt collar, Umali saw that there were two staircases on the right, one leading down, the other leading up. To the left were two doors; one was shut and padlocked while the second was labeled STORAGE and was not padlocked.

Inhaling through her nose and exhaling through her mouth, the way Sensei always had them do after a particularly strenuous workout in the dojo, Umali approached the desk, brushing aside her maroon jacket to show the gold shield clipped to the belt on her black jeans.

"I'm Detective Umali."

"You must be the newbie," Officer Hall said.

Umali raised an eyebrow. "Is it that obvious?"

Hall smirked. "Well, the movin' box is a big clue. Plus you ain't got the code for the keypad yet." She pointed at the staircase. "Go up to the second floor, talk to Jurienny. She'll get you squared away, including givin' you the code so I don't gotta buzz you in again."

"Thanks."

Umali went up the stairs slowly. She'd put in for this transfer not long after she'd made detective. On the one hand, she'd liked her chances, given that very few people actually wanted to be on the "Hallowe'en Squad," as her sergeant at the Two-Four kept calling it. On the other, there hadn't been an opening until now.

The stairs emptied out near the southeast corner of the building, revealing a much larger, open space that took up almost the entirety of the floor, broken only by the occasional support pillar. It looked like the place had been completely gutted and renovated from the crumbling old tenement it had been before NYPD seized it.

Most of what Umali saw before her was an array of desks, all with computer terminals, in-boxes full of file folders, and various personal tchotchkes—pretty much your typical squad room. Some desks were occupied, some weren't. Only one was completely empty; Umali figured that would be hers.

She realized that her heart rate had slowed to normal and she was breathing easy, and after a second, she understood why. *Special unit or not, place I've been dying to be transferred to or not—this is still a typical squad room. It's still the job.*

In the northwest corner, she saw a walled-off section with a door that had the words LIEUTENANT STANISLAUS MAJOROWICZ, UNIT COMMANDER stenciled on the frosted glass. That office had a window looking out over the squad room. Blinds hung on the office side of the window and were shut, as was the door to the office. Light shone in under the door and between the slats of the blinds, so the lieutenant was probably in there. In the northeast corner was a single-occupant bathroom, the door to which was currently wide open.

In the center, between the lieutenant's office and the toilet, was a SMARTboard that looked just like the ones in Umali's daughter's classrooms, as well as a more traditional whiteboard, which had a few pictures taped to it, accompanied by writing in various colors. About a dozen chairs were scattered in front of the two boards.

Behind her were four windows that looked out onto 106th Street. She could hear the traffic whizzing by on the two-way thoroughfare, punctuated by the occasional honked horn. Vending machines sat between the windows.

The desk closest to the staircase was occupied by a Latinx woman in her thirties. She wore a blouse decorated with sunflowers, and Umali could see that the clip that tied her long, dark hair back into a ponytail was also decorated with a sunflower. Next to the woman's computer was a vase containing three actual sunflowers. She was on the phone, but upon seeing Umali arrive at the top of the stairs, she said, with an accent that Umali placed as Puerto Rican, "Gotta go, Carlos. See you at lunch ... *Sí, sí ... Te amo.*" She hung up and favored Umali with a bright smile that accentuated the small mole on her cheek. "Can I help you, Detective?"

"Hope so. I'm Sofia Umali, I'm transferring from the 24th Precinct." She took out her ID and held it up.

"Oh, Detective Jiminez's replacement—good, you're here. And on time, too!" She stood up to peer at the ID, and Umali saw that she was wearing a solid brown ankle-length skirt that had a sunflower embroidered on it. Holding out a hand, she said, "Welcome to SCU. I'm Jurienny Feliz—I'm the admin for the day tour. I've got about a billion pieces of paperwork for you to fill out."

Umali chuckled. "I figured. This is *not* my first transfer."

Pointing at the empty desk, Jurienny said, "That'll be your desk, so you can put your box there. I'll get all your paperwork together, and Sergeant Hawkins can show you around." Turning toward a Black man sitting at the desk that was closest to the lieutenant's office, Jurienny cried out, "Hey, Hawk!" at a volume that nearly blew Umali back a few steps. "The new detective's here!"

Umali shook her head back and forth a few times in the hopes of clearing her ears.

Jurienny turned and smiled apologetically. "*Lo siento.* I got three kids, all in middle school, all trying to talk louder than the other two. I gotta keep up."

Hawkins was a very tall, very thin Black man who barely looked old enough to be a detective. His hair was cut close to his scalp, and he had a thin mustache and large brown eyes, which he was using to stare daggers at Jurienny as he approached.

"You do know how the phones work, right, Jurienny? There's an intercom function—"

"Which you guys always ignore, and I ain't leavin' a voicemail when I can just yell across the squad room. This is our new detective," she added before the sergeant could say anything else.

Turning to Umali, Hawkins gave her a warm smile that made him look much friendlier—and, oddly, much older. "You must be Detective Umali. Welcome. I'm Sergeant Simeon Hawkins." He put out a hand.

Accepting the handshake, Umali said, "A pleasure to be here, Sergeant. Or do you prefer 'Hawk'?"

"I answer to that, as well as 'Sarge,' 'Sergeant,' 'Simeon,' 'Hawkins,' and 'hey you.'"

"Good to know, hey you."

Jurienny barked out a giggle, which she swallowed quickly at Hawkins's look. She sat back down and started typing intently on her keyboard.

"Sense of humor's good to have, Sofia—it'll help you get through the crazy. You've already met Jurienny—technically, Lieutenant Majorowicz and I are in charge, but she actually runs the place during the day tour. You need anything, talk to her. Put your stuff down and I'll show you around."

After Umali set her box down on the empty desk, Hawkins led her to the next-closest desk. The young man sitting there, who had a shock of curly dark hair, was wearing a charcoal suit that was much fancier than anything she'd ever seen a detective wear during a normal tour. He wore no tie, and the first three buttons were undone on his light blue shirt, revealing a gold necklace resting on a hairy chest, making him look more like a stereotypical Mafia gangster than a detective. This was very obviously his desk, given the three pictures in a triple frame next to his computer monitor: on the left, him in dress uniform, probably his graduation photo from the Academy; in the middle, him with two older people, likely his parents given their looks; on the right, a sepia-toned picture of an elderly woman. The right-hand corner of the frame had a St. Michael medal draped over it.

He was reading a case file and closed it at their approach.

"Detective Second Grade Vincenzo Fiore, this is Detective Third Grade Sofia Umali."

"Call me Vinny," Fiore said, holding out a hand. "Welcome to the loony bin."

"Call me Sofia. That's, uh, that's a nice suit."

"Yeah, I paid wholesale. I got a guy." He turned to the sergeant. "Hey, Hawk, I got a text from Kevyn—he wants to meet."

"What about?"

"Fuck if I know, he didn't say—but he's always got the good shit."

"All right, go for it."

"I'll head out soon's Kiernan gets here with the cannoli."

Umali frowned. "Cannoli?"

Hawkins gave her the smile again. "Domenica lives in the Belmont section of the Bronx and usually brings in pastries from one of the bakeries in Little Italy. It's Thursday, so today we get cannoli."

"That's the thing from the *Godfather*, right? 'Leave the gun, take the cannoli'? I've never actually had one."

Fiore stared at her as if she'd said she came from Mars. "Really? You ain't *lived*, you ask me."

Putting her hands on her hips, Umali asked, "You ever had ube crinkle cookies?"

"I don't even know what that is," Fiore said.

"Then *you* ain't lived, Vinny. They're what you get at a Filipino bakery—and at my grandmother's house."

Hawkins asked, "Those are those purple cookies, right?"

Umali nodded.

Fiore made a face. "Why would anyone eat purple food?"

"I'm seeing my lola this weekend, so I'll get her to make some and bring 'em in Monday," Umali said.

As they started to walk toward another occupied desk, Hawkins said to Fiore, "You're not going out until after roll call."

"Ah, c'mon, Hawk, you can tell everyone I'm here."

"Nice try." He turned to Umali. "Trying to ingratiate yourself to the squad with dessert food, Sofia?"

Umali smiled. "Way to cops' hearts is through their sweet tooth, in my experience."

"That's kind of Domenica's racket, but she probably won't mind sharing."

"By the way, am I right in guessing this Kevyn person that Vinny was talking about is a CI?"

Nodding, Hawkins said, "Confidential informants are the lifeblood of this unit. Most folks still don't entirely believe that what we deal with is real—even after that vampire killed the mayor's aide."

Umali nodded. The SCU had been formed after a vampire named Bogdan Albescu killed a City Hall employee named John Rosario on the latter's way to work. The murder was caught on surveillance—both the part where Albescu used his oversize canine teeth to bite Rosario's neck and drain his blood, and the part right after, where Albescu turned into a huge bat and flew away.

She had still been in uniform at the time, but Umali had been utterly fascinated by the case, as well as the subsequent "coming out" of many beings and creatures previously assumed to be mythical.

"And then there's the nutjobs who believe that there's a lot more than what we deal with. CIs help weed out the crazies and also get us past the skeptics."

The next detective was a baby-faced man with curly, rust-red hair and an unusually dark complexion—in Umali's experience, redheads were usually much paler. He only had one picture on his desk: a woman with short brown hair, a large nose, and a bright smile.

"Detective Third Grade Liam Grullon, this is Detective Third Grade Sofia Umali," Hawkins said. "She's replacing David."

Unlike Fiore, Grullon actually stood up. "Welcome aboard, Detective. You got big shoes to fill."

"Oh?" Umali said.

"Not figuratively—literally. David has, like, enormous feet. He's a good guy."

"I hope I can live up to his example."

"Just don't get bit, and you'll do better than him."

Umali blinked. "Bit?"

Hawkins said, "By a galipote. Had to take a medical pension."

That brought Umali up short. "What's a galipote? Besides something that bites you?"

Looking up at the ceiling, Grullon started laughing. "Oh, this is great! I'm not the newbie anymore!" He looked back at Umali. "I was the one asking those questions when I got here. Don't worry about it—you'll *never* keep it all straight right away. Just work the cases, and if you have a question, ask the sarge here, or Basia."

"Who's Basia?"

"Our archivist. She's upstairs. We'll get to her in a bit," Hawkins said. To Grullon, he said, "You ready for IAB?"

"Just waiting for them—and Kiernan—to show up."

Umali gestured toward the picture on Grullon's desk. "She's lovely—is that your wife?"

"Not yet—getting married in two months."

"Oh, congratulations!"

"Thanks! You married?"

Umali shook her head. "Divorced."

"Great, now we're up to three divorced people," Grullon said with a chuckle.

For a moment, Umali considered asking but decided it would be rude. She knew that Ortega had a broken marriage. She'd find out who the third person was soon enough.

As they headed toward the lieutenant's office, Umali asked, "So what *is* a galipote?"

"Monster from the Dominican Republic—looks like a really weird dog. Guy out in Queens was using it to commit a bunch of nasty murders. It went after David when he was questioning the suspect."

Umali shuddered.

Hawkins continued, "There are two more detectives—our only first-grades."

"Kiernan and Ortega, right?" Umali said.

"Exactly." Hawkins sounded surprised. "You read up on us?"

"Kind of?" Umali said with a smile. "I served with Ortega at the One-Nine when I was in uniform. I'm guessing he's still always late?"

With a sigh, Hawkins said, "Yes. Always."

"Some things never change. Back at the One-Nine, he was only on time when he worked a double, and then only for the second tour. Why's IAB talking to Grullon and Kiernan?"

"Domenica discharged her weapon last night to subdue a domovoy."

Feeling incredibly stupid for having to do this a second time, Umali nonetheless asked, "What's a domovoy?"

"A shape-changer. This one committed assault and battery."

"Damn. I thought my comparative religion and mythology classes in college covered everything I'd need for this job, but apparently not."

"Yeah," Hawkins said, "it's not just vampires and werewolves and wizards. In fact, that's the least of it. Vampires are fairly easy to deal with—most of them stay off the radar and keep to themselves. Werewolves are only an issue once a month, and magic users are very rare, thankfully."

The door to the lieutenant's office opened as Hawkins finished. The man himself came out and said, "The sergeant's right, Detective. Whatever you think this unit's about, trust me, you're probably wrong."

Hawkins smiled. "Detective Third Grade Sofia Umali, meet Lieutenant Stanislaus Majorowicz, our boss."

"It's an honor to be here, sir," Umali said, shaking the lieutenant's huge hand, which looked even bigger due to his short arms.

"Well, we'll beat that notion out of you in a couple weeks, don't worry."

Majorowicz looked like two triangles, one small, one large, joined at the point and balanced on two thick sticks. His head, with squared-off steel-gray hair and a pointy chin, was the small triangle, while his torso, with narrow shoulders and a large pot belly, made the large one. He wore a white button-down shirt, a plain blue tie, khakis, and rainbow suspenders.

He looked at Hawkins. "IAB here yet for Kiernan and Grullon?"

Hawkins shook his head.

"I just got off the phone with Vondelikos and had to chew him a new asshole."

"Why?" Hawkins asked.

"Had breakfast with Lieutenant Patel of ESU this morning. He said that he had a squad free all afternoon yesterday."

Frowning, Hawkins said, "Lieutenant Vondelikos told Domenica that Emergency Services wasn't available to help arrest the domovoy."

"Hence my chowing down on his gluteus maximus. If ESU had been there, the takedown would've been smoother, Kiernan probably wouldn't have had to throw a shot, and I wouldn't have two detectives stuck at their desks until IAB clears them."

"And it was Domenica's last silver round," Hawkins added. "I'm gonna have her fill out a requisition for more as soon as IAB's done with her."

Umali asked, "Is that Elias Vondelikos, the Special Operations liaison?"

"Yeah," Majorowicz said, "and he thinks SCU's a waste of time and money and keeps fucking us on shit like this."

Quickly, Umali bit back what she had been going to say. She'd dealt with Vondelikos a few times at the Two-Four and had always found him to be reasonable. She'd already made an idiot of herself a couple of times today, she wasn't about to put her foot back in her mouth.

The lieutenant looked at Hawkins. "You show her around yet?"

"Just this floor. Still have to show her the rest of the house."

"Do it after roll call."

"Domenica and Luis aren't here yet."

Majorowicz closed his eyes and sighed. "Of course, they aren't." Opening his eyes, he regarded Umali with curiosity. "You served, right, Umali?"

Nodding, Umali said, "Yes, sir. Army CID. Did a tour in Afghanistan."

"I'll try not to hold that against you," the lieutenant said dryly.

"You're a Marine, sir?" she said without thinking.

Luckily, the lieutenant looked impressed. "Good guess."

Emboldened by that, she spoke with a bit more confidence. "Not a guess, sir, deduction. The haircut, for starters, and also you put a *lot* of disdain in your voice just now, so you had to be from another service, and Navy, Air Force, and Coast Guard are too wussy to be as disgusted as you were by my being a soldier, so you *had* to be a jarhead. Sir," she added after a second, having belatedly regretted using that term to refer to her superior officer.

"I can see why you got into Criminal Investigations in the sandbox," Majorowicz said with a chuckle. "And why you went for detective here."

"Yes, sir."

"You requested SCU when you got your gold shield last year. Most folks avoid it like the plague. How come you asked for it?"

Well, if he's gonna come out and ask me ... "The Albescu case, sir. I was really impressed with how the task force handled it, given how many unknowns there were. And I thought being here would be a greater challenge than being just a regular detective in a precinct."

"Oh, you'll get a challenge, all right, but probably not what you think."

Umali's briefly won confidence modulated back into uncertainty. "I don't know what that means, sir."

"You'll find out. Anyhow, you've got Jiminez's old desk. And good luck—you've got big shoes to fill."

"So I've heard, sir—he's got big feet." At the lieutenant's surprised look, Umali added, "Detective Grullon already told that joke, sir."

Looking past Umali, Majorowicz called out, "Hey, Grullon, stop stealing my jokes!"

"Sorry, Major!"

Umali smiled. "'Major'?"

"They started callin' me 'the Major' when I was a rookie back in the mists of prehistory when dinosaurs roamed the city. It stuck."

"Cannolis're here!" came a voice from behind Umali. It sounded like Fiore.

Turning, she saw that Fiore had bounded up from his desk and was practically running toward the staircase, where a very short woman with shoulder-length, dark brown hair and wide brown eyes had appeared, holding a box.

Umali's heart rate went up again. She hadn't actually answered Hawkins's question as to how she knew who Kiernan was, nor had she given a complete answer to Majorowicz's query as to why she transferred here.

What had impressed her most about the handling of the Rosario homicide had been the lead detective, Domenica Kiernan. Confronted with a murder that was unprecedented in the annals of NYPD, she had run a very impressive investigation. Umali had taken an interest both in her career and in the unit that formed in the wake of that case.

Now the target of her admiration was coming up the stairs with a white box tied closed by thin red string.

"C'mon," Hawkins said, "let's introduce you to Domenica and you can have your first cannoli."

The Major said, "You've never had a cannoli? You haven't *lived*."

"That's what Detective Fiore said, sir," Umali said quietly.

Shaking his head, Majorowicz said, "Everyone's stealin' my lines."

Hawkins quickly said, "It's a tribute to your leadership, sir."

"Right. Well, I hit my sugar limit for the day at breakfast with Patel, so I'm gonna pass. Roll call as soon as Ortega graces us with his presence." The Major retreated back to his office.

Hawkins led Umali to Jurienny's desk, where Fiore and Grullon had also gathered. Kiernan had put the box down on the desk, and Jurienny was using a pair of scissors to cut the string.

Hawkins, Grullon, Fiore, and Jurienny descended upon the pastries like vultures on a corpse. Umali took another deep breath through her nose, exhaled through her mouth, and walked up to Kiernan.

Shorter than everyone else in the squad room, she was also a bit on the chubby side—not pot-bellied like the Major, but with more curves than Umali herself. She had olive skin and very tiny wisps of hair on her upper lip.

She offered a hand to Kiernan. "Hi, I'm Detective Sofia Umali—it's my first day."

Kiernan nodded and accepted the handshake. "You're Jiminez's replacement. I'd say you got big shoes to fill, but you already met the Major, so you heard that joke."

"Actually, Detective Grullon made it first."

Looking over Umali's shoulder at Grullon, she said, "You cribbing the Major's jokes now, Grullon?"

Grullon, his mouth full of cannoli, just shrugged.

Kiernan gave her a pleasant smile. "Anyhow, welcome aboard. I read your file when your transfer was okayed. You were Army CID, right?"

Umali was briefly taken aback. *She read* my *file*? "Yes, I—I was."

"And you're a third-degree black belt in karate. You still train?"

Not expecting to be talking about this, Umali nodded. "And I teach kids once a week at our dojo. Do you train?" she asked, hoping for the commonality.

However: "Oh, fuck no, but my son does—up in Mamaroneck."

"I thought you lived in Belmont."

"I do. Bobby lives up there with my asshole ex and his bitch of a new wife."

Umali winced. This was the third busted marriage. "Bitter divorce?"

"Only very."

"Been there. But my ex-wife moved back to the Philippines, so I got sole custody of Liza."

"Lucky you. I only kept his last name 'cause it's easier to spell. I got *real* tired of people misspelling and mispronouncing Acquistapace."

With a chuckle, Umali said, "I get that. People make a mess of my last name all the time. Anyhow, I'm very happy to be here—" She hesitated, then thought, *Oh come on, just tell her.* "—and I'm really honored to be serving with you."

Kiernan surprised Umali by shooting her a very nasty look. "Why me?"

"You started this unit."

"I really didn't. I happened to take the call for Rosario's homicide."

"And that led to the unit being formed, mostly because of how well you handled one of the most difficult murder cases in NYPD history. In some circles, Detective—especially with other women on the job—you're kind of a legend."

Visibly shuddering, Kiernan said, "Yeah, and in a lot more circles, I'm the NYPD's equivalent of Fox Mulder."

Umali frowned. "Who?"

Kiernan sighed. "Never mind. Look, I appreciate it, but what we do here is policework just like everywhere else, okay?"

Before she could respond to that, Fiore walked over, holding a cannoli in one hand. "Only two left, Sofia, and Ortega gets one of 'em. Wanted to make sure you got to try one."

Kiernan regarded Umali with shock. "You've never had a cannoli?"

"Why is everyone so surprised by that?" Umali gingerly took the cannoli. It was a hard pastry shell filled with a white cream and bits of chocolate chip. She looked apologetically at Kiernan. "I'm sorry, but I have to ask—what's the filling made out of?"

"Whipped cream, mascarpone, powdered sugar, vanilla, and cinnamon."

One of those terms was completely unfamiliar. "Mascarpone?"

"It's kinda like cream cheese, only more wonderful," Kiernan said with a grin.

She handed it back to Fiore. "I'm sorry, I'm lactose intolerant. I can do a little bit of milk here and there, but *any* cheese and I'm spending all day in the bathroom."

Jurienny said, "Oh no, you can't do that—you gotta spend all day filling out paperwork!"

"Right. And lactose pills make me break out in hives."

Kiernan gave her an apologetic look. "Tomorrow's sfogliatelle, which has ricotta in it." She pronounced ricotta "ree-GOHT."

"Monday I'm bringing my lola's ube crinkle cookies."

Kiernan's eyes brightened. "Ooh, I love those!"

Umali smiled warmly. There was the commonality that mattered: love of food. That was a good start.

At the sound of footfalls, Umali turned to see the very familiar-looking form of Detective Ortega arriving at the top of the stairs. He had a completely bald head and a droopy mustache that he, after all this time, *still* insisted on dyeing black. The mustache complemented the hangdog expression that he always wore. The inspector at the One-Nine had once said that Ortega always looked like someone had just informed him that someone had run over his favorite pet.

He wore a beige windbreaker over a dark maroon shirt and a pale blue tie that had threads sticking out of it and coffee stains all over. He held a phone to his ear, and as he reached the landing, he said, "Got it. I'll talk to the Major," then touched the screen and put the phone in his slacks pocket.

Without preamble, Umali said, "Jesus, Ortega, you're *still* wearing that tie?"

Ortega broke into a huge grin that muted the dead-pet expression a bit. "Umali! Glad you made it!" He opened his arms, and she hugged him.

"Good to see you, you old fart."

"Good to be seen, you young squirt."

Fiore was chuckling. "You mean to tell me he's been wearing that tie since *before* SCU?"

"It's my lucky tie," Ortega said. "I wore it—"

Umali interrupted and finished his sentence in a sing-song voice. "'—the first day I got my gold shield and the one day I didn't wear it was the worst day of my career, and I've worn it every day since.'"

Grullon said, "We're *still* waiting to hear what happened on that worst day."

"You and everybody else," Umali said.

"Don't hold your breath," Ortega said as he snagged the last cannoli.

Across the squad room, the Major was back in his doorway. "Roll call, everyone!"

Umali walked across the squad room with Ortega. After swallowing the first bite of his cannoli, he said, "It's good to have you here, squirt."

"Thanks for putting in a good word with Majorowicz."

"Oh, that didn't matter. You got here on your own merits, trust me. And don't worry about the crazy here. Everyone goes on about how we're the spook squad or the monster squad or some other garbage, but it's just that—garbage. Crime is crime, and the policework here is just like policework everywhere else."

"That's pretty much what Kiernan said."

"Of course she did—I taught her everything she knows."

"But not everything *you* know, right?"

"Yeah, but that's only because I don't remember everything I know anymore."

Umali grinned. While the general challenge of SCU's cases and the presence of Domenica Kiernan were the primary reasons for her wanting the transfer, Ortega's presence was a very fortuitous side benefit. And she was sure that the good word he'd put in with the lieutenant—which she'd asked him to do at his sixtieth birthday party at Gleeson's Pub a few months back—played as big a role in her transfer going through as anything.

Everyone grabbed one of the chairs in front of the two boards, except for Ortega, who approached the lieutenant.

"Major, I just got off the phone with McSweeney at Midtown South. They got a body at the Port Authority they think is ours."

Before Majorowicz could reply, Hawkins rolled his eyes and said, "Is it really one of ours, or is this somebody trying to dump a case on us?"

Ortega didn't even look at Hawkins as he said to the Major, "McSweeney's a good police. If he says it's SCU, then it's probably SCU. We should look, anyhow."

"All right, head over there after roll call. Take Fiore."

"Can't, boss," Fiore said, "I got an appointment with Kevyn. Hawk already okayed it."

Ortega smiled. "Let me take Umali, break her cherry."

Now Umali was the one rolling her eyes. Ortega had his typical old-man moments, like that gross metaphor. She looked at Kiernan, hoping for some gender support, and the other woman shook her head and mouthed the word, *Men.*

Another commonality.

"Nah," Majorowicz said, "she's got a shit-ton of paperwork to fill out—and Kiernan and Grullon are stuck with IAB this morning. Hawk, you go with him."

"Wonderful," Ortega muttered.

"Happy to do it," Hawkins said.

Majorowicz took a seat in front of the SMARTboard. "All right, boys and girls, here's what's going on in crazytown today …"

Umali leaned back and smiled. She was looking forward to this.

FIVE

"I'm driving," Hawkins said as he and Ortega entered the garage on 106th Street, three doors down from SCU headquarters.

Ortega opened his mouth to argue, but Hawkins wouldn't let him get a word in.

"And before you start to argue, I will remind you that Support Services has your face on their dart board from all the vehicles you've damaged over the last forty years."

"The job requires aggressive driving." That was what Ortega always said, though he doubted Hawkins would ever accept it.

"And yet, *every other cop* in the unit has managed not to ding, damage, or destroy any car. Or stink them up, and you managed to do that twice just yesterday alone."

"I can't help what a kappa smells like," Ortega said defensively. "But fine, fine, you can drive."

Tilting his head, Hawkins said, "Gee, how kind of you to let your *sergeant* drive, Detective."

Ortega said nothing in response to the sarcasm. Sure, technically Hawkins outranked him, but that was because he was good at tests and did really well at all his desk jobs over the years. And he was a good administrator, Ortega had to admit that, though he'd never do so out loud in Hawk's hearing.

But going on the streets with him was never fun, because the sergeant had no idea what it was to be a real police.

The NYPD rented space for SCU's unmarked cars in the garage down the street and also allowed SCU staff to park their vehicles there if they drove to the office. The attendant, a young man named Imanol, who had a bald head and a thick beard, looked at Hawkins and said, "You're drivin', right?"

"Yeah."

"Good. After he stunk up both his rides yesterday, Sergeant Baney said I can't be givin' the detective here no more cars 'less I know for sure *he* ain't drivin'," he said, jerking a thumb at Ortega.

Ortega rolled his eyes as Imanol went to fetch one of the motor pool's many Chevy Malibus. "Baney does know that the car would've smelled like that no matter who it was who drove the kappa, right?"

"At this point, I don't think he cares," Hawkins said.

Once Imanol returned with the car, they climbed in. Hawkins pulled out of the garage and turned east onto 106th, and Ortega took his department-issue phone—which he'd been studiously ignoring since he'd gotten the call from McSweeney—out of his pocket. In the time since roll call, he'd gotten five text messages.

While most people on the job kept their personal stuff on their personal phones and used the NYPD ones for work only, Ortega had never had the patience for that. He just did everything on his department phone. It had caused problems a few times, when he'd had to turn his phone in as evidence, but he viewed those occasions as a break from the nonsense more than anything.

One of the texts was from his pharmacy, reminding him to pick up his meds, which he fully expected to forget all about by the time the tour ended. One was asking if he wanted to be part of a case study about erectile dysfunction, which he dutifully ignored.

He had done a drug trial, for cholesterol meds, ten years earlier, and they hadn't left him alone since.

The other three were from some of the women he'd married. He made a noise that was somewhere between a snort of disgust and a sigh of annoyance.

"Which ex-wife?" Hawkins asked, showing uncharacteristic insight into the timbre of Ortega's grumblings. They were now moving slowly down the FDR Drive, which ran down the east side of Manhattan. Skyscrapers towered over them on the right, while the East River, Roosevelt Island, and Queens sat regally on the left.

Grinning evilly, Ortega said, "Guess."

"Honestly, Luis, I *cannot* keep track. It could be any of them."

The grin fell. "Not *any.*"

At that, Hawkins had the good grace to wince. "I'm sorry, Luis."

This was why he hated going out with Hawkins. He was no kind of detective, or he would've remembered that Ortega's third wife was the only one of his five wives who hadn't been involved in divorce proceedings against him, by virtue of having died of breast cancer instead.

"It's fine," Ortega lied. "As it happens, I got a three-for: Maria, Estella, and Yzabella."

"Yzabella's the current one." Hawkins said it like he expected a prize for guessing right.

"A very temporary state of affairs, trust me. And technically, I didn't hear from her, I heard from her lawyer, who wanted to remind me about the deposition Monday afternoon. Speaking of that—"

"You've already asked for Monday afternoon off, and I already said yes."

"I did?" Ortega sighed. He'd been joking to Umali about how he'd forgotten some of what he knew, but there were times …

"Something I don't get, though—" Hawkins started.

Ortega restrained himself from commenting about how that was a long list.

"—why is Yzabella's lawyer contacting *you*? Shouldn't she be contacting *your* lawyer?"

"The text was to both me *and* my lawyer. I'll let Maxine handle it."

"Maxine's your divorce lawyer?"

"She is now. Her dad used to be, but he retired after I divorced Renata. I like her better anyhow—*much* more of a shark than Derek ever was."

"Good for you, I guess."

"Anyhow, Maria—that's my first wife—wants to know why there's no alimony payment because she—again—forgot that I don't get paid until tomorrow and the money direct-deposits into her account the Monday after payday. So I get to text her back—again—and remind her—again—about how this all works. It's only been thirty-eight years, I'm sure she'll get the hang of it soon enough ..."

"You had direct deposit thirty-eight years ago?"

Ortega ignored that, even though, in fact, back when the divorce was first finalized, he used to write alimony checks. Which Maria had always felt the urge to remind him to write, perhaps because it was rare that he remembered to do so. Which was what started them on this reminder merry-go-round they were still on after nearly four decades.

Hawkins—who was now getting into the right lane so they could get off at 49th Street—said, "Estella I know—that's number two, right?"

"And the only one I was stupid enough to procreate with."

"Oh come on, Ezequiel's a good guy." Hawkins smiled wryly. "Takes after his mother."

Ignoring that as well, Ortega said, "As it happens, Estella was texting to remind me that tomorrow is Ezequiel's thirtieth birthday. Which I had forgotten, so I need to get the kid a card. Probably should take him to lunch, too. And that annoys me."

"What, that you forgot his birthday?"

"No, that I'm grateful to Estella for reminding me, which pisses me off, because I hate being grateful to Estella."

"You'll get over it," Hawkins said as he drove across 49th.

Ortega didn't say anything but composed a text to Maria reminding her when he actually got paid and when, therefore, *she* got paid. Then he thanked Estella for reminding him.

He ignored the one from Yzabella's lawyer. Maxine could respond if she wanted to.

Estella texted him back:

You're welcome. Why don't you come for dinner tomorrow night? EZ's bringing his new boyfriend.

Ezequiel hated being called "EZ," but Ortega also knew that Estella hated how her phone kept autocorrecting "Ezequiel." He replied:

What happened to Bernardo?

I stopped asking those kinds of questions. Interrogations are your thing. I'm making pernil.

Ortega had already started typing his regretful refusal, but then he saw that Estella was making pernil. Slow-roasted pork had always been a weakness of his, and he'd never been able to resist Estella's version in particular. It was a big reason why he'd married her in the first place.

What time?

Hawkins had worked his way across Manhattan and was driving down Ninth Avenue. The block of 40th Street between Eighth and Ninth was closed off, but the patrol officers from Midtown South lifted the yellow crime-scene tape for the Malibu after Hawkins flashed his shield.

The Port Authority Bus Terminal was a giant edifice that took up the entirety of four city blocks. It was the primary terminal for buses going in and out of New York City.

About a third of the way down 40th, several blue-and-whites were parked haphazardly in the street, as was a van from the medical examiner's office. All of them were proximate to the entrance to one of the ground-floor garages that housed buses.

Hawkins pulled in behind one of the blue-and-whites and they both undid their seatbelts and exited the car.

Standing by the garage entrance were two men in button-down shirts, one Black, one Caucasian. The former was wearing a denim jacket and shivering, though sweat was beading on his bald head. The latter wore mirrorshades and had a thick mustache.

Without preamble, Ortega said to the Black one, "It's almost seventy out, DeLeon."

Before DeLeon could say anything, the other one said, "Don't get him started, please. Just wish this motherfucker'd put in his papers and move to New Mexico like he keeps sayin' he's gonna."

Ortega chuckled. "Sergeant Simeon Hawkins, meet Detectives Mason DeLeon and Dennis McSweeney."

"What've we got?" Hawkins asked.

"We think it's a vampire killing," McSweeney said.

Looking past them into the vestibule of the garage Ortega saw the body, currently being looked over by a coroner from the M.E.'s office. "Fuck, is that Jake the Jake?"

Hawkins turned to look incredulously at Ortega. "'Jake the Jake'? For real?"

Shrugging, Ortega said, "He's named Jake and he's Jamaican."

"That sounds—vaguely racist?" Hawkins didn't even seem sure.

"Maybe, but it's what everyone calls him."

"Not no more," McSweeney said. "Some vamp musta sucked his blood. And that vamp's prob'ly high as a kite now—Jake was a stone-ass junkie."

"How do *you* know him?" Hawkins asked Ortega.

"I met him when I worked the One-Seven. He helped me with some busts."

Hawkins nodded. "So he was your CI."

Shaking his head, Ortega said, "Nothing that formal—he was a good old-fashioned snitch. No paperwork, and the intel he gave me was always corroborated by someone I could actually put in a report."

"Uh-huh." Hawkins said those syllables disapprovingly.

Ortega tried not to roll his eyes.

The sergeant went to look at the body. McSweeney approached Ortega.

"Thanks for this."

"Hey, I owe Jake. He—"

Hawkins came back out onto the sidewalk. "Nice try, Detectives, but this is not an SCU case. The body is *covered* in stab wounds, two of which *happen* to be on the neck. They don't look a damn thing like bite marks." He looked angrily at Ortega. "I told you this would happen, Luis."

McSweeney took off his shades and rubbed the bridge of his nose between his first two fingers. "Fuck." He put the shades back on. "Okay, cards onna table. COMPSTAT is next week and our clearance rate is in the fuckin' toilet. We're still workin' that shooting in Bryant Park and the burglary at that comic store down the street, and we're absolutely nowhere on both. Now we got this. A fuckin' junkie. No witnesses, no surveillance."

"The garage doesn't have a camera?" Hawkins asked, surprised.

DeLeon sighed. "Busted. Work order's in for someone to repair it on Monday."

"What about forensics?"

McSweeney laughed at Hawkins's question. "You kidding me, Sergeant? Jake ain't had a shower since Obama was president. We ain't gonna find nothin' useful on him. It's a stone-cold whodunit, and our sergeant's gonna have our ass for this. Unless …"

Ortega sighed. "Unless SCU takes it. Our stats are counted separately as a special unit, and nobody gives a shit if our stats suck because half of everyone thinks what we do is bullshit anyhow."

DeLeon said, "Look, we will *totally* owe you guys one."

"No no no no," Ortega said with a big smile. "You will owe us three or four."

Hawkins stepped forward. "We are *not* taking this case, Luis."

"Look, Hawk, I owe Jake, okay? And our fellow detectives are asking us for a favor—one we can call in someday in the future. This is how being a police *works*—we *help* each other."

"No, how being a police works is closing cases."

McSweeney said, "Sergeant, we ain't gonna close this one. We ain't got the resources, and it's a fuckin' whodunit. Only thing that matters now is who gets the open case hangin' around their necks like that fuckin' bird."

"Albatross," Hawkins said absently. "It's from a Samuel Taylor Coleridge poem."

"Right, that thing." McSweeney raised an eyebrow. "That's from a poem?"

"You should try reading a book once, Detective." Hawkins sighed. "All right, fine, we'll take it."

Putting his hands together as if he was praying, McSweeney said, "*Thank* you, Sergeant! Like Mason said, we owe you one."

Ortega pointed a finger at McSweeney. "Like *I* said, you owe us *several*, McSweeney."

Hawkins stood facing Ortega with his hands on his hips. The sergeant probably thought it was an intimidating pose, but Ortega had to hold himself back from laughing. "You want this case, Luis? Fine. We'll take it. But *you* are doing every bit of paperwork yourself. No farming it off on Grullon. If I find out that this case isn't worked completely by the book, I'm tossing it back to MTS and your two friends here can go hang."

Putting his right hand on his heart, Ortega said, "I promise, Sergeant, that I will *not* make Grullon do my paperwork for me on this case."

"Good." He sighed. "All right, let's check the damn body."

As he and Hawkins went into the garage, Ortega smiled. He hadn't intended to fob the paperwork off on Grullon in any case. After all, he wasn't the squad's rookie anymore, Umali was. He could dump the paperwork on *her*.

SIX

As soon as she got back down to the second floor, Kiernan made a beeline for the vending machines. She had a rather ridiculous craving for corn chips.

Umali was sitting at what used to be Jiminez's desk, typing furiously using only her two index fingers.

"That," Kiernan said as she passed by on the way to fulfill her salt craving, "is the fastest I've seen anybody two-finger type."

"Years of practice," Umali said with a smile. "How'd it go with IAB?"

"My gynecologist is less invasive. And it was some new guy, so I had to explain fucking *everything* to him." She tapped her debit card on the snack machine's reader. It beeped and the display read CARD READ ERROR.

With a snarl, Kiernan swiped her card instead, then entered the code for the bag of corn chips.

The machine disgorged the small yellow bag of blessed, salty junk food into the bin in the bottom. Kiernan snatched it up and, as she headed for her desk, said to Umali, "Hopefully Grullon won't be as long up there. Hawk showed you around after roll call, right?"

Umali nodded. "Yeah. Went up to three and saw the kitchen and the interrogation and conference rooms. Went to four to see the regular holding cells. Went to five to see the bunks and lockers. Went down to one to see the big storage unit, the evidence closet, and the extra interrogation rooms for people who can't do the stairs or who we want to keep at ground level for whatever reason. And then he took me all the way down to the basement and showed me the *really awesome* special holding cells," Umali said that last with a big grin. Kiernan was starting to understand why the younger woman was so hot to join SCU. Beyond her ridiculous hero-worship of Kiernan herself, anyhow.

Sitting down at her desk, Kiernan smiled at the new detective. "They're pretty fabulous, right? The iron manacles, the silver manacles—oh, and I especially love the big-ass pentagram on the underfloor."

"There's a big-ass pentagram?"

Kiernan rolled her eyes as she popped a few corn chips into her mouth. After chewing and swallowing, she said, "Fuck, he didn't show you the pentagram? You push a button and the floor rolls back and there's this big pentagram in red on the underfloor. We need it to hold some kindsa monsters in place."

"Hawk said we're not supposed to use the word *monsters*."

Grabbing a tissue from the box on her desk to wipe the corn-chip residue from her fingers, Kiernan said, "He can say that all he wants, but anything that can get held in place by line art on the floor? That's a fuckin' *monster*. I mean, fine, we deal with plenty'a people I'd be happy to call *creatures* or *beings* or whatever, but if it's frozen by a fuckin' pentagram, then it's a monster." She ate a few more corn chips and added, "Please tell me he at least showed you the UV lights."

At that, Umali looked away, embarrassed. "Yeah."

"Lemme guess—you asked if that would burn the vampires to a crisp?"

She nodded.

"*Everybody* thinks that the first time—including me. Well, except Hawk, actually. But the whole idea of vampires bursting into flames from the sun comes from *Nosferatu*, which, it turns out, was just an unauthorized ripoff of *Dracula*. Everybody started doin' it after that in pop culture, but it was never part'a vampire folkore. Or, as it happens, reality."

"Wait, the bursting into flames thing is because of somebody's fanfic that everyone took seriously?"

Kiernan had to admit to loving that way of putting it. "Pretty much, yeah. The UV just keeps them at normal strength, instead of the super-strength they get at night."

As she tapped the space bar to wake her computer back up, Jurienny shouted across the squad room. "Domenica, line 2!"

"Thanks, Jurienny." She grabbed her phone, stabbed the button labeled "2," and put it to her ear. "Kiernan."

"Hey, Detective, it's Joe Lin from the One-Oh?"

"Oh, hey, Lin. How's Grabowski doing?"

"Nothing broken, just bruised ribs, but he'll be riding a desk for a week or two. IAB's talking to him now about discharging his weapon."

"Of course they are. Tell him I'm glad he's okay."

"Will do. Um, did you hear about the domovoy?"

Not liking the sound of that in the least, Kiernan slowly said, "What about the domovoy?"

"He—he got loose."

At a volume that was almost as loud as Jurienny's, Kiernan cried out, "How the *fuck* did he get loose?"

"A doctor came in and took the bullet out of his chest and then he snarled and tossed the doc around and ran off. They took shots at him, but he just shrugged them off and ran out into the street. There's a BOLO out and we've got a blue-and-white sitting at his place on 29th."

"Well, the BOLO's fucking useless, since he can change shape. And now that *he* knows that *we* know he committed the assault, no way he's gonna go back to looking like Leybenzon *or* going to that apartment." Then something rather important occurred to her. "After what the city paid to put in those specialized cells, how the *fuck* did he get out of one?"

"Um …" Lin hesitated.

Finally, when Lin's awkward pause threatened to go on forever, Kiernan prompted, "Lin?"

"They had him in a regular cell, not one of the new ones."

"*Madonna mia*, are you fucking kidding me with this? Why'd they do that?"

"I have no idea. Look, I only know what I do know because the report came in to us, since we brought him in. The DA's office was CC'd on it, but you guys weren't, so I figured I'd call. You want me to forward you the paperwork?"

"Please." Kiernan put a hand to her forehead.

The report was in her inbox almost before she hung up. She glanced over it, noting that yes, the suspect, Valery Leybenzon, had been placed in one of the regular cells. *Fucking idiots.*

She got up and went to the Major's office. The door was open, so she knocked on the frosted glass as she crossed the threshold.

"What's up, Kiernan?" the lieutenant asked.

"You're not gonna believe this." She filled him in.

The Major's first question was, "Why didn't they put him in one of the new cells?"

"That wasn't in the report, but my money's on 'they're fucking morons.' By the way, that report? They sent it to the One-Oh and the DA, but not to us. Luckily, I impressed the shit out of Lin yesterday on the bust, so the first thing he did was call me."

Majorowicz smirked. "Gee, Kiernan, it's not like you to *make* friends."

Kiernan casually replied with an upraised middle finger.

Chuckling, the Major reached for his phone. "All right, I'll call downtown and get into it. How'd it go with IAB?"

"The usual bullshit. Grullon's with him now."

"I'm sure it'll be fine. It was a clean shoot."

Kiernan hesitated. "Well, one of the things he asked was why I didn't try using a regular round before going to my backup weapon."

"Didn't one of the uniforms throw a shot already?"

"Yeah, which was in the report that this idiot didn't bother to fucking read. Anyhow, I don't trust that it'll come back clean from this *mammalucco.* Why couldn't they've sent Peña?"

"He's on vacation." The lieutenant, who had been holding the phone in his right hand for several seconds, finally started pushing buttons with his left. "I'll let you know what I get from the Tombs duty officer."

Grinning, Kiernan asked, "Can I listen in?" At the Major's dubious expression, she added, "C'mon, I love listening to you yell at morons. And I need cheering up after IAB's bullshit."

He sighed. "Fine, take a seat."

Still grinning, Kiernan plopped down on one of the guest chairs.

Someone answered the lieutenant's call, and after a second, the Major said, "Linda, this is Lieutenant Stan Majorowicz of the SCU. Who's the duty officer for you guys today? … Great, can you transfer me to him? … Thanks." Putting his hand over the mouthpiece, the Major said to Kiernan, "It's Frank Reilly. We were in uniform together in the Nine-Four a million years ago."

"Is that good or bad?" Kiernan recalled that the Major knew a third of the cops on the job and was on good terms with most of them, even the ones he thought were, in his words, "flaming-hot doofuses."

"I haven't talked to him in almost a decade, so it's hard to say." He uncovered the mouthpiece. "Frankie, it's Stan Majorowicz … I'm fine, thanks … Yeah, Hanna's doing great … No, Stan Junior's away at college. He's up at Cornell … I know, it feels like his confirmation was just last week. How's Mary? … Oh, damn. I'm sorry … Well, I'm glad it's amicable, at least … Good, arbitration's less painful than two lawyers going at it … Right, well, I got a problem with one of my cases … No, Frankie, I'm not at the Three-Three anymore, I run SCU … Yes, Frankie, it's real. That's why they built all those spiffy new cells in your basement."

Majorowicz looked up at the ceiling in supplication. Kiernan was squirming in the guest chair and practically biting her tongue to keep from laughing out loud.

"No, it's not for people high on PCP, it's for vampires and werewolves and domovoys—like the guy who got loose yesterday … Yeah, he was one of mine. I know officers from the One-Oh brought him in. That's 'cause we don't have room for him here. I only got four special cells, and right now they're full. I've got a naiad, a hugag, an awes-kon-wa, and a kappa … Basically, a mermaid, a funny-looking bear, Tinkerbell, and a slime monster with gas."

The Major's tone had been genial and friendly to start, but now he sounded very much like a Marine. "*No*, Frankie, I am *not* making this up. This is who we've got in holding until they can get arraigned. We ain't got space for any more, so we sent our latest collar down to you. Didn't you notice that Leybenzon looked like Bigfoot's cousin? … Cosplay, right. Look, Frankie, I know for a fact that the paperwork on Leybenzon said that he was SCU and that he should go in one of the new cells, and only *then* should the silver bullet be removed from his chest. The only part of that you got right was taking out the bullet. How is it you managed to see the part about removing a bullet but missed all the other parts? … Uh-huh … Uh-huh … Uh-huh … Actually, Frankie, yeah, it's *totally* your fault, and believe me when I tell you that the memo that I'm about to write to the commissioner will completely blame you. And you'd better hope the memo that I write on my computer is a helluva lot nicer than the one I'm writing in my head right now."

The Major slammed the phone down into the receiver. "What a flaming-hot doofus. Hope Mary takes him to the cleaners in the divorce."

At last, Kiernan felt comfortable enough to burst out laughing, which was good, because if she'd held it in much longer, her teeth would've exploded. Between guffaws, she asked, "Didn't he say it was amicable?"

"Yeah, but I hope she does anyhow." The Major also started to laugh, though he was visibly trying to keep control of himself. "It isn't really funny, y'know," he said between chuckles.

"Oh fuck no, it's tragic and pathetic and stupid." The straight face with which she said those words was fleeting. Kiernan let out another burst of laughter as she added, "But it's *also* funny. And frankly, after the rectal exam IAB gave me and finding out that your pal Frankie lost the domovoy, I needed the laugh."

"He is *not* my pal." Majorowicz shook his head. "This is why I buy the huge bottles of antacids. I'm gonna call Vondelikos and let him know we might need ESU if anyone ever finds Leybenzon."

Getting to her feet, Kiernan said, "Let's hope the asshole actually sends them this time. I need to go finish requisitioning new silvers." She refrained from mentioning that she hadn't even started filling out the forms. The Major was having a bad enough day …

Grullon was coming down the stairs as Kiernan came out of the lieutenant's office. The IAB inspector—whose name Kiernan refused to remember on principle—was right behind him. A short, squirrelly man with salt-and-pepper hair, a cheap suit, and a snotty attitude, he asked, "Is Lieutenant Majorowicz in his office?"

"He was a second ago," Kiernan said as she sat back down at her desk.

"Good." The IAB guy headed toward the lieutenant's office, then stopped and faced Kiernan. "By the way, Detective, I'm not supposed to tell you this, but you've probably got nothing to worry about. Once you explained what that thing was—and once I did a little reading on my phone between your interview and Detective Grullon's—it all made sense. This stuff you guys do is pretty wacked out, but it looks to me like it was a clean shoot."

With that, he continued into the Major's office.

"Damn," Kiernan said, "now I almost feel bad that I can't remember his name."

Grullon started to open his mouth, but Kiernan held up a finger. "*Don't* tell me what it is. I don't feel *that* bad."

Grullon chuckled. "Fair enough."

Kiernan tapped the space bar on her computer to wake it up, then started to fill out the paperwork for more silver bullets.

Let's hope they show up before I need them again.

She had only gotten through about a third of the form when a familiar voice said, "Excuse me, Detective Kiernan?"

Looking up, Kiernan saw a short, stout Latinx woman wearing a dark blue blouse, jeans, and flats. It took her a moment to completely recognize Catalina Mercado, as the woman's dark hair was much shorter than it had been the last time Kiernan had seen her. She still had a mark on her lip, though it was a scar now instead of the raw injury Kiernan had seen before, and all the bruising was gone. Even so, there were still some minor indications of swelling around her right eye.

Standing up, Kiernan said, "Ms. Mercado! I-I wasn't expecting you. Was I?" She added that last, worried that she had arranged to meet with the domovoy's assault victim and forgotten.

"No, no, Detective, I just—" Mercado took a deep breath. "I just wanted to see him in prison."

Kiernan winced. "Have a seat, Ms. Mercado. Can I get you something to drink?"

"The nice woman up front said she'd get me some tea."

Glancing at the front of the squad room, Kiernan saw that Jurienny wasn't at her desk.

Mercado sat down in Kiernan's guest chair. "I'm sorry to bother you, Detective."

Kiernan waved her off. "It's no bother, Ms. Mercado. It's good to see you. I like the haircut."

Smiling shyly, Mercado said, "Thank you. My son says it makes me look like a badass. My daughter says it's too butch."

Returning the smile, Kiernan said, "Well, I'm with your son."

Then Mercado's face hardened. "It's just, it's been so long since that bastard beat me up. Like I said, I want to see him behind bars. Or behind a steel door, I suppose? You don't have bars on your cells, do you?"

"We don't, no." Kiernan sighed. "The problem is, Ms. Mercado—the domovoy wasn't brought here. We're all full up, so the officers who helped us take him into custody took him to the Tombs downtown."

"Can you take me downtown to see him?"

Jurienny arrived with a mug of tea, which gave Kiernan time to figure out how, exactly, to tell this poor woman what had happened at the Tombs.

"Here you go, Ms. Mercado," Jurienny said as she handed the mug over. "*Cuidado, está caliente.*"

"*Gracias.*" Mercado gingerly took the mug by the handle.

Jurienny nodded, then also nodded to Kiernan before returning to her desk.

As Mercado blew on the tea and took a small sip, Kiernan said, "The problem, Ms. Mercado, is that—well—the domovoy isn't in the Tombs anymore."

"Did they transfer him somewhere else?" Mercado asked, sounding confused. Kiernan didn't blame her.

"Not exactly." Kiernan leaned forward. "I only just found out a few minutes ago myself. Someone down at the Tombs screwed up and the domovoy escaped. He's at large again. We've got a BOLO out," she said quickly as Mercado's left eye widened in horror; the right one hadn't healed enough to be able to do so.

"How does this happen?" she asked in a ragged whisper. "You said you arrested him."

"I did. *We* did. But, like I said, someone at the Tombs screwed up. They didn't put him in one of the special cells, so he was able to break out." She put a hand on Mercado's knee. "But he's on the run, Ms. Mercado. We've got officers watching his home and every cop on the job knows to look for him."

"Look for what? He can change shape, how are they supposed to find him?"

Kiernan had really been hoping that Mercado wouldn't have thought of that. "There are ways, Ms. Mercado. Trust me, we're professionals. We got this. We'll do everything we can to put him back—" She smirked. "—back behind bars."

"You promise?"

Again, Kiernan winced. "You know I can't do that. But I can promise we'll do our best."

Mercado took another sip of tea, then set the mug down on Kiernan's desk. "That's what you told me in the hospital, too."

"The good news is, we got a *lot* more information now than we did when you and I first met at St. Vincent's and I took your statement. We got a positive ID on the perp, complete with a DNA match, we got his movements and habits over the past six months, and we got a police force that gets cranky when people break out of our cells."

"And you think this is enough?"

"I think that when he assaulted you, we had limited options, and he had infinite ones. Now? It's the other way around."

Mercado closed her eyes and shook her head. "I hope you are right, Detective."

"Me, too," she said with an encouraging smile.

"What if he comes after me?"

"If you want, we can assign a car from—" Kiernan hesitated, trying to remember where Mercado lived—ah, yes, an apartment in the Corona neighborhood of Queens "—the 115th Precinct to your building."

"I would like that very much, yes."

Nodding, Kiernan said, "I'll get right on that."

After taking another sip of tea, Mercado got to her feet. "You will keep me posted, please? Even if there is no news?"

Also standing, Kiernan said, "Absolutely."

"*Gracias.*"

"C'mon, I'll walk you out."

She nodded, and the two women walked toward the staircase. As they passed Jurienny's desk, Mercado said to her, "*Gracias por el té.*"

Jurienny put her right hand over her heart and smiled.

As she walked the domovoy's victim downstairs, Kiernan hoped that everything she'd told Mercado was true and not a whole lot of bullshit to cover a rather massive fuckup.

SEVEN

Holding onto the Jesus bar in the Chevy Malibu for dear life, Grullon was seriously regretting his decision to let Umali drive down to the M.E.'s office.

It had seemed like a good idea at the time, he thought as she wove through the traffic on the FDR Drive like a skier down a slalom course. Now Grullon was certain in his very bones that they were going to die.

Grullon hadn't had much of a chance yet to get to know his successor as the squad's rookie. He'd had his IAB interview and then Hawk had him catching up on all the paperwork he'd fallen behind on. That task had been periodically interrupted by texts from his fiancée discussing the possibility of eloping, which had required Grullon to text back reminders that both families would disown them if they eloped, and Rachael replying that, for her, that wasn't really a deal-breaker right now.

Umali had had her own paperwork to fill out, plus Hawk had been showing her the various ropes. When the tour was over, Grullon had invited her out for a drink, but she'd had to go pick up her kid from afterschool.

This morning, right after roll call, and right after Fiore and Basia Pietri, the squad's archivist, had gone off to court, the Major had received a call from IAB. Kiernan and Grullon were officially cleared of any wrongdoing, so they could both go out on the street again. At the same time, Hawk had gotten a call from the Office of the City Medical Examiner that there was some news on Jake the Jake, and could a detective or two come down?

"I'll go," Ortega had said while eating one of the sfogliatelle Kiernan had brought in.

"No," Hawkins had replied without hesitation.

"It's my case!"

"Anastasia has made it clear you're not welcome down there, not after last time."

Ortega had frowned. "She was serious about that?"

"Extremely." Hawkins had shaken his head. "It's almost hard to believe you've had five wives."

"Fine, let Grullon go, then. I wanted him as secondary anyhow."

"You don't *need* a secondary on a drug murder that we took on for no good reason!" Hawk had cut off Ortega's objection. "Never mind. Liam, take Sofia with you. She should meet Anastasia in any case."

While they were walking down 106th to the garage, Umali had asked, "Mind if I drive? I get nauseous in the passenger seat."

Remembering all the times he'd been told no when he asked for things as a rookie—it was two months before anybody let him drive, for one thing, and it only happened that quickly because everyone felt sorry for him after the Van Cortlandt Park incident—Grullon had unhesitatingly said, "Sure." He didn't want Umali to go through the same hazing nonsense he'd been through.

Now Umali zoomed past the 34th Street exit, first in the left lane, then the center, then back to the left. Since the M.E.'s office was on 30th Street, Grullon found this decision curious. However, fear for his life had removed his ability to speak, so he didn't object.

The entire time, Umali had a very light grip on the wheel and seemed preternaturally calm. Indeed, the calmer she seemed, the more apprehensive Grullon got, and the more convinced he was that this trip was going to end in a fiery collision with an SUV.

Then she zipped across all three lanes to the 23rd Street exit, making the first right onto 25th. She decelerated into the turn and again as she approached a stop sign.

Grullon found his voice. "Wow."

"Wow what?" Umali asked as she sped up again, heading toward First Avenue.

"I didn't think you knew what a stop sign *was*."

Umali chuckled as she turned onto First. "Sorry, it's how my dad taught me how to drive."

"Your dad was a stock car racer?"

"No. He learned how to drive in the Philippines." She grinned. "Driving rules there are more like guidelines."

"That explains why you never signaled when you changed lanes."

As she pulled the Malibu into a spot right under a red NO STANDING ANYTIME sign, Umali said, "Dad always thought using the turn signal was giving information to the enemy."

"Uh-huh." Grullon opened the glove compartment and retrieved the NYPD credentials. He set them on the dashboard to keep the car from being towed.

They both got out of the car and Umali said as she beeped the Malibu locked, "Dad also said that you knew you could drive in New York safely if you could take the FDR without shitting in your socks."

"In that case, I wanna get a look at your socks," Grullon said.

Umali chuckled.

Now that he had his bearings and was no longer convinced he was going to die a horrible death, Grullon radioed in that they had arrived at the M.E.'s, and then said to Umali, "You've been here before, right?"

She nodded in the affirmative as the two of them entered the squat, rectangular edifice of bright blue bricks that was the Milton Helpern Institute of Forensic Medicine. The 1950s-era building housed the Office of the City Medical Examiner.

As they walked up the stairs to the glass door that would grant them ingress, Umali explained, "I was one of the secondaries on a triple homicide at the Two-Four last year, so I had to take a bunch of trips down here—plus I came a few times in uniform. But I don't know this Anastasia person?"

"Dr. Anastasia Klimchynskya. She handles most of the SCU's pathology cases."

They walked up another few stairs and then headed to the elevator. "Klimchink? I mean, Klim—"

Grullon laughed and cut off her attempt to pronounce the pathologist's last name. "We just call her 'Klimchee.' Except Ortega, he calls her 'Kimchee,' because he thinks it's funny to call her Korean coleslaw."

"Is that why he's banned from her presence?"

"Actually," Grullon said as they entered the elevator and he pushed the button for the appropriate floor, "I've got no idea why she's pissed at him. I mean, it's Ortega, pissing people off is kind of his super-power. Kiernan's, too."

"I don't know, I like them both. I mean yeah, Ortega's always been shit at making friends and influencing people, but he's also the best detective I've ever met. And Kiernan's just *amazing.* You should've seen her talking to the domovoy's victim yesterday. I don't think I could've kept the woman calm and reassured after what happened."

They arrived at the M.E.'s level and walked down the linoleum-floored hallway to a metal door with a nameplate reading ANASTASIA KLIMCHYNSKYA, M.D., PATHOLOGIST. Grullon knocked on the door.

A pleasant soprano voice said, "Come in" from the other side.

Grullon opened the door to a small, cluttered office. Facing them was a metal desk that was covered in file folders, a computer monitor, and a phone. Behind the desk, mounted to the wall were three more monitors, all of which displayed screen-saver images of the OCME logo.

Sitting at the desk, peering intently at the monitor in front of her, was a woman in her thirties with thick-framed red plastic glasses perched on her small nose. Her short, sharp, shock of hair had been dyed a bright red and she wore a white lab coat over light blue scrubs. The scrubs surprised Grullon, as Klimchynskya was usually dressed business-casual under her lab coat.

Tearing her gaze away from the monitor, she spoke in a voice that had only a slight Russian accent. "Hello, Detective Liam." She looked at Umali. "Who is this?"

Umali held out a hand. "Detective Sofia Umali. I just joined the unit."

"Dr. Anastasia Klimchynskya," she said, accepting the handshake as she stood up. "You are replacing Detective David?"

"Um, yeah." Apparently Klimchynskya wasn't big on last names.

The M.E. was staring at Umali's hand, which she still held. "What have you done to your knuckles?"

Grullon also looked and saw that the knuckles of Umali's index and middle fingers were swollen and callused. He was surprised he hadn't noticed that before now.

Umali smiled and broke the handshake. "Been practicing karate for eleven years now, and part of the training is doing pushups on my fists."

Eyes widening, Grullon said, "Seriously?"

"Yeah, it makes our punches stronger."

Klimchynskya snorted. "Okay, medically, that is probably correct, though also medically, it strikes me as incredibly irresponsible."

Grullon shook his head. "You told Hawk you had something for us?"

"I do."

"A prelim on Jake the Jake?"

"Not precisely."

The pathologist moved some file folders around on her desk, unearthing a small remote control. She pressed a button and the middle of the three wall-mounted monitors went from the OCME logo to a paused piece of security camera footage. It showed two young men in white lab coats standing over a metal table that held a zipped-up, black body bag.

"We received the body of Jacques Buddan—street name 'Jake the Jake'—this morning. It went yesterday to the morgue at St. Luke's for reasons known only to the gods themselves and was finally routed here today. This is what happened when we opened the bag."

Touching another button on the remote caused the video to play. One of the techs unzipped the body bag and gallons of a light brown liquid came pouring out onto the table and floor. Both techs jumped back in shock, their faces scrunched up.

After pressing pause on the remote, Klimchynskya regarded the two detectives. "What that video does not convey is the smell. Whatever liquid Buddan's body was turned into, besides being brown and roughly of the same viscosity as petroleum, had a stench that was among the worst any of us here have ever encountered. And when you consider that we all have spent our careers around corpses, you might imagine that our threshold for such is rather high. This is even worse than the cadejo."

Grullon looked blankly at the pathologist. "What's a ca-day-ho?"

Umali said, "That one I know—it's from Central American mythology. A kind of dog that either protects you or tries to kill you, depending on which folklore you read. And apparently real?"

Klimchynskya said, "It was from the early days of your unit. In any event, I am afraid that I am unable to perform an autopsy or determine cause of death for reasons that should be rather obvious."

Grullon said, "Well, Hawk's gonna be pissed that this really *is* an SCU case."

"I beg your pardon?" Klimchynskya asked, sounding confused.

"We only took the case as a favor to Midtown South. Jake was one of Ortega's CIs back in the day. But no way that—" He pointed at the monitor "—is natural, which means *super*natural, which means it's ours."

"And it is not alone," the doctor said.

"There's more?" Umali asked.

"Indeed. There is a reason why I am hyper-aware of the stench despite not being present for what you just witnessed. This morning, I was to perform the autopsy for a homicide victim named Elmore Hertweck." Klimchynskya touched another button on the remote and another monitor switched from the screensaver to security camera video, this of an autopsy room. Klimchynskya herself was standing over a dead body. The late Elmore Hertweck was apparently a middle-aged white male with short, salt-and-pepper hair both on his head and his chest, the beginnings of a pot belly, and long legs for his height. His neck was badly discolored and looked a bit off—probably a broken neck, likely the cause of death.

The pathologist was speaking on the video. *"Autopsy for Elmore Hertweck, case num— Chyort!"*

The Russian interjection was uttered as the body started to seemingly melt. Hertweck's facial features started to blur and flatten. His body collapsed in on itself, like an airbed deflating, and seemed to congeal and darken.

As the body fully turned to liquid, Grullon felt the sfogliatelle that he'd eaten back at the squad room well back up his throat.

Klimchynskya paused the video. "The smell has been lingering in my nostrils all morning. I had to throw away my breakfast. I do not like to waste food. I also had to burn the clothes I was wearing, as they were drenched in liquid lawyer."

"Sorry about that," Umali said weakly.

"It is not your fault, Detective Sofia, though I do appreciate the thought." The doctor sat back down at her desk and sorted through some file folders. She handed one to Grullon; it was labeled with Hertweck's name and the case number. "All yours, Detective Liam. I have already contacted the 17th Precinct and they will forward you NYPD's paperwork on the case."

"Thanks," he said, accepting the folder. "You said he was a lawyer?"

Klimchynskya nodded. "Corporate, I believe."

"Where was the body found?"

"In the basement of the apartment building on Sutton Place where he lived. For what it is worth, my opinion is that COD is a broken neck, with manner of death being homicide, but I am unable to provide evidence to support that declaration. Samples of both liquids are being compared to each other and tested for DNA, though I've no idea if they will even contain such."

Umali asked, "Does this mean we can't treat this as a homicide?"

"Strictly speaking," Grullon said, "it's corpse desecration."

"That's a Class E felony!" Umali sounded angry. "Which means it's pretty much just a misdemeanor with delusions of grandeur."

Grullon shook his head. "It doesn't matter."

"It doesn't?"

"We're a special unit, so we get to determine our own priorities. Even though this can't be classified as a homicide in the file, we can still run the investigation like it is one."

Umali nodded. "Okay. Good."

Looking at Klimchynskya, Grullon asked, "Anything else?"

"Has Detective Luis retired yet?"

With a chuckle, Grullon said, "Afraid not."

"Why? He is *very* old."

"Sixty is not *very* old," Umali said.

"Perhaps not for everyone, but it is for him. And he should consider a vow of silence. Or at least to be silent in my presence. And now I must return to work. It was a pleasure making your acquaintance, Detective Sofia. And Detective Liam, please give my warmest regards to Detective Domenica and Lieutenant Stanislaus."

"Will do," Grullon said.

As they headed to the elevator, Umali asked, "Just to Kiernan and the Major?"

"They're the only ones besides me she actually *likes*."

"So she doesn't like Hawk or Vinny, either."

"Nope. But hey, so far, she likes you."

"Lucky me." They rang for the elevator and one set of doors immediately opened. "You wanna get some food? I'm starving."

Grullon looked at her as if she had grown an additional limb—something he'd actually seen since joining SCU. "Are you nuts? After what we just saw? I ain't gonna be able to hold anything down for at least a day."

Umali shrugged. "I dunno, it just looked like what happened to Bruce Davison's character in the first *X-Men* movie. No big deal."

"If you say so." His phone buzzed and he immediately pulled it out of the pocket of his denim jacket.

"Why are you so nervous about a text?"

Grullon hadn't realized his apprehension was that obvious. "Lately, it feels like every text is something else going wrong with the wedding. But this one is just Rachael telling me she loves me and that she wants pizza for dinner tonight."

"Where do you guys live?"

"Crown Heights in Brooklyn. We got a great pizza place on Franklin Avenue. Oh!" Grullon added as he remembered something important. "I'm gonna need your mailing address."

Umali's face scrunched up in a suspicious expression. "Why?"

"So I can send you an invite to the wedding."

The elevator arrived at the lobby level and they headed back out to First Avenue and their parked Malibu. "Um—that's very kind, but—" She shook her head. "We only just met yesterday."

"Yeah, but I invited everyone in the unit, and it'd be awkward if you were the only one not there."

"Am I just taking Jiminez's spot?"

Grullon shook his head as they walked onto the First Avenue sidewalk. "Unlikely—he's the best man."

"Oh." She pointed the keys at the Malibu. Grullon stepped between her and the car.

"I'm driving," he said, holding out his hand.

"But—"

"No buts—I wanna live long enough to invite you to my wedding, and the only way I feel safe that's gonna happen is if *I* drive." Grullon cut Umali off as she opened her mouth to object. "And don't give me that I-get-nauseous-in-the-passenger-seat bullshit, either. If watching Hertweck turn into a stinky puddle didn't make you hurl, then my driving *definitely* won't. Gimme the keys."

Umali stared at him and Grullon wondered if he was going to have to fight her for the keys. Since she was a black belt, and Grullon wasn't, he didn't think that would work out well for him. And they were both third-grade, so he didn't outrank her.

Though she *was* the rookie. So he played that card: "If I let it be known that you, the rookie, refused to let me, not the rookie, drive, you will *not* hear the end of it from the rest of the squad."

Letting out a very long breath, Umali, with obvious reluctance, handed Grullon the keys. "Fine, but can we *please* stop and eat somewhere?"

"Okay, okay. You want breakfast or lunch?" It was after eleven, so it could go either way, and Umali hadn't been able to eat any of the sfogliatelle. He beeped the Malibu unlocked.

"Breakfast."

"Then we'll hit Un Grand Pâtisser. It's a French pastry place right near the house. Trust me, you'll love it. If it wasn't for Kiernan bringing in stuff from Little Italy, I'd be there every day." He got into the driver's side.

As Umali got into the passenger seat—still sulking a bit, Grullon noticed—she said, "Fine."

He started the car. "Since I'm driving, you get to call Hawk and tell him the good news."

Umali winced. "Can't I just text him?"

"Sure, but he'll just call you after he gets the text."

"I'll risk it." She started composing the text while Grullon pulled into the slow-moving First Avenue traffic.

As she was typing with her thumbs, she asked, "So Jiminez is your best man?"

"Yeah, we came up as uniforms together, and both made detective at the same time, too. I was best man when he married Chloe. He was put on that first case with the vampire killer that Kiernan caught, and she recommended him for the unit when it was formed. When the city gave us the budget for another third-grade, six months ago, he recommended me."

"That was good of him."

Silently Grullon thought that it wasn't *that* nice of him, given what had happened in Van Cortlandt Park, but he couldn't blame Jiminez for that.

Umali hit SEND on her phone with a flourish and said, "Done. Let's hope Hawk doesn't see it until we're back at the house."

"Anything can happen," Grullon said neutrally.

Turning to look at Grullon, Umali asked, "You sure it's okay to add me to the invite list? I mean, weddings are expensive, I don't wanna mess with your budget."

Grullon burst out laughing. "You *really* don't have to worry about *that*, Umali, *trust* me. Two-thirds of all the Jews in the New York metropolitan area are gonna be at this wedding on Rachael's side, and we won't even get into my gigantic Catholic family. It's gonna be *huge*, and nobody's even gonna notice one more person. Well, two more people, you can bring a plus-one."

"Are kids allowed?"

At that, Grullon sighed. "I was hoping not, but Rachael has seven nieces and nephews all under the age of thirteen and keeping them from the wedding was grounds for canceling the engagement. Unfortunately, that meant I had no excuse to keep my cousin Eddie away, so that little monster's gonna be there too, probably destroying everything in his path."

"Then my plus-one's gonna be my daughter Liza. She's seven, and she's the best-behaved little girl in the history of all creation, so she'll be fine."

"All of creation? Wow."

"Hey, when I have a kid, I don't screw around." Her thumbs started flying across her phone screen again. "Okay, I just texted you my address. We live up in Inwood—where's the wedding gonna be?"

"Place out on Long Island—in Massapequa."

"Think someone can give us a lift? We don't have a car, and I really don't wanna take the LIRR to a wedding."

"I would've ended that sentence at 'LIRR,' but yeah, you'll be fine. Kiernan lives in the Bronx and Ortega lives in Washington Heights, one of them oughtta be able to drive you guys out."

Umali's phone buzzed. She sighed. "It's Hawk."

"Better answer it."

"Can't I just let voicemail take it? I hate getting reamed by my boss."

"Hawk's a sweetheart, you'll be fine."

"Uh-huh." Umali slid a finger across the screen, then tapped the speaker icon. "Sergeant, you're on speaker with me and Grullon."

"How the hell did Luis's bullshit case turn out to be really SCU?"

Glancing sidelong at Grullon, Umali said, "Luck?"

"Yeah, all bad. And there's two cases now?"

Grullon explained. "Elmore Hertweck—corporate lawyer, lives on Sutton Place. Klimchee said the case file should be coming over from the One-Seven."

"Apartments on Sutton Place are *not* cheap," Hawkins said. "What's a lawyer who lives in the fancy part of the East Side got in common with a junkie?"

Umali said, "Rich people buy drugs, too, sir."

"Yeah. All right, get back here."

"We got some traffic, sir, it may take a bit," Grullon said.

Umali shot him a look—they were actually moving well up First.

"Just get here." Hawkins ended the call.

"Why did you lie to the sergeant?" Umali asked suspiciously.

"Because if I said we were going to Pâtisser, he'd insist on putting an order in and then asking everyone else what they want, and then making *you* pay for it, 'cause you're the rookie. Trust me, there's gonna be *plenty* of times when you will be responsible for feeding the entire squad room. I'm trying to spare you at least one of those occasions."

"Well, thanks." She hesitated. "And thanks for letting me drive down. I honestly didn't think you'd say yes."

Grullon shuddered. "If I'd known how you drive, I wouldn't have."

She chuckled. "And thanks for inviting me to your wedding. I promise, I'm not a horrible person who will make you regret that decision."

"Yeah, well, you're gonna earn it going forward. Because I'm telling you right now, you are going to be doing a *lot* of Ortega's paperwork."

EIGHT

Kiernan sat at her desk, pretending to read a case file on her computer, but actually watching the clock in the lower-right-hand corner of her monitor.

It was still seven minutes before the tour ended.

Seven interminable minutes.

At six minutes to end-of-tour, Fiore and Basia walked up the stairs.

"You're finally back," Hawkins said.

Ortega snorted from his desk. "Score another one for Sergeant Obvious."

Fiore was in one of the nice suits he got from his guy, with a tie this time for the court appearance. Kiernan was stunned that he'd kept it on once he'd left the courthouse.

As for Basia, she cleaned up well. The archivist, who was in her late twenties, had short, spiky hair that varied in color on a semi-regular basis—today, her hair was dyed a deep purple that almost looked like dark brown under fluorescent lights. Normally, she dressed in T-shirts that had reproductions of famous works of art on them, ripped jeans, and Chelsea boots. Today, for court, she wore a dark green, checkered dress, black lace stockings, and big, stompy, high-heeled boots that made her look taller than her usual four-foot-eleven. Kiernan envied her fellow short person's ability to wear those—her own weak ankles had never been able to support anything but loafers and sneakers and the occasional sandal. Basia also wore one of her smaller, daintier nose rings.

"How'd it go?" Kiernan asked.

"Shitty," Fiore said as he went to his desk, dramatically removing his tie and placing it in his top drawer.

Basia was a bit more forthcoming. "I've testified as an expert in court a *lot* since this unit was formed, and I have *never* seen so many sidebars and meetings in chambers as today. Including one time when I was on the stand and it got to the point that I pulled out a book and started reading every time the lawyers approached the bench."

"Didn't the judge complain?" Umali asked.

"Not after the third time. Anyhow, we were finally done about an hour ago, but traffic getting back up here from Center Street was murder."

"Speaking of murder," Hawkins said, "you wouldn't happen to know what could turn a corpse into a goopy brown liquid, would you?"

Grullon added, "That smells *really* bad."

Basia put a red-nail-polished finger to her chin as her blue eyes seemed to go blank for a second. Then she said, "Nothing off the top of my head. I can dig into it first thing Monday, though."

Umali said, "It's gotta wait until Monday?"

Basia pulled a phone out of one of her dress's pockets. "My tour ends in two minutes and the overtime freeze is still on. Besides, I've got to go home and then get to Penn Station to catch a train to Boston." She grinned. "I'm gonna go see Batteries Not Included at the Sinclair tomorrow night. Just gonna run up and get my stuff. G'night, all!" She headed upstairs to her office.

Umali said, "Okay, I'm pretty plugged into contemporary bands, but I've never heard of Batteries Not Included."

Holding up both hands, Kiernan said, "Don't look at me—all the music I listen to came out in a year starting with nineteen."

Grullon said, "Basia likes bands that nobody ever heard of. If they ever get a contract with a record label or get big enough to play a venue that can handle more than five hundred people, she loses interest."

Getting to her feet, Kiernan said, "Well, I'm outta here, too. Tim's droppin' Bobby off tonight and I still ain't done the dishes."

Fiore stared at her. "Seriously, Dom? Ain't a ten-year-old kid in the world who gives a shit whether or not you did the dishes."

"The ten-year-old doesn't," Kiernan said, having long since given up on getting Fiore to stop calling her "Dom," a nickname she despised. "But thirty-eight-year-old asshole ex-husbands give a shit, and I ain't giving him the ammo."

"Ammo?" Umali asked.

Remembering that Umali was new, and therefore hadn't been living with the saga of Kiernan's endless battles with Tim like everyone else, Kiernan said, "The reason why I live in a shitty one-bedroom in Belmont without a dishwasher or a washing machine or a dryer or consistent hot water is so I can save up for a *good* divorce lawyer and sue for more custody of Bobby than one weekend a month, plus Christmas. And the only reason I got Christmas is because my asshole ex is scared to death of my nonna, who was *not* gonna put up with doing the Seven Fishes without her great-grandson."

Umali's eyes had gone wide. "You only get one weekend a *month*? I don't care how bad your lawyer was, how'd the judge go for that?"

"Oh, didn't I mention that my asshole ex is a divorce lawyer? And that *his* divorce lawyer—who's now his second wife, by the way—works for the same firm and they're both tight with *every* family court judge in the Tri-State Area?"

"Ouch," Umali said with a wince.

"They also convinced their drinking-buddy judge that I was bad parenting material because of my job and that I went back on my promise to quit being a cop after we had a kid—a promise that only existed in my asshole ex's head, by the way, I *never* agreed to that. Mind you, I spend more time with Bobby on my weekends than those two do the other twenty-eight days of the month. The fucking nanny—who's great, by the way, I *love* Roseline—is the one raising him." She took a deep breath. "Fuck, now I'm all pissed off."

Getting up from her desk, Umali walked over and put a hand on her shoulder. "I am *so* sorry, Domenica."

"It's okay. Anyhow, the only lawyer who's willing to take those two on is *incredibly* expensive and won't even talk to me without a retainer the size of the GNP of Italy, not to mention their hourly rate. So I gotta save up."

The Major came out of his office, wearing a windbreaker that looked like it was a size too small. "What're you all doing here? Tour's over, get your asses home." He turned to Hawkins. "Who's on call tonight?"

"Vinny for evening tour, Luis for overnight."

"And who's on this weekend?"

"Sofia and Liam."

Nodding, the Major headed toward the stairs. "Good night, all." Everyone said their good-nights to the lieutenant as he departed.

Umali looked at Kiernan. "Grullon and I are the only ones working this weekend?"

Kiernan nodded as she slid into her leather jacket. "Unless there's a big all-hands-on-deck case, only two detectives work the weekends, and only the day tour. Hawk made the mistake of scheduling me for it on one of my weekends with Bobby *once*. He has *not* made that mistake a second time."

Umali grinned. "I bet. What about the on-call thing?"

"We always got one detective on call during the evening and overnight tours, just in case someone needs SCU when it's dark out."

"I would think that would happen more often than during the day, wouldn't it?"

"We thought that'd be the case when we first started the unit, but while a lotta stuff happens at night, it's usually not reported until daylight."

With a half-snort, half-chuckle, Umali said, "Yeah."

"If we ever get out of this stupid OT freeze, we'll work more than just weekday tours. Fucking Kogan."

Ever since City Comptroller Kogan had resigned in disgrace after admitting to embezzling funds from NYPD to put into one of Garth Ohlmeyer's Hudson Yards developments, there had been an overtime freeze while the department underwent a full financial audit. Originally, it was only supposed to last two weeks, but it had been a month now, with no indication of when things would return to normal.

"Well, I hope we start getting OT soon," Umali said. "I've got college tuition to save up for."

"From your lips ..." Kiernan slung her purse over her shoulder and headed to the staircase alongside Grullon and Fiore, with Umali a step behind. As they passed the admin's desk, Kiernan nodded to Jurienny. The admin was talking to Naomi, who covered the desk for the evening tour. Umali stopped to get introduced to Naomi, whom she hadn't met the previous day.

Downstairs, Kiernan said goodbye to Fiore and Grullon, who were both heading west, toward Lexington Avenue, to catch the train that would get them home to their respective neighborhoods in Brooklyn. For her part, Kiernan always drove to work in her battered, old Toyota Camry. The only decent parking she could find in her neighborhood was metered during the day, but as long as she got home after five p.m., she was fine. She could park in a metered spot and pay for parking until seven when the meters went out of service. She was always gone before the street sweepers came through at eight-thirty the following morning.

She could've just not had a car. It was an expense, even with the minimal insurance she had on it. But she'd always hated taking mass transit. More to the point, she hated being out of control of her transportation. Trains and buses ran at other people's whims. But *she* drove her car, dammit.

Not that I got a shit-ton of control right now, she thought glumly as she sat in bumper-to-bumper traffic on the Bruckner Expressway, inching her way northeast, a Bruce Springsteen CD blasting through the car's shitty speakers. The Camry was old enough to have both a CD player and a tape deck. Kiernan didn't own anything that would play on the latter, though her parents still had plenty that they insisted on still listening to.

She had bought a cradle for her smartphone that attached to the vent, so she could use the GPS to navigate traffic. As bad as the Bruckner was right now, it was still the fastest route home, and she had dishes to do, dammit. Which meant that when her mother called, she could see who it was … and even answer if she wanted.

Throwing common sense to the wind, especially since her mother was likely to ask if she'd been bitten by a vampire—*again*—Kiernan paused the CD, then slid her finger on the display to answer the call and put it on speaker. "Hey, Ma."

"Hi, Domenica, how are you doin'? Get bit by any vampires?"

Every damn time. "Not today, Ma."

"Good. You got Bobby this weekend, right?"

"Yeah, Ma." *I only told you fifty times.* "We're still on for dinner Sunday, right?"

"Of course! I'm makin' the sauce now. You give that grandson'a mine a big kiss from his nonna, okay?"

"Absolutely, Ma. You need me to bring anything?"

"Just some cannoli. For your father, not me."

Kiernan snorted. Her mother usually ate at least three cannoli, right after insisting she didn't want any, she was trying to lose weight. Well, maybe just one …

"Whatcha got planned, Domenica?"

"Movie tonight, Bronx Zoo tomorrow, Yankees game Sunday afternoon, then dinner with you and Dad."

"What movie? It's not gonna be an R-rated movie, he's only ten, you know."

Letting out a breath through gritted teeth, Kiernan said, "Yeah, Ma, I know how old he is. I happened to be present for the birth."

"Don't be snotty with me, Domenica."

Now she grinned. "Why stop now?"

"Ha ha ha. You wanna talk to your father?"

"Sure."

There was a pause, then, "Hello, *dolce figlia*."

"Hey, Dad."

"You shoot anybody today?"

"Not today, Dad, no, but IAB cleared me of Wednesday's shooting."

"Good. Maybe in the future, try not shooting people."

"He was beating up an officer, Dad. I had to do something. And this was a shape-changing creature that's immune to bullets."

"So then why'd you shoot it?"

"I used silver bullets."

"Like the Lone Ranger?"

She sighed. "*Yes*, Dad, like the Lone Ranger. And I had to requisition more silver bullets, and it's gonna take at least a month."

"Did you tell them that my *dolce figlia* needs her silver bullets to protect herself from shape-changing monsters?"

Chuckling, she said, "Not in so many words, but yeah, Dad, that was the gist. I mean, I left you out of it."

"Next time, tell them your father insists. It might help."

"Sure, Dad." Not that anything would make Moore Hill fulfill the requisition any faster, but there was no need to go into that with her father.

"Your mother wants to tell you something."

Of course she does. "Love you, Dad."

"Love you, too."

Her mother came back on. "Domenica, I almost forgot, your aunt Loretta's coming for dinner Sunday, too. She wants to see Bobby."

"That's fine, Ma." And it would be, mostly, as long as Loretta didn't try to set Kiernan up with someone—again. Loretta had always been Kiernan's favorite aunt, from childhood, but ever since the divorce, Loretta had been trying to set her up with "a nice Italian boy." This had led to a disastrous series of dates with guys who hit a 9.5 on the goombah scale. It was like going on a date with Fiore, if Fiore lost a hundred IQ points.

As she exited onto the service road to get her to the Bronx River Parkway, Kiernan said, "I gotta go, Ma."

"Okay, Domenica. All right. I'll see you and my wonderful grandson on Sunday."

"Love you, Ma."

"Love you, too."

The call having ended, she hit PLAY on the CD player, and Bruce started scream-singing about how he was going to spit in the face of these badlands. The traffic on the Bronx River was lighter and she got off at Fordham Road without incident. After driving around for ten minutes, she finally found a parking spot that was only two-and-a-half blocks from her apartment building on Hughes Avenue.

She walked up the three, cracked stone steps to the worn, black, metal front door of the five-story building where she rented a one-bedroom apartment. As usual, the key got stuck and she had to turn it back and forth before it finally got the door open. Her tiny mailbox was full, with three catalogues from stores she didn't shop at, two fliers from political candidates she didn't care about, and paperwork from her health insurance provider, which they kept sending no matter how many times she requested to go paperless.

As she trudged up the staircase to her third-floor apartment, a young, teenage girl went running past her. The girl was already at the door to 3A, at the far end of the third-floor hallway, calling, "Hi, Daddy, I'm home" as she unlocked the door, by the time Kiernan reached the third-floor landing.

Hadn't realized there was a teenager living down the hall. Must be new. Or I just haven't been paying attention.

At her own brown metal door, she unlocked all three locks and entered, relocking the door behind her.

Dropping the mail on the sideboard in the hallway along with all the other mail she'd gotten in the last week—which would all get recycled on Monday morning—she turned left and walked into the living room just far enough to get at the safe right under the fifty-five-inch TV that was mounted to the wall parallel to the front door. She entered the combination—four random numbers that had nothing to do with anything in her life, and which she had shared with no one—and put her department-issue nine-millimeter inside. She placed it right next to her currently empty backup weapon, which had been sitting in its holster in the safe since end-of-tour Wednesday.

After closing the thick metal door, Kiernan undid her shoulder holster and draped it over the top of the safe. She'd felt annoyingly vulnerable without the micro-nine backup the last two days and cursed Moore Hill and their slow fulfillment for the millionth time.

The necessary safety task completed, she kicked off her shoes and tossed her leather jacket onto the easy chair. Placing her purse on the same chair, she walked into the kitchen, where a pile of dirty dishes filled the sink in an accusatory manner. Kiernan didn't usually ascribe emotions to inanimate objects—not even after that time when a spell animated several things made out of bronze, including the Alice in Wonderland statue in Central Park—but right now, she felt like the dirty dishes were frowning at her, making fun of her, and saying she was a bad parent.

With a sigh, she yanked the single handle on the sink up and to the left, which theoretically turned on the hot water. It was ice cold to start, of course—the water needed several minutes to get warm—so she retreated down the hall to the bedroom. It was ready for Bobby: forty-five-inch TV with game controller attached, a stack of several of his favorite manga, the flannel bathrobe and *Star Wars* pajamas he favored, and, of course, his stuffed bunny rabbit, Usa-chan. When he'd turned eight, Bobby had insisted publicly that he didn't need to sleep with Usa-chan anymore, but every time he stayed here, he wound up snuggling the worn stuffie in his slumber.

Kiernan always slept in the living room—she didn't want Bobby to be icked out by sleeping in a bedroom that had Mom cooties—but stored her clothes in the bedroom. She stripped all the way down, not wanting a single piece of clothing that she wore to work to still be touching her person, then put on fresh underwear, the *Clone Wars* T-shirt that Bobby had picked out for her when they'd gone shopping at the Disney Store in Times Square over the summer, and yoga pants.

After tossing her work clothes into the hamper in the bathroom, she padded barefoot into the kitchen and put her hand under the streaming water. It was *almost* hot enough.

Pulling out her phone, she touched the music icon and put it on shuffle. She had half an hour before the time Tim said he'd arrive, which meant in reality she had forty-five minutes to get the dishes done.

As the dulcet tones of Bob Seger singing "Lookin' Back" came out of the phone's tinny speaker, Kiernan attacked the dishes. Forty minutes later, she finished the last of the silverware, having spent an inordinate amount of time taking a bit of steel wool to the Dutch oven that she'd burned the chicken in three days earlier. Janis Joplin was just finishing up "Me and Bobby McGee" when she put the final spoon in the silverware bin of the drying rack. She dried her hands and went to the bathroom, taking her music-playing phone with her.

Naturally, Tim rang the doorbell while she was on the toilet. *And if that isn't the best metaphor for our marriage, I don't know what is.*

Finishing quickly, she flushed, pulled her pants up, washed and dried her hands, and dashed into the hallway to push the TALK button. "Who is it?"

Static and some distorted sounds that vaguely resembled her ex-husband saying, “It’s Tim,” came through the ancient speaker.

Kiernan pushed the DOOR button, which made a mild buzzing noise, unlocking the building’s front door.

She unlocked and opened the apartment door and stood on the threshold waiting for them, stopping the music in the middle of Patti Smith’s “Because the Night,” hoping that her body language would make it clear that she didn’t want Tim to enter.

Bobby came up ahead of Tim and ran down the hall, his backpack bouncing.

“Mom!”

He barreled into her, and she barely was able to stand her ground as he grabbed her in a hug. Bobby had inherited his father’s blond hair and his mother’s brown eyes. He also had Tim’s father’s cheekbones, thank goodness, and the same cleft in his chin that most of the Acquistapace men had, including Kiernan’s father, uncles, and grandfather.

“Hey there, kidso.” She had accidentally mispronounced “kiddo” as “kidso” one time when Bobby was four, and it had stuck. When he finally broke the hug and pulled back, she gave him a bright smile. “Geez, are you taller than you were a month ago?”

Tim approached, looking winded from the three flights of stairs. His hair was cut in the same, corporate-looking, short-back-and-sides style as Bobby’s, but Tim’s was noticeably thinning.

“Couldn’t you have rented a first-floor apartment?” he asked, not for the first time.

She regarded him with annoyance. “Bobby’s big enough to climb stairs on his own, Tim, you don’t have to come up every time.”

Tim looked apologetic. At least Kiernan assumed it was apologetic—he so very rarely was regretful about anything, despite the legion of things for which he *should* have been, that it was hard to be sure. “I’m sorry, Domenica, but I *really* need to use the facilities. We were in traffic forever.”

Bobby shot his mother a look. “He took the Cross Bronx again.”

Kiernan gave her ex a what-the-*fuck* look. "Why would you do that? The Cross Bronx is *always* borked. It's a universal truth."

"Fine, whatever, can I *please* use your restroom?"

With a very dramatic sigh, Kiernan stepped aside and let Tim into the apartment. He immediately turned right down the hallway toward the bathroom.

"Sorry we're late," Bobby said. "I *told* him not to take the Cross Bronx, to just cut across Pelham Parkway, but—"

She put an arm around her son and led him into the apartment, closing but not locking the door. "It's okay, kidso. He's always late dropping you off, but he's also always late picking you up Sunday night, so it works out."

"We havin' dinner with Nonna and Nonno Sunday?"

Nodding, Kiernan said, "Yeah, Nonna's already making the sauce." Remembering something else Ma said on the phone, she grabbed Bobby by the sides of the head and planted a big kiss on his entire face.

"Mom!" Bobby cried out, pulling away and wiping his face with his palm.

"That was from Nonna."

"Figures."

Tim came out of the bathroom. "Thanks, Domenica. And hey, the apartment looks almost habitable this time."

"Gee, thanks," Kiernan said dryly.

Bobby said, "I'm gonna go put my stuff in my room so you two can argue where I can't hear it." With that, Bobby went down the hall and into the bedroom, closing the door behind him.

"When did that kid get so smart?" Tim asked, shaking his head.

"He always was. Takes after his mother."

"If you're the smart one, why am I living in a house in Mamaroneck while you're living in this dump?" He added quickly, before she could reply: "I'll pick him up Sunday night at ten-thirty, okay?"

"If you want to pick him up earlier, you can get him at my parents' place. We're having dinner with them."

"No, thanks, then I'd have to talk to your mother." Tim shuddered. "Or, rather, *listen* to your mother. I wouldn't wish that on my worst enemy."

"Really? I would."

"Besides, Julia and I have a thing Sunday night. We won't be any earlier than ten-thirty."

"It's okay, you won't make it until eleven anyhow."

"Just try not to get him bitten by a vampire or something."

Rolling her eyes, Kiernan said, "I'm off-duty till Monday morning, Tim. He'll be fine. The unit's covered, so unless a portal to hell opens, I'm all Bobby's this weekend."

"Good. Oh, speaking of your job, I—" Tim hesitated. "Wait, you said you'd wish seeing your mother on your worst enemy right after you invited me to—" He sighed. "Very funny, Domenica."

"Aw, and I thought you were the smart one! Took you half an hour to get that joke."

"I get jokes that are actually *funny*."

"Laughed all through your second wedding, didja?"

Tim closed his eyes and took a breath. "Look, this is serious."

"What's serious?"

"What I want to talk to you about. I heard that a friend of mine from law school, Elmore Hertweck, was killed."

That drew Kiernan up short.

Tim went on. "What's more, I heard that his body turned to liquid in the morgue. So I assume that's now one of your cases?"

Normally, Kiernan wouldn't discuss a case with a civilian, especially when that civilian was her asshole ex, but she also knew that Tim wouldn't leave until she gave him the answer he wanted. "Yeah, we caught it. I don't know the specifics, though, it's Ortega's case."

"So the turning-to-liquid thing is true?"

Kiernan nodded.

"Damn." Tim stared off into space for a second, then shook his head. "Well, tell Ortega—that's the bald one with the dyed mustache, right? Tell him that I had lunch with Elmore last week, and he was complaining about how he thought Jack Taylor—one of the other partners in the firm—was embezzling funds."

"I can pass that on, but we'd need a formal statement. Ortega might have to call you in for that. I wouldn't wish that on my worst enemy."

"What, is Ortega worse than your mother?"

"No, I meant I wouldn't wish talking to *you* on my worst enemy. I *like* Ortega."

"Very funny. Anyhow, it's fine, he can call me, I'll make a statement, whatever."

"I'll text him tonight, but he won't be in touch until he's back on the clock on Monday."

"That's fine." Tim then called down the hall. "Bobby! I'm leaving!"

Bobby called through the door, "Bye, Dad!"

"Don't I get a hug?"

After a lengthy pause, during which Kiernan prayed the reply would be "no," Bobby opened the door and came out. He gave Tim a much more perfunctory hug than the near-tackle he'd given Kiernan.

As Kiernan let Tim out, she said to Bobby, "You never replied to my e-mail—where you wanna get takeout from tonight?"

"Takeout?" Tim said as he walked out into the hallway. "You're not cooking?"

"I'll cook tomorrow—I'm wiped tonight." Before Tim could respond, Kiernan said, "Bye, Tim," and closed the door in his face.

"You enjoyed that, didn't you, Mom?"

"I don't know what you're talkin' about," Kiernan said with a smile, then led her son into the living room. The room was bisected by a couch, which faced the wall with the TV and the weapons safe.

The couch was currently covered in a virtual nest of unmatching throw-pillows, none of which matched the plain, dark red of the couch itself. Gathering up most of the throw-pillows in her short arms, Kiernan tossed them over the back of the couch. A large futon lay flat on the floor between the couch and the back wall of the apartment. Kiernan used that as her bed, and the throw-pillows could stay there while she and Bobby watched TV and ate dinner.

In front of the couch was a large red trunk—bright red and a completely different shade from the couch—that served both as a coffee table and a place to store bed linens. Next to the couch was a wooden end table with a worn finish that held the TV remotes and a basket filled with menus. Indicating the basket as she sat on the now-clear couch, Kiernan said, "Pick a restaurant, let me know what you want, and I'll go pick it up."

"They'll probably deliver."

"Food'll stay hotter if I get it." She didn't add that she didn't have to give as big a tip if she got it herself. "So pick something. And when that's done," she added, grabbing the TV remote, "tell me what you wanna watch tonight while we eat."

Bobby said, "You *know* what we're watching."

"*My Neighbor Totoro* again?"

The boy just grinned.

Kiernan laughed. "Fine." She turned the TV on and worked her way through the various menus until the animated movie in question was ready to go.

Bobby picked Joseph's on Arthur Avenue, which suited Kiernan fine, as it was her favorite of the many great restaurants in the area. He selected chicken parmigiano and a potato croquette on the side. He also wanted fried calamari, but Kiernan convinced him to go for a burrata instead. Fried calamari didn't work well as takeout food, the fish got all slimy and the breading went soft.

Kiernan called Joseph's—Yvonne answered the phone and recognized Kiernan's voice—and ordered Bobby's food, as well as a lasagne and side salad for herself.

"Chicken parm? You got your kid this weekend, honey?" Yvonne asked.

"Yeah."

"Whyn't you come in? We got Martino singin' tonight."

"No, thanks," Kiernan said quickly, "we're just gonna do a nice mother-and-son night in and watch a movie."

"Okay, honey, I understand. Should I use the credit card on file?"

"Yeah."

"Great, I'll put that in now. Give Bobby my best, and come on by in twenty minutes for pickup, okay?"

"Thanks, Yvonne."

Kiernan set a timer on her phone for fifteen minutes, since it would take five minutes to walk over.

"Yvonne sends her best," Kiernan said.

Bobby grinned. "I heard. You keep the volume way up on your phone, I heard the whole call. Why can't we go hear the singing at the restaurant?"

"Because Martino is the worst singer in the history of the world."

Eyes wide, Bobby asked, "Worse than Uncle Louie?"

"Okay, second worst. And he sings all those Italian songs your great-grandmother loves: Sinatra, Bennett, Carosone, Prima."

"But I thought we liked those songs. That's why I learned them on the clarinet."

Kiernan chuckled. Bobby had taken up the clarinet and played in the school band. He had learned the clarinet parts for several old Italian classics, which he'd played for Nonna when he'd visited her over the summer. "I love 'em! That's why I don't wanna hear Martino sing them in the key of Q. It hurts my heart."

"Oh, okay." Bobby gave an approving nod.

They watched the first fifteen minutes of the film. When the timer went off, Bobby ran into the bedroom and pulled out his tablet so he could play games until Kiernan came back.

As she slid into her Mary Janes and her leather jacket and grabbed her purse, Bobby said, "Don't get killed by a tengu!"

Kiernan chuckled. "In this neighborhood? Never happen. Maybe a strega would put a hex on me, though. So I'll watch out for that, okay?"

"Okay."

Bobby went back to his tablet, and she locked the door behind her.

Joseph's was only four and a half blocks from her building, a nice short walk. The late September weather was a little chilly, though it would be just like New York to get a heat wave before—or during—October.

Soon enough, Kiernan entered the vestibule at Joseph's, where they had the coat check and a little table. Another door led into the main part of the restaurant, where she could hear Martino massacring "Tu Vuò fà l'Americano."

Someone was already standing in the vestibule. He was very tall, though Kiernan had been forced by biology to think of most of humanity that way. She looked up to see short, curly dark hair atop a soft, circular face. His thin beard was trimmed in just the right way to accentuate a near-perfect pair of cheekbones. His skin was the color of cappuccino, and his almond eyes were wide and inviting—and also, just at the moment, vexed, his eyebrows turned downward, knitting a small vertical line in the middle of his forehead. Additionally, he was shifting his weight from foot to foot. Whether that was because he was eager for his food or because he couldn't stand the desecration of a Renato Carosone song from 1956 coming from the restaurant's interior was an open question.

One of the servers, Stefano, came out and said, "Domenica, *bellissima*! How are you? You need a table?"

Before Kiernan could reply, the tall man said, "Excuse me, but I am still waiting for my takeout order." He had a deep, resonant voice, with just the slightest trace of an accent. Based on his coloring, he probably traced his ancestry to southeast Europe, possibly Italian, more likely Greek or Albanian, all three of which were well represented in the neighborhood.

Stefano was brought up short by the tall man's comment and looked befuddled for a second. "I'm sorry?"

Kiernan stepped in quickly, saying to the other customer, "He's a server, he doesn't do takeout." To Stefano, she said, "I don't need a table, I'm picking up takeout, too. Is Yvonne around?"

Nodding, Stefano said, "I will bring her." He shot an annoyed glance at the tall man and went into the main room.

"Sorry," Kiernan said, "I'm a regular here, so they know me."

"I've never been here before. I just moved to the neighborhood, but my students all rave about the place, so I thought I'd try it. But I've got two *very* hungry girls at home who are likely to eat the furniture if I do not return with dinner soon. I called in the order an hour ago."

She winced. "Oooh, and you've had to listen to Martino this whole time? That's the guy singing."

"Whatever that man is doing, the verb 'to sing' is a very generous description of—of *that*."

Kiernan laughed just as Yvonne came into the vestibule from the restaurant, carrying two shopping bags, each with a receipt stapled to the side. The grand-daughter of the Joseph for whom the restaurant was named, Yvonne was a medium-height woman with straight dark hair, thick eyebrows, and a big nose. She wore a black blazer over black slacks and a white blouse.

With a bright smile showing off the bridgework Kiernan knew she'd paid through the nose for last year, Yvonne said, "Hi, honey, I've got your order." She turned to the tall man. "Are you—" She peered at the receipt on one of the bags. "—Mar-cage?"

"Markaj," he replied, pronouncing it "mar-KAHJ."

Yvonne handed him the shopping bag. "Here you go. Sorry for the delay, but they made veal parm by mistake, and I remember you saying your daughter is allergic to tomatoes, so I had to send it back. It's the veal scaloppine, I promise."

For a second, Markaj had looked like he was going to complain, but Yvonne's explanation seemed to calm him. "Thank you." He put the bag on the table, then reached into his back pocket and pulled out a wallet from which he extracted a credit card, handing it to Yvonne. "Here you are."

"Great." She took it and handed the other bag to Kiernan. "Honey, this is for you. If you could sign the receipt inside?"

Grabbing the bag, Kiernan saw a credit card machine printout with a pen clipped to it. "Got it."

To Markaj, Yvonne said, "I'll be right back."

Martino had moved on to "Tintarella di Luna," which was a slight improvement only insofar as he got the pacing right on the 1959 Mina song, though he retained his love-hate relationship with key.

Kiernan put the receipt on the table, quickly figured out a fifteen percent tip, added it to the slip, then wrote the total and her signature. If she'd been eating in the restaurant, she'd have tipped twenty or twenty-five percent, ditto for delivery.

As she finished, she said, "So whaddaya teach at Fordham?"

Markaj shot her a look. "How do you know I teach at Fordham?"

"You said 'my students all rave about this place,' and in my experience, grammar-school kids aren't all that big on restaurant recommendations. But this place is always full'a Fordham students … and the semester started three weeks ago."

"Not bad. You should be a detective."

"Yeah, prob'ly," she said with a smirk.

"I teach cultural anthropology."

"Nice."

Yvonne came back with a receipt for Markaj to sign and took Kiernan's. After saying goodbye, Kiernan walked out.

She went down Arthur to 189th, then turned right to get to Hughes. As she made that right, she was surprised to see Markaj walking down Hughes, crossing at 189th.

When she got to the corner and turned left, she saw Markaj struggling with the key to open the door of her own building.

"Two things," she said without preamble as she approached. "One, you gotta twist the key a few times, it sticks constantly. Two, how the hell did you get ahead'a me?"

Markaj chuckled. "Well, for starters, my legs are about twice as long as yours."

She looked up at him with mock annoyance. "Yeah, fine. But at least I don't hit my head on chandeliers."

"Good point—the struggle *is* real." He finally got the door unlocked. "Eureka!"

"Haven't seen you 'round the building before," she said as they entered the main floor.

"We only moved in at the start of the school year. I wished to be closer to work so I could be home for the girls. I've been on my own for a year now. More than that, really."

"Divorce?"

Markaj shook his head. "No, my wife—she died. Endometrial cancer. It was rough."

"I'm so sorry."

They trudged up the stairs together. "Thank you. We also have family in the neighborhood. And Violeta's thirteen now, so she can take care of herself, but Mimoza's only nine."

"My boy's ten. I got him this weekend. Divorce," she added as they turned at the second-floor landing and went to the stairs up to three.

"Your ex-husband has custody?"

"Except for one weekend a month and Christmas. Do *not* get me started." She could see Markaj was about to ask the same questions Umali had been asking earlier. "The food'll get cold if I start in on it."

Markaj laughed. Kiernan found herself liking his very musical laugh.

They both went straight ahead on three, and she realized where he had to live. "You're in 3A?"

He nodded.

"Your daughter ran past me on the steps this evening."

"That sounds very much like Violeta." Again the lovely laugh. "I'm Sabri." He pronounced it with emphasis on the first syllable.

He also put out his hand, and she accepted it, saying, "Domenica."

"Enjoy your dinner."

"You, too—the veal scaloppine is always excellent."

"Is that what you ordered?"

"Nah, I was in a lasagne mood."

"I didn't know there was such a thing as a lasagne mood. What are the symptoms?"

"A desire to stop standing in the hallway keeping my kid waiting for dinner so I can eat the lasagne."

Once more, the great laugh. "Right, of course. My apologies. Same here, truly. Hope to see you again soon, Domenica."

"Back atcha, Sabri."

His mouth fell open. "You pronounced it properly!"

She put her key in the lock. "You just said it, like, three seconds ago."

"That doesn't always help."

"My maiden name's Acquistapace, so I feel your pain." She opened the door.

"You kept your husband's name?"

"I don't have to spell 'Kiernan' to people quite as often."

"Fair enough."

Bobby's voice came from the living room. "Mom?"

"Gotta go," she said.

"Bye," he replied.

She went into the living room and put the shopping bag on the coffee table/trunk. "Let's eat." When he'd heard her key in the lock, Bobby had, as usual, gotten napkins, forks, and butter knives from the kitchen, along with two bottles of Ramune, a soda Bobby loved. Kiernan had bought two variety ten-packs from one of the Japanese grocery stores in Industry City in Brooklyn; she'd been out there a lot when those trolls were wreaking havoc under the Gowanus Expressway.

Bobby had set out a strawberry for her and an orange for himself.

"Who were you talking to?" he asked.

"New neighbor. He was getting dinner for his kids at Joseph's, too."

"Nice," Bobby said as Kiernan laid out the food. "Any stregas? Or tengu?"

"Negative on both."

Within minutes, they were continuing *My Neighbor Totoro* while munching on Italian food and drinking Japanese soda.

Even though he had the movie completely memorized, Bobby was utterly rapt by the film. At this point, Kiernan had memorized it, too, even though she'd only seen it a tenth of the number of times her son had.

But she loved watching it with him, because it brought such joy to her Japanophile kid, especially if he also got to drink Ramune and eat food from one of his favorite restaurants at the same time. From what Roseline, the nanny, had been telling her, Bobby was a generally happy kid, but he rarely was joyous when he was with his father and stepmother.

She couldn't wait to take him to the zoo tomorrow.

NINE

Ortega was in the third-floor kitchen, holding an empty mug and staring angrily at the coffeemaker, which wasn't brewing nearly fast enough to suit him.

Umali and Kiernan both came up behind him. "There coffee?" the latter asked.

"Workin' on it," he muttered.

Umali was on his left, holding a Tupperware container in both hands. Kiernan was on his right.

"You look like crap, Ortega," Umali said.

Managing to scrape up the energy for a wry smile, Ortega said, "Gee, thanks, Umali. I'd hate to feel this shitty and not look the part."

Kiernan said, "He had dinner with Estella Friday night."

"Oooh." Umali's entire face scrunched up. "How much did you drink on Saturday?"

Ortega sighed. "I stopped counting. Mostly because I forgot how."

"Why did you have dinner with Estella?"

Kiernan answered as she got on her tiptoes to reach up to the white cabinet over the coffeemaker. "It was Ezequiel's thirtieth birthday." She grabbed two white mugs with the NYPD logo on them, handing one to Umali.

"And she made pernil." Again, Ortega sighed. "What can I tell you, I'm weak."

"No, I get it," Umali said. "You always used to rave about her pernil. That plus Ezequiel's birthday? You couldn't resist that. This might help." She opened the lid to the Tupperware to reveal a pile of purple cookies.

Ortega managed a ragged smile, which was difficult in his pre-caffeinated, hung-over state, but the sight—and smell—of the Tupperware's contents made it worth the effort. "Y'know, when I found out you were assigned to SCU, my first thought—" He snorted. "Well, my first thought was, 'When the hell did she make detective?' but my *second* thought was, 'Damn, I hope her grandmother still bakes.'"

"She does. Help yourself to some ube crinkle cookies." Umali put the Tupperware down on the counter next to the coffeemaker. "Also, I had made detective when I asked you to vouch for me to Majorowicz at your birthday party."

As Ortega grabbed one of the purple cookies, he asked, "You weren't still in uniform, then?"

"No, I've been a gold shield for two and a half years now."

"Huh." He popped the cookie into his mouth.

Kiernan asked, "How the hell is Ezequiel thirty?"

"The same way I'm sixty, Kiernan," he snapped. "It's just math and time."

He instantly regretted his tone, but Kiernan, as usual, was unbothered. "I guess. I mean, I don't see how Bobby could possibly be ten, either."

"How was your weekend with him?" Umali asked.

Kiernan grinned widely, which was a very rare expression for her, in Ortega's experience. "Fuckin' fantastic. We watched his favorite movie Friday night—"

Ortega said, "Oh God, he made you watch that cartoon about the gray teddy bear *again*?"

Laughing, Kiernan said, "*My Neighbor Totoro.* And Bobby is all about the anime and the manga. Has been since he took up karate. He's even thinking of trying to learn Japanese."

"That's fantastic," Umali said in what seemed to Ortega to be an unnecessarily enthusiastic tone.

"Anyhow, we went to the zoo Saturday, which was great, even though it was *packed*, and I made stuffed pork chops for dinner. Sunday was fabulous. First, we saw the Yankees game, which not only were they kind enough to win, but they were also giving away a bobblehead that a friend of Bobby's is dying to get his hands on. My son said he can trade it for a Funko Pop that he's been dying to get *his* hands on, so it was win-win all around. And then we went for dinner at my parents'."

"You survived that?" Ortega asked, remembering that Kiernan dreaded parental dinners with almost the same fervor that Ortega dreaded seeing any of his surviving ex-wives.

"Oh, yeah, it's always fine when Bobby's there. They dote all the fuck over him. Even Aunt Loretta who—miracle of fuckin' miracles—did *not* try to set me up with anybody."

An annoyingly cheery voice piped up from behind. "Good morning, everyone!"

Ortega turned to see Basia coming into the kitchen, holding a mug with a teabag in it. She was in her usual art T-shirt—this time, some painting Ortega didn't recognize—and ripped jeans. She had re-dyed her hair over the weekend, so it was now bright green, and was wearing a nose ring with a sparkly little diamond.

"Hey, Basia," Kiernan said. "How was the concert?"

"Not bad. Batteries Not Included was great, but the sound system was *awful*. Saw another band on the bill called Epic Grit Bowls that was pretty good, and they're coming down here to play Duff's in Brooklyn next week, so I'm gonna try to catch them there. Oh!" She added that exclamation at a volume that rattled Ortega's poor, hung-over brain. "I got to go to a game at Fenway Park. Domenica, you'll be happy to know that the Red Sox lost."

Nodding sagely, Kiernan said, "Excellent. Always a good day when the Yankees' rivals lose."

For his part, the only sport Ortega cared about was horse-racing, and he'd given that up as a promise to Mayli on her deathbed.

"Are those ube?" Basia asked, staring hungrily at the Tupperware.

Umali nodded. "Homemade."

"You made them?"

"Oh, God, no, I don't even *touch* my stove. They're from my lola."

Basia took one. After her first bite, she said, "Mmmmm, these are delish! Thank you!" She shook her head. "Between your grandmother and Domenica, I'm gonna gain fifty pounds working here."

Ortega was going to make a snide comment about how Basia was skinny enough to fit in one leg of his trousers and maybe gaining a few pounds wouldn't kill her, but the coffeemaker made a final gurgle and then was quiet, so his focus shifted back to that. He eagerly started pouring the blessed elixir into his mug. Just the smell as it sloshed into the ceramic made him feel better.

Basia took a sip of tea while the other two detectives grabbed for the coffee. "By the way, Luis, I've got some leads on the liquefying corpses thing."

"Shit!" Kiernan said. "I've got something for you, too, Ortega—but go ahead, Basia, just don't let me forget to tell him."

Nodding, Basia said, "I did some research last night at home, and I double-checked when I got in this morning. It had to have been a spell."

"So we're looking for a Gandalf," Ortega said.

"A Gandalf?" Umali asked, sipping coffee.

Kiernan waved a hand back and forth. "That's what we call magic-users."

"Well," Basia said, "this isn't just any Gandalf. We're talking about a *very* powerful spell—and on top of that, whoever cast it on Hertweck had to have done it from a distance, but still with precision. There are *maybe* half-a-dozen Gandalfs in the world who could pull that off."

"I don't suppose you could tell me who those six *are*?" Ortega asked.

"I wish."

He held up a hand. "It's okay, I know just who to talk to. Thanks."

"No problem."

The archivist retreated to her office on this floor, while Ortega and the other women headed for the staircase and the squad room. Umali left the cookies on the kitchen counter.

"I also may have a lead for you," Kiernan said as they went downstairs, "from my asshole ex, believe it or not."

Ortega shot her a look. "I *don't* believe it, actually."

"He went to law school with Hertweck."

"Okay, maybe I do believe it."

"You should call him. Hertweck told him some office gossip when they had lunch a little while ago."

"What gossip?"

They had arrived on the second floor and Kiernan said firmly, "No, no, no, you talk to him directly. I don't want no official part of this."

"Fine." Ortega looked right at Umali. "*You* call him."

"Why me?" Umali asked defensively.

"Two reasons. One, because everyone else in the squad room knows him and hates him. You don't have any history with him."

"And two?"

"Because I said so, squirt."

Kiernan chuckled. "I'll give you his work number."

All three detectives went to their respective desks. The Major had gone to a meeting at One Police Plaza this morning, so they were skipping roll call, which suited Ortega. His head hurt enough without dealing with the lieutenant's brash, ex-Marine voice.

Ortega pulled out his phone and called an informant. It went straight to voicemail. "This is Lane. Do the thing after the beep. Or just send a text like normal people."

Snorting, Ortega ended the call without leaving a message and composed a text:

Need to talk today.

Lane texted back within a minute:

Meet me in an hour at Belvedere Castle.

Ortega looked up quickly, an action he instantly regretted. After sipping some more coffee, he called out to the sergeant. "Hey, Hawk, I got something from Basia, but I'm gonna need to follow up with Lane."

Nodding, Hawkins said, "Yeah, okay. Take Sofia, she should meet Lane."

Umali asked, "Who's Lane?"

"Lane Thibodeaux," Hawkins said. "One of Luis's CIs and one of SCU's most reliable. They're plugged in to the magic-user community."

"So he's gonna ID our Gandalf, maybe?"

Hawkins glared at Ortega. "She's been here less than a week and you've already got her using that stupid term?"

"You're the only one who thinks it's stupid, Hawk," Ortega said. "Everyone else in the unit uses it, including the Major."

"A million people may say a stupid thing, and it's still a stupid thing." Hawkins sighed. "Anyhow, take her with you."

Ortega stood up slowly, hearing his knees crack. He gulped down the rest of his coffee, which he instantly regretted as it burned his tongue. Shaking his head back and forth, he took a second to get his bearings, then said, "Okay, let's go."

Umali was staring at him with concern. "You okay, Ortega?"

"I'm fine." He smirked. "Don't get old."

"Screw that," she said, "it beats the hell out of the alternative."

"Can't argue with that," he said while shrugging into his windbreaker.

At that, Umali grinned. "That's never stopped you from arguing before."

"Maybe when I was back at the One-Nine, but I was younger then. Now I need to save up my arguing energy for Maria, Estella, and Yzabella."

"Not Renata?"

"We haven't spoken since she married that idiot."

They started moving down the stairs. "You've met her new husband?" Umali asked.

"No."

"Then how do you know he's an idiot?"

"Look who he married."

"Um—"

"Yeah, I know, I married her, too, but I wised up and divorced her. Renata is the only one of the women I married that *I* served with divorce papers."

"Why do you sound proud of that?"

As they hit the first-floor landing, Ortega said, "It shows growth?"

"It'd show more growth if you hadn't married Yzabella."

Ortega shrugged. "Eh. Growth is a process."

"Uh-huh."

They stepped outside. A cold breeze cut through the air, coming in off the Harlem River to the east. Ortega zipped up his windbreaker though Umali left her flannel-lined denim jacket hanging open as they walked to the garage. Umali's phone buzzed and she glanced at the display.

Imanol looked at them as they entered the garage. "She's driving, right?"

Ortega said, "No way," at the same time that Umali said, "Yes."

"Excuse me, but I'm the senior detective," Ortega said, glowering at Umali.

"In the whole NYPD, yeah," Umali replied with a grin.

"Damn right, squirt, and that means I get to drive when I say so. Besides, Grullon warned me about how you nearly made him ralph."

"Okay, first of all, Grullon exaggerated. He showed absolutely *no* signs of barfing. Secondly, it's not like I've ever actually hit anything while driving, which puts me one up on you. Thirdly ..." Umali held up her phone.

Ortega, whose reading glasses were buried in his shirt pocket under his still-zipped-up windbreaker, had to squint to read what was apparently a text from Hawkins.

> Don't let Luis drive. If he argues, tell him it comes directly from me and the Major.

"Look, sometimes a guy gets a rep—"

Imanol, however, interrupted. "Fourthly, I *still* can't let you have a car 'less *she's* drivin'. In fact, Sergeant Baney called me, texted me, *and* e-mailed me this morning to make sure I wouldn't sign out a car to you unless someone else was driving."

"Fine, fine, she's driving."

"Cool." Imanol retreated to fetch their Malibu.

Umali was grinning. "Didn't Support Services have you on speed-dial when you were at the One-Nine?"

Ortega ignored the dig. "You realize that text was bullshit, right? The Major isn't even in yet. You know Hawk just said that the orders came from the Major 'cause he knew I wouldn't take it seriously just coming from him."

Sounding confused, Umali said, "He's the sergeant."

"If you're in plainclothes, sergeant is just a consolation prize for not being able to cut it as a detective."

"By outranking detectives and getting to boss detectives around?"

Ortega waved a dismissive arm. "You wouldn't understand."

"That's for sure."

Imanol pulled up in the Malibu, and Umali moved quickly to the driver's side. With as dramatic a sigh as he could manage, Ortega gingerly climbed into the passenger seat.

"Head to the Central Park Precinct on the 86th Street Transverse. We can park there and walk to the castle." He yanked the door closed.

As Umali fastened her seatbelt, she said, "There's really a castle in Central Park?"

Ortega stared at her. "How did you not know that?"

"Only parts of Central Park I've been to are Bethesda Fountain and the flower garden. Oh, and I saw a concert on the North Lawn once."

"Belvedere Castle overlooks the Great Lawn, and it's right next to that open-air theater, the Delacorte. It also overlooks the Turtle Pond, which is where the naiad we've got in holding was living."

Umali pulled into traffic. "A naiad lived there?"

"No, half a dozen naiads *live* there, present tense. One of them was mugging people in the park."

"How'd you catch him?"

"Her—all naiads are female. And I didn't catch her, it was Kiernan's case, but she closed it the way you always close a case: gather evidence, talk to people, make an arrest. Just because some of that evidence is soaking wet and the people you talk to are water creatures that communicate via sign language, the methodology don't change."

Umali reached Fifth Avenue and turned left. Traffic was slow, but Umali was weaving around cars with the verve of a cab driver.

As she cut off an SUV while changing lanes, Umali asked, "Wait, naiads use ASL?"

"Two of them did—they have their own language, which is all gestures and stuff, but a pair of them learned American Sign Language on their own. Their mouths can't form words, so we had to use one of the department's interpreters to interview 'em, and we—*Christ!*"

Umali had swerved around a yellow cab that was pulling over to pick up a passenger, then swerved again to avoid a delivery bicycle.

"I thought you said Grullon was exaggerating!" Ortega cried out as he clenched his eyes shut, not particularly willing to observe his imminent death.

She slowed down for a red light, and only then did Ortega open his eyes. "Christ," he muttered.

"Oh, stop it. I haven't hit anything."

"Yet."

"In all the time I've been in NYPD—and, for that matter, for all my time in the Army—no vehicle I've driven has even had a *scratch.* I had to drive myself to investigations when I was in CID. You think New York roads suck, try driving around Kandahar."

"I'll take your word for it." Ortega closed his eyes again as Umali stomped on the accelerator.

Within a few minutes, they arrived at the Central Park Precinct. They checked in with the watch commander to let them know that they were meeting a CI at Belvedere Castle and radioed dispatch that they'd arrived.

It took almost twice as long to walk from the precinct to the castle than it had to drive from the house to the park, but at least it was a nice, sunny day, if a bit chilly. Besides, the walk gave Ortega a chance to reset his heart rate after surviving Umali's driving.

They walked past the various softball fields on the Great Lawn; nobody was currently playing a game. The park was filled with people, though, on the grass or on one of the many benches alongside the paved walkways. Some were talking, some were reading, some were working on laptops or tablets or listening to music or playing catch or jogging or walking their dogs or just wandering about.

Umali watched a jogger pass between them. "All these people in the park. How did nobody notice that there were a bunch of naiads living in the Turtle Pond?"

"Who says they didn't?" Ortega said. "It just didn't get reported. Or if it did get reported, nobody believed them. That's one of the things the unit's been good for. People can report the weird stuff to us, and we'll actually believe them instead of laughing at them or calling for a psych consult. Anyhow, from what the naiads told Kiernan a couple weeks ago, they only started living in the lake in the last thirty years or so—before that, the lake was too gunked-up to live in."

"Pollution?"

"And too much algae, plus there were tons of dragonflies. Naiads are allergic to dragonflies. But the Conservancy drained and redid the Turtle Pond in the late nineties. That's when the naiads moved in."

"So who is this CI we're going to see?"

"Lane's plugged into the whole woo-woo community, even more than Basia is. They know a lot of the Gandalfs—most of whom, I should add, are little better than Penn-and-Teller wannabes. Not that many people can do seriously powerful magic, thank God. The Gandalfs have a whole community that's still pretty under the radar, and it's a pretty tight one."

"If Lane's more plugged in than Basia, why aren't they working directly for us like she is?"

"Because Lane's a major hustler and grifter. I arrested them a few years back. The department frowns on hiring ex-cons, but they can be CIs, and Lane's been a great one."

"So Basia's more legit?"

"Oh yeah. For one thing, besides being an expert in our little sub-section of the world, Basia's also a tech wizard and has a library degree. Kiernan brought her on as a consultant during the Rosario case and pushed to hire her when the unit was formed."

Ortega led Umali to the right of the pond, around the Delacorte Theatre, to the uneven stone staircase that led up, past the Shakespeare Garden, to the castle.

Halfway up, Ortega had to stop. It was getting hard to breathe, pains were shooting through his shins and feet, and suddenly he was *very* warm inside his windbreaker. "Hang—hang on." He bent over, putting his hands on his knees, and tried to breathe slowly.

Umali, two steps further up, came down to stand next to him. "You okay?"

"You want the honest answer or the polite answer?"

"The honest one."

"I'm fine."

Umali snorted. "Seriously? What if I'd asked for the polite answer?"

"I'd have said, 'I'm fine, thanks.' Like I told you before, don't get old."

"And like I told you before, I don't like the alternative."

Ortega straightened. "C'mon."

"You sure you're all right?"

"Did you miss the part where 'I'm fine' was the honest answer?"

"Yeah," Umali said with a grin, "I just don't believe it."

Ortega pointed up the stairs. "Move your ass, squirt."

Holding up both hands in an I-surrender gesture, Umali said, "All right, all right."

At the top of the stairs, they stepped into a courtyard.

The first time Ortega had come here, he was a little kid. Back then, Turtle Pond was called Belvedere Lake, and it was choked with algae and insect life. The Great Lawn was more brown than green, the park was covered in litter, and the courtyard he was standing on was cracked and badly maintained.

More than five decades later, he felt like he was looking at a postcard. The sun shone down on the miniature castle, a small stone edifice that looked like it belonged in the Scottish countryside. To the left was a large, slant-roofed gazebo where Ortega knew lots of weddings had taken place since they'd fixed this area up.

Between them was a waist-high stone wall that provided a truly magnificent view of the lush greenery of the Great Lawn and the clear blue-green waters of the Turtle Pond. Ortega had always loved that this pastoral magnificence had been created in the middle of the city.

The one thing he couldn't see was Lane, but that was mainly because he didn't have his glasses on and couldn't really make out faces. He pulled out his phone and texted the CI:

Where are you?

After a moment, he got a text back:

At the wall over the lake. I'm looking right at you.

"C'mon," Ortega said as he led Umali forward.

Once they were close, he had no trouble making out Lane. They had a dark-skinned face with a tiny nose and thin lips. They were dressed in a denim jacket over a white button-down shirt and tight black jeans. The shirt was untucked, shirttails sticking out under the jacket, which was apparently the fashion now.

Ortega remembered Ezequiel asking him once, "Who tucks in their shirts?" as if the very concept was absurd. Ortega had replied at the time: "Grown-ups."

However, Ortega had mostly made peace with the fact that he was sixty years old and most people whose age was a smaller number did things he just wasn't going to understand. Accepting that had enabled him to cut down considerably on his drinking.

As they approached, Lane said, "Jesus fuckin' Christ, Ortega, you still wearin' that damn tie?"

Ortega said, "It's my lucky tie" at the same time that Umali said, "*Don't* get him started."

Lane laughed and pointed at Umali. "Who's this?"

"Our newest detective. Sofia Umali, this is Lane Thibodeaux."

"It's Thibodeaux."

Ortega frowned. "That's what I said."

Umali glanced sidewise at him. "No, you said Thibodeaux. It's pronounced Thibodeaux."

"I'm not hearing a damn bit of difference between either of the things you said."

Speaking slowly, Umali said, "You said '*tih*-boh-doh,' and it's '*tee*-ba-doh.' "

He stared blankly at Umali. "I'm still not—"

"Forget it," Lane said. "If we gotta correct every stupid-ass thing Ortega here says, we'll be here all day, and I got shit to do. So what's up?"

Since Lane was a good CI, Ortega let the insult pass—this time—and instead explained about the liquefied corpses and what Basia had told them about Gandalfs who might be capable of successfully casting the necessary spell from a distance.

Lane let out an appreciative whistle. "Damn. My girl Basia's right, that's some serious shit right there. Buncha folks could cast that spell easy if they was in the room, but long-distance? And gettin' it right? Only two people I know who live in the Big Apple can pull *that* shit off. Amanda Cornwell and Garth Ohlmeyer."

That brought Ortega up short. "Wait, *the* Garth Ohlmeyer?"

Lane looked back and forth, confused. "I guess?"

"Isn't that the guy who's got that development in Hudson Yards the DA's looking into?" Umali asked.

Ortega nodded. That was a name he had *not* expected to turn up in an SCU case. "That's him. Venture capitalist, real-estate developer, corporate magnate, drug kingpin. The first three are general knowledge, but the fourth one is something Narcotics, Major Case, and the One-Seven have been trying and failing to prove for ages. I was part of the team tryin' to build a case against him at the One-Seven back in the day. Sonofabitch got half our evidence tossed and the DA dropped the case. Now they're goin' after him for that comptroller mess in Hudson Yards, but he'll probably skate on that, too, like he always does. Why am I not surprised that he's a Gandalf?"

"Y'know what surprises *me*?" Lane asked. "That you never asked me about his ass before."

"Never came up. Hell, I ain't hardly even thought about Ohlmeyer since I transferred out of the One-Seven. But he's been the white whale for half the damn department *and* the DA's office, and now we find out he's a Gandalf?" Ortega sighed deeply. So much about Ohlmeyer was making more sense now.

Umali looked at Lane. "What about the other person you mentioned, Amanda something?"

"Cornwell," Lane said. "She one crazy-ass bitch, I tell you that, but I don't see her for this."

"Me, either," Ortega said.

"You know her?" Umali asked.

Ortega nodded. "She's big in the Wicca community, gives speeches, writes books. She's also got a bug up her ass about SCU—but yeah, Lane's right, she's not the type who'd go around desecrating corpses. Or making someone into a corpse in the first place, for that matter."

Lane smirked. "Yeah, she's all about the sanctity of life and shit."

"It's the 'and shit' that always gets you," Ortega said. "Anybody else you know can do this?"

"One's livin' up in Canada, contemplatin' his navel or somethin', and the others are all in Asia and Africa. I'll text you the names if you want, but I ain't heard that none'a them traveled no place."

"Text me the names, definitely," Ortega said with a nod. "Thanks, Lane."

"Hey," Lane said, "you wanna hear somethin' funny? While I was waitin' for your ass to show, I was talkin' to this dude. You know this place is a weather station? Whenever they say on the TV or the radio that the temperature in Central Park is whatever degrees, this is where they measure it. That's some cool-ass shit."

"If you say so." Ortega put out a hand. "Thanks again, Lane, this is a big help."

Lane accepted the hand. "Hey, long as y'all keep fightin' the good fight—and keepin' my Black ass from goin' back to jail—we're always cool."

Umali also offered a handshake. "Good to meet you."

"Back atcha, Detective. See if you can buy this motherfucker a new tie."

As they headed back to the staircase, Ortega's phone buzzed. He stopped walking, pulled it out of his windbreaker pocket, and held it close to his face so he could read it.

It was from Maxine:

Deposition moved up to 11. Can you make it?

It was a little after ten now.

Absolutely. Still at Scumbucket's office?

It is at the office of my respected colleague, Genisea Grant, Attorney-at-Law, yes.

Ortega snorted.

Right, Scumbucket. See you there.

Umali was watching him with her arms folded. "Everything okay, old fart?"

"Yup. Guess what—you get to drive back alone."

"Oh?" Umali dropped her arms as her face fell.

Jerking a thumb eastward, he said, "I'm gonna walk over to Fifth Avenue and catch a cab down to 61st Street. I gotta give a deposition."

"This is for the divorce?" Umali asked.

Smiling wryly, Ortega asked, "How'd you guess?"

"If it was for the job, we'd go there in the Malibu. If you're paying for a cab out of your own money, then it has to be personal. And since you don't actually have a life outside the job, the only personal thing you could be giving a deposition for at a Lenox Hill law office is your divorce."

Bowing his head with mock-appreciation, Ortega said, "It's almost like you're a detective or something, squirt." Umali was right, too. In fact, when he was honest with himself—which wasn't all that often—his inability to have any kind of life outside the job was the primary reason for each of his divorces. The only one who hadn't gotten pissed about how dedicated he was to the job at the expense of a home life was Mayli, God rest her soul.

"Anyhow, you can take the Malibu back to the house, which means that when you die in a mass of twisted, fiery metal, you'll only be taking yourself out, and not me."

"I keep telling you—" she started in a sing-song voice, but Ortega cut her off.

"You've never crashed a vehicle. Yet. With my luck, I'll be your first victim, and no thank you."

"Oh, trust me, old fart, when I kill you, it'll be on purpose." She laughed to make it clear she was kidding, though Ortega knew that already.

He grew serious as they proceeded down the stone stairs. "I'll radio in that I'm 10-89," he said, which would indicate that he was unavailable for a reason that wasn't mechanical or a meal break, "and tell Hawk that we got a break. You give him the specifics in person—and the Major if he's back."

"We're gonna jump on Ohlmeyer?"

Ortega gave her an *are you kidding?* look. "Oh, no no no no *no*, we are going to move *extremely* slowly and carefully and meticulously on Ohlmeyer and we're going to double check everything and do it all by the book. And even then, it probably won't help. Ohlmeyer pays good money for his army of lawyers, and he's already loaded for bear with this Hudson Yards investigation. I'll forward you Lane's text when he gets me the other names. We're going to run Cornwell and all the other people Lane's given us."

Umali frowned. "What, even the ones in other countries?"

"Damn right." They got to the bottom of the stairs, right behind the Delacorte. "Because if we don't check every single lead provided by our confidential informant, that army of lawyers I mentioned will say that NYPD did not investigate *every* possibility, that they singled out their client at the expense of pursuing other leads. We will therefore pursue every other lead."

"So we're gonna jump on Cornwell?"

Pointing at Umali approvingly, Ortega said, "*Now* you get it." They had gotten to the paved walkway that passed in front of both the Delacorte and the Turtle Pond. "All right, I'm going this way," he said, pointing east.

"I'll head back to the Central Park Precinct. Good luck with the deposition. You gonna be okay?"

"You kidding?" Ortega let out a huge grin. "I'm in a position where I'm *forced* to tell the truth about my soon-to-be-ex-wife, and on the record, no less! I'm looking forward to this!"

HOT

TEN

Kiernan had been in a very good mood. The weekend with Bobby had been wonderful, she'd survived dinner at her parents without her mother being too annoying or her father being too ridiculous, and Aunt Loretta hadn't tried to set her up with anyone.

The new detective was looking like she'd turn out okay. Kiernan had been nervous about Umali. Part of that was because Ortega spoke so highly of her. While Ortega was one of the best detectives Kiernan had ever known, his ability to judge people *as people* was suspect at best, with Exhibit A being his marriages.

And part of it was the way Umali got all goofy when she and Kiernan were first introduced, treating her like some kind of fucking celebrity. It wasn't the first time that had happened, but it *was* the first time it'd happened within the unit.

However, after four days on the job, Umali was doing great. Over the weekend, she and Grullon had gotten a lead on a string of thefts of grocery stores in Chinatown going back several weeks.

When the thefts had first started back in August, witnesses had described a four-legged creature covered in green scales. It had a deep, wide mouth filled with sharp teeth, a flattened snout, and beady eyes located on its shoulders.

The locals all said it was a Taotie, at which point the 5th Precinct eagerly dumped the case on SCU. Fiore had caught the case, and it had been slowly going cold. The squad had been getting daily phone calls from Dolly Chao, a septuagenarian resident of Chinatown who claimed to represent a group of concerned citizens, asking what kind of progress was being made, as well as weekly phone calls from the city council member representing District 1.

On Saturday, however, Chao's phone call was informational rather than accusatory: the Taotie had been sighted breaking into a restaurant. Umali and Grullon checked it out, and while the Taotie was long gone, there were several witnesses, including a busboy who had taken video with his phone. Umali and Grullon interviewed the new witnesses and reinterviewed the old ones, and on Sunday, they determined that all the places the Taotie had hit were clustered around the corner of Pell and Doyers Streets. So when Chao called on Sunday, they had actual news for her.

This morning, Fiore and Grullon had gone down to Chinatown to follow up and had brought in a couple whom everyone in the neighborhood now was saying kept the Taotie as a pet. Grullon had asked why this hadn't been mentioned before, which had prompted Fiore to say, "Forget it, Grullon, it's Chinatown," which had prompted Grullon to smack Fiore on the arm.

Fiore was now upstairs interrogating the couple, with Umali observing after returning from her field trip to Belvedere Castle with Ortega.

Meanwhile, Hawkins was looking into Garth Ohlmeyer's financials—mostly records already subpoenaed by the DA's office—while Kiernan and Grullon had spent the afternoon chasing down the other Gandalfs that Lane Thibodeaux had mentioned to Ortega and Umali. Kiernan had determined that Amanda Cornwell had been in New Zealand for the last six months, researching a book. Basia had confirmed that even the most powerful Gandalf couldn't cast the liquefication spell from a different hemisphere, so she, at least, had an alibi.

Overall, it had been a good few days, even accounting for the drag effect of the Tombs losing the domovoy and having to regularly give negative updates to Catalina Mercado. In general, though, Kiernan was feeling great.

Two hours before the tour ended, the Major managed to utterly destroy her good mood with fourteen simple words: "Kiernan, I need you go to down to Plaisir Douleur and talk to Valapart."

"For fuck's sake, *why*?" she asked plaintively.

The Major was standing in the doorway to his office, hands on his rather expansive hips, giving Kiernan a stare that probably used to intimidate the shit out of his fellow Marines, but which Kiernan—a veteran of the myriad looks Italian mothers and grandmothers were capable of—was wholly unaffected by. "I would think, 'Because I said so' would be a good enough reason, what with me being a lieutenant and all."

Smiling gamely, Kiernan said, "You'd think that, wouldn't you?"

"Since I'm feeling generous, I'll give you another answer: because Valapart probably can get us a line on the domovoy."

Kiernan was pretty sure the Major wasn't being generous at all, but was tap-dancing since his stern disapproving look was not working.

But he was also right. Valapart, a three-hundred-year-old vampire, was a useful source of intel, going all the way back to the case that got the SCU started.

And Kiernan really didn't want to send another "no news yet" text to Mercado.

Majorowicz continued, "Plus, I got seven separate phone calls today asking for help in tracking the domovoy—one from the One-Oh, one from the Tombs, one from the chief of detectives, one from the commissioner's office, and one each from three different deputy commissioners. I'm guessing that the victim isn't all that thrilled and been calling regularly?"

"Texting, but yeah," Kiernan said quietly.

"Even though it isn't our fuckup, everyone wants us to fix it. So you're gonna go talk to Valapart and start working to fix it."

However, Kiernan wasn't ready to give in just yet. "He's gonna hit on me again."

"Detective Kiernan," the Major said firmly, and now Kiernan flinched, because when the lieutenant started referring to you by your rank *and* your last name, you were in trouble, "are you telling me that a police officer of your talents isn't capable of dealing with a little flirting?"

"It's not 'a little flirting'! He comes on *extremely* strong, so much so that I wanna punch him in the throat and stick a stake in his heart and cut off his head. And if I do that, he'll never tell us anything about the domovoy."

Grullon stood up. "I can go talk to him."

"You've never even met him," Kiernan said.

"Yeah, but you guys talk about him all the time, and if he's that important a CI, I should probably meet him."

The Major nodded, always an amusing sight given the thickness of his neck. "Fine, you can both go."

Kiernan winced and pointed angrily at Grullon. "C'mon, Major, he just said he'd go!"

"And *I* just said you're *both* going. Guess who wins." Before Kiernan could object again, the Major cut in, "Look, forget everything else—it's Valapart. He's not gonna talk to Grullon. For that matter, he's not gonna talk to Fiore, especially after what happened last summer, and Ortega refuses to go into the place. But he *will* talk to you, because he wants you to join the club, and he knows you'll never join if he doesn't do what you ask."

"I'll never join if he does, either," Kiernan said with a shudder.

"Yeah, but he doesn't need to know that."

Kiernan sighed. "I know, I know, but—"

Holding up one hand, the Major said, "Ah ah—no buts. Despite your best efforts to act otherwise, this is a direct instruction from your unit commander." That same hand pointed to the staircase. "Get your ass to Plaisir Douleur."

"Fine." Kiernan put her computer to sleep, grabbed her leather jacket, and said, "Let's go, Grullon."

Grullon had a deer-in-the-headlights look. "So I *am* going?"

"*Madonna mia, yes,* you're going. The Major's right, you should meet Valapart. If nothing else, having you there will *probably* keep me from beating him about the head and shoulders."

"Yeah," Grullon said as he got up and put on a trench coat, "I don't think keeping you from doing something stupid is one of my super-powers."

In a long-suffering tone, the Major said, "Nobody has that power."

Kiernan stuck her tongue out at the lieutenant and said, "Both of you can kiss my entire ass."

They headed downstairs and then out to the garage.

"So where are we going, exactly?"

"It's a club Valapart owns down in SoHo."

Grullon chuckled. "And we're going in daylight?"

Kiernan rolled her eyes. "Vampires don't—"

"I *know* vampires don't burn up in sunlight, they just don't like it, and they're not super-strong during the day. I'm talking about *a club in SoHo* being open in daylight."

Kiernan had to give him that one. "There'll be people there getting the club ready for tonight, at the very least."

"It's also Monday," Grullon said, as if Kiernan didn't know that. "Half the clubs in town don't bother opening Monday or Tuesday."

"Club's in the basement of a residential building on Sullivan Street between Prince and Spring. Valapart lives in an apartment on the first floor. If he's not in the club, he'll be in the apartment. He's always at one or the other."

They signed out a Malibu, Kiernan allowing Grullon to drive, for which he was grateful. "Nothing personal, Kiernan, but I still got PTSD from the last time I was a passenger in a unit car."

"Umali's that bad?"

Grullon shuddered. "Worse. I thought I was being too hard on her when we went to the M.E.'s, so when we went down to

Chinatown on Saturday, I let her drive again. Swear to God, I saw my life flash before my eyes."

Kiernan smiled and got in on the passenger side.

Grullon got in on the driver's side, they both put on their seatbelts, and he pulled out into traffic. "So who is this Valapart guy?" he asked while driving hilariously cautiously westward on 106th. "I've heard you guys all mention him a buncha times."

"Back when Rosario was killed, we had eight million cranks coming to us, claiming to be vampires or to know about vampires or some other bullshit. The vast majority of them were full of shit, Cosplayers or goths with delusions of grandeur or people who were just plain nuts. And then there was Valapart, who really *was* a vampire, which he proved by turning into a giant bat, hefting a file cabinet with one hand, and making Mecozzi cluck like a chicken."

"Mecozzi?" Grullon asked.

"Detective from Brooklyn who got assigned to the task force. He got, like, four hundred nicknames after that: Cluck-Cluck, Chick-Fil-A, Feathers, Beak, KFC, you name it. Soon as the case was closed, he couldn't put in his papers fast enough. He's a PI out on Long Island now. Anyhow, Valapart proved that he was the real deal, and he helped us track down Albescu. He's been one of our better CIs since. If there's any kinda creature, monster, cryptid, or what-the-fuck-ever in town, he probably knows about it or can find out about it."

"But you don't like him."

"He's a CI, Grullon, we ain't supposed to like 'em."

"True." Grullon turned down Fifth Avenue. "Wait, you said he never leaves his building."

"Yeah, but he's got a phone, a tablet, a laptop, and a desktop. It's the twenty-first century, Grullon, you don't gotta be out in the world to be out in the world."

"I guess. My mentors all said 'your CIs need to be on the streets.'"

"Old-school bullshit. Whole fuckin' world's on the Internet, especially the monsters. Safer for 'em there. Especially after Albescu forced a lot of them out in the open. Most of 'em were able to get by unnoticed, and they liked it that way. But the Rosario case made them visible to a lotta people for the first time."

Again, Grullon said, "I guess."

Kiernan heard a buzz from her personal phone and pulled it out to see a text from Bobby. He'd successfully traded the bobblehead for the Funko Pop. She texted him back to congratulate him on the successful barter.

They eventually made it down to SoHo, with Grullon parking in front of a hydrant two doors down from the building that held the club.

As they got out of the car, Grullon stared at Valapart's large brownstone. A big stone staircase led up to the first floor and two shorter staircases on either side headed down to the basement. There were three windows on either side of the front door, which meant each floor had at least two apartments, possibly three, which made it on the large side for your average brownstone. "You sure this is the right place? I don't see a sign."

Kiernan smiled. "It's a private club. Members only."

"Just for vamps?"

"Not exactly." Kiernan walked to the side of the stoop and opened the wrought-iron gate that led to one of the down staircases. Right in the middle, underneath the stoop, was a big metal door with a small, sliding peephole that was eyes height for most folks, but several inches over Kiernan's head.

She knocked on the door with the side of her fist.

The rectangular peephole slid open, and a voice that was not Valapart's said, "We closed."

Kiernan reached up to hold her badge level with the peephole. "NYPD."

"Yo, c'mon, we ain't doin' nothin' illegal here. Look, talk to Vice, talk to the 10th Precinct, hell, talk to Lieutenant Majorowicz of that Supernatural Crimes Unit thing they got goin'."

"Who do you think sent me, dumbshit?" Kiernan said. "I'm with SCU. Open the fuckin' door."

"A'ight, a'ight." The peephole slid shut, there was a massive clunking sound, and then the door slowly opened inward to reveal a tall, skinny, dark-skinned man in a Los Angeles Dodgers ballcap, gray hoodie with the words PLAISIR DOULEUR emblazoned on the front, tight black shorts that hugged a very shapely butt, in Kiernan's considered opinion, and flip-flops. "Whatchy'all want?"

"We need to talk to Valapart."

"A'ight, he inside. Well, c'mon, you lettin' the cold in!"

It was forty-five degrees outside, which was hardly Kiernan's notion of "the cold," but she said nothing as she entered, Grullon following.

Gray Hoodie led them down a darkened hallway, lit only by tiny purple, fluorescent lights on the ceiling, to a door that had the same PLAISIR DOULEUR logo that was on the hoodie. There was a desk next to the door where, Kiernan knew, people had to check in before entering.

Through that door was a wide-open space, broken only by a few support pillars. The walls were all a very unfortunate shade of light green, making it almost look like the basement of a public school in the 1970s. To the right were a few doorways that Kiernan knew led to small rooms with beds. To the left was a bar; the shelves behind it held only clean, empty glassware.

Scattered throughout the room were various pieces of somewhat odd-looking furniture made of wood, leather, or metal. If you looked closely at the benches, platforms, and chairs, you could see O-rings, boat cleats, or short straps attached to them. That, along with the chains and ropes hanging from the ceiling and support pillars, gave the room a somewhat sinister air, though the whole space was scrupulously clean.

Valapart was at one of the pieces of wooden furniture, making adjustments on it with a wrench. Gray Hoodie led them toward him.

Grullon's face had gone pale. "What—what is this place?"

"I told you," Kiernan said, "it's a private club."

"What *kind* of club?"

"BDSM," she said matter-of-factly.

Grullon stopped walking. "Seriously? A bondage club?"

Kiernan also stopped and stared at her colleague, resisting the urge to remind him that there was also domination and sadomasochism. "Yeah, seriously. What's the fuckin' problem?"

"Shouldn't we be—I dunno, raiding this place or shutting it down or something?"

That got Gray Hoodie's dander up. "Motherfucker, I *told* you, we ain't doin' nothin' illegal here!"

Valapart straightened. He was very tall and wiry, moving with a certain restrained grace, and didn't so much stand up as unfold. His dark brown hair was cut very short, and he had high cheekbones and almost hypnotic gray eyes. He wore a plain black T-shirt, black jeans, and black boots, which was pretty much the uniform of lower Manhattan. Kiernan had actually found him very attractive when she first met him, but that had burned itself out pretty thoroughly after he started talking to her.

Now he gave Kiernan a small, pleasant smile, just enough to show off his oversized canine teeth, bowed his head, and spoke with only the faintest trace of a French accent. "Detective Kiernan, it is always a pleasure to have your loveliness grace my presence." He turned to Grullon. "You, I do not know, and yet you speak ill of me. You must not be part of Detective Kiernan's unit."

"Actually, he is," Kiernan said. "Pasquier Valapart, meet Detective Liam Grullon. He joined SCU about six months ago."

"In that case, I bid you welcome, Detective Grullon. As my assistant Eric here has said, the activities in this club are all within the confines of the laws of both the city and state of New York. Those who come here enter freely and of their own will."

Kiernan rolled her eyes. Valapart never passed up a chance to quote *Dracula*.

Valapart continued, moving slowly closer to her, "All acts performed within the club's walls are consensual, and we have paperwork from all participants verifying that. Full nudity is permitted, but the sale of alcohol is not, again in compliance with the law. Our members do not drink—wine."

Again, Kiernan rolled her eyes.

"Acts of sexual intercourse take place only in the side rooms, with the doors closed and locked, and therefore are not in a public space, and no money changes hands. The only people allowed ingress during hours of operation are members of the club. Any financial transactions occur between the member and club and are separate from the activities contained herein. The only things people pay for inside the club are the non-alcoholic drinks and merchandise—T-shirts, shot-glasses, ballcaps, hoodies, and the like. Should we violate any local or state ordinances, I am sure that the various officers of the constabulary who are club members will inform us of such."

That, Kiernan noted, brought Grullon up short, and he looked even more disgusted. "There are cops who are members?"

"A bunch, yeah," Kiernan said. "What's the big deal?"

"It's immoral."

"To you, maybe. But nobody's doin' nothin' here that they don't wanna do. And in my experience? Most people don't got any control over what turns them on. And also in my experience, people who repress themselves and don't do what they enjoy 'cause some asshole told 'em it was immoral are the ones who usually go out and do shit that we gotta arrest 'em for later."

Valapart's smile grew wider. "As usual, Detective Kiernan, you show wisdom and brilliance. You should come back this evening, we are having a—"

Kiernan held up a hand. "Don't care."

"You haven't even heard what this evening's events *are*."

"Still don't care." Then, in deference to the Major's desire for her to play nice to a degree, she added, "I'm here on business, not pleasure."

Valapart put an elegant hand to his cleft chin, nodding approvingly. "Aaaaah, so you do admit to there being pleasure to be found here at Plaisir Douleur."

Grullon—who looked like he was going to jump out of his skin—muttered, "Oh, God."

Choosing her words—and her tone—very carefully, Kiernan said, "I admit that I need to ask you something as one of SCU's best informants."

Chuckling, Valapart muttered something in French, then said, "First you tease me, then you flatter me. Very well, Detective, please pose your query."

"There's a domovoy on the loose. He stole the identity of someone named Valery Leybenzon, who died ten years ago, and recently assaulted a woman from Queens. We arrested him on Wednesday, he got loose on Thursday, and here it is Monday, and we ain't found him yet. My fellow police officers, the DA, and especially his victim, are a little pissed off about this."

"And you believe that I may have intelligence with regards to his whereabouts."

She put on a sweet smile. "May you?"

"I may—but alas, I do not at present. However, I will, as the saying goes, put my ear to the ground, as unsanitary as that sounds, and will inform you if I learn anything that will aid you in finding him."

Nodding, Kiernan said, "Thanks, Pasquier. It means a lot."

"There is no need to thank me with mere words, Detective, when you could simply accept my invitation to join us for tonight's festivities. Before you say no," he added quickly, just as Kiernan was about to, in fact, say no, "please be aware that Monday is Movie Night. We clear away all the paraphernalia, put out comfortable chairs and couches, and project films onto the back wall."

Kiernan chuckled. "No wonder you don't paint the walls something darker."

"Well, people come here to observe as much as they come to play, and the brighter walls allow for better viewing. So, will you join us?"

"Let me guess," Kiernan said, "a marathon of Jean-Luc Godard's most pretentious films?"

Valapart looked nauseated. "Hardly. I met Godard once, you know—he was what I believe young people today refer to as a poser."

"Not so much young people anymore," Kiernan said.

"I'm three hundred and twenty-one years old, Detective, to me, you are *all* young people," Valapart said dismissively. "In any event, no, the movies we shall show will be all three of the *Bill & Ted* movies with Mssrs. Reeves and Winter."

Unable to help herself, Kiernan giggled. "Okay, I did *not* expect that."

"Why? I find the two titular characters to have a most worthwhile philosophy: be excellent to each other and party on, dudes!" He said the last three words while thrusting his hands upwards with his first two fingers unfurled, the same way Abraham Lincoln did in the first film. It was a very incongruous gesture.

"I appreciate the offer," Kiernan said, almost meaning it, as she loved those particular movies, "but I'll still pass."

"What of you, Detective Grullon?"

Grullon once again looked like a deer in headlights. He'd been practically cringing while Kiernan talked to Valapart, and now that the vampire was speaking directly to him, he looked ready to run screaming from the club. "What *of* me?" he asked in a wobbly voice.

"Would you like to attend our Movie Ni—"

"*Shit*, no. I don't ever wanna set foot in here again. Can we go?" he asked Kiernan.

"You gotta excuse my partner, he's Catholic."

"So're you," Grullon said defensively.

While Kiernan was fairly spiritual and still prayed to God and the Virgin Mary on the regular, she was about as lapsed a Catholic as you could be. However, this was neither the time nor the place to get into *that* with Grullon—or with Valapart, for that matter. "We do gotta get going, though. Call SCU if you find anything."

Valapart smiled. "I could simply call you, Detective."

"Nice try, but you ain't gettin' my number."

"I live in hope. Please do give my regards to Lieutenant Majorowicz and tell him that we look forward to seeing him and Madame Majorowicz on Saturday night."

Grullon's eyes went as wide as saucers. "The hell?"

Kiernan turned toward the exit. "Let's go."

"What?" Grullon just stared at her for a second. Then he recovered, said, "Gladly," rather emphatically, and practically ran to the hallway.

Kiernan waited until they were down the hall, out the main door—which Eric closed and locked behind them—and on the sidewalk before she turned on Grullon.

Grullon, though, beat her to the punch. "You're telling me *the Major* is a member of that shithole?"

"And Hanna, yeah. The Major vouching for Valapart is part of why I was able to convince the bosses to use him on Rosario. For that matter, I think part of why they tapped the Major to head up the unit is because he already knew about vampires from being a member here."

"I can't believe it."

"And I can't believe you ever made it to detective being so fucking stupid."

Grullon straightened. "What?"

Pointing at the brownstone, Kiernan said, "What happened in there was the most embarrassing display I've seen by a detective in all the years I been on the job. That's the sorta bullshit I expect from a rookie in uniform, not a gold shield."

"How the hell am I *supposed* to act in a place like that?"

"Like someone who's trying to get something out of an informant. That means you check your bullshit at the door. I don't like the asshole either, y'know—he was practically drooling on me—but I played along, up to a point, so we could get the info. You almost blew the whole fuckin' thing! Lucky I was there for him to focus his googly eyes on, so he didn't really concentrate on giving you shit."

Indicating the brownstone with both hands in an almost-flailing gesture, Grullon said, "What goes on in there is assault and battery!"

"Nice try, but assault and battery comes with intent to harm. What goes on in there is purely for pleasure and enjoyment, and everyone signs a consent form before they walk in the door. It ain't my thing, but like I said before, we can't control what turns us on."

"I just—" Grullon threw up his hands. "I don't even know what to think. Especially knowing that the Major's some kind of deviant."

"I fucking *dare* you to call him that to his face."

Grullon swallowed audibly, as he obviously thought through the consequences of making such a declaration to the lieutenant.

"But," she continued, "you absolutely should talk to the Major about this. Get his point of view. He's always been open about it. Well, as open as he ever gets, anyhow. But talk to him, maybe you'll pry your closed mind loose."

"That's not fair."

"Life ain't fair, Grullon. You're a cop, you should know that. And you should also know better than to judge anyone before knowin' all the facts—especially workin' this unit, and *especially* after what happened to you four months ago."

Grullon looked away.

Kiernan went on, "It's *real* obvious that you got *no* idea about the lifestyle that goes on in Plaisir Douleur and other places like that. You should find out more before gettin' all high and mighty."

"Yeah, but *cops*? Especially someone like the Major?"

"Everyone's got secrets, Grullon. Including you."

Grullon just stared at Kiernan. Then he turned toward the Malibu, beeping it unlocked without another word.

ELEVEN

As he and Hawkins sat outside Judge Kisenwether's chambers in the Criminal Courts Building on Center Street, Ortega decided to say the same thing he'd said a dozen or so times already: "We don't have enough for a warrant."

It was worth it for the way Hawkins's nostrils flared when Ortega spoke. And, to be fair, Hawkins had good reason to be annoyed, since Ortega had lost the argument.

At roll call Tuesday morning, Hawkins had said they should get a warrant for Ohlmeyer's office and home. Ortega had responded by saying, for the first time, that they didn't have enough. While the squad room was not a democracy, the Major asked the two other detectives present what they thought. Kiernan also thought it wasn't enough for a warrant. Fiore agreed with Hawkins that they should take the shot.

Because Grullon and Umali had worked the weekend, they had Tuesday off. Though Ortega figured it would have remained even, as Grullon was likely to agree with Hawkins, while Ortega and Kiernan agreeing on a course of action meant that Umali would be right there with them.

The Major decided to break the tie by agreeing with Hawkins. Because it was Ortega's case, he was the one who had to see the judge, but because Ortega wasn't really feeling it, the lieutenant had Hawkins go with him to make sure the warrant got signed. While Ortega couldn't really blame the Major for saddling him with Hawkins yet again, he didn't have to like it. And his way of dealing with not liking it was to annoy the shit out of the sergeant by reminding him, repeatedly, that he didn't think they had enough for a warrant.

Hawkins was sitting on the edge of the wooden bench set against the cream-colored wall, tapping his foot impatiently on the marble floor. Ortega was leaning back on the bench, trying to remember if he'd taken all his medications this morning.

The clerk came out and told the pair of them that the judge would see them, and led them through a large wooden door, first to the clerk's own tiny section, then through a metal door to the judge's chambers.

Ortega recalled the first time he had visited a judge's chambers as a member of NYPD, decades earlier. It had been very disappointing, especially given how spectacular the more public areas of the courthouse were, with their impressive Romanesque architecture, with big stairs and columns leading to the entrance, and their glorious, colorful Art Deco interiors. Ortega had, perhaps naïvely, expected a city judge to have a lavishly appointed office with a big wooden desk and maybe a wet bar, plus a picture window with a view of the Manhattan skyline.

But most judges' offices were like Kisenwether's: tiny and cramped, with barely enough room to fit two guest chairs, an industrial metal desk, a desk chair, and a tiny window with a view of a stone wall of one of the other buildings on Center Street.

The walls were, as one might expect, covered with floor-to-ceiling shelves containing books relating to the legal profession, although her honor had dedicated a single shelf to various mystical and supernatural topics that the judge had encountered during the past few years.

Kisenwether herself was seated behind her small metal desk, peering at her computer through a pair of what looked to Ortega like off-the-shelf reading glasses. She was wearing a blue suit, and her robes of office were hanging on a wooden coatrack behind her desk.

Removing her glasses and tossing them uncaringly on the desk, Kisenwether folded her hands and regarded the pair of them. The judge had a round, pleasant face that could fool you into thinking she was in a good mood. If she ever had such moods—Ortega had never seen one.

"Sergeant, Detective—I'm assuming you've got a warrant for me to scribble on?" She held out an expectant hand.

Hawkins handed over the warrant—Ortega didn't even want to touch it—before removing his topcoat and draping it over the back of one of Kisenwether's guest chairs. Ortega took the other seat, not taking his windbreaker off. He had a feeling they weren't going to be here all that long.

Putting her glasses back on, the judge started poring over the document.

Hawkins sat calmly in his chair while Ortega fidgeted. He really couldn't remember if he'd taken all his meds, which was starting to annoy him.

After about ninety seconds, Kisenwether removed her glasses and tossed them angrily back onto the desk. "Seriously, guys?"

Hawkins's face fell. "Is there a problem, your honor?"

Ortega tried not to smile and mostly failed.

"No, there's not *a* problem, Sergeant," the judge said slowly. "There are six or seven problems. Just because I presided over *People* v. *Albescu* back in the day, doesn't mean you guys have any kind of 'in' with me."

Defensively, Hawkins said, "That's not why we come to you, your honor."

"Bullshit," Kisenwether said. "I'm still the judge that's friendliest to you guys, because I actually believe the evidence of my own eyes, unlike way too damn many of my colleagues. But that doesn't mean I'm gonna give you a break on a thin warrant. I'd have thought you'd have learned your lesson by now, Detective," she said, looking directly at Ortega. "I mean, it's a nice touch, dragging your sergeant along to make it look good, but—"

Ortega was about to object, but Hawkins was kind enough to take the blame. "Excuse me, your honor, but *I* typed up that warrant."

"I *did* learn my lesson, your honor," Ortega added, figuring he'd twist the knife a little, what with being right and all. "I'm only here under protest, because it's my case, and because my sergeant insisted."

Hawkins shot Ortega an angry look, which Ortega ignored. Sure, it was the Major who'd insisted, but it was more fun to throw Hawkins under the bus.

The judge held up the warrant as if it was a diseased rat and gave Hawkins a scowl. "So *you're* the one who thought this nonsense was worth wasting time I could've spent doing something *useful*?"

"Your honor, the PC is good, the—"

"Sergeant, this is some of the most improbable probable cause I've ever seen. Plus, you're going after *Garth Ohlmeyer*. The man has the best litigators in the state on retainer. They'd tear this apart. In fact, they've spent the last several months tearing apart much better warrants than this from the DA's office."

Under his breath, Ortega muttered, "I tooold you."

Kisenwether went on, "You want to go after Ohlmeyer for murder based on the word of a single informant that he happens to be a magic-user?"

"That informant's intel has always been reliable, your honor."

"Even if it is, so what? The only thing your informant has confirmed is that Ohlmeyer is a magic-user, which isn't actually illegal."

"But he's one of only five people who could've destroyed the corpses from a distance like that, and that's verified not only by our CI, but also by our in-house expert."

"Great, so you've got four other suspects. Where's the warrants for their offices and houses?"

"None of the other four are in New York at the moment," Hawkins said. "So they have alibis."

"I thought you said that this was done from a distance. 'Out of town' doesn't strike me as much of an alibi."

Hawkins sighed and started squirming in the guest chair. Ortega was having tremendous trouble not bursting out laughing. "It can't be done from that much of a distance," the sergeant said. "Besides that, Ohlmeyer has some financial dealings we found in the DA's discovery—they're not pursuing it for Hudson Yards, but it might be relevant to us. He's part-owner of a film production company whose CEO, as far as we can tell, doesn't exist and whose social security number is stolen. The company has yet to produce a single movie despite being in business for a decade."

"Whoop-de-doo, Sergeant." Kisenwether tossed the warrant aside. "Did it occur to you that the DA's office isn't using that information for a reason? You need a *lot* more than this if you want to go after someone for murder. Being part-owner of a movie company that hasn't made a movie doesn't make you a suspect for murder. Neither does identity theft. We don't even know that whoever liquefied the corpses of—who are the victims again?"

Ortega said, "Jacques Buddan and Elmore Hertweck."

Kisenwether did a double take. "Really? One of the victims is named Elmore?"

"Parents are cruel people, your honor," Ortega said with mock solemnity.

"Right." Kisenwether shook her head and scoffed. "Anyhow, we don't know that whoever did this is the murderer. We don't even know for sure that Hertweck was murdered—the M.E.'s report was inconclusive."

"Because of the destruction of the corpse!" Hawkins said a bit too loudly.

Kisenwether gave him a nasty look that indicated that he was dancing on the edge of the appropriate way to talk to a judge. Ortega struggled mightily to keep a straight face.

Lowering his voice, Hawkins continued, "Look, the fact that he destroyed the corpses before proper autopsies could be performed means he probably had good reason."

"He *possibly* had good reason. But we don't give warrants on possible cause, Sergeant."

That nearly broke Ortega. He allowed himself a small snicker, figuring that was safe since the judge had made a funny.

Hawkins said, "Look, this isn't enough for a murder charge? Fine—it's truly a case of corpse desecration and obstruction of justice. Not to mention the identity theft. Surely we have enough for *that*."

"If that's all you're going after, then this warrant goes from being too thin to being horrendously excessive. If you're talking these lesser charges, you've only got enough to question Ohlmeyer, not search his house or his office. The minute the questions get hairy, his lawyers will have him out of your interrogation room in nothing flat. And you *know* that, Sergeant, so I gotta ask you again: why are you wasting my time with this?"

"We've got two murders—and," he added quickly, "yes, I know Hertweck isn't officially a murder, but we have pictures from the crime scene, and Hertweck's neck was broken. He was murdered. And Buddan was *definitely* murdered, Detective Ortega and I saw the corpse ourselves. Evidence has been tampered with, and Ohlmeyer is our best suspect."

"Not based on what you've shown me. What we've got here, Sergeant, is evidentiary leapfrogging and wishful thinking. All you've got is someone *capable* of doing this, without any evidence to indicate that he *did* do it. Plus, I say again …" She cupped her hands around her mouth to amplify her voice. *"We're talking about Garth Ohlmeyer."* She dropped her arms to the desk. "You need a case that's watertight, and all I see here is a leaky boat, which Ohlmeyer's lawyers will sink like a stone." She picked up the warrant and held it out to Hawkins. "Come back when you've graduated from possible cause to probable cause, and maybe I'll sign it."

With a sigh, Hawkins took the warrant back.

For his part, Ortega made a mental note to use that possible/probable metaphor in the future, though he knew that he'd probably forget. He got to his feet and said, "Sorry to have wasted your time, your honor."

"It's hardly the first time, Detective." She stared at him. "By the way, wasn't a collection taken up to get you a new tie?"

"I have plenty of ties, your honor," Ortega said defensively, "but this is my *lucky* tie."

The judge looked to the ceiling in supplication. "Save me from superstitious cops." She looked back at them. "Why are you both still here?" She extended her arms and bent her hands downward, fingers sweeping out and up like a broom. "Shoo! Shoo! Go get some *evidence*!"

"Yes, your honor," Hawkins said, standing, grabbing his coat, and moving quickly toward the door.

"Thank you, your honor," Ortega said as he followed.

In the corridor, Hawkins held up a finger after shrugging into his coat. "Do *not* say a word."

Ortega put a hand to his chest. "Why would I say a word when I don't *have* to say a word? The judge summed it all up *very* nicely, I thought."

Hawkins went to the elevator and stabbed the down button with much more force than necessary. Seeing the sergeant's hissy fit at being stymied made the whole trip worthwhile as far as Ortega was concerned.

"We need some kind of direct connection between Ohlmeyer and the victims." Those words from Hawkins brought Ortega back to Earth, as it were. They still had a case, after all.

"No shit. But we haven't found one so far."

The elevator came and they both entered. There were five other people in the elevator, so Hawkins stopped discussing the case. When they got to their Malibu, in the basement parking area, Hawkins radioed in that they were done with the judge and heading back to the house.

Then he turned to Ortega. "You used to have a CI when you served in the One-Seven—Emilio Jerez."

Ortega frowned and put a finger to his chin. The name rang a bell.

After a moment, he dredged it up from the inner recesses of his brain. "Oh yeah—Emilio! He was a slinger on the east side back in the day. I busted him for possession with intent and he started feeding me intel after he did his time. He never dealt with Ohlmeyer directly, but it was an open secret that Ohlmeyer was in charge. Still, it wasn't open enough for there to be any actual evidence." Ortega tried not to think too hard about the fact that he could remember the name of a CI from years ago but not if he'd taken all the right pills this morning.

"Think he might be able to shed some light on Ohlmeyer?" Hawkins asked.

Shrugging, Ortega said, "Couldn't hurt to ask. Haven't talked to him in a few years, so he may be out of the game, but it's worth a try." He hesitated, then decided to throw the sergeant a bone. "That was a good idea, Hawk."

Hawkins said nothing as he pulled out of the basement lot with a sour look on his face, like he didn't want the compliment. That made it even more worth doing, in Ortega's opinion.

His phone started buzzing. Pulling it out of his windbreaker pocket, he frowned at the display, then accepted the call and put the phone to his ear. "Detective Ortega."

"Is this Detective Ortega?"

Hawkins obviously could hear the voice of the man on the other end; he let out a quick snort of laughter. Ortega rolled his eyes and said slowly, "Yes, this is he."

"I got a message you called my office, so I'm returning that call. What is it you want, Detective?"

"That's—that's difficult to say, sir, as you have yet to identify yourself."

"Oh, I'm sorry—I'm Jack Taylor."

Ortega sat up straighter. This was Hertweck's co-worker, the one that Kiernan's ex-husband had heard was embezzling funds. Ortega had called the number Umali had given him right after she'd talked to Tim Kiernan but had had to leave a message.

"Ah, yes, thank you for calling me back, Mr. Taylor. I'm investigating the death of your co-worker, Elmore Hertweck."

"I figured it was something about that. Such a tragedy. I'm afraid I've been in St. Louis on a business trip for the last week. I'm coming back home tonight, but my flight doesn't get into La Guardia until after midnight. Can I talk to you tomorrow afternoon?"

"That would be perfect, Mr. Taylor. We're on East 106th Street between 2nd and 3rd. Can you come by at noon tomorrow?"

"Um … I guess that'll be okay?"

"Great. We'll see you then."

After the phone call ended, Ortega noticed that he had two new text messages. One was from Ezequiel. "Christ," he muttered after reading it.

"What is it?" Hawkins asked.

"Text from my idiot son. He and Marcos—the boyfriend I just met for the first time last Friday, and with whom, I might add, he was talking marriage—have broken up."

"I'm sorry."

"Don't apologize to me—I'm not even surprised. If anything, *Marcos* is the one who dodged a bullet."

"So you're saying that Ezequiel inherited his father's proclivity for screwing up romantic relationships?"

Ortega turned and stared at the sergeant. "I'm trying to come up with a nasty reply, but the fact is, you're pretty much right. Poor kid." He looked back down at his phone and read the other text, which was from the office of one of his doctors. "I need Friday morning off."

Hawkins nodded. "I know, you have an endocrinologist appointment. You asked me yesterday when they texted you a reminder and I approved the time off. Did they send you another one?"

With a very deep sigh, Ortega said, "Yeah, and they'll send another one tomorrow, and I'll probably ask you for Friday morning off then, too."

"Something to look forward to," Hawkins muttered.

Ignoring Hawkins, Ortega started scrolling through the contacts on his phone. "Aha!" he said, finding Emilio's contact info. "Thought I still had it. God bless technology."

"Still had what?"

"Emilio's number. Finding it in your phone's contacts beats the shit outta the old days when you had to flip through eight hundred filthy Rolodex cards that've faded with time, covered in crappy handwriting, and not filed in any meaningful order."

Hawkins visibly shuddered. "I don't know how cops managed to keep track of stuff in the old days, without computers or smartphones."

Rolling his eyes, Ortega said, "Yeah, it was rough keeping track of stuff on stone tablets." He called the informant's number.

Without preamble, the tinny speaker sounded with a deep voice that had a slight accent. "Holy shit, Ortega, that you?"

"It's me, Emilio. How you doing?"

"Gotta be honest, *hermano*, I'm doin' shitty, but hey, I'm alive, so fuck it, I'm good. What's got you puttin' my digits in your phone after all this fuckin' time?"

"Need to talk to you about the game, Emilio."

"Shit, I ain't in the game no more, Ortega. That's some young'un shit, and I ain't a young'un no more."

"I know the feeling."

"Yeah, I bet you do. Shit, motherfucker, you was old when I *met* your bony ass, and that was, what, ten years ago? Fuck, man, why ain't you retired yet?"

"And give up this glamorous life?"

That, Ortega noted, got a chuckle out of Hawkins.

He continued, "Look, Emilio, I need some up-to-date intel, and you may not be in the game, but I don't believe for a second that you don't know what's up."

"Damn fuckin' right, I know what's up—shit, my nephew's all up in the game now, and he one stupid motherfucker, so I gotta be keepin' an eye on his dumb ass. But I ain't doin' this shit over no phone."

"Didn't think so. Where can we meet? That coffee shop on Third and 38th?"

"Nah, *hermano*, that's a Starbucks now, and I don't do that shit."

"Me either—if I want crappy coffee, I'll stick with what we have in the squad room, I'm not paying for it."

Hawkins shot Ortega a look of confusion. Probably because Ortega was lying through his teeth, as he loved Starbucks and the squad room kitchen had a *good* coffee maker, something Ortega himself had insisted upon. Ortega knew that Hawkins didn't understand that you lied to CIs to make them comfortable.

Emilio said, "Tell you what, whyn't you buy my ass some lunch? There's a pizza place on Second and 33rd."

"All right, we'll be there in about fifteen minutes or so."

"Wait, what's this 'we' shit?"

"I got a new partner I'm breaking in. We just had a meeting with a judge where he fucked up a warrant. My sergeant'll have my ass if I don't bring him along here, too—supposed to be a learning experience or something."

Now Hawkins gave Ortega a glance of anger that made him look somewhat constipated as he merged into northbound traffic on Lafayette Street from Cleveland Place.

Emilio sounded pained. "You can't leave his stupid ass in the car or some shit, like you did with that rookie—what was his name?"

"Rueber. He was a pain in my ass, let me tell you. But I won't get away with that this time—he'll just complain to the sergeant, and he's already pissed off at me." He said that last bit with a sweet smile at Hawkins, who still looked constipated.

"Okay, *hermano*, I'll see you there."

As soon as Ortega ended the call, Hawkins asked, "What the *hell* was that?"

Holding up both hands in a defensive gesture, Ortega said, "Take it easy, Hawk, I'm just working my CI. That 'rookie' we talked about? Rueber? He was a ten-year vet, but he had a baby face, so everyone assumed he was fresh outta the Academy. One time I brought him along so Emilio and I would have someone young to bitch about. It's his thing. All I need you to do when we get to the pizza place is sit there and look intimidated and maybe ask a few stupid questions that I can answer snidely." Then he grinned. "Y'know, like usual, except I mostly won't mean it this time."

"I suppose you think that's funny."

"Oh, I *know* it's funny." He sighed. "Look, this is how it works with Emilio. I gotta play his game."

"All right, all right," Hawkins said quickly. "If it's what gets us intel on Ohlmeyer, I'm all for it."

Hawkins parked under a red sign on Second Avenue that read NO STANDING ANYTIME and radioed in that they were meeting an informant, while Ortega got their credentials out of the glove compartment and set them on the dashboard.

Waiting for them outside the pizza place was a short Latinx man with a shaved head, a thick mustache, and a pot belly. He wore a denim jacket over a flannel shirt, both unbuttoned, revealing a plain white T-shirt underneath. His jeans were threadbare, and his boots were unpolished. He'd had a full beard and a full head of hair last time Ortega had seen him, plus he'd been about twenty pounds lighter, but this was still definitely Emilio.

As they approached, Emilio shook his head and started laughing. "Motherfucker, you are *not* still wearing that *fucking* tie."

Showing an unexpected ability to throw himself into the part, Hawkins said to Ortega, "You've been wearing that tie since you were at the One-Seven?"

"It's my good luck tie!" Ortega said, cranking his usual defensive tone up a bit. "Emilio, this is the guy I was telling you about on the phone, Simeon Hawkins."

"Hi." Hawkins put out a hand.

Emilio ignored the hand and scowled at Hawkins. "Do us both a favor, motherfucker, you feel the urge to talk? Ignore that shit. We got things to be talkin' about." He gestured to himself and Ortega as he spoke.

They went into a cramped, dimly lit space that smelled of garlic. On the right was a large, glass-topped counter covered with prepared pizzas, most of them missing varying numbers of slices. On the far-right wall, behind the counter, was a large pizza oven, the heat emanating from it almost overwhelming in the narrow space.

Jammed against the left-hand wall were several tiny tables with two chairs; they could only fit two people if both were very short and neither exhaled. Past the register, however, Ortega could see a more open dining area in the back.

Hawkins ordered a Sicilian slice and a cola, while Emilio got two pepperoni slices and a black cherry soda. Reluctantly, out of deference to the army of medical professionals he spent way too much time visiting, Ortega got a slice of white pizza and a diet cola.

When it was time to pay, Ortega said, "Get this, will you, Hawk?"

For a second, Hawkins looked surprised, then he sighed and pulled out his wallet. Ortega suspected that *that* at least was not acting.

The back dining room was only moderately crowded. Ortega noticed some people in scrubs and/or wearing ID cards from NYU Langone's Tisch Hospital, which was just a block away. The three men quickly found an empty table.

"So whatchoo wanna know about, *hermano*?" Emilio asked before biting into his pepperoni slice, which was folded between his fingers, the orange grease from the meat dripping onto both his chin and his paper plate.

"Ohlmeyer."

Shaking his head, Emilio swallowed and said, "Shoulda fuckin' known. You're with that new spooky unit, right?"

"SCU," Hawkins said primly.

"What-the-fuck-ever," Emilio said with a sneer at Hawkins. "So you know about Ohlmeyer?"

"You mean *you* know about Ohlmeyer?"

"What, that he casts spells and shit? 'Course I know, every-fuckin'-body who's worked for his rich ass knows. How you think the motherfucker keeps the troops in line?"

Ortega had been about to take a bite of his white pizza, but now he unceremoniously dropped it back onto the plate. "And you never told me this before?"

"Last time you and I talked, *hermano*, you was on 51st Street, and it was, what, five, six years before that vampire motherfucker killed the mayor's aide? Would you've believed my ass if I told you that Ohlmeyer was a wizard and shit back then?"

With a heavy sigh, Ortega said, "Probably not."

"Definitely not," Hawkins said.

Emilio pointed at Hawkins with his pizza slice. "Did anybody ask for your opinion, motherfucker? Speak when spoken to, okay? Fuckin' children, man …"

Ortega put what he hoped looked like a comforting hand on Hawkins's forearm. "Let me handle this, okay, Hawk?"

"Yeah, 'Hawk,' let the grownups fuckin' talk," Emilio added.

"So what can you tell us about Ohlmeyer?" Ortega asked before finally taking a bite of his white pizza.

"Whatchoo wanna know?"

"Well, for starters, what's he up to these days? Besides being investigated by the DA?"

"Dunno about that shit. All's I know about real estate is I ain't got any. But here on the street, what he been up to is amplifyin' the fuckin' product." Emilio took another bite of pizza, washed it down with soda, and went on. "Found himself a fuckin' spell, masks the high, but also makes it more powerful and shit. So you feel great, but it ain't so fuckin' obvious that you're high. I mean a lotta junkies, they don't give a shit about hidin' it, but your more upscale clients love that shit. They can do a bump on their lunch break and nobody in the office even fuckin' notices. 'Less they look at their eyes, anyhow."

Ortega frowned. "Their eyes?"

"Only giveaway—the eyes get all funky and shit, the black part in the middle, what's that shit called?"

"The pupil," Hawkins said.

"Right, *that* shit," Emilio said without looking at Hawkins. "It's like the eye's all color and no pupil."

Ortega nodded. "Okay. You wouldn't happen to know if any of those upscale clients is named Elmore Hertweck?"

"Nah, I don't know that motherfucker. But I know Ohlmeyer's pissed about some other uptown junkie, though—Taylor's the name, I think."

That got Ortega's attention. *Good thing Jack Taylor's coming in tomorrow.* Aloud he asked, "Why's he pissed about Taylor?"

"Dunno—my dumb fuckin' nephew just told me that Ohlmeyer was pissed about Taylor and also about one'a his dealers, Jake the Jake."

"Jake the Jake?" Ortega repeated.

"Yeah—why, you know him, *hermano*?"

"He's one of my cases—a homicide. They found Jake dead in Port Authority last week." Ortega left out the part about Jake being a CI. The "C" stood for *confidential*, after all.

Emilio's face scrunched up. "Aw, fuck, man. I always liked that stinky motherfucker." He took another bite of pizza.

"So, wait," Ortega said, "Jake was one of Ohlmeyer's dealers?"

"Yeah, the last couple years or so. He been workin' the PA, mostly. Hittin' up commuters and homeless motherfuckers. He started up with Ohlmeyer after Ray-Ray's crew got busted up."

That surprised Ortega. "They got Ray-Ray?"

Nodding, Emilio said, "Yeah, Narcotics got his ass and some other east side dealers."

Hawkins said, "Ray-Ray is Raymond Porter, right?" At Emilio's nod, Hawkins continued, "I remember that operation. Narcotics spent two years on that. Took a lot of big players out."

"Left a lot of unemployed slingers, know what I mean?" Emilio drank some soda, then let out a really big belch. "'Scuse me. Buncha folks got themselves hired by other crews—especially Ohlmeyer, since he got, like, a fuckton'a new territory after that bust."

Shaking his head, Ortega said, "Figures."

"What figures?" Hawkins asked.

Again, Ortega admired Hawkins's ability to play the role. They'd had this argument a thousand times before and Hawkins wouldn't have prompted it again, but it would help sell their mentor/mentee act to Emilio and also help Ortega reestablish his bond with the CI.

Ortega swallowed a bite of pizza and answered the sergeant's question. "Wipe out a buncha drug dealers, some new drug dealer's gonna come in and take over, because the *problem* isn't that people sell drugs illegally, the problem is that people *want* to *buy* drugs illegally. Supply and demand."

Giving his usual response, Hawkins said, "It's still illegal. What, we're supposed to just ignore it?"

Emilio answered before Ortega could. "Abso-fuckin'-lutely, motherfucker. Who gives a *fuck* if some junkie wants to get high? What harm that doin'?"

"Lots if they kill people for a fix."

"Yeah, but that shit's homicide. Of course you investigate *that* shit. But why you gotta be pickin' on people who's just providin' a public service? Fuck, you see all the damn smoke shops around town now that weed's pretty much entirely fuckin' legal?"

"If it's such a great public service," Hawkins said, "why does Ohlmeyer need to use magic to cover up the high?"

In reply, Emilio held up his right hand, palm-out, and shoved it near Hawkins's face. "Don't fuckin' talk to me no more, motherfucker, 'cause I am fuckin' *done* talkin' to you." He flipped his hand so that his thumb pointed at Hawkins. "This right here is why the police is fucked, *hermano*."

"I can't really argue with that," Ortega said, then dragged the conversation back to the subject at hand. "Any other uptown junkies you can think of?"

Emilio gave them a few more names. It was the smart play, as Hertweck's death might not have been related to Taylor, especially since Emilio wasn't sure of Taylor's first name.

Once he finished providing his intel, Emilio got to his feet. "I gotta bounce. It was good to see your ugly, fuckin' face again, Ortega."

Grinning, Ortega said, "I was gonna say the same thing to you."

"And you," Emilio said to Hawkins, "if you're gonna be stuck followin' this motherfucker around, see if you can talk his ass into buyin' a new fuckin' tie."

With that, he took his leave.

Once Emilio was out on the street, Ortega said, "I gotta give you credit, Hawk—you were a perfect callow youth."

"I'm not even gonna dignify that with a response." He ate the crust of his Sicilian slice. "Finish your slice, Luis, we need to get back to the house and I need to write up a new warrant. Emilio's still under contract as a CI, right?"

Nodding, Ortega said, "I'll call my old lieutenant at the One-Seven, have him forward Emilio's paperwork."

"Good idea. Now we've got direct connections from Ohlmeyer to Hertweck *and* Jake."

"Hertweck's still iffy," Ortega said, "since we don't know if Emilio's Taylor is the same as Kiernan's ex's Taylor, but Jake? That's solid, coming from Emilio. And now we've got *two* corroborating witnesses to Ohlmeyer being a Gandalf."

At that, Hawkins winced. Knowing that he hated that term, Ortega made sure to use it in front of him as often as possible.

But they had better PC for the warrant now. Even Judge Kisenwether might have to sign this one.

Maybe.

"Also," Ortega said as he finished his pizza, "I was thinkin' 'bout somethin' the judge said. Or, really, what you said about Ohlmeyer's fake film company—does it have any assets?"

Frowning, Hawkins furrowed his brow while biting down on his last bit of crust. "A few … and they also rent a storage unit in the South Bronx."

Pointing a finger at Hawkins, Ortega said, "You gotta include that storage unit in the warrant. Shoulda thought of it sooner, but I was too busy thinking that we didn't have enough for the warrant to actually think about what should go in it."

"How very counterproductive of you," Hawkins said dryly, then added, "Why a storage unit?"

"Because Ohlmeyer's not stupid enough to keep anything incriminating in his office or apartment, but he might think that he's clever enough to keep something incriminating in a storage unit rented by a film company that he thinks nobody knows about because he hid it under a stolen ID."

"Fair enough." Hawkins got to his feet. "Let's get out of here. I want to rewrite that warrant."

TWELVE

It had taken the entire rest of the tour to rewrite the warrant, which now included more detailed information on Ohlmeyer's ID theft and corporate shenanigans with the film company, Augurer Productions. Kiernan thought that an odd name until Basia explained that it was an old-fashioned word for a magic-user. Basia had also used her skills as an archivist, as well as some of the material from the DA's investigation, to make some forensic accounting connections which also bolstered Hawkins's warrant. So did having a direct connection between Ohlmeyer and Jake the Jake.

The warrant listed three places that needed to be searched: Garth Ohlmeyer's home, a penthouse apartment on East 54th Street and York Avenue; the corporate offices of Ohlmeyer Inc. (Kiernan's comment upon learning the corporation's name was, "Up all fuckin' night comin' up with that?") on Sixth Avenue and West 43rd Street; and a unit rented to Augurer Productions in a storage facility on Bruckner Boulevard.

Since the audit-induced overtime freeze was *still* on, all the detectives had to go home at end-of-tour, but the Major was a lieutenant and not hourly. He could therefore go back downtown and catch Judge Kisenwether on her way out the door.

For her part, Kiernan went home. She was just inserting a key into one of the locks on her door when Sabri came out of his apartment down the hall.

"Domenica, hello!"

Turning, Kiernan smiled. "Hi, Sabri!"

"Just getting back from a hard day's work?"

"Something like that."

He walked toward the staircase, passing close by her. "I have to get Violeta from basketball practice. Also, I found out that you really *are* a detective."

Looking at the floor abashedly, Kiernan said, "Yeah. I don't usually tell people that unless they really push, y'know? Changes the whole conversation once they find out I'm a cop. We won't even get into what *kinda* cop I am."

Sabri smiled. It was bright and pleasant. "Yes, part of the Monster Squad."

Now she rolled her eyes. "*Madonna mia. Yes,* I'm with SCU."

"Not just with—you were the lead detective on that vampire murder a few years back." Now it was his turn to look abashed. "I, ah—I may have Googled you a bit." Then he winced. "This doesn't mean you will be running a background check on me, does it?"

"Uh, no." Kiernan finished unlocking her door and pushed it open. "We can't really do that unless it connects to a case. That's the sorta thing that gets you suspended. And I need the cleanest jacket possible right now."

Holding up a finger, Sabri said, "Let me guess—you want to sue for more custody?"

That took Kiernan aback. "No fuckin' way that came up on Google." Quickly, she added, "Pardon my French." While profanity was second nature to Kiernan as both a Bronx native and a cop, she tried to avoid it when talking to strangers and new people.

But Sabri just loosed another of his very lovely laughs. "Please, I live in a city and I teach college students. Even my attempts to shield my daughters from foul language have, thus far, proven to be an abysmal failure. As for your desire for more custody, that was a guess, based on the vehemence of your 'do *not* get me started' when we spoke of it over the weekend."

"Okay." Kiernan smiled. "Guess I'm not the only detective on this floor."

"Well, good luck with that. And now I must go, I was already running late. Take care!"

"Bye."

The smile still on her face, Kiernan put her weapon away, changed into yoga pants and the *Princess Mononoke* sweatshirt Bobby had gotten her for Christmas last year, then went to the kitchen. She snatched a beer and leftovers from Sunday dinner out of the fridge, put the latter in the microwave, and poured the former down her throat.

Once the microwave beeped, she sat on the couch watching the Yankees game until she fell asleep.

She didn't wake up until Wednesday morning, still on the couch, the television still going, and with a painful crick in her neck. A hot shower mostly took care of the ache. Afterward, she threw work clothes on, ran to the bakery to get some rainbow cookies for the squad room, then drove to 106th Street and heard the good news that Kisenwether had signed the warrant.

As they sat at the front of the squad room, the box of rainbow cookies being passed around, Hawkins was holding forth. "I've alerted the 17th, Midtown South, and 40th Precincts, and they'll all have officers waiting to serve the warrants when we get there. Luis, you and Liam will serve the warrant at Ohlmeyer Inc. Vinny and Sofia will take the penthouse, and Domenica and I will hit the storage unit."

Ortega's face was twisted in a rictus of annoyance. "Wait a minute. Wait a minute. This is *my* case. I should get the storage unit—you didn't even *think* of including it until I brought it up!"

"First of all, it's *our* case. Second of all, would you even know what components to look for? Because I do know."

"That's what Basia's for," Ortega said weakly.

Kiernan snorted. Ortega usually had better arguments than that. "She's a civilian and can't go on the raid."

Now Ortega smirked. "That's what cell phones are for."

"Besides, Ohlmeyer's probably going to be at the corporate offices. Don't you want to rub his face in the warrant?"

"That's ... a fair point," Ortega said slowly.

The Major, who'd been standing to the side with his short arms folded over his large chest, unfolded his arms and clapped his hands once. "All right, let's gear up."

Kiernan approached Ortega. "You realize you just lost an argument with Hawk, right?"

"Ah, I let him win. Once it was obvious he wasn't gonna back down on going to the storage unit, I let it go. I've already ridden with him twice in the last week, which is three more times than I'm entirely comfortable with."

Kiernan chuckled. "Fair enough."

"Plus, much as I hate to admit it, he's right—I *do* want to rub Ohlmeyer's nose in it."

"Enjoy. I'll let you know what we find in the storage unit."

They all went out, wearing vests and sufficiently armed—though Kiernan had yet to receive her resupply of silver bullets. Jurienny had, thus far, been unable to convince the reps at Moore Hill to expedite delivery. Not that Kiernan expected to need them for this particular raid; it was the principle of the thing.

She let Hawkins drive, mostly out of a desire to avoid listening to him complain about the route she took, which he had done every damn time she drove with him somewhere.

Out of curiosity, she asked, "What's the *real* reason why you got me comin' with you instead of Ortega?"

Sounding defensive, Hawkins asked, "What makes you think the reason I gave wasn't the real one?"

"Because I don't believe for a second that you did it as a favor to *him*."

Hawkins tilted his head in acknowledgment as he turned left, up First Avenue. "Look, I've ridden with Luis twice in the last week. I am *not* in a rush for number three."

Kiernan had to hold in a belly laugh at that, as Hawkins would ask why she was laughing so hard at so innocuous a comment. But she thought it was best that neither Ortega nor Hawkins knew how much their reasons for wanting to avoid each other's company matched.

Mind you, she had every intention of sharing it with the rest of the squad …

The storage unit was only about a ten-minute drive from the squad room. Four patrol officers whose collars bore gold "40" pins were waiting for the detectives outside the facility's office.

To the officers, Hawkins said, "I'm Sergeant Simeon Hawkins, SCU. This is Detective Domenica Kiernan."

The POs all introduced themselves, though they all had nameplates on their chests: Holcombe, Roberson, Stevens, and Lagdamen.

Pointing to the office, Hawkins asked, "Manager inside?"

Holcombe nodded. "He's expecting you."

"Good. Wait here."

Hawkins went in, Kiernan following.

A middle-aged man who looked like he was of Indian descent was sitting behind the desk reading the day's *New York Times*. At their entrance, he folded the paper and put it on his desk, getting to his feet. "Hello, are you the detectives from the strange unit?" he asked in a heavily accented voice.

"We're from SCU, yes," Hawkins said testily. "I'm Sergeant Hawkins, this is Detective Kiernan, and this …" He handed the manager the warrant. "… is a warrant to search unit 248, rented by Augurer Productions."

The manager took the warrant and read it over. Finished, he said, "I am afraid I cannot provide you with a key."

"That's fine, the warrant gives us permission to break in."

Kiernan noticed the state-of-the-art security camera in a corner of the ceiling. "You got cameras like that all 'round the place?"

"No, ma'am, only in this office, so the owners may keep an eye upon the employees." The manager spoke with a certain bitterness. "There are lesser cameras at the elevator bays, but they are non-functioning, and only there so that the owners may claim on their insurance that they have them." He hesitated. "I should, perhaps, not be saying this to police."

Before Hawkins could go all dedicated-peace-officer on the man, Kiernan quickly said, "Ain't our problem. We're just here to serve a warrant. Anyone from Augurer ever come here?"

"Not to the office, at least not while I have been on shift. But they could have gone straight to their unit, and I would not know, and they could have come when I was not working."

"Thank you," Hawkins said, and he and Kiernan went back to talk to the uniforms.

"Someone's taking pictures?" she asked.

Holcombe, Roberson, and Lagdamen all pointed at Stevens.

"He's got the steadiest hand," Holcombe said.

Roberson added, "And I can't frame a shot for shit."

Kiernan chuckled. "We're gonna need to bust in."

Holcombe nodded and said, "I'll get the clippers."

Tossing her keys to Roberson, Kiernan said, "We got evidence boxes in the trunk of our Malibu. Get 'em out, please?"

"Sure, Detective," Roberson said, catching the keys one-handed and heading for the car.

Lagdamen, the only woman of the quartet, said, "Excuse me, but are you *the* Detective Kiernan?"

Madonna mia, she thought, *here we go again*. "Maybe?"

"You busted that vampire. That was so amazing!"

Stevens was rolling his eyes. "Jesus, Lagdamen."

"It was a team effort," Kiernan said quietly.

Holcombe came back with a set of giant metal clippers that should break whatever padlock was on the storage unit door. Roberson carried a dozen flat-pack boxes; they needed to be assembled, but that could wait for now.

The six of them rode the very slow, very rickety elevator up to the second floor. As they disembarked, Kiernan said, "Ohlmeyer's got all this fuckin' money. He can't spring for a storage unit built *this* millennium?"

"He *is* trying to hide it," Hawkins said as they approached unit 248.

Holcombe went to the door and peered at the lock, scoffing. "Cheap-shit padlock. I could take it out with pliers." He hefted the metal clippers, set the blades on either side of the lock's shackle, then closed the large handles. The blades sliced through the metal easily and the lock clanged to the floor.

Roberson reached down, grabbed the handle at the bottom of the door, where it touched the floor, and yanked upward. With a mighty rattle, the door rose, revealing a dark unit. Hawkins searched for and found a light switch and flipped it.

The light showed exactly what you'd expect to find in the storage unit of a film production company: video and sound equipment and a few file cabinets.

"Ohlmeyer isn't even trying," Hawkins said.

"Whaddaya mean?" Kiernan asked.

"Most of this stuff is ancient—from the nineties. Nobody reputable would be trying to make a professional film with any of this."

With a snort, Kiernan said, "Nobody reputable rents this thing." To Stevens, she said, "Start takin' pictures of *all* this." To Roberson, she said, "Once he's got all the pics, box *everything*."

Hawkins gave her a look. "What for? This junk doesn't have anything to do with our two murders."

"We don't know that," Kiernan said, "and besides, it'll piss Ohlmeyer off. Angry perps make mistakes sometimes. The warrant allows us to take anything we think might be of interest in our case against Ohlmeyer, and part of our case is identity theft and fraud. *This*—" She waved her hand, indicating the contents of the storage unit "—is all evidence that Augurer Productions is bullshit."

"I guess."

Kiernan rolled her eyes.

Three of the four patrol officers assembled evidence boxes and started putting things into them. Stevens took pictures of everything they did on his department-issue phone.

Hawkins started going through the file cabinets, glancing at the file folders in each drawer.

"Geez, look at this," Lagdamen said, looking at a plastic tub. She pulled out a VHS tape. "Talk about relics from the nineties."

Kiernan walked over and peered into the gray tub. She saw a pile of blank VHS tapes.

Roberson said, "Y'know, people used to record TV shows and movies on those."

Something struck Kiernan as off. "Take 'em all out."

Lagdamen regarded her with confusion. "Can't we just take the tub?"

"Oh, we're gonna, but I want you to empty it first."

"Um, okay." Lagdamen took out the rest of the tapes.

With a grin, Kiernan reached into the tub and pulled out a false bottom, placing it on top of the pile of VHS tapes.

Eyes widening, Lagdamen said, "I didn't even *see* that!"

"Geez," Holcombe whispered to Stevens, "Lagdamen's gonna cream her panties now."

Whirling angrily on the PO and giving him Nonna's nastiest look, Kiernan said, "You got somethin' to say, Holcombe?"

Flinching visibly, Holcombe said, "Uh, no, Detective, I got—I got nothin' to—to say, no, ma'am."

Satisfied that Holcombe would shut the fuck up from now on, Kiernan turned her attention to what was under the false bottom. "Hey, Hawk, I got four candles here and some other crap that looks promising."

Hawkins came over and peered into the tub. Then he smiled. "We got him."

"We do?" Kiernan couldn't believe it was that simple.

"This is most of what you need to do the spell Ohlmeyer used on Jake and Hertweck's bodies."

Wincing, Kiernan said, "I don't like the sound of 'most.'"

Hawkins pointed at a large green gemstone that was covered in nicks and chips. “We’ve got moldavite.” He pointed at a Ziploc bag filled with what looked like a pile of yellow-orange stones. “Benzoin resin.” A plastic bag filled with long, skinny green leaves. “Yucca leaves.” And four candles, which had been partly consumed, a blackened wick sticking out of each. “An obsidian candle, a ruby candle, a gold candle, and a plain white candle. You need all four for a transmutation spell this powerful.”

“What *don’t* we have?” Kiernan asked.

“Mushrooms, a lemon, and some spinach, kale, or lettuce. Any leafy green will work. And you can get those at any supermarket.” He turned to Stevens, who had continued to take pictures. “You got all this?”

“Yes, sir, Sergeant.”

“Good. This stuff goes in its own box.” He turned back to Kiernan. “We *got* him.”

Kiernan held up a hand. “It’s a *start.* Ohlmeyer’s skated on better evidence than this. Right now, all we can prove is that he’s got the components for the spell. We ain’t got no way of provin’ he used ’em.”

“There’s no good reason to have all this stuff together—especially the four candles—unless you’re casting a powerful transmutation spell. And the candles have obviously been used.”

Kiernan admired Hawkins’s passion but doubted that it was going to hold up by itself. “Like I said, it’s a start. If nothin’ else, it’ll give us a way in when we interrogate him.” She sighed. “Assuming he doesn’t just lawyer up and make good use of his right to remain silent.”

Hawkins folded his arms defiantly. “I guess we’ll see, won’t we?”

“Yup.” She turned to the four POs. “Let’s box the rest of this shit up.”

THIRTEEN

The third floor of SCU headquarters included the kitchen, Basia's office, four interrogation rooms, and two conference rooms. The latter two were on the street side of the floor, with windows that looked out onto 106th. The rooms were designed to put the occupants at ease, as they were used for interviews with witnesses, victims, relatives, and such. Each space had a black steel laminate table in the center, surrounded by comfortable chairs; the walls were painted a pleasant shade of blue, the overhead lights that supplemented the natural light from the windows were not harsh or buzzy, and the doors were generally left unlocked.

This was in direct contrast to the interrogation rooms, which had no windows. Those walls were painted a dull beige, the lighting was stark, the furnishings were industrial metal tables that wobbled and deliberately uncomfortable chairs. The doors locked automatically when closed and could only be unlocked from the outside.

That day, one of the conference rooms had been taken over by seized evidence, which was laid out and stacked up on the table. There were file folders, laptops, tablets, video equipment, and boxes of more stuff, including all the books from the single bookcase in Ohlmeyer's apartment. According to Umali, they were almost entirely books about Zoroastrian mythology, which she found odd enough that she and Fiore decided they were worth taking. Umali had studied the subject in college and felt that Ohlmeyer being a Gandalf meant any interest in mythology was a legitimate avenue of inquiry. Most of the books were in good shape, with absolutely no dust on them, indicating that they'd been acquired recently.

However, what mattered most was the box in the center, which contained the spell components.

Kiernan watched Basia review those components. The archivist would remove an item from the box, put it on the table next to her tablet, make notes on the tablet, then move the item to the middle of the table so she could check the next thing. Ortega, Hawkins, and Umali all looked on as well.

"Okay," Basia said, "this is good. The fact that the yucca leaves are part of this, and that he's got four candles, points to a long-distance transmutation of organic matter."

"Wait," Umali said, "organic—as opposed to inorganic?"

Basia nodded. "So this is based on an attempt at a transmutation spell from the ninth century by the alchemist Jābir ibn Ḥayyān. It didn't work on inorganic matter."

Umali's head tilted. "So this alchemist tried to turn lead into gold and it didn't work?"

With a smile, Basia said, "Alchemy is a lot more complicated than that. It was about trying to get at the heart of what matter *is*. In fact—" She hesitated, then took a breath, and shook her head. "In fact, this has nothing to do with two people who got murdered and whose corpses turned to gunk, so I'll stop now, but if you want to talk more about this after work, Sofia, I'm *totally* down."

Kiernan put in, "I always thought alchemy was a thing in medieval Europe."

"It *was* practiced there, but it goes back to ancient Greece. The term actually comes from the Arabic word *alkhimya*, and we know a lot more about Islamic alchemists, 'cause they kept better records."

In a long-suffering tone, Ortega asked, "Can we get back to the case, please?"

Hawkins smirked at him. "Worried you might learn something new, Luis?"

Ignoring the sergeant, Ortega looked at Basia. "So this is definitely what can be used to make what happened to Hertweck and Jake happen?"

"Most of it, yeah."

Ortega's face fell. "What's missing? We can't have *anything* missing, this is fucking *Ohlmeyer* we're dealing with."

"*Madonna mia*, Ortega, calm your fuckin' nerve endings," Kiernan said. "All that's missing is shit from the produce section."

The phone rang with the staccato breeting noise that indicated an internal call, from elsewhere in the unit. Umali was closest to the phone, so she went to pick it up.

Hawk added, "The other spell components are mushrooms and a lemon and some kind of leafy vegetable. He wouldn't keep that in a storage unit."

Ortega shook his head. "We don't have enough to bring him in for questioning yet."

"We still have to process all of this," Hawkins said. "We'll take our time, see what we find."

Umali hung up the phone. "You get to talk to him anyhow. That was Jurienny. Garth Ohlmeyer just showed up, accompanied by two lawyers."

"Only two?" Ortega made a *tch* noise. "He's getting soft—he used to bring four or five when he came to the One-Seven."

Hawkins pointed to the phone and said to Umali, "Call Jurienny back, tell her to tell him that we're still processing the evidence, and he can come back tomorrow."

Kiernan winced. "Don't fuckin' do that."

"Excuse me?" Hawkins asked frostily.

"Jurienny's a civilian. Yeah, she can handle herself, but it ain't fair, makin' her deal with someone like that. They don't pay her enough."

"Besides," Ortega said with a vicious grin, "I'd rather tell him myself."

For several seconds, it looked like Hawkins wanted to argue, and Kiernan could see the different emotions play on his face before he slumped his shoulders. "Fine, you two go tell him."

"Good." Ortega walked quickly out of the conference room, followed by Kiernan.

They went downstairs, to where three of the most boring-looking men in suits Kiernan had ever seen were standing in front of Jurienny's desk. From newspaper and TV news reports, Kiernan recognized the one not wearing a tie as Ohlmeyer. He was the shorter of the three, with a nearly rectangular head and an expensive haircut that diligently tried to mask the fact that his light brown, flecked with gray, hair was thinning on top.

He was flanked by two taller men Kiernan didn't know, one dark-skinned with a crew cut and a very thick, full beard, the other pale and bald, with a thin mustache. These were probably two soldiers from Ohlmeyer's army of lawyers.

As the detectives approached the desk, Ohlmeyer looked up at them and laughed. "Good Lord, if it isn't Detective Ortegas, as I live and breathe. And still wearing that horrible tie, I see."

"It's his lucky tie," Kiernan said, to save him the trouble.

"And it's Ortega, no S," he added.

Dismissively, Ohlmeyer said, "Whatever." To Kiernan, he said, "I'm Garth Ohlmeyer, and these are my attorneys, Farid Anand and Nicholas McManus."

"I'm Detective Domenica Kiernan," she said. "What can we do for you?"

Anand, the one with the beard, stepped forward. "Our client respectfully requests his possessions back. They were illegally obtained."

"We disrespectfully refuse," Ortega said with a sweet smile. "And they were *legally* obtained, which you should know, Mr. McManus," he added to the bald one, "because I gave you a copy of the warrant this morning."

McManus made a *tut-tut* noise. "Judge Kisenwether has overstepped her bounds—hardly the first time. These activist judges seriously need to be stopped."

"And so does this joke of a unit," Anand added. "The DA's case against us is falling apart, as there's nothing to it, so now they get the NYPD to take yet another shot at us. It's never worked before, so this time you hide behind this nonsense task force of yours. Magic-users? Vampires? Utter bullshit."

Kiernan looked at Ortega. "Wanna show him the kappa you arrested?"

"The what?" Anand asked with a confused squint.

Ortega said, "It's a slime monster. You three ought to get along perfectly with it."

"The point is," Anand said with a huff, "you have our client's possessions from his home and his office, and we'd like them back."

"We'll return whatever isn't germane to our case after we've processed it," Ortega said.

Ohlmeyer chuckled. "'Germane'? You actually read a book some time in the last ten years, Ortegas?"

"Ortega," he corrected, "and bite me."

"That sort of language is unbecoming of an officer of the NYPD," Anand said, shaking his head.

"Wouldn't be the first time," Ortega said.

Kiernan said, "I'm guessin' you want the stuff from the storage unit in the Bronx, too?"

"Please," Ohlmeyer said dismissively, "only time I've even set *foot* in the Bronx is to go to Yankee Stadium."

Kiernan felt nauseous as she realized that she shared a fandom with this *mamalucco.*

Then he continued, "And even then, I only go when they're playing the Red Sox, so I can root for Boston."

That made Kiernan feel so much better.

"Our client owns no property in the Bronx," Anand said, "so anything you may have found at that storage unit mentioned in your warrant is of no interest to us."

"Nice try, chuckles," Kiernan said, "but we already got a paper trail that links your client here to Augurer Productions. Cute name, by the way—fancy old word for 'magic-user,' which is funny, 'cause you guys were just talkin' about how that was bullshit."

"It is," Anand said. "We've never heard of this production company you mention. We just want our client's possessions back."

Ortega said, "And I want my hair back. But like the song says, 'you can't always get what you want.'"

"That song is a relic," Ohlmeyer said, "like you, Detective."

Looking at Kiernan, Ortega asked, "That what passes for funny in the rich-white-asshole crowd?"

Kiernan shrugged. "Hell if I know, I mostly don't talk to 'em."

Turning back to Anand, Ortega said, "Either way, request denied. Our warrant's legit, so unless you get a court order—and good luck with that—we're keepin' the stuff until we're done with it."

McManus leaned forward. "Oh, we'll get that court order. In fact, thanks to you and the DA, we now have a case for harassment."

"I've been saying all along," Ohlmeyer added, "that this unit is preposterous, and I've been saying it since John Rosario's murder, when you arrested some delusional fool who claimed to be a vampire."

"No," Kiernan said, "we arrested an *actual vampire*, which we know 'cause'a the footage of him turnin' into a giant bat right after he killed Rosario and 'cause'a the way he tossed around the officers who tried to arrest him the first time. He died before he could go to trial because they didn't serve blood in the chow hall in Riker's. They do now, by the way, thanks to us."

Ohlmeyer shook his head. "Pathetic that you're trying to sell these—these *delusions* to the public. It's a waste of the taxpayers' money. I suspect the civil suit that I'll be filing against the police department will lead to finally shutting down this waste of space."

With that, the three men turned and went down the stairs that would take them to the ground floor.

"Nice work, you two," came the Major's voice from behind them once the trio was out of sight.

Kiernan turned around to see that the unit commander had been standing nearby, but not too close. "You there the whole time, Major?"

Majorowicz nodded. "Ready to step in, in case you needed some brass. But you two have plenty of brass of your own."

"Damn right," Kiernan said with a grin.

Since the departure of the trio, Jurienny had been muttering a series of curses in Spanish. Now, she looked at Ortega. "Before those *pendejos* got here, a Jack Taylor called. He said he and his wife are taking an Uber here from their place in Williamsburg. They'll be here in half an hour or so."

Kiernan frowned. "He and his wife?"

"That's what he said. Stephanie's her name."

"Have them put in Interrogation 2 when they get here," Ortega said.

At that, Kiernan shot him a confused look. "I thought Taylor was a witness?"

"My old CI from the One-Seven said he might be somebody Ohlmeyer was pissed at. Between that and what your ex said, Jack Taylor is looking at lot more like a suspect than a witness."

The detectives went back to the conference room, where Kiernan said to Hawkins, "Jack Taylor and his wife should be here in an hour."

Ortega stared at Kiernan. "Jurienny said they'd be here in half an hour."

"Coming from Williamsburg? In the middle of the day? By cab? It'll be an hour, at least."

"All right," Hawkins said, a wave of his hand indicating all the confiscated items laid out on the conference-room table, "we need to keep going through all this. Sofia, Basia, and I will handle that. You two interview the Taylors when they get here."

Kiernan was grateful that Hawkins wasn't going to make either her or Ortega go through the evidence. Ortega was terrible at that sort of thing, especially with his poor eyesight. As for Kiernan, one of the many reasons why she fought so hard to get promoted to detective first-grade was so that she could get second- and third-grades to do this sort of shit work for her.

She had been worried, because Umali was the only lower rank available. Grullon had today off as his other day to make up for working the weekend. Umali, Kiernan knew, had taken a day between her last day at the Two-Four and her first day at SCU, so she could stay on the clock today, but Fiore was still working the Taotie down in Chinatown and was not available to help. Luckily, Hawkins liked this sort of detail work, and Basia was like a kid in a candy shop with this stuff, too.

Thinking about Fiore in Chinatown made Kiernan think of all the good restaurants down there, which made her hungry. "I need to grab a bite."

"I'm starving," Basia said, nodding in agreement.

Hawkins said, "I could eat. Who's working downstairs today?"

With a sigh, Kiernan said, "Roney." The front desk reception was usually staffed by an officer on desk duty from the 23rd Precinct. It was ever-changing, and they never knew who they would get from one day to the next. However, you had to pass right by the officer in question when you walked into the house, so Kiernan didn't see how Hawkins could never recall who was there.

"Let's have Roney put together an order from Zhong Hua," Hawkins said, referring to the Chinese place across the street.

Kiernan was grateful Hawk had suggested Zhong Hua, as she'd been thinking about Chinese anyhow. She went back downstairs to take care of that. Roney got everyone's order and collected everyone's money, either in cash or electronically.

Ortega and Kiernan ate in the other conference room, along with the Major and Officer Athena Tsekhanovich, one of the three uniforms who stood guard over the holding cells. Kiernan was just finishing her pepper steak when her phone buzzed with a text from Jurienny, who was eating her pork fried rice at her desk:

Taylors here.

To Ortega, who was popping the last of his steamed dumplings into his mouth, Kiernan said, "We're up."

Nodding, Ortega swallowed his dumpling.

Tsekhanovich looked up. "You need me to guard the door, Detectives?" Because the interrogation rooms could only be opened from the outside—a necessary precaution to keep suspects from leaving on their own—someone needed to be stationed outside to let the detectives out when they were done.

Holding up both hands, Kiernan said, "Once we're inside, yeah, please, but for now, could you and the Major stay here and keep eating? We need a good excuse why we're puttin' 'em in a shitty interrogation room instead of a nice pretty conference room."

"Only reason I'm eating here instead of in the privacy of my own office," Majorowicz said with a smirk as he speared some sweet and sour pork with a plastic fork.

Ortega gave a mock-bow. "Your sacrifice is appreciated, Major."

"Don't bullshit me, Ortega, just get something out of these two. Preferably without a lawsuit threat."

"Hey, c'mon, Major," Kiernan said, "that lawsuit threat from Ohlmeyer was fuckin' fabulous."

"How you figure?" the lieutenant asked.

"He wouldn't'a said that if he wasn't scared. 'Sides, at this point, we're pretty sure his whole empire is built on the fact that he's a Gandalf, and that's also why he's been able to skate so easily on every single charge and wriggle out of every single investigation. SCU's the biggest threat to him NYPD's got. And he knows it, which is why he's throwin' his weight around."

"Maybe," Majorowicz said, "but he *has* the weight to throw, so watch your asses."

"Always do," Kiernan said.

"Bullshit—if you did, I wouldn't have agita."

"Nah, you've got agita 'cause you keep eating pork against your doctor's orders."

Pointing angrily at the door to the conference room, Majorowicz said, "Go talk to your suspects, Detective."

Chuckling, Kiernan went out with Ortega.

Two more of the uniformed officers assigned to the unit were walking toward them from the interrogation rooms. Both were named Sam Jones. One was a Caucasian with sandy blond hair, whose full name was Samuel Adams Jones. While his parents had named him after the Founding Father, the name was better known because of the beer, so he had acquired the nickname, "Hops." The other was bald, Black, and had a goatee. *His* full name was Samwise Jones, after the character in *The Lord of the Rings*, which naturally led to the nickname, "Frodo," after the main character in that famous J.R.R. Tolkien trilogy.

The two men had become best friends after being partnered up in the Two-Three. They'd finally stopped cursing their parents for saddling them with ridiculous full names. After all, if they'd both just been named Samuel Jones, it would've been much harder to tell them apart …

Hops said to Kiernan, "They're in Interrogation 2 like you guys asked, Detectives."

"Thanks, Hops," Kiernan said.

Ortega added, "If you guys could give Hawk and Umali a hand in the conference room sorting evidence, we've got a shit-ton of stuff from the Ohlmeyer warrant."

"You bet," Frodo said, and the pair of them went to the conference room.

Ortega reached into the pocket of his slacks and pulled out a carabiner with a ton of keys on it. He started going through them one by one. "This is how you measure how old you are, y'know—by how many keys you accumulate. Now *one* of these is for the interrogation rooms …"

"*Madonna mia*," Kiernan muttered, barreling past Ortega and pulling out her own keychain. She actually had more keys than Ortega, but she kept them in an order that made it easier to find the right one. The interrogation room key was right next to her car's ignition key.

She unlocked the big metal door with a thud and pushed it open.

Two people were sitting behind the metal table under the flickering fluorescent lights. All the other rooms in SCU HQ had state-of-the-art lighting that was easy on the eyes and lasted a long time, which made life easier on the people working and visiting. But the interrogation rooms were not there to make life easier on the people inside them. They were meant to be uncomfortable and unpleasant.

In addition to their other unlovely features, each interrogation room had a clock on the wall that didn't work. To the people in Interrogation 2, it was always thirteen minutes past four. Those people, currently, were a pair of very ordinary-looking Caucasians. Jack Taylor had thinning, brown hair and a double chin; he was wearing a button-down shirt that was mildly stained with sweat, thanks to the stuffiness of the interrogation room. He was staring intently at his phone, stabbing angrily at the screen with a pudgy finger, while constantly shifting his weight in the chair.

Next to him was Stephanie Taylor. Unlike her husband, Stephanie sat ramrod straight and stared straight ahead. She wore a plain blue T-shirt and had moderately long hair that was dyed a very deep shade of red and tied back in a ponytail.

"Mr. Taylor, Ms. Taylor, I'm Detective Luis Ortega, we spoke on the phone?" Ortega offered a hand.

"Hi." Jack put his phone in his pants pocket as he stood up and shook Ortega's hand. "This is my wife, Stephanie. She works with Elmore also, so I thought she should come along."

"I'm Detective Domenica Kiernan—sorry to have kept you waiting, and, uh, sorry to put you in here. Normally, we'd talk to you in a conference room, but they're both occupied."

"It's—it's fine," Jack said, sitting back down. "It's a little stuffy, though."

"Yeah," Kiernan said as she sat in the seat opposite Jack, "they don't let us run the AC after Labor Day. It's annoying."

Ortega took the seat opposite Stephanie. "Thanks for coming in."

"It's just—it's terrible what happened to Elmore. And especially what happened to his body! Why would anyone do that?"

"We're wondering that ourselves," Kiernan said.

"For that matter, *how* would anyone do that?"

At that, Kiernan smiled. "That we don't need to wonder. It's a spell."

Stephanie finally spoke. She had a very quiet voice, barely audible. "I guess you deal with that sort of thing a lot?"

"That's what the S in SCU stands for," Ortega said. "What is it you do at Hertweck and Associates, Ms. Taylor?"

"I'm a computer programmer. It's what I did in the Marines, and after my discharge, I got a job at Jack's firm." She smiled shyly. "It's been very nice."

Kiernan asked, "What kinda discharge did you get from the Marines?"

"Medical," she practically whispered. "I was wounded in Baghdad."

Wincing, Kiernan said, "Oh, I'm sorry."

"It's okay. It wasn't that bad, and I've had physical therapy, so I can walk normally again, finally."

"That's great." Then Kiernan added, "Thanks for your service."

Stephanie nodded and looked away, seemingly embarrassed.

Kiernan actually hated the near-rote use of that phrase, but she'd wanted to see how Stephanie responded to it. The embarrassment indicated that she didn't like the fact that she was medicaled out.

Ortega looked at Jack. "Can you think of any reason why someone would want to kill Mr. Hertweck? Did he have any enemies?"

"Not ones who wanted to kill him, no. Look, I know you guys think that corporate lawyers are the scum of the earth …"

"We don't think that at all." Ortega broke into a grin. "We think *criminal defense attorneys* are the scum of the earth."

Jack chuckled. Stephanie, Kiernan noted, did not.

"Be that as it may," Jack said, "Elmore wasn't a shark. I mean, yeah, he made sure that we always did right by our clients, but he was also picky about who he chose to represent in the first place. Our client list isn't the kind you hear about in nasty news stories about evil corporations and the like."

"Might there be clients he refused to represent that resented being turned down?"

"Possibly? But we haven't taken on any new clients—or been offered any new clients—in a few years. We've got a pretty good stable and we don't have as many lawyers as we used to. A few retired and Elmore hasn't hired anyone to replace them at the lower levels."

Ortega nodded. "What about the embezzlement?"

Stephanie was shifting uncomfortably in her chair, in much the same way her husband had been a few minutes earlier. To be fair, it could just have been the chair itself causing that, as it was designed for discomfort.

Jack replied, "There was no embezzlement—where did you hear that, Detective?"

"It came up during the investigation."

"Well, whoever brought it up to you had bad info, I'm afraid. Elmore *thought* there was some embezzlement, but it was just a computer glitch." He glanced at his wife. "In fact, Stephanie was the one who found and fixed the glitch!"

"I did, yes." Stephanie was still squirming, and her voice had, amazingly, gotten quieter. "We had just gotten new Wi-Fi routers, and they didn't have the best security on them—we got hacked."

"Luckily," Jack said with a smile, "it was just financial stuff for the company. Client records are stored on air-bubbled laptops."

Closing her eyes and sighing, Stephanie said, "Air-gapped, dear."

"Right, right." Jack waved an arm back and forth. "You know I don't get all this computer stuff. I can barely turn mine on."

Ortega suddenly got to his feet. "Okay, will you excuse us for a second, please, Mr. Taylor? Ms. Taylor?"

Stephanie nodded, while Jack said, "Uh, sure, I guess. Will this take much longer?"

"We just need to check something. If you need anything, Officer Tsekhanovich is right outside."

Kiernan rose while Ortega knocked on the door to the tune of "Shave and a Haircut." Two seconds later, the door unlocked with a thud and Tsekhanovich let them out.

Ortega zoomed past the uniform while Kiernan stopped to say, "Check and see if they want anything."

Tsekhanovich nodded, then shoved her head into the interrogation room to ask the Taylors what they needed.

Ortega was going downstairs to the squad room. Kiernan jogged to catch up with him on the steps. "Ortega, what the fuck?"

"I gotta type up a warrant."

"For what?"

"The Taylors' apartment."

"C'mon, no way Jack Taylor killed anyone. The guy's a fuckin' marshmallow."

They got to the second floor, Ortega making a beeline for his desk. "You're right, it ain't Jack."

"So why the fuck—"

Ortega took a seat at his desk and tapped the space bar. As his monitor lit up, he said, "Emilio told me that Ohlmeyer was pissed about something involving someone named Taylor, but my snitch didn't have a first name or a gender. He also told me that Ohlmeyer's latest batch of junk to hit the streets is magically enhanced to hide the high. Only way you can tell it's being used is the user's eyes. The pupils go down to almost nothing."

"Okay ..." Kiernan still wasn't entirely following.

Pointing at the staircase, Ortega said, "Stephanie Taylor was a Marine, so she's trained in combat, and I'm willing to bet all of Grullon's money that she's totally capable of breaking someone's neck the way Hertweck's was. I was looking her right in the face the whole time we were talking, and not *once* could I make out the pupils in her blue eyes."

Kiernan blinked. "Fuck."

"I'm betting that Hertweck found out that Stephanie was working while high, she killed him, and maybe killed Jake the Jake, too, and she got her dealer, the Gandalf, to cover it up with his fancy-ass spell."

Again Kiernan said, "Fuck. All right, let's get us a warrant."

FOURTEEN

Ortega wrote up the warrant in record time. Unfortunately, Kisenwether was in court all day, so they had to try another judge. At this stage, plenty of judges were on board with the types of crimes and perpetrators that SCU dealt with, but there remained some who were at best skeptical and at worst convinced that it was a big con job.

Kiernan and Ortega sat at Jurienny's desk while the admin checked her computer for the various judges' schedules.

"What about Fiorello?" Ortega asked.

Wincing, Kiernan said, "If it's him, you're going alone. I don't need another lecture on how divorce is a mortal sin."

"You think he won't lecture *me* on that?"

"No, because it's always the wife's fault with him."

Jurienny tapped some keys, then shook her head. "On vacation this week."

"Small favors."

Ortega started snapping his fingers. "Who was the judge in the Henby case with the *chupacabras*?"

"Nakashima."

"Right, her."

Again, Jurienny shook her head. "In court all day, like Kisenwether."

Recalling her recent testimony in the skoffin's murder trial, Kiernan said, "What about Steinberg?"

"Which one?" Jurienny asked.

"Please God," Ortega muttered, "not Danny Steinberg."

Kiernan chuckled, remembering that Daniel Steinberg had been a pain-in-the-ass defense lawyer for years before becoming a judge, and after that, he'd had Ortega cited for contempt-of-court twice. "No, I mean Michael."

Jurienny sighed. "Judge Michael Steinberg's been out sick all week."

"Dammit."

Ortega sighed. "It's too bad O'Connor retired. Our PC's all about magical enhancement of drugs, and she's always been a hawk on drug crime."

"She isn't retired yet," Jurienny said. "She's still on the bench, until the end of the year." She grinned after tapping some keys. "And she's on call for a deposition, so she should be in her chambers all day!"

"Let's go," Ortega said, getting slowly to his feet. Kiernan winced when she heard his knees crack.

As they went to grab their respective jackets, Kiernan said to Jurienny, "Tell Tsekhanovich to tell the Taylors that we'll be back with them soon."

Still grinning, Jurienny said, "The usual stalling bullshit?"

"Exactly," Kiernan said, with an answering grin.

A quick trip to the chambers of Judge Alice O'Connor later, they had a signed warrant. Kiernan and Ortega headed to Williamsburg with some uniforms from the 90th Precinct to serve the warrant at the Taylors' co-op. The building manager very kindly let them in.

After ten minutes in the place, Kiernan called HQ and made sure one of the uniforms read both Taylors their rights and had them sign the paperwork that made it clear that they knew their rights.

The tour was nearly over by the time they got back to 106th Street. Because the Taylors were still technically witnesses, they couldn't really justify keeping them overnight in an interrogation room without charges but doing that before talking to them would spoil any shot at a confession.

"All right," the Major said, "I'll sign off on enough OT to interview those two, but only for you two and Basia. Everybody else has to go home." Basia was in charge of video recording interrogations, so she needed to be on the clock along with the detectives.

Kiernan nodded. "Good."

They went back into Interrogation 2. Shift change meant that Officer Jurgen Fischer was now guarding the door. He let them in.

Stephanie looked nervous. Jack looked pissed.

"Detectives," Jack said, "forgive my language, but what the *hell* is going on here?"

Kiernan managed to keep a straight face at Jack's adorable notion of foul language. She held the ever-growing file folder with all their casework so far in her right hand. "What's going on here is the search warrant we just served on your co-op." She pulled a copy of the warrant out of the folder and tossed it onto the table.

"What? Why?" the lawyer asked, snatching the warrant off the table.

Ortega was leaning against the wall behind Kiernan. "Officer Jones did all the paperwork with you?" he asked Stephanie. "You understand your rights?"

Stephanie nodded quickly.

"And you've waived your right to have an attorney present."

Jack said tightly, "She *has* an attorney present. I can protect her rights. What I don't know is what I'm protecting her *against*. Your Officer Jones didn't specify what she's being charged with."

Once again, Kiernan controlled her reaction, which she could do with the ease of long practice. Jack was *not* a criminal lawyer, and he was Stephanie's husband. Those facts made him woefully ill-equipped to protect Stephanie's rights. But it wasn't up to her to keep the perps from being stupid.

"Well, for starters," she took three photos from the folder, "possession."

She laid out the pictures, each of which showed a sealed plastic bag. The one full of pills, they'd found in the tank of the toilet in the large bathroom; the one full of a tan-colored powder, they'd found in the tank of the toilet in the small half-bath; the one of white powder had been at the back of the pantry.

"We did a quick-test on the two powders, and they're definitely cocaine and heroin. The pills're at the lab now, but we're guessin' oxy, especially since you were prescribed oxycotin after you got wounded in Iraq."

Jack was staring angrily at Stephanie, who was practically shrinking into her chair. "What the *hell*, Steph? You told me you were done with the drugs! You went to rehab! To NA meetings! What happened?"

Stephanie stared at her husband like he was nuts. "What do you think happened, Jack? I'm an addict. I took more drugs. It's what I *do*! God!"

"I—I don't understand." Jack was shaking his head. "You—you've been clean!"

"Not exactly." Ortega moved closer to the table. He leaned forward and put his hands on the desk so that he loomed over both Taylors. "She just found a better way to get high."

Kiernan added, "The drugs she's been gettin' have a spell put on 'em that masks the high. She still gets to feel good, but she don't *look* high."

Tears welled up in Jack's eyes. "Why? Why would you do this to yourself? You were getting help!"

"The rehab didn't work, Jack, okay?" Stephanie sounded defensive. "It still hurt."

"What hurt?" Kiernan asked.

"*Everything*! My legs, my head, my damn *brain*! The only time it doesn't hurt is when I'm high! And, oh my *God*, the new drugs that Jake was selling me? The high was *so much* better."

Bingo, Kiernan thought. That was their in to the real meat of the case. "Jake is your dealer?" she prompted.

"Yeah. Everyone calls him Jake the Jake. Not really sure what that means."

"'Jake' is a slang term for Jamaican," Ortega said.

That seeemed to surprise Stephanie. "Really?"

"Jake is also dead," Ortega said.

"What?" Jack sat up straighter. "Dead? We're talking about dead people now?"

"Murdered people, Mr. Taylor," Kiernan said, taking another picture out of the folder.

This one showed a switchblade stained with blood. It had been under the mattress in the Taylors' guest room.

Jack's eyes widened. "Oh my God."

"That knife belonged to Jake," Ortega said. "He used it to defend himself. Never actually stabbed anyone with it, as far as I know."

Kiernan told a bald-faced lie. "The knife's being tested against Jake's blood." Jake's body had been hit with the transmutation spell before any tests could be done or samples taken, so they had nothing to compare to the blood on the knife. And according to the latest word from Klimchynskya, they still hadn't determined if the goo Jake and Hertweck had turned into even *had* DNA. But Stephanie—if she was innocent and ignorant of what happened—had no way of knowing that.

"No, it isn't," Stephanie said confidently. "Jake's body was destroyed!"

There it is. Kiernan's favorite part of interrogations was when the interviewees walked right into the rhetorical trap.

Ortega stood up straight and folded his arms. "And how do you know that, Ms. Taylor?"

Jack stared at his wife. "How did you even know he was dead? My God, Steph, you—you didn't kill him, did you?"

"I—" Stephanie seemed to collapse in the chair, like a marionette whose strings were clipped. Her arms fell onto the table and then her head collapsed onto her arms. Kiernan could hear her whimpering.

Kiernan leaned forward and spoke softly. "Why'd you kill him, Stephanie?"

Raising her head, Stephanie looked Kiernan in the eyes. "He—he wouldn't give me anything. I *hurt* so much, but he said that Mr. Ohlmeyer cut me off."

"You mean Garth Ohlmeyer?" Kiernan asked in as calm a voice as she could manage. Once again, Stephanie had led her to the next part of the interrogation without prompting.

Stephanie nodded.

"He was Jake's supplier?"

"Yeah. Well, I mean, Quinn was the supplier, technically, but everyone knows it's really Mr. Ohlmeyer."

"Who's Quinn?" Kiernan asked.

Ortega said, "He's Ohlmeyer's latest beard, a banger who's the public face of his drug operation. Ohlmeyer's gone through about a dozen. Whenever we get too close, the banger-du-jour takes the fall and goes to jail, and some other asshole is anointed in his place. According to Narcotics, Quinn Markham's the latest."

Nodding, Kiernan looked at Stephanie. "Go on, please."

"The new drugs are a lot more expensive, and my—my extra income stream got cut off."

Had Jack truly been there as her legal counsel, he would have told her to shut up some time ago. But because he was really there as Stephanie's husband, he instead prompted her to say more incriminating things. "What income stream?"

"I—" She got nervous again.

Ortega held up a hand. "Wait, let me guess. That fake embezzlement you guys told us about—it wasn't so fake, was it?"

Jack looked like *he* was going to break down and cry now. "Oh my God, Steph? It was you?"

"It was just—" Stephanie let out a very long breath. "It was a few hundred here and there. We have, like, billion-dollar clients, I didn't think anyone would notice."

"But they did notice," Kiernan said, "so you came up with your bullshit story about gettin' hacked, and you 'fixed' it. But you still needed to pay for your drugs, and it had to be in a way your husband wouldn't know about, right?"

Stephanie sighed. "At first, I thought I could just power through, y'know? Maybe even go back to rehab. But then the pain—Jesus, the pain got *so bad*! And then Elmore called me."

"Elmore?" Jack frowned. "What's he got to do with—" Then it finally occurred to him. "Oh God. All right, Steph, enough, don't say *anything else*, please."

Was wondering when he'd start being a lawyer again. Aloud, Kiernan said, "That's your right, Stephanie. We can stop this interview any time but keep somethin' in mind—we got you on Jake's murder, as well as possession. That's basically a done deal. But we also know you couldn't possibly have been the one to dispose'a his body with a transmutation spell. And Elmore's body was hit with the same spell, so we already know the two murders're connected."

Tears were now streaming down Stephanie's cheeks. She turned to Jack. "Sweetie, I—I have to."

"No, Steph, you don't. We need to stop this and—"

"I killed Elmore, too," she said.

"Steph! Jesus!" Jack threw up his hands.

"I've never killed anyone before, Detectives," Stephanie said in a ragged whisper. "Was trained, did boot camp in Parris Island, but I never saw any kind of real combat—at least, not until I got wounded. But that day when I met Elmore in the basement of his building ..."

Ortega asked, "What were you doing in the basement?"

"He called. Said he wanted to meet in private, away from the office, so I went to his apartment. He was doing laundry, so we went down to the basement, where the washers and dryers are." She chuckled. "Guy owns a damn law firm, and he still does his own laundry. Couldn't believe that. He's such a good guy—*was* such a good guy. He said he found out what I did, and he was gonna fire me, but he wanted to know why.

"That's when the pain got *really bad*, and I tried to explain things to him, but he wouldn't listen, and then the pain got *worse*, and I—" She blew out a long breath. "I lost it. I don't even remember doing it, I was just—I was in pain, and then his body was on the floor in front of me. But the pain—God, the pain was awful."

Kiernan said gently, "So you went to Jake for a hit?"

She nodded. "He wouldn't help me. He said Mr. Ohlmeyer cut me off." Shuddering, she said, "He whipped out that switchblade when I wouldn't take no for an answer, and he attacked me and—and training took over, I guess. I disarmed him and stabbed him with his own weapon."

"Eight times," Ortega said. "I saw the body before you had it turned to gazpacho soup."

"Which brings us to the next part," Kiernan said. "You had the bodies disposed of."

Stephanie seemed to curl up into herself again. "I think I'd better stop there."

"Good," Jack said. "You've already said too much. We should get a criminal lawyer."

"Yeah, see," Kiernan said, "there's this problem. I mean, sure, two murders, possession, that's all pretty bad—but we're the *Supernatural* Crimes Unit, and what got our attention was the transmutation spell that turned two dead bodies into goop. And we're guessin' it's the same guy who was selling you drugs that let you get high without your hubby here or your coworkers finding out."

Ortega once again went back to leaning forward, hands down on the desk, looming over Stephanie. "I can't imagine Garth Ohlmeyer would cast that spell—and give you drugs, since you were high as a kite when you came in here—without getting something in return."

"I—I really think my husband's right, I should—"

Kiernan reached into the folder. "And then there's the receipts we found in your place." She pulled out pictures of the receipts in question; Kiernan was grateful that Stephanie was the type who preferred paper receipts. "You bought a moldavite rock from a mineral store near your place in Williamsburg, you got four mushrooms, one lemon, and a bunch of kale at a fruit-and-vegetable stand across the street from the mineral store, you bought benzoin resin from a cosmetics place in midtown near your office, you got yucca leaves at a place in Union Square, which is down the street from an electronics store that we know is a front for selling magic supplies and is probably where you got the four candles. Ain't surprised there's no receipt for that, but we're gonna have detectives go down there to see if anyone recognizes your face. And—aside from about half a bunch of kale, which you had in your fridge—none'a that stuff was in your apartment."

Jack looked completely befuddled. "What is all that?"

Kiernan looked at Stephanie. "You wanna tell him?"

Stephanie's response was to curl into herself more.

Looking at Jack, Kiernan said, "It's what you need to do the transmutation spell that got used on your boss and her dealer. It's also what we found in a storage unit belonging to Garth Ohlmeyer."

"Now," Ortega said, straightening, "we can book you for two murders and three counts of possession. You've confessed to the murders, and we found the drugs in your co-op, and even if you decide to recant, we've got evidence, and we'll get more. We're still waiting on lab results from the building on Sutton Place, and I'm willing to bet that—since you were in *so much* pain—you didn't clean up after yourself after you killed Hertweck."

"Or," Kiernan said, "we can talk some more. You bought this stuff for Ohlmeyer, right?"

Stephanie looked confused. "I—I don't—"

"Fine." Kiernan stood up to stand next to Ortega. "Stephanie Taylor, you are under arrest for the murders of Elmore Hertweck and Jacques Bu—"

"Hold it, wait, wait!" Stephanie cried out.

"For the love of God, Steph," Jack said, "shut the *hell* up!"

"You don't understand, sweetie," she said. "Just—just let me—"

Ignoring his wife, Jack looked at the detectives. "My wife is invoking until we can get a criminal lawyer in here."

But then Stephanie blurted out, "He needs me to consult on something! Something that's happening this weekend!"

"Steph!"

"I'm sorry, I just—I'm scared, sweetie, I don't know what he's gonna do!"

Jack got to his feet. "I'm serious, Detectives, get the hell out of here. We'll talk again when our lawyer gets here." He was pulling a phone out of his pants pocket.

"All right. Officer Fischer is right outside the door if you need anything."

Running a finger across the phone's screen, Jack said a very insincere, "Thank you," then put the phone to his ear.

Ortega knocked on the door and Fischer opened it to let them out.

Basia, the Major, and Hawkins came out of the former's office, which included video surveillance on every room in the building. "I killed the video feed," she said.

Kiernan nodded. Jack had identified himself as Stephanie's lawyer, as specious as that was, and if they were alone in a room, their conversations were still privileged, at least until a new lawyer showed up.

"What do you think?" the Major asked.

"I think she's drowning," Kiernan said. "She said it herself, she never killed anyone before, and it's makin' her nuts. Plus the pain she's talking about—I don't know how much of that is real and how much is psychosomatic, but it also don't matter. She's hurting. A lot. And Ohlmeyer's the one providing the stuff that keeps her from hurting, so he's gonna have power over her."

Basia said, "Anything Ohlmeyer wants one of his junkies to 'consult' on can't be good."

Ortega looked at Basia. "Didn't you tell us that the new moon is this weekend?"

Eyes widening, Basia said, "Wow, Luis, I didn't think you actually *read* my memos."

"I don't." He grinned. "Umali mentioned it."

"Figures," Kiernan muttered.

Nodding, Basia said, "Well, you're right, Saturday night is a new moon, and that means the ley-lines are hot as hell. It's a great time to perform a magic ritual."

"I can't see any ritual Ohlmeyer wants to perform being good for anyone," Ortega said.

Hawkins spoke up. "A lot of your bigger rituals require a certain amount of power."

Basia nodded. "Simeon's right, if you want to do something *really* big, using the—well, the life-energy of a human body can add to the power. It's what Chinese martial artists call *qi*."

"Catholics usually just call it *the soul*," Kiernan said.

"Same principle," Basia said. "The Bible uses the Greek terms *psyche* and *pneuma*, which mean *soul* and *spirit*, though both are usually translated into *soul*, and it's pretty much the same idea as *qi*. For that matter, the Quran also uses two different Arabic words, *rûh* and *nafs*. Hebrew has five different words for it, Sikhs call it *atma*, and—" She stopped, closed her eyes, winced, and said, "Sorry! I'm going on again."

"It's fine," the Major said in a tone that implied that it wasn't fine but that he wasn't interested in discussing it further, either.

"Thing is," Kiernan said, thinking it through, "if you wanna do a big ritual with humans for batteries, your best recruits for that are junkies who won't be missed—or it won't be all that surprising to anyone if they just disappear."

"Kiernan's right," Ortega said.

"Wait," Kiernan said with a grin, "lemme get my phone out so I can record you sayin' that!"

Ortega shot her an annoyed look, then went on. "But none of what we're talking about is evidence. We gotta get her to wear a wire."

"Which means we need to do a deal," Kiernan said. "She ain't gonna go for bein' charged with two murders if we want her to wear a wire, especially now that she's getting a *real* lawyer."

Hawkins scowled. "I don't like plea-bargaining with a killer."

"You know what I like less?" Ortega asked. "Letting Ohlmeyer skate *again*. This is the closest we've come to him in years."

"I agree with Ortega," the Major said before Hawkins could say anything else, for which Kiernan was grateful, as she didn't really want to sit in on another Ortega-Hawkins fight. "You guys all go home. We're gonna hold her overnight on the charges we already got. I'll leave a message at the DA's office, get someone up here first thing in the morning. And I'll call Narcotics, too, see if they can do the surveillance."

Kiernan nodded. SCU didn't have the staff to do the kind of full-time surveillance that would be required if they were going to wire Stephanie up.

Assuming she took the deal.

The Major headed toward the stairs, Ortega and Hawkins following. Kiernan hung back a second and looked at the archivist. "Basia, first thing tomorrow, can you put together a list of some of the possible rituals we're lookin' at here?"

"It's a *long* list, Domenica," Basia said with a certain passion.

"Then it's a long list. But we gotta start somewhere."

"Okay."

They all went home. As Kiernan drove north on the Bruckner, in much less traffic than usual, since it wasn't rush hour—she wondered what Stephanie Taylor would do.

Thursday morning, Kiernan brought her usual box of cannoli to work. The Major, Fiore, Ortega, Hawkins, Jurienny, and Hops devoured them. Grullon, Umali, and Frodo weren't present; the former two had gone straight down to Leon Persaud's magic shop—the one that masqueraded as an electronics store—on 14th Street, while the latter was upstairs guarding the interrogation room.

While eating her cannoli, Jurienny said, "The Taylors' lawyer and Yvette Wood from the DA's office both got here about half an hour ago. They're all in Interrogation 3 now."

Kiernan nodded. Wood was a good prosecutor who had worked with SCU before.

Ortega's phone buzzed as he stuffed a cannoli in his mouth. "It's Grullon," he said with his mouth full, a sight Kiernan never needed to see.

Kiernan followed Ortega to his desk, and the Major and Hawkins joined them. Ortega tapped the speaker icon, and after swallowing, said, "Grullon, I've got you on speaker with Kiernan, Hawk, and the Major."

Grullon had to shout over the wind. "Umali and I just left Persaud's place. He recognized Stephanie Taylor right away. Said she came in with a shopping list and paid with a generic gift card. He e-mailed me a copy of the transaction report."

"Good," Ortega said.

"Persaud said that she barely spoke a word, just handed over the list, then the card, muttered a 'thank you,' and practically ran outta the place."

"That's in character," Kiernan said.

"Mind you, I had to practically pry Umali outta there," Grullon added, and Kiernan could hear his snarky smile.

"That place was cool, okay?" Umali sounded defensive as she, too, shouted over the wind. "I didn't know there were shops like that!"

Hawkins said, "There's at least two dozen that we know of in the five boroughs. Since the Rosario murder, a few of them have been more open, but most of them have fronts like Leon's."

"Good work, you two," the Major said. "Get back up here."

"This should give us enough to arrest Ohlmeyer," Hawkins said.

Ortega rolled his eyes. "We're not even in the same zip code as having enough to arrest Ohlmeyer."

"Oh, come on, Luis." Hawkins put his hands on his hips. "We've got our murderer. We've got that same murderer buying the spell components needed to liquefy the corpses. And we've got those same components, minus the produce, in a storage unit owned by Ohlmeyer under a shell corporation."

"Ortega's right, Hawk," Kiernan said before Ortega could say something stupid. "It ain't enough. Nothing on that shopping list of Stephanie's is unique. Hell, aside from the candles, it's all stuff you can get at regular stores."

Nodding, Ortega added, "And even the candles are just there to help focus the energy. They're special, but they're also a dime-a-dozen, at least in a shop like Persaud's."

Majorowicz folded his arms. "If these items are all so common, why can't just anyone cast the spell?"

Hawkins had an answer for that. "The power comes from the person. The components direct the spell to make it work the way you want it to, but the energy, the juice—that comes from whoever's casting it. It needs someone strong—with a lot of that *qi* that Basia was talking about last night."

"The point is," Kiernan said, "Ohlmeyer's asshole lawyers'll insist that there's no link between Stephanie's purchases and what we found in the storage unit, and pretty much any judge'll agree. We need solid fuckin' evidence, and what we got is still Swiss cheese."

After all but one of the cannoli were consumed, Kiernan and Ortega went upstairs to Interrogation 3, with Kiernan holding the last cannoli wrapped in a paper napkin. She handed the sweet to Frodo, who grinned, said, "*Thank* you, Detective," and opened the door.

In this interrogation room, it was always eleven-oh-three. Wood, a short, slight Black woman in her twenties, sat facing the Taylors, who had been joined by a tall, thin Indian man in his thirties. This was Chandan Venkatesh, from the law firm of Hooper, Nissen, & Bonina.

"How we doin'?" Kiernan asked.

Wood said, "The people have agreed to lower the charges to first-degree manslaughter, to which Ms. Taylor will plead guilty, assuming that she agrees to wear a listening device and also testifies against the target, Garth Ohlmeyer, should this matter come to trial. She will serve a sentence of twenty-five years in a medium-security prison."

Jack was squirming in his seat. "I don't know about her testifying, Dan. Isn't that dangerous?"

Putting a hand on Jack's shoulder, Venkatesh said, "I wouldn't worry about it, Jack—this is *very* unlikely to come to trial. Garth Ohlmeyer is the type who will take a plea bargain of some manner rather than face the publicity of a trial. And since the DA's office is already going after him for Hudson Yards, this will likely be folded into that."

Kiernan thought it was even more likely that Ohlmeyer's lawyers would find a way for him to skate on the charges. Or that the DA would cut a deal as part of the Hudson Yards thing, like Venkatesh said. Or that the double murderer they were counting on to get them evidence would flake. Either way, though, still no trial ...

Stephanie was reading over the plea agreement Wood had written up. "There's one problem," she said very quietly.

Could be worse, Kiernan thought, *she could be saying that* after *she signed.* "What's the problem, Stephanie?"

"Won't Mr. Ohlmeyer find a wire?"

Ortega answered that one. "If we had been havin' this conversation back when I was a detective at the One-Seven, that would've been a problem, but you're in luck! You're currently being taken care of by a nice, well-funded special unit that gets access to some of the better, cutting-edge toys."

Kiernan leaned forward to put her hand on Stephanie's. "We've got a thing of lipstick that has a mic in it that's shielded from any detector on the market. It's on loan from the FBI."

"We'll be monitoring you," Ortega said. "So if anything goes wrong, we'll come a-runnin'."

Strictly speaking, a rotating crew from Narcotics would be handling all that. But, based on what the Major had told them when

Kiernan had arrived that morning, that entire unit was salivating at the prospect of finally nailing Ohlmeyer, so they were more than willing to lend a hand.

Stephanie had yet to pick up the pen to sign the agreement. "I don't know if I should do this," she said in a whisper.

"Oh God, Steph, *please*!" Jack shouted, leading Ventakesh to put a hand on his shoulder.

Wood stared right at Stephanie. "If you don't agree to this, Ms. Taylor, we're going to charge you with two counts of murder in the first degree—to which, I might add, you have already confessed—as well as three counts of possession of a controlled substance in the third degree. I doubt we'll have much difficulty getting a conviction, at which point you will serve two consecutive life sentences in maximum security."

"Steph," Jack said in a more even tone, "twenty-five years is better than never, and medium security is better than maximum."

Kiernan had to admit to being impressed. All she saw in Jack's face was love—and, to be fair, pity—for his wife. It would've been easy to just walk away once he found out that she was still a junkie and a murderer besides. But he still wanted what was best for her—and for them as a couple.

Wish I had a partner like that ...

Tears again welling in her eyes, Stephanie signed the agreement.

Kiernan got to her feet. "I'll call and get the wire sent over."

Wood followed her out of the interrogation room. "This is good," the ADA said after Frodo closed the door. "Another criminal charge can only help the bigger case."

Kiernan shot her a look. "You're saying a real-estate mess is the bigger case than the double murder? 'Cause I'm pretty sure it's the other way around."

"To you and me, maybe, but thanks to the shit with Kogan, my bosses are all over the Hudson Yards thing, and they're who I gotta answer to."

With a sigh, Kiernan said, "Figures."

"Oh, and Simon Delaj asked me to ask you what was happening with the domovoy."

Kiernan sighed again. "We're lookin' for him."

"What's taking so long?"

"Hard to find a shape-changer in a city of eight million. If Delaj has a problem with that, tell him to talk to Frank Reilly at the Tombs."

"Simon's been ducking phone calls from the victim."

Kiernan winced. "I been talkin' to Mercado. I'll ask her not to bug him, since he can't tell her anything."

"He'll appreciate that."

They took care of everything that needed to be done, and before the end of the tour, the Taylors were sent home with a new lipstick in Stephanie's purse. They'd also talked to Sergeant Abajian in Narcotics, who would set up the surveillance team during the overnight tour.

With that all handled, Kiernan was looking forward to going home, broiling the lamb chops she'd been marinating in hickory smoke salt and Worcestershire sauce all day, and watching the Yankees game.

While driving home, she put her phone on speaker and called Mercado.

"Detective Kiernan?" the woman said, answering on the first ring.

"I don't have any new news," she said quickly, not wanting Mercado to get her hopes up. "I just wanted to let you know that the ADA assigned to the case isn't gonna answer your calls."

"But I have questions about the case!"

"He doesn't have any answers. He's got eighty bajillion cases on his docket, and this ain't one of 'em yet, and it won't be until we recapture the thing. Don't worry, he'll be available to you once the case actually starts, but the domovoy hasn't even been arraigned yet."

"All right, I'm sorry, I just—I'm so eager to—"

"Forget it. You got nothin' to apologize for. Look, you wanna bug someone, bug me."

"I'm already bugging you, Detective."

Kiernan grinned. "Then bug me some more."

"This is just so frustrating."

"I know what you mean."

Mercado let out a long breath. "All right, thanks for letting me know. Have a good night, Detective."

"I promise I'll call or text if there's any new news."

"Thank you, Detective."

She drove the rest of the way home, changed, and put the lamb in the broiler.

Just as she sat down on the couch, having set the timer for eight minutes, at which point she would need to turn over the lamb chops, her personal cell phone rang. The display showed an unfamiliar 914 number, which likely meant Westchester County. Tim and Bobby and Tim's stupid new wife lived in Mamaroneck, so it might have been something related to them.

She sat down at the kitchen table and answered. "Hello?"

A pleasant, scratchy voice asked, "Is this Domenica Kiernan?"

"Yes," she said slowly. He had pronounced it "dom-en-ICK-uh," rather than "doh-MEN-ick-uh."

"I'm Detective Eddie McLain with the Village of Mamaroneck Police Department. I need to ask you some questions about your son, Robert."

"What about Bobby?" Kiernan got up and started pacing in the tiny kitchen.

"Just some questions we need to ask in situations like this."

"Situations like *what*?"

"I'm—I'm sorry, didn't your ex-husband call you?"

Getting a very cold feeling in the pit of her stomach, Kiernan said in a very tight voice, "I haven't heard from my ex since Sunday. What the *fuck* is going on, Detective?"

"I'm so sorry, Ms. Kiernan, he said he talked to you." McLain took a breath. "Your son is missing."

FIFTEEN

Kiernan had no memory of the rest of her conversation with McLain. She answered all his questions on autopilot. After she ended the call, she saw that her phone now identified the number as belonging to "Det. Eddie McLain VMPD," so she must have saved it at some point during the call, though she had no memory of doing that, either.

The lamb chops were cooling on top of the stove, also, which meant that she must have turned them and taken them out while talking with McLain.

Apparently, her brain had suppressed all of those memories, consumed as it was with one thought: *I can't believe he's missing.*

Her appetite shot, she ignored the lamb chops and called her asshole ex.

Roseline, the nanny, answered the phone. "Ms. Domenica, I'm *so* sorry!" She sounded like she was in tears. Not that Kiernan could blame her, as she would've been in tears herself if she wasn't so off-the-charts furious.

"What the hell happened, Roseline? And why are you answering Tim's phone?"

"He lent me his. Mine was stolen. I have been calling people trying to find Bobby."

Thinking about it—which she was barely even capable of doing, as she was so livid—Kiernan was glad it was Roseline she was talking to, as it would've been harder to talk to Tim right now, focused as she was on wanting to rip his face off.

In a gentler tone, she again asked, "What happened, Roseline?"

"I told you, my phone was stolen. Whoever did that texted the school and said that someone else would be picking up Bobby today, and it would be early, right when school ended, that they needed him to come home before band practice. They even sent a picture of the person who would do it. It came from my phone, so they believed it."

That told Kiernan a lot right there—including that Bobby was taken from school. It was possible that McLain had told her that, but she no longer recalled.

The school had a system set up to avoid releasing a child to an unknown person, so it would take a fairly elaborate scheme to kidnap a child from there. Texting from the nanny's phone would definitely get around the protocols, especially only a couple weeks into the school year, when many kids didn't have settled routines yet.

Which meant that Bobby had been very specifically targeted by someone with smarts and resources.

"It's okay, Roseline, this isn't your fault."

Roseline sounded miserable. "It's *all* my fault, Ms. Domenica! Oh, I know Mr. Tim is gonna fire me."

"He's not gonna fire you," Kiernan said with almost no confidence. "Could you put him on, please?"

"Of course."

A few moments later, Tim's voice came over the speaker. "What is it, Domenica? I'm kinda busy right now."

Intellectually, Kiernan had every intention of talking calmly to Tim, but emotionally she was all over the place, so she practically screamed, "When the *fuck* were you gonna tell me that our son got kidnapped, you *stupid* fucking *fuck*?"

"Calm down, Domenica, I didn't want to worry you. How did you find out?"

"How did—" *Why did I marry someone this stupid?* "I just got off the phone with Detective McLain!"

"Dammit. I told him I'd already talked to you. He shouldn't have called you."

Kiernan swallowed a retort that he had lied to a police officer. That was his fucking problem, and she had bigger fish to fry in this conversation. "Yeah, Tim, he should've called me. Wanna know *why* he should've called me? Because when a child of parents who had an acrimonious divorce gets kidnapped, the first person they call is the non-custodial parent to check their fucking alibi for the kidnapping, 'cause guess who's the prime suspect in cases like this?"

"Oh." She heard Tim swallow. "I, uh—I didn't think about that. I've been a little distracted."

"In case you're wondering, I got an alibi."

"I assumed as much. You were still on the clock when Bobby was kidnapped, and I'm fully aware that they account for your whereabouts at all times. So you don't have to worry. That's why I told the detective that I talked to you already."

"*Madonna mia*, of *course* I have to worry, you jackass, he's *my* son too! What the fuck happened?" She'd already heard it from McLain, though his account had fled her brain completely, and Roseline, but she wanted Tim's version.

"Roseline lost her phone—or at least that's what we thought. She was going crazy looking for it, and then she finally gave up and went to pick Bobby up after band practice. But he wasn't there. The security guard, what's her name, um—"

"Monique."

"Right, her."

I can't believe he still *can't remember Monique's name.* She might excuse his forgetfulness due to the stress of the situation, but the fact was that he *never* remembered Monique's name, even though she'd been the front-desk security guard at their son's school since Bobby was in kindergarten.

Tim continued, "She said that Bobby was picked up at dismissal, just like Roseline said he would be, by that friend of the family. Roseline, of course, had no idea what she was talking about. Monique showed her the texts from her phone, all time-stamped after she lost it."

"I'm guessing they tapped your phone and are waitin' for a ransom demand?"

"Yes, there are two detectives here now—not McLain, two others. They said there'd be an Amber Alert, too."

"You get that I *see* all Amber Alerts in the New York Metro Area, right? And that they're public?"

"Really? But this isn't NYPD's jurisdiction."

Kiernan rolled her eyes. "Kidnappers don't always stick to one county, Tim."

"I guess not. Look, the detectives need me for something. Can I put Julia on?"

"I—"

"Thanks," Tim said before Kiernan could voice her objection.

A moment later, Julia's nasal voice came over the speaker. "Don't worry, Domenica, we'll get him back, I promise, we won't let anything bad happen to our boy."

Julia always called Bobby "our boy," as if she had any claim to him. Well, okay, she had *some* claim to him, but Julia barely took her duties as "person who lives in the same house" seriously, much less "stepmother." Roseline was more of a maternal figure to Bobby than Julia had ever even attempted to be.

"Not really up to you—or to me."

"I know, but we can take care of any ransom demand. We'll get him back. And I'm sorry Tim didn't call you. I told him he should let you know right away, but—well, you know how he gets."

"Yeah." Kiernan made that word several syllables long. "We just gotta hope—"

"I'm sorry, Domenica, Tim needs me. Gotta go. Bye!"

She ended the call.

Kiernan stared at her phone for a few seconds and then threw it across the room.

The little device clattered against the kitchen wall and fell to the tile floor. She'd bought a high-quality protective case because her job sometimes resulted in abuse to her phone, which also made it handy when she needed to throw it angrily across the room.

I can't believe he's missing.

I can't believe someone took him.

The lamb chops had gotten cold, and Kiernan's appetite was gone, so she put them in a Tupperware and shoved them into the refrigerator. Then she went to the wine rack in the living room, which was about half full, all Italian red wines. She hadn't purchased any alcohol since the divorce, but plenty of others had bought her drinks, both in glasses in bars and in bottles as presents.

She thought about opening the Brunello that Uncle Hermenegildo had given her after his last trip back home to Italy. But no, he'd said to save that for a special occasion. While this occasion could be called *special*, it wasn't celebratory.

Instead, she grabbed the bottle of red from the Friuli province in the north of Italy that Aunt Loretta had given her. It was a harsh wine, fitting her mood.

She nearly split the cork with the corkscrew, and some bits of cork fell into the bottle. Normally, she'd find a strainer if that happened, but she had no shits to give at this point, so just upended the bottle into one of her larger wine glasses, filling it with about a third of the bottle's contents.

Plopping down on the couch, and uncaringly spilling wine on it—the wine was red, the couch was red, who'd even notice?—she tried to watch the Yankees game. But she couldn't focus on it, having to constantly check the MLB app on her phone to remind her of what she had just watched happen on the television. Which she did between obsessive checks of her text messages to see if there was any new news from Tim or from McLain, of which there continued to be none.

Finally, she gave up and turned the game off. The wine had made her a bit sleepy—though she doubted she was going to sleep well, if at all—so she put a stopper in the bottle and shoved it in the fridge, then brushed her teeth, stripped off her clothes, turned out the lights, and lay down on the futon behind the couch.

I can't believe he's been taken.

She checked her phone once more before plugging it in overnight—

—and nearly dropped it when she saw an e-mail with the subject line, *Bobby missed band practice today.*

"Fuck," she muttered.

Reluctantly—mostly because she didn't want to know—she tapped a finger on the e-mail to open it.

> *Dear Detective Kiernan:*
>
> *Despite the deal you have with the Taylors, I suggest that you back the hell off from the case you're pursuing. There's no evidence—at least not anymore—so why drag it out? And if you DO drag it out, your son Robert will be in serious trouble.*

The e-mail was from a Hotmail account. Kiernan didn't even realize Hotmail was still a thing. There was no way to verify who owned the account—the user ID before the @ sign was just some numbers—but nonetheless Kiernan immediately forwarded the e-mail to the Computer Crimes Squad to see if they could track the e-mail address. They probably couldn't, but she had to at least take that step.

She considered and rejected forwarding the e-mail to McLain. The e-mail was almost definitely from Ohlmeyer—he was the only one who could possibly know about SCU's deal with the Taylors. If so, McLain would be *way* out of his depth. And if the e-mail was bullshit and Ohlmeyer had nothing to do with it, or if he didn't really have Bobby and had seen the Amber

Alert and was messing with her, it was a crappy lead that McLain shouldn't waste his time with.

After she finished sending the e-mail to CCS, she screamed, "*Fuuuuuuuuck!*"

A few seconds later, someone knocked on her door. "Domenica?" came a muffled voice from the other side of the door. "It's Sabri, are you all right?"

Kiernan sighed. She should've realized that her loud voice, combined with the building's thin walls, would enable her profane exclamation to reach the hallway.

Glancing around, she tried to remember where she'd put her bathrobe. "I'm okay," she yelled as she clambered to her feet, padding across the living room to finally find the robe draped over the easy chair. Shrugging into it and tying it shut, she opened the door to Sabri, who was wearing a fleece jacket over a pair of slacks and well-polished shoes.

He looked genuinely concerned. "Are you all right?"

"Not even a little bit. But I'm sorry I disturbed you—you just comin' in?"

Nodding, he said, "I just got back from a function at the university." He frowned. "You look *terrible*, Domenica, what happened?"

She shouldn't have been surprised that she looked like shit, all things considered. "The short version is my kid got kidnapped."

Sabri's entire body tensed. "Oh my goodness, Domenica! Is there—is there anything I can do? What happened? How'd it happen? I—" He shook his head. "I'm sorry."

"No, it's okay, I just—" She shivered a bit—it was cold out in the hallway, and she was only wearing a flannel robe. "This is way too much to go into in my doorway, you wanna come in?"

He hesitated, then pointed in the direction of his apartment. "I need to just check on my girls and make sure they're okay. Can I come back in a few minutes?"

"Yeah, sure. I'll leave it unlocked, just come right in."

He nodded and then went down the hall. Domenica shut the door and had to stop herself from locking it out of habit.

She padded to the bedroom, undid the robe and dropped it to the floor, climbing into sweatpants and a nice, baggy Yankees sweatshirt, as putting a bra back on didn't bear thinking about.

Sabri opened the door and came in just as Kiernan was walking back down the hall toward the living room. He had removed the fleece jacket so she could see that he was wearing a very nice, dark blue, button-down shirt.

He seemed befuddled at the sight of her. "Was that what you were wearing a minute ago?"

"Uh, no. I changed."

"Okay, good." He shook his head. "I'm so sorry, I've had a bit to drink and I'm not thinking straight."

"S'okay, neither am I. I'd offer you a glass of wine, but if you ain't thinkin' straight ..."

"A glass of water would be lovely—perhaps hydrating will get my brain in order."

"I'm way past that." She went into the kitchen, opened the fridge, and got out both the bottle of red she'd poured earlier and the pitcher of water, the one with the filter.

Moments later, she was sitting on one end of the couch with her wine and Sabri was on the other with his glass of water. She had turned on only the floor lamp next to the couch, so the apartment was still mostly dark; the halogen bulb in the floor lamp highlighted Sabri's very attractive, bearded face.

She told him the first part of the story: that Bobby was kidnapped, and how she found out about it.

"I—" Sabri shook his head. "I'm sorry, I don't know what to say. Anything I can think of would be horrendously inadequate."

"Everything about this is horrendously inadequate, believe me," Kiernan said after gulping down some wine.

Sabri took a sip of water, regarding her with a mix of confusion, compassion, and care. His eyebrows were slanted in, once again creating that vertical line in the middle of his forehead. "I'm surprised you were trying to sleep. I'd imagine you'd be driving up to—where is it you said, Mamaroneck?"

She nodded.

"And trying to find him."

Shaking her head, Kiernan said, "Oh, every nerve of my body is screaming at me to do that, but absolutely no way. I've worked three child kidnappings on the job, one when I was in uniform and two as a detective. The one thing they all had in common was that the thing that most kept us from finding the kid and closing the case were the parents, who kept stickin' their fuckin' noses into the investigation. When I was pregnant, which was right after the first one of those cases, I swore to St. Michael that, if God forbid, my kid was ever kidnapped, I would *not* be one'a those asshole parents who got all up in the detectives' faces. I'm better off stayin' right here outta the way." She tried to smile and almost succeeded. "And you do *not* break a promise to St. Michael."

Sabri's soft face had settled into an expression of sadness. His almond eyes were wider than ever, and his mouth was an uneven line inside his thin beard. "I'm afraid that, despite being employed by a Jesuit university, my knowledge of the saints is incomplete. Which one is Michael?"

"He's the archangel Michael, to be precise, and, among other things, he's the patron saint of cops. And there's enough Irish, Italian, and Latin cops that St. Michael's medallions're all over every precinct. I ain't the most religious person on the planet, but even I don't fuck with St. Michael."

"Fair enough, but I also imagine you wish to drive to Mamaroneck and strangle your ex-husband for not telling you."

"Oh, definitely," she said emphatically. "But I kinda always wanna do that?"

He favored her with that laugh, which brightened his face as well. "Fair enough."

She sighed. "And then there's the e-mail."

"What e-mail?"

Her phone was plugged in on the end table next to her. She called up the e-mail in question, unplugged the phone, and handed it to Sabri.

Sabri's complexion went very pale after reading it. The vertical line was back on his forehead. "My goodness, Domenica—who sent this? I mean, the kidnappers, obviously, but—"

She took the phone back and plugged it in again. "There's a case we're workin' right now—can't really talk about it. But the guy we're lookin' at's got serious juice. And if he knows about the deal we made this afternoon, it means he's got a way of knowin' what's happening in our house—uh, in SCU HQ," she added, in case Sabri wasn't up on his cop lingo.

"That's—that's not good."

"No, it ain't. That's why I yelled 'fuck' at the top of my lungs."

"Shouldn't you tell this Detective—McCain, was it?"

"McLain, and prob'ly, but if I do, the bad guy'll probably find out about it. I gotta be real careful. And I don't know who to trust right now."

Sabri gulped down all of the rest of his water. "I'm flattered that you trust me."

"Yeah, I probably shouldn't, since I've only known you for a week, but I needed a sounding board, and you were nice enough to knock on my door. Besides you ain't part of—" She waved her arms back and forth. "—all this."

"No, I'm not, and the next time I find myself frustrated by the inanities of academia, I will remind myself of tonight for perspective." He sipped more water. "But shouldn't you talk to someone who *is* part of—" He mimicked her gesture. "—all this?"

"What do you mean?"

"Your fellow Monster Squad detectives should be able to provide some guidance, especially as it apparently relates to their case."

"You really gotta stop callin' it the Monster Squad."

Smiling ruefully, Sabri said, "Apologies, but it's too good a name to *not* use."

She snorted. "Y'know, one of the names they floated when they formed the unit was, I swear to God, the Magic and Monster Investigation Unit, figuring we could just call it the M&M Unit. Luckily, the commissioner's office said no."

"I agree, that was not a good name. And Supernatural Crimes Unit is descriptive, certainly."

A thought occurred to Kiernan. "It can't just be a mole in the department. Or even in the unit."

"Why not?"

"The timing. The paperwork on that deal the e-mail mentioned had only got started being processed before Bobby got kidnapped. It wasn't finished and in the system until later in the evening. The only way our target could know about the deal is if he's got some way of eavesdropping on us. He musta started the kidnapping as soon as he heard us *talking* about the deal. We gotta do a sweep."

"For bugs?"

"Not just bugs. Our guy's a Gandalf—sorry, a magic-user—so he could have some kinda magic doodad in the house."

"I assume 'doodad' is a technical term?"

She chuckled. "Yeah." Then she let out a long breath. "Listen, Sabri—thank you. I ain't been thinkin' straight since McLain called me, but talkin' to you has helped me focus a little. It probably won't last, but I appreciate it. Unfortunately, that means I gotta kick you out. There's some calls and texts I gotta do."

Putting the now-empty glass down on the coffee table and holding up both hands, Sabri said, "I understand completely." Getting to his feet, he looked down at her, still seated on the red couch. "Do what you have to do. And, um—you're welcome, I suppose. If there's anything else I can do to help, please don't hesitate to call."

"Tough to do without your number."

Sabri tilted his head. "I didn't give you my number? Or ask for yours?"

"Nope." She unplugged her phone again and went to where she could add a contact. Then she got up and handed the phone to him. "Put it in."

He not only entered his ten-digit phone number but also put his name and e-mail address in the appropriate spots.

"Thank you," she said when he handed it back, and immediately sent a text message:

This is Domenica.

"My phone is in the jacket I was wearing, so I won't see what you sent until I get home."

She walked him to the door. "Thanks again, Sabri."

He went over the threshold and then turned to face her. His wonderfully expressive eyes were an endearing mix of concern and helplessness. "I'm glad I could help. I'd say 'good night,' but that seems inappropriate—and inadequate."

"Lotta that goin' 'round," she said with a ragged smile. "I hope at least one of us sleeps well."

He favored her with one final smile before she closed and locked the door.

First, she texted everyone in the squad to let them know that Bobby had been kidnapped and provided all the details she actually knew.

Then she called SCU HQ. It wasn't yet midnight, so Naomi was still working the desk.

"NYPD Supernatural Crimes Unit."

Kiernan almost smiled. Both Jurienny and the overnight admin, Marjorie, just said, "SCU" when they answered. "Naomi, it's Detective Kiernan."

"What can I do for you, Detective?"

"I need you to send two e-mails. One to IT to ask them if someone can come over and sweep for bugs." There was always the possibility that Ohlmeyer was using a good, old-fashioned, electronic listening device. "Then I need you to e-mail the Gitaus and tell them we need a magical sweep of the house ASAP."

"I'll e-mail IT right away, but shouldn't I check with Lieutenant Majorowicz or Sergeant Hawkins about hiring the Gitaus first?"

With a sigh, Kiernan said, "Just do it, please, Naomi? If Hawk and the Major don't approve using the Gitaus, *I'll* pay for it."

"Um—okay, I guess."

"Thank you."

Jimiyu and Wanja Gitau were a husband-and-wife team of licensed private investigators who specialized in the supernatural. Before the SCU existed, they'd been one of the primary go-tos for people in New York who had issues with magic and monsters and had been laughed at by the police. The Gitaus had consulted on the Rosario case and the SCU had continued to use them as consultants periodically. Which was the least the SCU could do, given that the formation of the unit had seriously cut into their business.

She was tempted to just call them herself, but if they weren't out on a job, they were both asleep at this hour, and they wouldn't be able to actually do the sweep until morning in any case. Best to do it through official channels.

Next she composed another group text, this one just to Ortega, Fiore, and Grullon. She considered and rejected including Umali. After she started writing, she realized she also needed to include Basia.

While she waited for her colleagues to get back to her, she got a phone call from Detective McLain.

"Just wanted to give you an update, Detective Kiernan."

McLain had been calling her "Ms. Kiernan" at the start of their conversation earlier—she must have corrected him at some point. "Okay."

"We found the car that was used to take your son. It was left at Harbor Island Park. It was reported stolen this evening by a married couple who live on Valley Place."

"This evening? That's kinda suspicious, it being reported stolen *after* Bobby got taken?"

"We were hoping so when we saw the time of the report, but the two owners have jobs in Manhattan and commute via Metro North—and their house is right by the station. They didn't know the car was missing until they got home from work."

"Oh." Kiernan had stupidly allowed herself to hope that this was a lead, but Ohlmeyer's flunkies probably stole the first available car after they swiped Roseline's phone.

"We're gonna check those two out, but I'm pretty sure they're just two more victims in this. And we're processing the car, hoping it gives us something. Oh, and Bobby's phone, backpack, and clarinet were all in the car. The phone was turned off, which is why we hadn't been able to track it. They're in evidence right now."

"Okay. Well, thanks for the update, Detective. I'm gonna try and fail to get some sleep."

"Of course, Detective. Have a good night."

While Kiernan had been on the phone with McLain, Grullon, Basia, and Fiore had all responded, and Ortega did just after she ended the call. They agreed to meet tomorrow morning, an hour before the tour started—or, in Ortega's case, an hour and a half before his endocrinologist appointment—at the bagel place on 118th Street.

She undressed and climbed back into bed, plugging the phone back in.

Laying on her back, she stared at the ceiling.

I can't believe they took my little boy.

SIXTEEN

"Sorry I'm late," Ortega said as he came in from the cold morning and approached the big table in the corner of the bagel place. Kiernan had gotten there first, quickly followed by Basia, then Grullon and Fiore. They had all gotten food and drinks at the counter before sitting down. Kiernan had purchased two coffees and a poppy-seed bagel. She'd taken only a single bite of the bagel but was already down to the dregs of her first coffee.

"Are you *really* sorry?" Grullon asked as Ortega took off his windbreaker and sat next to him. "I mean, doesn't being sorry imply that you didn't mean it and you'll try not to do it again? We all know *that* isn't true."

Ortega rolled his eyes at Grullon. "Shut up and drink your coffee."

Kiernan found that she was grateful for the banter. Except for Basia, everyone at this table was an experienced cop, and they were used to dealing with insane situations in a calm, professional manner. This was what they *did*. And she needed that calmness and especially that professionalism right now. That they were her friends and colleagues was important—that was why they were all here before their tour—but that they were detectives who'd been there and done that was even more so.

Basia asked, "Aren't you going to have anything, Luis?"

"Can't," Ortega said. "They're gonna be takin' blood at the doctor this morning, so I can't eat or drink anything." He turned to Kiernan. "How you doing, Domenica?"

Kiernan was taken aback. She could count on the fingers of one hand the number of times Ortega had called her by her first name. "Terrible. Got a call from Detective McLain this morning—that's the VMPD detective handling Bobby's case. No new leads, no ransom demands."

Fiore swallowed a bite of his sesame bagel with cream cheese and said, "I'm guessin', since we're all meetin' here, and Hawk and the Major ain't part of it, that this is off-book?"

"Is that a problem?" Kiernan asked pointedly.

"Nah, I just wanna make sure I know where we stand. I got your back, Dom, you know that."

"We all do," Ortega said.

Basia said, "Forgive me, but why just us? Why not Simeon, Sofia, or the lieutenant? I mean, I understand why this is off-book, like Vinny said—it's not NYPD's jurisdiction, and it's your kid, so you can't be involved officially—but ..." She shrugged and took a sip of her tea.

Kiernan gulped down the last of her first coffee. "Hawk's too straight an arrow. He wouldn't sanction this and would probably report it. Umali's too new—I don't know her well enough to know how she'd respond. As for the Major... ." She sighed. "Ohlmeyer got inside info. Now he may've gotten it magically—that's why I asked Naomi to call in the Gitaus. But he's also a wealthy, powerful asshole, so he might have a high-up source in the department. I can't take the chance that someone the Major reports to'll have loose lips."

Nodding, Basia said, "Okay. Like Vinny said, I have your back, I just wanted to understand the situation."

Kiernan took another small bite of her bagel, then looked at everyone in turn. "Look, this is risky as hell. We could all get fucked by this. I'm willing to take the chance for Bobby, but—"

Ortega got an *are you kidding?* look on his face. "Will you stop it with that? If we didn't want in, we wouldn't be here. And it's *Bobby.* So let's get on with it."

"Thanks." Kiernan tried for a grateful smile, but her face—and brain—wouldn't cooperate. "So where are we with the official investigation?"

"Nowhere until Ohlmeyer contacts Stephanie Taylor," Ortega said. "I got a text twenty minutes ago from Abajian. Narcotics got set up on the Taylors late last night, but they got nothing useful yet. Just the pair of 'em fighting like cats and dogs."

"At this point, she's probably going through withdrawal, so there's gonna be a lotta that." Kiernan sighed.

Fiore wiped cream cheese off his lips, then asked, "Hey, shouldn't we check the Taylors for bugs, too? Ohlmeyer could have *her* tagged as part'a the 'thank you for disposin' of two bodies' thing."

Ortega nodded. "Good idea. I'll text Abajian."

While Ortega fondled his phone, Kiernan said, "All right, you guys can just clock in like normal and do what you gotta do."

"You guys?" Basia asked.

Kiernan sighed. "The Major told me to take the day when I called him this morning. I tried fightin' him on it, but—"

"It's department policy," Ortega said, "and it's a smart one. You're in no shape to work today, Kiernan."

"I'm in no shape to fuckin' *breathe.* And now I gotta sit around my shitty apartment and come up with worst-case scenarios all day."

Basia put a hand on Kiernan's. "Maybe go to the zoo or the botanical gardens? Decompress a little?"

"Maybe." Kiernan's apartment was walking distance from both the New York Botanical Gardens and the Bronx Zoo. Basia had gotten Kiernan a membership to the former as a birthday present this past spring, and one of the few things she still shared with Tim was the family zoo membership.

There was no chance of her going to the zoo. She'd just been there with Bobby this past weekend and the memory was way too raw. But maybe the botanical gardens …

"Anyhow," she said, "we gotta figure out a way to find Bobby, if Ohlmeyer really is the one that has him." Looking at Basia, she asked, "Can we use a locator spell?"

Quickly shaking her head as she spread some strawberry jam on a muffin, Basia said, "No chance. Someone as powerful as Ohlmeyer would be warded against that."

"And if something hits the wards, he'd know that, right?" Grullon asked. Basia nodded.

"Then that's out," Ortega said. "We can't do anything he'd notice, he might kill Bobby."

"Hey, man, easy," Fiore said.

Kiernan held up a hand. "It's fine. I know the stakes. And honestly, I'd rather we *didn't* fuck around with pretty language to try to make me feel better. I *ain't* gonna feel better, so we may as well be as blunt as fuckin' possible."

Grullon was chewing on his everything bagel with lox, then spoke as he swallowed. "Hang on a second. Whatever Ohlmeyer's got planned for tomorrow night is probably also heavily warded, right?"

"Yeah," Kiernan said.

"Basia, what about a spell to detect wards?" he asked before washing down his bagel with coffee.

Eyes and smile both widening, Basia said, "That would work! It's a low-level spell, just something that tells you where wards are."

"Ohlmeyer wouldn't be able to detect it?" Kiernan asked.

"No—but …"

When Basia's hesitation threatened to go on forever, Kiernan prompted, "But what?"

"There are wards *all over* the city. The spell we're talking about won't be able to distinguish one set from another."

"So we cross reference with Ohlmeyer's properties," Ortega said. "I'm supposed to be getting a full list of those from the DA's office."

Grullon said, "We should also check anything owned by Augurer Productions."

Pointing an approving finger at Grullon, Kiernan said, "Good idea."

"So we just hire a Gandalf to—" Grullon started.

Ortega interrupted him. "Shit. We can't use any of our regulars."

Grullon asked, "Huh?"

Kiernan realized the problem. "This is off-book. Anyone we'd normally hire for this, like Nikolaeva, Stein, or Uduwana, would have to get paid by the department. We can't have a paper trail."

Fiore smiled as he swallowed the last of his sesame bagel. "No problem. I got a guy."

Normally, Kiernan wouldn't even ask—Fiore *always* seemed to have a guy—but this was her son. "What guy, Vinny?"

"A guy. Don't worry about it, I'll take care of it."

Kiernan gave him one of Nonna's looks.

Holding up both hands as he wilted before her grandmother's gaze, Fiore said, "Okay, okay, it's my second cousin Maria's first husband, Nicky. He owes me big-time."

"And he's a Gandalf?" Kiernan asked.

Fiore nodded. "Maria don't know that, though, 'cause if she did, she'd'a taken his ass for everything in the divorce and not agreed to joint custody of little Anna. For that matter, Nicky's second wife don't know, either." He grinned. "My silence ain't cheap."

"Or common," Ortega muttered.

Pulling his phone out of his suit jacket pocket, Fiore said, "I'll text him now—but I won't get an answer till noon. Nicky don't do mornings."

"Okay, good. Thanks, Vinny." Kiernan let out a very long breath, then decided to take a third bite of her bagel. "And thanks, all of you."

"We'll find him," Ortega said.

Fiore finished his text and said, "We should prob'ly get to work."

Grullon quickly ate the last of his bagel, Fiore gulped down his coffee, and Basia finished her muffin. Ortega regarded Kiernan with concern.

"Do me a favor, you guys?" Kiernan asked as they all started to get up and put their coats on. "Check up on me a few thousand times today? Even if you don't got any progress, I just—I need to hear from people. I ain't okay, y'know?"

Ortega nodded. "We know, Kiernan."

"Do you guys mind schlepping up to the Bronx after the tour's over? I'm feelin' real exposed talkin' about this stuff here. I think our next get-together should be at my place. We can order in from Joseph's."

"Works for me," Fiore said. He lived in the Bensonhurst neighborhood of Brooklyn but loved going to Belmont for Italian food. He slid into his designer fleece coat and said, "I gotta head back down to Chinatown for my Taotie thing."

Ortega stared at him. "You still ain't found it yet?"

Fiore shook his head. "The couple that kept it said they can't find it, and we already searched their home and work. But I got a call from Ms. Chao last night with a lead, so I'm gonna go follow up."

"Wait," Kiernan said, "she called you last night? You gave her your cell?"

"Yeah. She was startin' to make Jurienny and Naomi both a little crazy, y'know? So I figured I'd take the heat off and let her call me directly."

Grullon was shuddering. "I talked to her a couple of times, and she's *really* intense."

Shrugging, Fiore said, "So're all my aunts and grandmothers and great-grandmothers. I'm used to it. Anyhow, I'm gonna head downtown."

"By yourself?" Ortega asked. Kiernan agreed with his surprise, as the Major preferred detectives to pair up.

"Nah, Umali's comin' with. I texted her, she's gonna meet me down there. Hey, Grullon, can you sign us both in?"

"Sure," Grullon said.

Putting her motorcycle jacket on over a T-shirt that had a rendition of Demuth's *I Saw the Figure 5 in Gold*, Basia said to Kiernan, "If you go to the botanical gardens, send me pictures, please?"

Kiernan nodded. "You bet."

Grullon put a hand on her shoulder as he followed Basia out. Fiore just put a hand over his own heart before departing.

Ortega stayed behind, though. "I still got time before my appointment."

Sighing, Kiernan said, "I've got nothing *but* time. Until something happens. And something better fucking well happen, because I *cannot* deal with this shit. That goddamn motherfucker took my boy, and I can't do a *fucking* thing about it because he's Mr. Rich-and-Powerful Fuckface, so we gotta be sneakin' around and meanwhile we don't know shit and there's no ransom demand and my asshole ex can't even be fuckin' bothered to *call* me and I just want to rip everybody's *fucking* face off and *I can't do a goddamn fucking thing!*"

She had been gesturing more and more wildly the longer her rant had continued, and on her last word, knocked her half-eaten bagel off the table.

Suddenly incredibly self-conscious, Kiernan swallowed, then leaned over to pick the bagel up off the floor. The other customers were very quiet and very studiously *not* looking at the crazy woman at the large table.

Naturally, Ortega took it all in stride. "Feel better?"

"Not even a fuckin' little bit. And now I can't eat this bagel."

Getting to his feet, Ortega said, "I'll get you another one."

"Thanks," she said quietly.

Ortega went to the counter to get another bagel. She wondered what explanation—if any—he gave the person behind the counter as to why she'd suddenly started screaming her head off.

She drank the last of her second coffee. She considered asking Ortega for another, but the last thing she needed was to be *more* hyper right now.

No, the last thing I needed is for Bobby to be kidnapped. Fuckin' Ohlmeyer.

I can't believe he took him.

NYC

SEVENTEEN

As soon as Grullon and Basia reached the second floor, Marjorie Park, who covered the desk overnight, said, "You've got a call on line 2, Detective Grullon." Basia nodded to Marjorie and Grullon and continued up the stairs, to her office on the third floor.

"Thanks," Grullon said as he passed the admin's desk, adding, "Why you still here?"

Marjorie, who had a trace of a Korean accent, as she was born in Uijeongbu, said, "Jurienny had a thing this morning and I don't have class until eleven, so I said I'd cover until she came in."

Grullon nodded and said, "Can you sign me, Fiore, and Umali in? They're going down to Chinatown, but they're on the clock."

"Okay."

That taken care of, Grullon headed to his desk. As he sat down, he smiled at the picture of Rachael. Then he picked up the phone and stabbed the button for line 2. "Grullon, SCU."

Rachael's lovely voice greeted him. "Hi, Grullon, SCU, it's Haimovitch, Olson Investment Partners."

Chuckling, Grullon said, "Hey, sweetness. Why didn't you call my cell?"

"I did. It went straight to voicemail. Probably 'cause you forgot to take it out of airplane mode."

Reaching into the pocket of his slacks, Grullon pulled out his phone to see that it was indeed still in airplane mode. He always switched to that when he rode the subway, as the constant going in and out of service underground chewed through the phone's battery life. Disengaging airplane mode, he put the phone down on his desk. "I did, in fact, totally forget."

"It's fine, my love. I just wanted you to know that the invitation to your new coworker went out."

"Thank you."

"How's Domenica doing?"

Grullon blew out a breath. "Not great. There's been no news, and—well, let's just say the news we already had kinda sucks."

"Damn. Please give her a hug from me?"

"I will. Oh, speaking of that, we're getting together again tonight at her place in the Bronx. We're getting takeout from Joseph's. Want me to get you something?"

"Yes, please!" Rachael said enthusiastically. "Lasagne!"

"Will do."

Rachael's voice got distant. "What's that? Okay." Her voice got louder. "My love, I have to go, just wanted to let you know about Sofia Umali's invite. Oh! And I got an e-mail notification—those silver manacles for the basement should arrive today."

Grullon shuddered. It wasn't going to be an issue for another couple of weeks, but it still annoyed him that he needed silver manacles. Regular manacles were not proving as useful as he'd hoped.

"Take care, my love," Rachael said. "See you whenever you get back from Domenica's."

"Bye, sweetness."

As he hung up the phone, he heard a couple of familiar voices. Turning, he saw that Jimiyu and Wanja Gitau had just come up the stairs.

Marjorie said, "Hi, Jim! Hi, Wanja!"

Jim, who had a broad smile and a large round head that he kept shaved, looked at the admin through a narrow pair of glasses. "It is good to see you, Marjorie."

"Is Jurienny not in?" Wanja asked. She was the same height as her husband and had steel-gray hair that she kept cut short. Both of them wore black turtlenecks, black slacks, and black boots, and each carried a black pack. Grullon knew that under their turtlenecks, they wore body armor which had runes of protection carved into the surface.

In response to Wanja's question, Marjorie said, "Jurienny has a thing with her kids this morning. She'll be in around ten, and I don't have class until eleven."

"You are in your second year now, yes?" Jim asked.

Marjorie nodded.

"Still pre-med?"

Chuckling, Marjorie said, "So far, yeah."

Wanja shook her head. "I do not comprehend how you can work here all night and go to class all day."

With a shrug, Marjorie replied, "I sleep in the evenings. And it's usually quiet overnight, so I do my homework here." She smiled. "Just don't tell Sergeant Hawkins."

Both Gitaus grinned and Jim said, "Your secret is safe with us."

"And hey, I don't comprehend how you guys fight monsters and stuff."

Laughing, Wanja said, "We do not fight them, child. At best, we trick them."

With a nod, Jim said, "Guile is our greatest weapon."

"That, and silver bullets," Wanja added.

"You have an appointment?" Marjorie asked.

Grullon had, by then, gotten up and walked over to the desk. "Kiernan asked them to come in and do a sweep."

"And your timing is very fortunate," Wanja said. "We are down to our very last Bondarenko Charm."

Grullon smiled. "I'm guessing that's what you use to sweep the place?"

Hawkins came over. "Yes, it is. And I'm wondering why, exactly?"

Wanja smiled at the sergeant. "Hello, Simeon. How was your date with Vernetha?"

Suddenly, Hawk looked very embarrassed. "Uh, I'll call you later to talk about that, okay?"

Jim was giving his wife an annoyed look. "Come now, Wanja, you know the boy doesn't wish to discuss his personal life at work!"

While they talked, Grullon thought very carefully about how to answer Hawkins's question. "It was Kiernan's request. She got an anonymous e-mail that seemed like it came from Ohlmeyer, and he knew about the deal we made with the Taylors. She was worried that he left a magical bug behind."

"It could just have been a regular electronic bug."

Nodding, Grullon said, "She put in a work order with IT, too."

"Okay, good." Hawkins turned to the Gitaus. "Have at it, I guess."

Reaching into his pack, Jim said, "Just go about your business. We have enough juice left in the Bondarenko to do all five floors and the basement."

"Barely," Wanja added.

"I'm afraid that means the bill will also have to cover the purchase of a new one."

Hawkins waved a hand back and forth. "It's fine. The department generally doesn't even understand most of our requisitions, so they won't know the difference."

That got another of Jim's big smiles. Then the Gitaus got to work.

Grullon looked at Hawkins. "Who's Vernetha?"

"None of your business, Liam," Hawk said firmly.

"Oh, come on, Hawk. Everyone in this squad knows the intimate details of my upcoming wedding, but we don't get to even know about your date?"

"That's right, you don't." With that, Hawkins walked back to his desk.

Grullon sighed and started toward his desk, stopping when Marjorie let out a small cry.

Turning, he saw that her desk lamp was glowing blue.

A similar blue glow was also coming from the inside of Grullon's desk drawer. The St. Michael medal that hung on Fiore's picture of his great-grandmother was also glowing, as was a paperweight on Hawkins's desk.

The Gitaus were standing at the center of the squad room, beside Kiernan's desk. Together, they were holding something that looked like a big rock with shimmering blue highlights. There was a blue glow coming from under their turtlenecks as well as the insides of their backpacks.

Jim said, "The glowing items are all magical."

Holding up his now-blue paperweight, Hawkins said, "This is an equanimity charm I bought last month."

Grullon wondered how well that charm worked, given that Hawk and Ortega had been arguing pretty constantly since he'd joined the unit six months earlier, and it hadn't gotten noticeably better in the last few weeks.

Wanja indicated Fiore's desk with her head. "And that, of course, is Detective Vinny's St. Michael medal."

Jim was staring at Grullon's desk. "What is in the drawer, Detective?"

"Special handcuffs with runes," he said quickly, hoping they would ask no further questions. Of those present, Hawkins and Majorowicz were the only ones who knew exactly why he needed those cuffs.

Marjorie was now standing up and looking apprehensively at the glowing lamp. "I don't know why the lamp is glowing."

The Gitaus exchanged a look, then walked over to the reception desk. While Jim held the rock, Wanja reached into her pack and took out a pair of gloves. Grullon had seen them before and knew that normally they were yellow, though they were glowing blue right now, creating a rather garish visual.

The Major came out of his office, holding his phone in his hand—it, too, was glowing blue. "Doing a sweep, I see," he said dryly.

Hawkins stood up. "Domenica asked for it. She was worried about Ohlmeyer gaining intel on the unit."

Grullon was staring at the Major. "Your phone is magic?"

"The case is," the lieutenant said. "Long story."

Wanja closely examined the still-glowing lamp before pulling a small, flat disc out from inside the shade. The disc continued to glow blue while the lamp itself reverted to its ordinary incandescence.

"What is that?" the Major asked, walking across the squad room toward the Gitaus, accompanied by Hawkins.

"I am not sure," Wanja said, "but I believe it is a scrying stone."

Shaking his head, Hawkins said, "Damn, Domenica was right."

Having set down the charm, Jim was rooting around in his pack. He pulled out a small case that was also glowing blue. He opened it, Wanja put the disc inside, and Jim snapped the case shut.

"It will not function while in this case," Jim said.

Hawkins turned to face the Major. "If that really *is* a scrying stone, whoever put it there has seen and heard everything that's happened in this squad room."

Majorowicz was, Grullon noticed, looking more than a little tense. "Can you verify that that's a scrying stone? And where it was scrying *to*?" he asked the Gitaus.

"Absolutely," Jim said.

"But," Wanja added, "that will be an additional fee."

"I don't *care*," the Major said. "Someone was eavesdropping on us, and I want to know who. I don't give a good goddamn *what* it costs. And that someone was probably Garth Ohlmeyer, in which case we need to know *yesterday*."

"It may not have been Ohlmeyer," Hawkins said.

Pointing at the lamp, Majorowicz said, "Wednesday, when Ohlmeyer was here with his lawyers? They stood right there. Any one of the three of them could've slipped something that small into the lampshade without anybody noticing."

Wanja and Jim exchanged a glance. "We should do the rest of the building," she said.

"But assuming we don't find anything else untoward," Jim added, "we can have a full report for you by end of business today."

"And before you ask," Wanja said, "we cannot do that any sooner. The determination process is very specific and very complicated. The fastest it can happen is within the next eight hours."

"Understood." The Major stared down at his still-glowing phone. "How much longer does *this* go on?"

Once again, Jim provided his wide grin. "About ten minutes."

"Wonderful," Majorowicz muttered.

Hawkins said, "I'll go with you. Let's check upstairs first."

Jim stowed the case, Wanja picked up the charm, and the Gitaus and Hawkins moved toward the stairs. Grullon heard Wanja saying, "So how *did* it go with Vernetha?"

As the Major turned to head back to his office, the phone rang. Marjorie just stared at it, as if not entirely sure what it was.

Gently, Grullon said, "You want me to get that?"

Shaking her head as if coming out of a trance, Marjorie said, "No, no, I got it." She picked up the phone. "SCU … Sure, one second." She turned around and called out, "Lieutenant?" just as the Major was about to cross the threshold.

He turned to give her an inquisitive look.

"Line 3."

Nodding, Majorowicz continued into his office.

Majorie sat down and stared off into space.

Grullon stood next to her. "You okay?"

"Hm?" She looked up at him, and her eyes looked haunted. Grullon knew that look well; he'd seen it in the mirror most days since Van Cortlandt Park.

"You okay?" he asked again.

"Not really?" She sighed. "This is why I work nights here. We get a few calls, but not many. Sure, there's the occasional crazy all-hands-on-deck thing, like the last full moon?"

"I, uh—" Grullon coughed. "I wasn't here for that; I had that night off."

"Oh, right. Well, it was crazy town. And it was fine—it was actually kinda fun to get some chaos for a change, but—" She shuddered. "This is different. This is someone listening in on me when I'm doing my homework or video chatting with my mother in Korea or—" Again, she shuddered. "Damn. I need to get some tea. I'll be right back." She got up and went to the staircase, then turned to look back at Grullon. "Thanks, Detective."

"No problem. And hey, while you're up there, see if you can find out who Vernetha is."

Laughing, Marjorie said, "I'll try."

Just as she was going upstairs, the Major stuck his triangular head out of his office. "Grullon! Get in here."

"Okay, boss."

Taking a seat in the chair facing Majorowicz, Grullon noticed that his phone, which was on his desk, was still glowing blue.

"Any word on Bobby?" Grullon asked.

The Major shook his head. "No. I've got a call in to VMPD for an update. And I texted Kiernan, but I haven't heard back yet."

She was probably still driving home from the bagel place, but Grullon said nothing, since the Major hadn't been in on that meeting.

"I need you to head back down to Plaisir Douleur. More specifically, to Valapart's apartment above the club. He's gonna have something for us about the domovoy in about an hour or so, and he said it needs to be at his place."

Grullon shifted uncomfortably in his seat. "Can't he come here?"

With a smirk, Majorowicz said, "I'm pretty sure Valapart has only left that building three or four times since Stonewall."

"And you'd know," Grullon muttered.

Even as he spoke, Grullon knew he was making a mistake. And if he hadn't known, the sudden shift in the Major's tone would've told him. "What was that, Detective?"

"Nothing, sir," Grullon said quickly.

"Nice try, Detective Grullon, but that was most definitely *something*. So let's try this again. What *was* that, Detective?"

"I—" Grullon was at a loss for words.

Or, more accurately, he was at a loss for any words that would improve his situation.

"Are you, Detective, perhaps making a snotty comment about the fact that I'm a member of Valapart's club?" Every over-enunciated syllable of "Detective" was like a knife in Grullon's gut. "And yes, to answer your next question, Kiernan told me about how you reacted to that intel at the club on Monday. She also told me that she told you to talk to me about it. I can't help but notice the lack of conversation on the subject over the past five days."

"I'm sorry, sir, I just—" Grullon fidgeted. "I don't see how you can—can *do* that stuff!"

"Not that it's an *iota* of your business what I do in my personal life, Detective ..."

Grullon winced every time the Major used his rank in a sentence. He got to his feet. "It's okay, sir, you're right. It's none of my—"

"Sit your ass down, Detective."

Swallowing, Grullon did as he was told.

"When I finished my bit in the Marines, I was—let's just say, I wasn't in the best shape. I met Hanna and she and I clicked—and we found that we were both interested in similar activities. It gave me an outlet I pretty desperately needed at the time, especially after what I saw right before I came home. And no, I can't tell you what that was, suffice it to say that it's classified."

"I wasn't gonna ask, sir," Grullon said, though he had to privately admit to being curious.

"What Hanna and I do at home—and what we do in the club—relaxes both of us. It's our form of stress relief. Most sex is like that—or at least it should be—whatever form it takes."

"It is," Grullon said, thinking in particular of how many times a bad day at the office for either him or Rachael, or both, had worked itself out in the bedroom that night.

"It's not something I talk much about. but it's not a secret either. So I'm curious as to why you didn't take Kiernan's advice."

"I'm sorry, sir, really. I shouldn't have—"

"Judged? Thought less of your superior officer because of his private life?"

Grullon got to his feet. "I should go."

"Just keep something in mind, Detective—we all have secrets. Including you."

Feeling defensive, Grullon said, "But what happened to me wasn't my fault!"

"Neither was what happened to me overseas."

That brought Grullon up short.

The Major's phone case stopped glowing blue. Grullon was shocked to see that the room was now slightly dimmer.

"About damn time," Majorowicz said. "All right. Now, Valapart doesn't have the intelligence directly, but he said someone's meeting him at his apartment."

Grullon practically got whiplash from the sudden subject change. "Um, okay."

"The meet's in an hour at his place, so get your ass down there."

"By myself?"

"Has to be, every other detective is out, and Hawkins is helping the Gitaus, and besides which, I need him to stay here and work the Ohlmeyer case."

Grullon was not surprised that it had become "the Ohlmeyer case," given the perp's prominence—and his apparent bugging of the squad room—rather than "the Hertweck and Buddan murders."

"Besides," the lieutenant added, "Valapart requested you specifically." He smiled. "Well, he requested both you and Kiernan, as part of his ongoing attempt to get into her pants, but I told him that Kiernan was out today. I didn't tell him why, and you won't, either."

"Of course not, sir."

"Instead of going down to the club, go up the stoop and ring the bottom doorbell."

Grullon left the lieutenant's office, grabbed his trench coat, and headed downstairs.

The walk to the garage was a chilly one, with a cold breeze blowing in off the Harlem River. While he waited for Imanol to bring him a Malibu, Grullon texted Kiernan to see how she was doing.

Since it was still rush hour, it took him the full hour to drive all the way to the club, what with the traffic on the FDR Drive.

Probably woulda got here in half the time if Umali was driving.

He parked in front of the same hydrant he'd parked in front of Monday, put the NYPD credentials on the dash, and radioed that he had arrived to meet with an informant. As instructed, he went up the stoop and rang the bottom bell for the first-floor apartment.

"Who is it?" Valapart's voice sounded clearly over the speaker, which surprised Grullon. Usually apartment-building speakers were incomprehensible. The one in his and Rachael's building was broken half the time. *It's good to be rich.*

"Detective Grullon."

"Ah, excellent. Enter freely and of your own will."

A low buzz came from the door and Grullon pushed it open. He walked into a carpeted hallway. There were doors on either side and a staircase leading up to the higher floors.

The door on the left opened to reveal Valapart. He was wearing what looked like a silk bathrobe—okay, it was the kind of thing that would probably be called a dressing gown, really, but Grullon had always thought that was a pretentious name for a bathrobe—over an ascot, slacks, and, bizarrely, pink bunny slippers.

"Detective Grullon, I bid you welcome. I'm so very glad you could be spared. It's only a pity that Detective Kiernan could not accompany you."

Grullon entered the apartment, stepping into a huge living room. Like many older apartments, the place had *very* high ceilings—Grullon glanced up and figured the ceiling was about ten feet.

He'd been expecting something out of a museum, a place filled with a ton of antique furniture. Instead, Grullon found himself staring at a ridiculous mish-mash of stuff from multiple eras: a dark blue beanbag chair, a power recliner with a charging station, a wooden rocking chair with cushions in a soft paisley pattern, a ceramic floor lamp with a wide, white shade, an end table with a mosaic pattern that genuinely looked like it belonged in a museum, another end table that was made out of plastic, and a couch that was assorted shades of green Grullon had last seen in the puke of transients they'd arrested at his old precinct.

"Have a seat, Detective. My informant will be here shortly. May I offer you a drink?"

"No, thanks," he said as he sat on the ugly couch. "And you get that Kiernan's not interested, right?"

"Do you not appreciate the thrill of the hunt, Detective?" Valapart asked, taking a seat in the recliner.

"Not really, no."

"Now I find that impossible to credit, given your particular circumstances."

Grullon frowned. "What circumstances?"

"Oh, come now, Detective, do not be coy. I knew what you were the moment you walked into my club on Monday."

Grullon started to panic. "I don't know what—"

"I am *nosferatu*, Detective, and I'm quite familiar with the scent of a lycanthrope."

Closing his eyes, Grullon sighed. He supposed he should have realized that. "Fine, yes, I'm a werewolf. Not that it's any of your business."

"You keep your other self a secret, then?"

"Let's just say that the right people know."

"Is the rest of your stalwart squadron aware? Or do you hunt your own kind in secret?"

"Don't give me that. 'My own kind' are my family and fellow cops, thanks. And the Major and Hawk know—so do Ortega and Kiernan, since they were there when I got bit."

Valapart nodded. "Ah, so you were brought into the fold, not born into it."

That surprised Grullon. He thought that all werewolves were the result of being bitten. "Born to it?"

"Lycanthropy is an inherited condition, were you not aware of that?"

Grullon swallowed and looked away. He wasn't aware. In fact, he'd been avoiding doing any research about lycanthropy, which he intellectually knew was stupid, but he just couldn't bring himself to face what he would be dealing with.

To make matters worse, he and Rachael had been planning to have kids someday. If this was hereditary …

The doorbell interrupted them. "Ah," Valapart said, gracefully getting to his feet and gliding to the intercom, "that would be my informant." Pressing the button, he asked, "Who is it?"

"Wei."

"Excellent. Enter freely and of your own will." He buzzed the door open.

Moments later, a short, unassuming Asian man entered the apartment. He wore a brown topcoat over a red sweater, jeans, and sneakers.

"Detective Liam Grullon, this is Zhang Wei. Wei, the detective is the one who desires the intelligence I asked you to provide. I take it your quest was successful?"

Zhang nodded. "Yes, but I wish to dispense with this form. I find it distasteful."

A moment later, the human in front of Grullon was gone, replaced by a four-legged creature that stood at over six feet at the shoulder. A large, unicorn-like horn was protruding from his head, which looked very much like that of a lion. His legs and torso were scaly; the former ended in very large paws while the latter had a lengthy tail that whipped back and forth behind him.

Grullon wasn't surprised or put out. This change didn't even crack the top ten of strange things he'd seen since joining SCU. He looked at Zhang. "How'd you cast the illusion?"

"You do not believe him to be a shape-changer?" Valapart asked.

"Shape changers actually *change* shape—it's a process." Grullon had just seen the process last week with the very domovoy he had come for information about, not to mention his own travails every full moon.

Zhang said, "I have a charm that allows me to be seen as I wish to be seen—though not as I *want* to be seen, but one must make compromises to survive in the world."

Valapart smiled, showing off his oversized canines. "It is a cross we all must bear—so to speak." To Grullon, he said, "Wei is a lù duān. He is a creature of truth—he can detect any prevarication and is also compelled to answer any query truthfully. And he owes me several favors."

"I now owe you one fewer," Zhang said.

With a chuckle, Valapart said, "That depends on your answer to this question: have you found the domovoy that Detective Grullon and his compatriots are searching for?"

"Yes."

Grullon got to his feet. "Where?"

"He has been hiding in Central Park, on the western edge of the park, just north of the West 81st Street entrance. There are rocks and trees where he takes cover, aided by his ability to change his shape."

"Thank you," Grullon said emphatically to Zhang, then added to Valapart, "both of you."

Valapart bowed his head. "It is our pleasure, Detective. Malefactors such as this domovoy—and that fool Albescu—make life far more complicated for all of us. You of all people should be aware of that."

"What does that even mean, 'me of all people'? Yeah, I'm a werewolf, fine, but that doesn't mean I'm not a cop or a *person* anymore."

"Are you implying that we are not people, Detective?"

"No, I just—" Grullon shook his head. "Forget it. I'm having a bad day. A friend of mine's kid got kidnapped, and it's got my head all messed up."

"If I may ask, what friend?"

Grullon allowed himself a tiny smile. "Well, Zhang Wei here can tell if I'm lying, so I'm just gonna not answer that, okay?" He took out his phone. "I need to call this in. Can I have some privacy?"

Pointing to the rear of the living room, "Make a right at the window, it will lead you to a dining room, and beyond that, the kitchen. We shall remain here and grant you the privacy you request."

"Thanks." Grullon followed Valapart's instructions to a huge kitchen. He leaned against the island in the center of the kitchen, thinking his *abuela* would kill to be able to cook in a place like this, and looked at his phone.

There was a text from Kiernan:

> Made it home okay. No news from Mamaroneck yet.
> Gonna go to bottle gardens.

Right after that:

> *botanical. Stupid phone.

He texted back to her:

> Enjoy!

Then he added:

> We got a lead on the domovoy,
> finally. Friend of Valapart's.

Once he sent that, he called the Major's department-issue cell.

After two rings, the Major said without preamble, "Talk to me, Grullon."

"We got him. Valapart's informant says the domovoy's hiding in the rocks and trees in Central Park above the Ramble, near Summit Rock. Around 82nd, 83rd Streets or so on the west side."

"Good work, Grullon. I'll get ESU up there, but I want you with them. Umali and Fiore, too—I'll call them and have them go straight there from Chinatown."

"Roger that. Oh, and hey, sir?"

"Yeah?"

"Valapart outed me—apparently vampires can tell if you're a werewolf by our scent."

"Imagine that."

Grullon blinked at the Major's dry tone. "You knew?"

"Of course, I knew."

"Why didn't you tell me?"

In a very even, very scary tone, the lieutenant said, "You're a detective in the Supernatural Crimes Unit, Grullon, you shouldn't need me to tell you this stuff."

"Sir—" Grullon took a very deep breath before continuing. "After Van Cortlandt Park, you said you'd respect my decision to keep my—my lycanthropy secret."

"I did say that. Remember what else I said?"

Frowning, Grullon said, "I—"

"I said you'd have to accept the consequences of that choice. Welcome to the consequences of that choice. Now hang up the damn phone so I can call Vondelikos and make sure he really sends me ESU this time."

"Yes, sir." He ended the call.

Kiernan had responded to his text:

> Nice to know he's still a good CI, at least. Thanks, I'll let Mercado know. Be a nice distraction to talk to someone else going crazy.

After texting a thumbs-up emoji to Kiernan, Grullon went back to the living room. Valapart was alone, lying on the fully-reclined recliner, legs straight in front of him and back tilted nearly flat.

"Where's Zhang?"

"His business was concluded. As is mine with you. He departed, and I will ask you to do the same. It is morning, and time for me to sleep." He held a remote control in his hand, which he pointed at the giant television mounted to the wall opposite the recliner. He began scrolling through menus. "It is ridiculous—I was alive for centuries before television was even invented, yet now I cannot sleep without it playing."

"Rest well, I guess."

"I must ask, Detective Grullon—do you have a haven? A place where you can be safe? I know it is far too soon for you to have control of the beast."

That surprised Grullon. "I didn't even know control was *possible*."

"Oh yes. But not for several years at least, and even then, it is not guaranteed. The beast can be—difficult."

"Yeah, that much I know."

"There is much I may teach you, if you would like." He smiled again. "If you are comfortable seeking guidance from a deviant."

Now Grullon was on his guard. CIs were there to be used, not to be trusted. "And what do I have to do in return?"

"Well, we may discuss that at another time."

That set off every alarm in Grullon's head. "Fat chance. I'll muddle through on my own, thanks. And I'll see myself out."

"Muddle away, Detective, but don't say I didn't warn you."

Shuddering, Grullon left Valapart's apartment, hoping that next time they needed intel from the vampire, they'd send someone—anyone—else.

NYC

EIGHTEEN

As the Malibu worked its way slowly up Eighth Avenue toward Columbus Circle, Umali asked Fiore, who was driving, "You hear from Kiernan today? How's she doing?" Umali had barely slept last night; she kept getting up to check on Liza, who was, of course, sleeping peacefully in her bed every time.

"She's doing shitty is how she's doing." Fiore shook his head as he changed lanes to get around a double-parked car. "I texted her about an hour ago, and she didn't seem no worse, at least."

"Should I text her? Or call?"

"Text. If she gets a call, and it ain't from VMPD about her kid, she'll go ripshit, y'know?"

Umali nodded in understanding. "Yeah, if someone took Liza, I'd be bouncing off the walls. But I'd also want my friends to check up on me." She didn't add that she was bouncing off the walls anyhow. Pulling out her phone, she composed a text:

> Hope you're doing okay. We're all thinking about you.

Then she winced at the clichés she'd just spouted. Still, it had the benefit of being completely true.

"You ever work with ESU before?" Fiore asked.

"Yeah, a couple times—once with Sergeant O'Malley's team, once with Sergeant Attico's."

Fiore inched his way around the fountain in the middle of Columbus Circle, slowly working his way toward Central Park West. "I don't know Attico, but O'Malley's not *too* bad a dude."

"I thought he was fine—really knew his stuff."

"Yeah, but his taste in women sucks—he married my cousin Bella."

"Don't like your cousin?" Umali asked with a smile.

"Nah, I love Bella to death, but she's fuckin' crazy. She eats men alive. Honestly, somebody combat trained is prob'ly what's best for her, but I wouldn't wish her on nobody, y'know?"

"Do we know which squad we're getting?"

"No clue. Long as it ain't Herrera's squad."

"What's wrong with Herrera?"

"Nothin', Herrera's great. Good guy—captain'a the softball team, and it's 'cause'a him we beat FDNY every year." Fiore finally merged into the traffic on CPW. "Nah, the sniper on his squad is my stupid-ass second cousin, Enzo. Total fuckup, that guy."

"If he's a fuckup, how'd he get on ESU?"

" 'Cause the one and only thing he's good at is shooting. Fucker can hit the wings off a fly. But every time I see him, he's got some 'investment opportunity,' which is always a fuckin' useless thing that loses money. Last one was a gadget that's supposed to detect vampires."

"I'm guessing it didn't detect vampires?"

"It just checked body temp, and if you were less than 98.6, it said you were a vamp."

"Ninety-eight-six is an average," Umali said. "And not a very accurate one at that."

"Yeah, you know that and I know that. Enzo? Not so much. If my great-aunt didn't keep bailin' his stupid ass out ..." Fiore swerved around a cab that was trying to cut him off. "So how you likin' the unit?"

"I like it so far. Hell, a lot of it's the same old, same old. Today was a perfect example—our 'big lead' on the Taotie was just some guy with an iguana."

Fiore snorted. "Yeah, I'm startin' to think I'm never gonna find the stupid fuckin' thing."

"On the other hand," Umali said, figuring she should change the subject, "it hasn't even been two weeks, and we're already going after a white whale."

That got a laugh out of her fellow detective. "Yeah, Ohlmeyer's some serious shit. There was some bad heroin goin' 'round about six years ago that everyone was pretty sure was from him. Not only that, but I got an uncle used to work for one'a his legit investment companies. Said he was a nice guy in person, but a scumbag to work for."

ESU had set up a command center on 81st Street, just in from CPW, in front of the entrance to the Rose Center for Space and the museum's parking lot. Their large, blue-and-white truck was parked on 81st and a tent had been set up on the sidewalk. Central Park West was cordoned off at the south side of 81st Street, with patrol officers from the 20th Precinct diverting traffic.

One of those POs let them by once Fiore badged her, and they parked near the truck. Grullon was already there, talking to a cop in full tactical gear. There were five other tac'd up cops with them.

They got out of the car, each putting their phones into airplane mode, then pulled their vests out of the trunk. Umali put her flannel-lined denim jacket on over it, noticing that Fiore tossed his fleece jacket into the back seat.

"You're gonna be way too fuckin' hot in that *and* the vest," Fiore said.

Umali shrugged. "It's fine. I always wear a heavy-duty gi in the dojo, too. I don't mind a little sweat."

"Yeah, but I gotta sit in the car with you bein' all sweaty when we're done. Whatever, let's go."

They moved toward Grullon and the ESU officers. As they approached, Umali recognized one of the latter, and he glanced at her and did the same. Fiore peeled off to join Grullon at the truck while Umali headed for her old friend.

"Shit, Umali, that you?"

"Been a while, Jessup."

Dean Jessup's broad smile nearly split his dark-skinned face. He was a little bit taller than Umali and even under all the tac gear, she could see that he was pretty cut—much more so than the last time she'd seen him. "When the hell'd you wind up with the Goon Squad?"

"I'm in week two. How'd your fat ass get into ESU?"

One of Jessup's fellow ESU officers, a broad-shouldered Latinx man, said, "Who's this, and how does she know what your ass looks like?"

Holding out a hand, she said, "Sofia Umali, SCU. Jessup and I shared a patrol car in the One-Seven."

"José Mota, ESU," he said, returning the handshake.

"To answer your question, Jessup here had a cookie fetish when we were on patrol together, and—well, let's just say his butt would *not* have squeezed into that getup then." She gestured at his tac gear. "When I got him to sign up for my dojo, he gave up after a month."

"You have a dojo?"

"I train at a karate dojo in the Bronx, it's not actually mine. I'm a third-degree black belt."

Jessup grinned more widely. "She thinks it's hers, though. And washing out of karate is what got me here, actually. I got pissed at myself for fucking it up, so I started training at a gym. I also don't *touch* cookies no more, except at Christmas." He held out his arms. "And look at me now."

Umali chuckled. "I can barely see you under all that crap."

"Hey, how's Liza doing? She's what, three now? Four?"

"Seven."

"Shit, really? Damn, time flies. How's Analyn?"

"She moved back to Kalibo after we got divorced."

Eyes widening, Jessup said, "You two split up?"

Mota was now laughing. "You are seriously steppin' in it, *hermano*."

Not wanting to dwell on her broken marriage, Umali changed the subject. "Hey, you know who else is in SCU? Ortega."

Jessup winced. "Please tell me that motherfucker ain't wearin' that tie, still."

"He's wearing that tie, still."

"Fuck." Jessup shook his head. "Not surprised his crazy ass wound up in the Loony Bin Squad."

Mota said, "If you're such a badass, Umali, you should try out for ESU. Beats being in the Bullshit Squad."

Umali was starting to get weary of this. "You got any other stupid nicknames for my unit?"

"Oh, I got dozens," Mota said. "We all do. I mean, c'mon, vampires and werewolves and stuff? It's *all* bullshit."

Putting her hands on her hips, Umali said, "You *do* know you're here to chase down a shapechanger, right?"

"And we're supposed to believe that?" Jessup asked.

"Talk to Grabowski down at the Nine. The domovoy beat him something fierce. You guys are using silver rounds, right?"

Mota rolled his eyes. "Yeah, 'cause I'm the Lone fuckin' Ranger. Trust me, ain't none of us botherin' with *that* shit."

"Dammit." Umali broke off from them and went over to where Grullon and Fiore were talking with an ESU officer wearing sergeant's stripes.

Fiore saw her approach and said, "Umali, this is Sergeant Dylan Herrera. He's in charge of this op."

"Oh, so he's the one who didn't pack any silver rounds?"

Both Fiore and Grullon shot Herrera a look at that.

"Say the fuck *what*?" Fiore asked.

"We packed them," Herrera said. "We pack everything. Who told you we didn't?"

She indicated Jessup and Mota. "Mota just told me, and I quote, 'Ain't none of us botherin' with that shit.' "

Grullon said, "Which means your weapons are useless. The domovoy'll shrug off your rounds."

"Maybe from a nine," Herrera said, indicating his M4 Carbine rifle, "but these—"

"It doesn't matter." Grullon threw up his hands. "The only thing that affects the domovoy is silver. I don't believe this. Sergeant, I know for a fact that Lieutenant Majorowicz told Lieutenant Vondelikos to tell you this."

This time it was Herrera who rolled his eyes. "Vondelikos didn't tell us shit, except where to roll out."

Fiore's and Grullon's radios sounded with a voice. "2E33, we're set up on the roof of 230 CPW."

Grullon said to Umali, "Channel 4."

Nodding, Umali adjusted her radio to pick up that frequency.

Herrera said, "2E30, status."

"Got a little bit of movement in the trees, Sarge, but no clear shot."

Fiore asked, "Is that Soo?"

"Yeah," Herrera said, "he's your cousin's spotter."

Putting the radio to his mouth, Fiore said, "Soo, this is Fiore. Tell Enzo to load up with the silver rounds."

Another voice said, "2E34, say again?"

"You fuckin' heard me, Enzo. Silver rounds are the only thing that'll stop this thing. Load up."

Herrera said, "You heard the man, Annichiarico. To all 2E30 squad, switch to silver rounds."

Mota and another ESU officer walked over looking pissed off. "You fuckin' kiddin' me with this, Sarge?"

Herrera was pulling the magazine from his M4. "Mota, how long you been under my command?"

"I—" Mota squinted in obvious confusion at the question. "It's been two years, Sarge."

"Right, and in those two years, have you *ever* known me to kid on duty?"

"Well, no, sir, but—"

Herrera walked over to the truck. "So shut the fuck up and load the fuck up."

Soo's voice sounded over the radio. "2E33, we got movement. Looks like a dog, but it's bigger than any dog I ever saw."

Fiore spoke into his radio. "He can change shape; he can't change mass. He's gonna be the same basic size no matter what."

Herrera had put a light gray magazine into his M4. "Really?"

Umali said, "Conservation of mass and energy is still a thing, Sergeant. That's why vampires only turn into *really, really* big bats."

Soo continued, "Still in the trees twenty feet in from the wall, thirty feet south of 83rd. Moving slowly east."

"You have a shot?" Herrera asked.

After a second: "Negative. Too much foliage, and he's half behind a rock."

Herrera nodded. "You get a clean shot, take it." There was no reply, so he added, "Acknowledge, 2E33!"

"2E33, acknowledge," Soo said.

Grullon turned to Fiore and said, "How come we wait eighty years for our silver rounds from Moore Hill, but these guys have piles of it?"

Before Fiore could answer, another ESU officer—a short, broad-shouldered Caucasian with a blond mustache, who was practically rectangular in shape—said, "Because we're the ones who do the violence. If you guys need to fire a silver round, it means shit's gone sideways." He and the other four members of the squad—a Black woman, a very tall Latinx man, and Jessup and Mota—had all joined them at back of the truck, swapping out their black magazines for gray ones.

The Black woman laughed and said, "'Do the violence'? Really, Simms?"

Holding out both hands, palms-up, Simms said, "What's the problem, Okonta? We *do* do the violence."

"Not last week," Grullon said. "When we arrested this very same guy, Detective Kiernan had to throw a silver round 'cause you guys weren't there."

"Shoulda called us," Simms said.

"So we could do the violence," Okonta added with a smirk.

"We did," Grullon said angrily.

Fiore added, "Fuckin' Vondelikos said you all were busy."

"Well, that explains it," said the very tall one, whose uniform nametag read DOMINGUEZ. "That *maricón* is always fuckin' shit up."

"Speaking of fucking shit up," Simms said, "if you arrested the target, why are we chasing his ass through Central Park?"

Umali looked right at Mota. "Tombs lost him because they thought that we're a bullshit unit and didn't put him in the new cells designed to hold creatures like him, and he escaped."

Mota looked as if he was going to respond, but then Herrera asked, "Everybody locked and loaded?"

Everyone sounded off one after the other. Simms said, "2E31, affirmative."

Then Mota: "2E32, affirmative," though he said it with very little enthusiasm.

Okonta was much more emphatic when she said, "2E35, affirmative!"

Dominguez said, "2E36, affirmative."

Finally, Jessup: "2E37, affirmative."

Herrera turned to the three SCU detectives, offering them three Glock nine-millimeter magazines, also gray. "These are for you guys. For the record, we don't get 'em from Moore Hill, we get 'em from Striker. May wanna let your unit commander know. Meantime, you can keep those. We got plenty."

Mota muttered, "Yeah, 'cause they're stupid."

The SCU detectives quickly swapped out the magazines in their department-issue Glocks.

Once they were all locked and loaded, Herrera said, "All right, we're gonna move in. Mota, Jessup, you approach from the south. Simms, Dominguez, go with them, then keep going and come around to approach from the east. Okonta and I'll come from the north. Detectives, you stay on the sidewalk in case the target runs west and out onto the street. Any questions? No? Let's move!"

Umali looked over at Jessup. "He *ever* give time to ask questions?"

Chuckling, Jessup said, "Nope."

The nine of them jogged onto Central Park West, which was eerily empty of traffic or pedestrians north of 81st. More officers from the Two-Oh had blocked off access to and from 82nd, 83rd, 84th, and 85th, with another barricade visible on the south side of 86th.

Herrera and Okonta ran up to 83rd and hopped a short stone wall that separated the park from the sidewalk, while Simms, Mota, Jessup, and Dominguez did the same at 82nd. Umali stood on the distinctive hexagonal asphalt pavers that made up the sidewalks that bordered Central Park on all sides.

"Watch this guy," Grullon said. "He's fast and he's *strong.* Tossed me and four guys from the Nine around like we were nerf balls."

"Wasn't Kiernan with you, too?" Umali asked.

"Yeah, but she didn't mix it up with the domovoy, she stayed back and threw a shot with her backup piece. Which is what actually stopped him."

Fiore grinned. "Always said Kiernan was the brains'a the unit."

"I don't doubt that for a second." Umali sighed. "I hope she's okay."

"She ain't," Fiore said. "Nobody'd be okay with their kid took."

"I feel that," she whispered, thinking about Liza.

"But she'll manage," Fiore added. "She's stronger'n dudes twice her size."

"Good thing, 'cause *everyone's* twice her size," Grullon said with a grin.

Over the radio, Simms said, "2E31 in position."

A second later came, Herrera's voice. "2E30 in position."

Then Soo said, "2E33, target still holding position, still no shot."

Finally Jessup said, "2E37 in position."

"Stand by," Herrera said.

"2E33, he's moving! Taking the shot!"

Umali knew that they'd never be able to hear a shot from a sniper rifle on the roof of one of the apartment buildings across the street, so she imagined the sound of the silver bullet whizzing through the air to strike the domovoy.

"Got 'im!" Enzo said over the radio. "Wait—fucker's still up and movin' around!"

Soo talked over him. "2E33, target is mobile and heading— Shit! He just changed color! Now he—he—fuck!"

Herrera was sounding very pissed now. "Confirm 2E33, did you hit the target?"

"Aim was true, Sarge, but nothing happened to target, and now we've lost visual."

"Everybody move in!" Herrera cried out.

Fiore put his radio to his mouth. "You sure you hit the thing, Enzo? Silver round should've taken his ass right out and kept him from changin' shape like you saw."

"I was using *real* bullets, Vinny, Martina don't like it when I use weird-ass ammo."

Umali mouthed the word *Martina*?

Grullon shrugged, but Fiore said, "Dumbass named his rifle after his high school sweetheart. Who, by the way, is married to someone else now."

Now Umali could hear rustling in the underbrush as the ESU personnel closed in on where the domovoy was.

Or, apparently, where he had been. "2E30, no sign of target, say again, *no* sign of target. Fan out, find the damn thing! And Soo, Annichiarico, when this is over, the three of us are having a talk that you won't enjoy one bit about what an order from your squad leader is."

Fiore was shaking his head. "Fuckin' idiot."

Grullon had his head in his hands. “I don’t believe this. We’re never gonna catch this guy.”

Umali saw some movement on the other side of the park wall. At first it seemed to be a tree blowing in the breeze, but then she realized there *was* no breeze.

She acted at almost the same time as the camouflaged domovoy, who had altered his skin to look like it was made of trees and rocks. The domovoy was going for Grullon, whom the creature probably remembered as one of the ones who had subdued him the previous week.

Umali dove to knock Grullon out of the way while thrusting out a side kick to the domovoy’s belly. It was an awkward move, and as a result, she and Grullon both collapsed onto the sidewalk in a heap, but at least she stopped the domovoy from striking Grullon.

Shaking off the blow, the domovoy raised a fist to hit Umali, but she managed to roll away from both the fist and Grullon.

The report of a Glock nine-millimeter rang out, echoing off the park wall and the buildings across the street.

Glancing up and back, Umali saw that Fiore had fired his nine.

Looking in front again, she saw the domovoy doubled over in pain, wheezing and whimpering, a wound in his left arm.

Herrera and his five squad members all came leaping over the wall a second later, weapons at the ready.

Fiore held up both hands. “Easy, Herrera, we’re one under,” he said, indicating that they’d made their arrest.

Umali tried to stand up, but her right foot wouldn’t support her weight, so she collapsed to the sidewalk again.

Fiore immediately got on the radio and called for an ambulance. Grullon, meanwhile, walked over to the domovoy—who was in human form, albeit with his skin the colors of trees and rocks—and put his cuffs on him.

Holding a hand out, Grullon said, “Give me your bracelets.”

Umali tossed hers to him and Fiore handed his over.

"Three sets of cuffs?" Herrera asked.

Grullon snorted. "That *might* be enough, yeah. We'll take him back to our house." They had three free cells now. The naiad had been arraigned and was now out on her own recognizance, awaiting trial, and the hugag and the awes-kon-wa had each made a plea deal. The domovoy would get the cell next to the kappa.

"You gonna read him his rights?" Okonta asked.

"Not while the silver's in him." Grullon got to his feet, leaving the domovoy curled up on the sidewalk. "Right now, he's in so much pain that he can't understand these rights as we've explained them to him."

Simms, meanwhile, came over to Umali. "Lemme take a look at your foot."

"You a medic?" Umali asked.

"Field medicine is part of what I learned in Coronado."

Umali shook her head. "You're a SEAL. Shoulda known you were Navy."

"How's that?" Simms asked as he knelt down to take a look at her foot.

"'We're the ones who do the violence'? That's the kinda thing I'd expect you cab drivers to say."

Simms chuckled. "Okay, you can form sentences, so you can't be a Marine. Army?"

She nodded. "CID."

"Figures. Where'd you serve?"

"Afghanistan."

"Next question: does any'a this hurt?" Simms was touching different parts of her foot.

Shaking her head, Umali said, "Nope."

"Nothing's broken and it don't hurt. You prob'ly just strained it. Try standing again—slow this time."

She got to her feet. Her right foot still hurt, but she could put at least some weight on it. "I think it's okay."

"Walk it off, you should be fine. If it acts up—"

"Mt. Sinai is just a few blocks from our house. Thanks."

Simms let loose with a huge grin under his mustache. "No problem."

Fiore canceled the ambulance, then turned to Herrera. "So I gotta ask—what the fuck did we need you assholes for?"

Umali, who was limping around in a circle, which was working the pain out, said, "Hey, c'mon, Vinny, that's not fair. If your cousin had put in the silver rounds, ESU would've taken care of this in nothing flat. As it is, they flushed him out so you could shoot him."

"He nearly killed me," Grullon said. "Thanks for the save."

Jessup was chuckling. "That was a nifty move there, Umali—what do you call it? Falling on your ass?"

"Falling on my ankle, actually," she said, grinning back.

"Well, you saved my ass," Grullon said, "and my ankle. I didn't even see him coming. How'd *you* see it?"

Umali shrugged. "Caught movement, went on instinct."

"Well, thanks. Seriously. I know what that guy could've done to me." He turned to Fiore. "I'm gonna go bring my car over here so we can put the domovoy in the back."

Fiore nodded.

As Grullon jogged down Central Park West toward 81st, two more people in ESU tac gear approached from one of the buildings across the avenue. One was Asian and one looked like a younger version of Fiore, so she assumed they were Soo and Fiore's second cousin, Enzo.

Herrera immediately got into the latter's face. "You realize we almost lost the target because of you two?"

"I'm sorry, boss, but—"

"Shut the fuck up, Annichiarico, this is not a *discussion*. Our job is to protect the detectives and get their asses out of the fire. Instead, they had to get *our* asses out of the fire, because you're too fucking *stupid* to follow an order. Both of you are getting written up for insubordination. Now get the fuck out of my face."

Mota walked over to Herrera. "Hey, c'mon, Sarge, give them a break, they—"

Herrera fixed Mota with a fierce look that was almost as nasty as Kiernan's. "Be very, *very* careful how you finish that sentence, Mota. Bear in mind that you are in serious danger of defending a fellow officer who nearly let an extremely dangerous fugitive escape due to his inability to obey the chain of command. Now—what kind of a break, exactly, should I give them?"

Mota said nothing, just turned and walked away.

Jessup said, "I'll talk to him, Sarge."

"Ain't nothin' to talk about." Herrera turned to Fiore. "Sorry for the fuckup."

Shrugging, Fiore said, "We're used to it. People don't believe this shit until they see it. Sometimes not even then. Hell, if I wasn't in the unit, I ain't sure *I'd* believe it."

"We certainly saw it today. Never seen nothin' like that in fifteen years on the job." Herrera blew out a long breath. "You need anything else, Detective?"

Fiore said, "We gotta drive this guy back. Can you clear the scene?"

"You got it." He turned to the snipers. "Annichiarico, Soo, you two help the POs clear the scene and pack up the sawhorses."

The two of them looked like teenagers being grounded, but wisely said nothing, just went to assist the patrol officers from the Two-Oh.

"Let's move," Herrera said, and jogged back toward 81st Street.

Simms said, "Hey, Umali!"

"Yeah?"

"You ever get tired'a chasing ghosts and shit, think about ESU. We could use someone with those instincts you were tellin' us about." He glanced over at Soo and Annichiarico. "Besides, I'm guessin' we're gonna have a coupla openings soon."

With that, he jogged off after his squad commander.

She pulled out her phone and took it out of airplane mode. Immediately it buzzed with a text from Kiernan:

Thanks. Spent some time at botanical gardens, drank some cappuccino, ate some cannoli, and screamed a lot. No news yet.

Good

Umali texted back.

And, hey, some good news! We got the domovoy back in custody.

She'd had to retype *domovoy* after her phone autocorrected it to "Donovan."

Fiore was also reactivating his phone. "You ever think about joinin' ESU? I mean, you bein' a black belt and ex-Army and all."

"Not really. I don't train in karate for the ability to fight, I do it to center myself, to stay in shape, and to blow off steam. And I like being a detective. It's why I was in CID and why I lobbied to transfer here." She grinned. "I'd rather *not* be the one who does the violence."

Fiore chuckled. "Yeah, me either. I'm a lover, not a fighter."

"I could tell that from the shot you threw. Seriously, you were only, like, two feet away, and all you could do was wing him in the arm?"

Shrugging, Fiore said, "I ain't a great shot. Like I said, I'm a lover—"

"—not a fighter, right."

"'Sides, thanks to that guy's silver allergy, all I *had* to do was wing him." His phone buzzed and he read the display. "Shit. Hey, Umali, can you ride back with Grullon? I just finally heard back from a CI about a thing, and I need to go talk to him."

"Is this about the Taotie?" She was really hoping, for his sake, that they would finally get a break there.

"Nah, somethin' else."

Umali's phone buzzed with a text from Kiernan:

About ducking time.
At least I can give Mercado good news.

Then:

*fucking

Unable to help herself, Umali laughed as Grullon pulled up in his Malibu.

"It's fine," she said to Fiore, "I'll go with Grullon and the prisoner."

"Great, thanks."

"And hey," she added, "good thing I kept my jacket on, huh?"

Fiore laughed. "Yeah, and now I don't gotta sit in a car with you all sweaty." He ran back toward 81st.

"Where's he going?" Grullon asked as he got out of the car.

"Has to meet a CI."

"Okay. Help me get the domovoy into the back seat? And into one of *our* holding cells, so maybe we'll keep him?"

Umali nodded. "You bet."

NINETEEN

"You can go in now," Ohlmeyer's new assistant, whose name was Sabrina, said without preamble, startling Farid Anand where he sat on the couch outside Garth Ohlmeyer's office.

With a heavy sigh, he got to his feet. Next to him, Nick McManus also rose and shot Anand a look. "The fuck are you sighing for?"

Anand looked at his fellow attorney as if he'd grown a second head. "Seriously? Have you not been paying attention?"

"I'm doing my job."

"Yeah." Another sigh, and then Anand pushed open the heavy door with the dragon's head on it.

Ohlmeyer was leaning on the front of his desk. "Come on in," he said, putting two fingers to his temple and closing his eyes. After he reopened his eyes, he said, "Okay, the wards are up."

"What happened to Jada?" McManus asked.

With a sigh, Ohlmeyer said, "I had to let her go. She was the one who put the spell components in the storage unit."

"She wasn't supposed to?" Anand asked.

"No. She thought I might need them again to cast another transmutation spell and assumed that no one would ever find them in the Augurer storage unit. While her instincts were good, the results were not. If she had simply thrown them away, we'd be in much better shape. So I let her go. I'm sure that Sabrina will do just fine."

Anand tried not to think about what being "let go" meant, exactly.

A breeting sound came from Ohlmeyer's suit jacket pocket. He retrieved a cheap flip phone, opened it, and put it to his ear. "Yes, Quinn … You got the bus? … Okay, just make sure all fifty of them are in the supermarket by midnight tonight. That's when the possession spell will take full effect. Stay long enough to make sure they're not going anywhere, but after that, you can leave. The wards will keep them in and everyone else out … *Yes*, the wards are set to let you in and out, Quinn … Yes … Yes … *Yes*. Now I have to go."

He closed the phone and put it back in his pocket. "How's the kid?" he asked McManus.

"Still sedated."

"Good. Him waking up would be awkward. Make sure he's at the supermarket before midnight, too."

"Of course," McManus said with a nod.

Anand asked, "Why did you kidnap a cop's child? I thought you were gonna use one of the junkie's kids for this."

Ohlmeyer smirked. "It's supposed to be an innocent youth, and I'm not entirely sure any of the fifty's kids qualify for that." The smirk fell. "Besides, it helps keep SCU at bay."

"How do you figure that?"

"They're all distracted with worry about Detective Kiernan's son. And they'll hesitate to act because it didn't happen in their jurisdiction, plus they want to keep the little moppet safe, so they'll be cautious. Besides, Kiernan's the brains of the outfit, and by kidnapping little Robert, we've taken her completely off the table."

"It's true," McManus said. "NYPD policy is for her to take personal time until the kid gets found, so she's not on the clock."

With an approving nod toward McManus, Ohlmeyer added, "Which means SCU is down their best person. All they have left is that relic, Ortegas, and I've been running rings around his wrinkled ass for years."

Anand thought about correcting his boss's mispronunciation of Ortega's last name, then decided not to bother.

Ohlmeyer continued, "It's like with the DA's office, Farid, we just need to delay until the new moon. After that, nothing's gonna matter, because everyone will be too busy dealing with hell on Earth."

Somehow, Anand wasn't comforted much by those words. Ohlmeyer hadn't been particularly forthcoming about this ritual, though Anand assumed it had to do with his recent, near-obsessive interest in Zoroastrian myth and legend.

The only things he knew for sure was that it required a bunch of junkies to help power it and that an innocent child had to be sacrificed. One of the reasons why they'd agreed to have the sacrifice be a junkie's kid was that that particular victim wouldn't be missed. Such a child's disappearance likely wouldn't even be reported or investigated.

He decided to throw caution to the wind and say what he was thinking out loud. "What happens if the ritual doesn't work?"

In a very quiet, very menacing tone, Ohlmeyer said, "Excuse me?"

"During the vernal equinox last year, that binding spell didn't work. Neither did the masking spell you tried during the harvest moon."

"True." Ohlmeyer said with obvious reluctance. "But those spells failed due to unforeseen circumstances—and all my *other* rituals have worked. I know what I'm doing, Farid."

Anand wasn't giving up that easily. "But what if it does go wrong? Or you can't tap into the ley lines properly, or the detective's son isn't innocent enough, or there's some *other* unforeseen circumstance? You're the one who always says that you have contingencies for everything, and that's why you're so successful. So what's your contingency for this?"

Ohlmeyer stared at Anand with a pitying expression. "Then we go on as before. The only witnesses will be a bunch of catatonic junkies and a dead ten-year-old boy."

"Whose mother is a cop. You'll be getting much more attention from NYPD, and you *know* how cops get when you involve their families." Before Ohlmeyer could reply, Anand quickly said, "Yes, I know that Mamaroneck isn't in NYPD's jurisdiction, but you really think that's gonna matter if you've killed a detective's son? That's exactly the kind of move you say you never make because you don't want to draw undue attention. And we've already *got* undue attention because of Kogan and Hudson Yards."

Now Ohlmeyer was standing with his hands on his hips. "Are you finished?"

Anand blew out a breath. "I'm just trying to do my job, Garth, and represent you and your interests which is hard, considering I still don't even know what this ritual is or what it's supposed to accomplish."

The smirk came back. "Put it this way, Farid. Right now, in purely objective terms, I'm one of the most powerful people on the planet. But everyone thinks I'm just another one-percenter. After tomorrow night, everyone will *know* that I'm one of the most powerful people on the planet and will treat me accordingly—or pay the price." He put his fingers to his temple and closed his eyes for a moment. "Okay, wards are down. Get outta here, I have a meeting with the mayor to get to."

Anand and McManus both walked out behind Ohlmeyer. The latter said to Sabrina as he passed her desk, "I've got that meeting at Gracie Mansion."

"Your car's already waiting at the front door."

"Is Manfred driving?"

Sabrina nodded.

"Good. He knows how to get through midtown traffic." He shook his head. "I wish I could teleport over, but that tends to draw attention from security details, and as my lawyer just reminded me, it's not a great idea to draw undue attention."

Anand bowed his head in acknowledgment. He started to follow Ohlmeyer to the elevator, but McManus put a hand on his bicep.

"Hang back a minute, Farid."

Ohlmeyer got into an elevator, giving the attorneys a jaunty wave as the doors closed.

As soon as the doors closed, McManus turned on Anand. "What the *fuck* is wrong with you, Farid?"

"Nothing's wrong with me, Nick. Like I said—and like *you* said—I'm just trying to do my job." He blew out a breath, and then, after glancing at Sabrina, drew McManus into the conference room where the CNN interview had been filmed the previous week. He could have talked freely in front of Jada, but he didn't know Sabrina well enough.

Once they were inside, with the door closed, Anand said, "I'm trying to protect him, same as always. This whole thing has been *completely* reckless. Hudson Yards is poisoning everything. I couldn't get *any* of our usual judges to walk back Kisenwether's warrant. Then kidnapping a *cop's* kid? That's insane, and if this ritual goes bad, he's seriously screwed. And I'm really not liking the sound of something that involves murdering a child and people kowtowing to him."

McManus shrugged. "It's what he's always really wanted, anyhow. I think Trump getting re-elected really pissed him off. He wants that kind of love from people who admire him. And since when did you grow a conscience, anyhow?"

"Look, I don't give a damn about the drugs. It's just supply and demand. And the Hudson Yards nonsense is just that—nonsense. But kidnapping and killing a kid? Hell on Earth? People treating him with deference or else? I'm not comfortable with any of that."

"We aren't paid to be comfortable, Farid." McManus's phone buzzed and he took it out of the pocket of his slacks. "Oy—Tamara says they have questions about the subpoena. C'mon, let's go hold the associates' hands."

"Yeah." Anand followed McManus out of the conference room and toward the elevator.

I hope to hell this stupid ritual works.

TWENTY

Kiernan couldn't remember the last time—if ever—she'd had so many people in her apartment.

Ortega had driven himself, Basia, and Grullon up to the Bronx when the tour was over. Fiore had to meet his off-the-books Gandalf, and said he'd get a cab up to Kiernan's place.

They had all texted their orders from Joseph's, allowing Kiernan to have their food waiting for them when they arrived. She had put everything except Fiore's and Rachael's out on the coffee table. Fiore's had gone into the oven to keep warm, while Rachael's was in the refrigerator. Grullon would take it home to her when they were done.

Catalina Mercado had called while Kiernan was waiting for the food to be delivered. The domovoy's victim was abject in her gratitude. Kiernan accepted it as best as she was able to under the circumstances. And she was able to take a tiny bit of solace from the fact that, while this was the worst couple of days of her life, it was now one of the best days of Mercado's.

Now, Ortega was sitting in the easy chair—which Kiernan had cleared of the sweatshirts, bras, and coats that tended to live on it—eating spaghetti with oil and garlic. "I got a complete list of every property Ohlmeyer owns and every property that Augurer Productions owns."

Basia, who was sitting on the couch, eating fettucine with broccoli rabe, said, "I put them all onto a map." She patted her laptop, which was currently closed and resting on the couch between her and Grullon.

"Wait," Grullon said as he bit down on his chicken parmigiana, "how many properties does Augurer Productions own?"

"More than you'd think," Ortega said, "given that they haven't produced a movie yet. Or optioned a script. Or done, you know, any of the things movie production companies do."

Basia grinned. "I think they mostly do lunch and have pitch meetings and focus groups."

Kiernan was sitting cross-legged on the floor, eating veal saltimbocca. "What does Augurer own?"

Ortega leaned forward and grabbed a piece of paper from a folder that he'd put on the coffee table. "A warehouse in Queens near JFK, an apartment building in Sunset Park in Brooklyn that's currently completely empty, and a commercial property on Boston Road in the Bronx that they're renting to a bunch of small stores."

Grullon was shaking his head. "They've got a warehouse and an empty apartment building, why are they renting a storage unit?"

Basia added, "And why an empty apartment building in Sunset Park of all places? Rents are through the roof there."

"I'm guessing a tax write-off," Kiernan said bitterly.

Ortega said, "And he's probably renting the warehouse to someone unsavory. We should pass that on to the One-One-Three, let them look into it."

Kiernan stared at Ortega. "'Unsavory'?"

Shrugging, he gestured expansively and said, "It's all this food."

The doorbell buzzed. Kiernan put her veal on the coffee table, untangled her legs, got to her feet, went over to the intercom box, and buzzed the door open.

"You're not gonna see who it is?" Grullon asked.

"It's gotta be Vinny," she said with a shrug, heading back to her dinner.

Grullon was not placated. "Or it could've been somebody trying to get in and ringing bells at random, hoping somebody'd just let him in without asking."

Giving Grullon one of Nonna's looks, Kiernan said, "And any other fuckin' day, I'd probably be worried about that."

That made Grullon practically shrink into the couch. "Okay, fine."

A minute later, there was a knock at the door. "It's open!" Kiernan cried out.

Fiore opened the door.

Normally, as a single woman in a big city, she'd have kept the door locked, but there were two—now three—other cops in her apartment. She liked her chances against any theoretical persons who would try to enter her place right present.

Holding up a poster tube, Fiore said, "Nicky came through—I got a map with all the wards in the city."

Pointing toward the kitchen, Kiernan said, "Your reward is the sausage, peppers, and onions sitting in the oven. Potholders are hanging from the cabinet, silverware's in the drawer under the drying rack. You can hang your coat in the closet next to the kitchen doorway."

Grinning, Fiore put the poster tube on the coffee table. "You're the best, Dom."

As Fiore went into the kitchen, Ortega said, "Oh, I also talked to some buddies in Narcotics and talked to Emilio some more. Ohlmeyer's dealers—" He rolled his eyes. "—that is to say, his *alleged* dealers, are all *way* more in evidence than usual, the last twenty-four hours. Like Ohlmeyer's prepping for something."

Basia said, "That also points to him doing some kind of ritual on the new moon tomorrow night."

Fiore came back into the living room, no longer wearing his fleece coat and holding a takeout plate in one hand and a knife and fork in the other. He was using one of Kiernan's potholders as a makeshift tray, to protect his hand from the heat. "Where do I sit?"

Basia, who had finished her fettucine, stood up. "Sit here, Vinny. I need to stretch my legs anyhow." She grabbed the poster tube and pulled out its contents.

Fiore sat on the couch. "My guy cast the spell and put the locations on that map."

Ortega sighed. "Woulda been nice if he could've put it on an electronic map that you could've e-mailed all of us."

"You can actually do that," Basia said as she unrolled the map, "but it's a much stronger spell. Ohlmeyer would probably detect that."

"'Sides," Fiore added, "Nicky ain't got that kinda mojo."

Kiernan got up to help Basia with the map. They used the TV remote, a half-empty bottle of Ramune, a book about the Yankees that she still hadn't gotten around to reading even though it'd been sitting on the coffee table since April, and Grullon's glass of water to hold the four corners of the map down and keep it flat. Kiernan usually didn't drink the Japanese soda when Bobby wasn't with her but had felt the urge to do so tonight.

Fiore's "guy" had provided them with a street map of all five boroughs, as well as bits of lower Westchester, Nassau County, and northeastern New Jersey.

However, it looked like an ordinary street map. "Uh, Vinny?"

"Shit, I forgot. You gotta activate it with a charm. I got one in my coat pocket."

Basia nodded. "I'll get it."

"Thanks, Basia," Fiore said. "Front right pocket."

She went into the hall; moments later, she returned, holding what looked like a spherical ruby. "It's a Qian charm. Haven't seen one of these in ages—people usually use a Farrell or a Yadav. It's weird, because the Qian is cheaper *and* more effective, but—"

Ortega interrupted her. "Can you activate it?"

"Hm?" Basia shook her head. "Oh, yeah, sorry. You just touch it to the map …" She married that statement to action. The ruby glowed briefly, and bits of the map started to glow red. The red blobs of light were different shapes and sizes and varied in depth of color and brightness.

"The bad news," Fiore said, his mouth full of sweet sausage, onions, and red bell peppers, "is that there's *lotsa* wards all around the city."

"Not surprising," Basia said. "A good set of wards is better than locking your door, and you can tailor them. The problem is, they're hard to come by."

Staring at all the glowy red on the map, Kiernan said, "That don't look that hard to come by."

"Sorry, I meant *good* ones are hard to come by." Basia pointed at the map. "See all the light ones, that are more like pink or magenta?"

Ortega squinted at the map. "They all look red to me."

Before Basia could reply to that, Kiernan held up a hand. "Do *not* get him started on colors, or we'll start having the yellow versus orange argument about the color in the middle of the traffic light, and then I'm gonna have to shoot all of you."

Basia grinned. "Right. Well, the ones that everyone who isn't Luis can tell are pink or magenta are low-level wards, which are probably just to warn you if someone comes in. They won't stop you or do anything to you, just alert the caster that something's come past it."

Kiernan pointed at 106th Street on the map. "Should I be worried that the wards at the house are only light red?"

"They're good enough for what we need." Basia pointed at Morningside Heights. "Those light red ones are where the Gitaus live, and if it's good enough for them …"

"I guess," though Kiernan didn't feel reassured by that.

Grullon was peering at the map. "I'm seeing six dark red ones."

"Right," Basia said. "Those are the big-time wards; they're basically force fields and Faraday cages. You can't get through them unless the caster wants you to go through, and radio waves or cell phone signals or anything like that are also blocked—again, unless the caster lets them in. Thing is, something that strong is like the transmutation spell, you need to be incredibly powerful to cast it and maintain it."

"It's gotta be maintained?" Ortega asked.

Nodding, Basia said, "Or at least reinforced every couple of weeks or so." She grabbed her laptop and put it on the coffee table next to the map.

"Can I ask a question?" Grullon said, holding up a hand.

Rolling her eyes, Kiernan said, "*Madonna mia*, Grullon, this ain't high school, you don't gotta raise your hand. What is it?"

"Okay, I get why we were being all secretive and stuff before, in case Ohlmeyer had a bug in the squad room. Well, he did have a bug, and we got rid of it. The Gitaus confirmed that it was a scrying stone *and* that it was broadcasting to Midtown. They couldn't pinpoint it exactly, but the area they gave us includes Ohlmeyer's office on Sixth. So why are we still doing this all behind Hawk and the Major's backs?"

"Because," Ortega said, "we're not a hundred percent sure that Ohlmeyer's the one who planted the bug, and we're not even seventy-five percent sure that that bug the Gitaus found is the only bug in HQ, or his only source of intel. Ohlmeyer's got juice—one of our investigations of him back in the day got quashed by the commissioner his own damn self right after Ohlmeyer played a round of golf with him and the mayor."

"Yeah, he may not need a scrying stone to get inside info." Kiernan blew out a quick breath. "Plus, I can't be part of any official investigation right now."

"With good reason." Grullon quickly added, before Kiernan had a chance to apply Nonna's look, "I'm just saying, Kiernan—you don't have the best judgment right now."

"That's why I got you guys here. You all gotta be my conscience—and my rationality. Which," she added with a sigh, "is why I'm actually glad you said that. You're all takin' a big risk here. If Hawk finds out or—"

"He won't," Ortega said, "he's not that bright."

Kiernan said more emphatically, "Or if *the Major* finds out, and he *is* that bright, we could be fucked."

Fiore said, "I ain't worried about the lieutenant. He's one of the best shit umbrellas in the department."

Basia stared at Fiore. "Shit umbrella?"

Kiernan said, "When shit comes from on high, he protects us from it."

"Ah," Basia said with a nod. She turned her laptop screen toward Kiernan. "Well, of those six really powerful wards, one is about nine hundred square feet on West End Avenue and 72nd Street, one is a smallish bit on Sixth Avenue between 42nd and 43rd, one is a very tiny one in the middle of Co-op City in the Bronx, and one is in the middle of a storage unit in Long Island City in Queens. There's another tiny one on 54th Street and York Avenue and there's a gigunda one on 125th Street."

"The one on 54th and York is where Ohlmeyer lives," Fiore said. "And his office is on Sixth between 42nd and 43rd."

"The one on 54th is really small," Basia said. "I'd guess he uses it like a safe, to protect really important stuff. It might even surround his safe. And the one on Sixth is a little bigger, maybe the size of a conference room or a big office."

"My money's on the big office," Kiernan said.

Grullon said, "West End and 72nd is where Amanda Cornwell lives. Nine hundred square feet … it's probably her whole apartment. And according to the alert I got from DHS a couple hours ago, she's flying back to the States today, should be in at JFK tonight."

"Vinny and I are on this weekend, so we'll question her first thing tomorrow morning," Ortega said. "Also, that storage unit in Queens probably isn't Ohlmeyer's—except for the Augurer Productions one in the Bronx, all the ones he's rented, under his own name and through Ohlmeyer Inc., are in Manhattan."

Kiernan said, "So that leaves Co-op City and 125th Street."

"The Co-op City one is in the middle of the shopping center," Basia said, "and I'm not sure what it is. But the one on 125th matches perfectly the shape and size of a supermarket that closed five years ago, right after Ohlmeyer Inc. bought it."

Peering at Basia's laptop, Kiernan saw that the map of Ohlmeyer's properties showed a big one on 125th Street, between Malcolm X Boulevard and Adam Clayton Powell Jr. Boulevard. It was a perfect match for the reddest of the glowy red bits on Fiore's map.

"Big space, abandoned for years, got the magical equivalent of a force field around it." Kiernan looked at her comrades. "Looks like a good place to have a magic ritual and not be disturbed."

"It's a perfect place for a magic ritual tomorrow night, especially," Basia said quietly.

"Why's that, Basia?" Kiernan asked.

"One of the reasons why both the new moon and the full moon are good times for certain rituals is because that's when the ley-lines get particularly hot."

Ortega rubbed his bald head. "You mentioned that back when we arrested Taylor. Remind me what those are, again?"

"Basically, ley-lines are a latticework of magical energy conduits. They vary in strength depending on a number of factors, including the waxing and waning of the moon. As it happens, the new moon that starts tomorrow night is going to make the ley-lines especially hot because it's close to the autumnal equinox. And one of those ley-lines? In fact, the most powerful ley-line in New York, and one of the three or four most powerful in the northeast?" Basia put her finger on the part of Fiore's map that indicated Ohlmeyer's heavily warded property. "The 125th Street fault line."

"There is absolutely no way," Ortega said slowly, "that it's a coincidence that Ohlmeyer owns an empty supermarket on the most powerful magical zappy thing in town and he's got it warded up the wazoo."

"Really?" Grullon asked. "Magical zappy thing?"

"I dunno, it sounds like the right way to describe it to me," Fiore said with a shrug.

"So how do we get in there?" Grullon asked.

With a snort of derision, Basia said, "We don't. Warded up the wazoo means you'd have an easier time breaking into an adamantium dome."

Grullon smirked. "You know adamantium's fictional, right?"

Throwing up her hands, Basia said, "Fine, breaking into a six-foot-thick steel dome, then."

"But it's not a six-foot-thick steel dome," Kiernan said. "It's magic. So what we need to get through is more magic."

"I mean, theoretically, sure, but—" Basia sighed. "Ohlmeyer's an *incredibly* powerful magic-user. And tomorrow night, thanks to those hot ley-lines, he's gonna be *even more* powerful. We're not gonna be able to get through these wards with anything we have laying around, or anything we can get at a shop."

"Yeah, but Ohlmeyer's not the only big-shot Gandalf in the city." Kiernan pointed at the deep red glow on 72nd Street and West End. "Grullon, when's Cornwell supposed to be landing at JFK?"

"About nine."

Kiernan nodded. "By the time she gets through customs and gets her luggage and gets from JFK to the Upper West Side, it'll probably be close to midnight." She looked at Ortega. "We could go now, wait at her place, catch her when she gets home."

"Or we could interview her tomorrow like we already planned."

"Fuck that, this is my *kid*, Ortega! I ain't waitin'!"

"And we want to actually get Bobby back." Ortega leaned forward in the easy chair. "What exactly do you want to do with Cornwell when you meet her at her apartment late tonight?"

"Get her to bring down Ohlmeyer's wards."

"Right—out of the goodness of her heart. So, to be clear, you want to ask a powerful Gandalf for a favor. You really think the best plan is to ambush her, at home, at midnight, after she's flown halfway 'round the world, gone through customs, waited for luggage, and sat in a cab for an hour in traffic on the Van Wyck and the Triboro? All while you're off-duty, mind you ..."

For a few seconds, Kiernan stared angrily at Ortega as she tried and failed to come up with an answer to his question that wouldn't be pathetic.

Finally, she said, "I hate it when you're right and I'm wrong."

"I keep telling you, just agree with me more." Ortega's light tone quickly turned serious: "And hey, we're gonna get Bobby back. But we gotta be smart. Ohlmeyer's been skating on his bullshit for *years*."

"Yeah, 'cause the fucker's rich and nobody knew he was a Gandalf," Fiore said. "We know now, so he ain't got that no more."

"But he's still richer than God," Ortega said, "and that pays for the best lawyers, not to mention the best politicians and judges that money can bribe. And we're already doing a rogue investigation here. We gotta be *extra* careful."

"Yeah." Kiernan just stared at the map, specifically at the dark red glow on 125th Street. She imagined her little boy in Ohlmeyer's clutches. Then she looked at Ortega. "We also gotta get him back before Ohlmeyer does whatever shit he's doing tomorrow night. So you'd better talk to Cornwell *first* thing."

"We will," Ortega said.

Fiore leaned forward and put a hand on Kiernan's shoulder. "We got you, Dom."

"Thanks, Vinny." She looked at all of them in turn. "All'a you, thanks."

TWENTY-ONE

Ortega didn't bother to go to SCU HQ in the morning, as he wanted to talk to Amanda Cornwell as soon as possible. He texted Fiore to meet him at the apartment building on West End Avenue at 72nd Street at nine a.m.

Fiore messaged back:

She's jet-lagged, she might still be asleep

Ortega's reply:

YOU want to explain to Kiernan why we didn't go there first thing?

After several seconds came a simple response from Fiore:

See you at 9.

In addition, Ortega called the house to inform the reception desk officer—today, a patrol officer Ortega didn't know and whose name he forgot the moment the call ended—that he and Fiore were talking to a person of interest in the Ohlmeyer case. He asked the desk officer to please sign the two of them in, which the PO said he would.

As Ortega sat on the 1 train that took him from his home in Washington Heights to the 72nd Street station that was only a block away from Cornwell's building, a text came in from Hawkins:

Who's the POI you're interviewing?

Ortega sighed. That meant that either Hawk was in the office today or he was checking up on things from home. The latter was preferable, but the former was more likely, which was just going to make the weekend go that much more slowly.

Amanda Cornwell.
She flew back from NZ last night.

Hawk texted back:

Good. Keep me posted.
I'll be home all day, but I've got my phone with me.

Grateful that Hawkins at least wouldn't be underfoot in the squad room, Ortega texted back a thumbs-up emoji.

When he got out at 72nd, he regretted his decision to wear his windbreaker. In the half-hour since he'd taken the elevator down to the platform at 181st Street, the temperature had gone up to nearly seventy degrees, which was a good twenty-five degrees warmer than it had been the day before. By the time Ortega had walked down to West End, he was sweating.

Fiore was already waiting in front of the fifteen-story apartment building. He was staring straight up the building's façade. "Gotta say, I'm disappointed," he said without preamble as Ortega walked up.

"Good morning, Vinny, and how are you?"

"Sorry, I'm good."

"How'd you get here before me?" Fiore lived in Brooklyn, at least an hour away by subway.

"Was already in the neighborhood, so I just walked over. Y'know, I figured, hotshot author/activist chick living on the Upper West Side, she'd be in an Art Deco building."

Ortega stared at the rectangular red brick building that looked like practically every large apartment building in the city. "This isn't Art Deco?"

"Nah. Right time period, pre-war, but this is Colonial Revival. Some of the coolest architecture in history's goin' up all over town back then, but this one set'a assholes decide, 'Hey, let's go back to that boring shit from the eighteenth century.' "

Ortega looked at Fiore again. "That's the same suit you wore yesterday."

"Yeah, I ain't been home yet."

"Didn't you have a jacket?"

Fiore nodded. "I'll pick it up later."

"From where?"

"Place on 68th and Columbus, where I slept last night." Then he grinned. "Well, I slept eventually, y'know what I mean?"

"I do, yes," Ortega said with a sigh. "I remember when I was young and could work a whole tour, meet with my fellow detectives in the evening, and then go to a bar and pick up a random woman and spend the night. Well, okay, I only did that last part when I wasn't married. Mostly."

"Kaitlyn wasn't random. She played a mean game of eight-ball. I almost lost once."

That was high praise. Fiore's prowess at pool was legendary. Where his high-school classmates all had part-time jobs for extra money, Fiore spent his time in bars he was too young to legally be allowed in, hustling pool against guys twice his age.

Fiore began to go on about the previous night, but Ortega held up a hand. "Much as I would *love* to hear all about your night of passion, he says, lying through his teeth in the interests of camaraderie, we've got an interview to conduct." Fiore nodded and fell silent.

They went in through the glass-and-brass door. The lobby was huge, with two couches, two easy chairs, and a huge TV that was currently showing a news channel.

Between the front door and the elevators was a large desk, behind which sat a man in a maroon suit. His nametag read JEAN AUGUSTINE. "Can I help you gentlemen?" he asked, with a mild Haitian accent.

Ortega said, "We're here to see Amanda Cornwell in 7C."

Augustine winced. "I'm sorry, Ms. Cornwell specifically asked not to be disturbed."

Unclipping his badge from his belt, Ortega held it up. "I'm afraid disturbing her is what we're here for."

"I'm sorry, but I can't—"

Ortega interrupted. "Look, Jean, I understand that you're just doing what you were told. But so are we. If we don't get to talk to Ms. Cornwell right now, I'm gonna have to go to all the trouble of getting a warrant, and then our conversation with Ms. Cornwell is going to be *incredibly* unpleasant."

"That is likely to happen regardless." Augustine smirked, then grabbed the phone. "I will call her."

"Thank you."

As he entered a number onto the phone's keypad, he asked, "What are your names, please?"

"Detective Ortega and Detective Fiore."

"Hello, Ms. Cornwell, it's Jean downstairs ... I am sorry to have awakened you, but there are two plainclothes police officers here to see you, Detectives Ortega and Fiore ... They did not say ... They say that if you do not see them, they will obtain a warrant ... I assume for your arrest ... Very well, Ms. Cornwell, good-bye." He hung up, then looked at Ortega and indicated the elevator bank with a hand. "Go ahead, Detectives. She's on seven."

"Thank you," Ortega said.

They rode the elevator up to seven, and as soon as they set foot on the landing, a voice said, "Who the hell are you?"

Turning to his left, Ortega saw a six-foot-tall woman with a mane of dark brown hair with purple highlights, a pointed nose, and long arms and legs. The arms were resting on her hips, which were clad in a flower print bathrobe over what appeared to be a tank top and yoga pants. Her feet were bare.

Again holding up his shield, he said, "I'm Detective Luis Ortega. This is Detective Vincenzo Fiore."

"Call me Vinny," Fiore said with a smile.

"I don't think I will, thanks," the woman said.

"You're Amanda Cornwell?" Ortega asked.

"I am. And you're with the fraud squad, I'm guessing? You guys are always coming around and fishing, and—"

"We're not investigating a fraud, Ms. Cornwell," Ortega said. "We're with SCU."

Cornwell rolled her eyes. "Oh, Hel's teeth, that's worse. All you people have done is make it harder for people like me."

"Making your life easier isn't really NYPD's job, ma'am."

"No, but putting innocent creatures in jail just for performing according to their nature is not doing a damn bit of good."

Fiore surprised Ortega by speaking up rather passionately. "Now, that's some bullshit. You know who's in our cells right now?" Fiore enumerated points on his fingers as he talked. "We got us a domovoy that committed assault and battery and also stole a dead guy's identity. And we got a kappa who killed another kappa, and a third kappa is the star witness. Ain't nothin' there got to do with 'nature' or some shit, it's just a couple assholes who happen to be supernatural creatures, but who also broke the fuckin' law."

Ortega quickly said, "Can we come in, please, Ms. Cornwell?"

Cornwell was staring daggers at Fiore. "Conveniently, Detective, you left out the naiad who's out on her own recognizance, and against whom the evidence is very weak." At Fiore's surprised look, she added, "I still had the Internet in New Zealand, and for obvious reasons, I keep up with what you guys are doing. I'm friends with the naiad community in Turtle Pond, and I'm fairly certain your interpreter misconstrued what the naiads said. It wouldn't be the first time."

Before Fiore could respond or Cornwell could continue her rant, Ortega said, "If you're following our cases, then you probably know that we're investigating the murders of Elmore Hertweck and a drug dealer called Jake the Jake."

"I did know that, though I've no idea why it's *your* case."

"Because the bodies of both victims were liquefied by a transmutation spell—one that was cast expertly and from a distance."

Cornwell made a noise like a bursting pipe. "And you think *I* had something to do with that?"

"You're one of the few people on Earth powerful enough to. Which is why we need to eliminate you as a suspect."

Closing her eyes and shaking her head, Cornwell said, "I've spent the last six months in New Zealand, Detective. And even I couldn't cast that spell from halfway around the world."

"I know that, and you know that, but a jury might not, and our actual suspect has very good lawyers, and we need to be able to show that we checked into you."

"Oh, so you can harass some *other* magus? Please."

"The other Gand—The other magus in question is Garth Ohlmeyer."

That brought Cornwell visibly up short. Then she put her fingers to her temples and closed her eyes. After a moment, she opened them and said, "Come in."

"You were instructing the wards to let us in?" Ortega asked as he crossed the threshold into a decent-sized living room with a very aggressively expensive-looking living room set. There was a sectional couch and a reclining easy chair upholstered in the same flower pattern; a glass coffee table sat in front of the sectional, and there were beautiful wooden end tables on either side of it.

The floor was quality hardwood, with area rugs in various spots, which was typical for the neighborhood. To the left was a hallway that seemed to lead to the kitchen. To the right was a closed door that Ortega assumed went to the bedroom. One entire wall was taken up with bookshelves that were full to bursting with books. Ortega had seen plenty of homes with bookcases where the books were neat and orderly and apparently hadn't been touched in years. But it was obvious that Cornwell consulted her books regularly.

Other walls had paintings hung on them, including one of a dragon menacing a boat, another of a spacescape. These were original paintings, not prints, Ortega could make out the brushwork—which meant they were a lot more expensive than prints. The back wall had a large window that looked out over West End.

When Cornwell closed the door, Ortega saw, hanging from the back of it, a poster from Barnes & Noble that advertised a signing of Cornwell's first book, *The Many-Shadowed Paths: One Wiccan's Journey to Enlightenment.* The date of the event was fifteen years ago.

"I'm impressed," Cornwell said, pointedly not offering them a seat or something to drink, "I didn't think anyone in your unit knew what a ward even *is*."

"We don't know everything," Ortega said, "but we're learning, and we're getting better."

"I find that impossible to believe."

Ortega smiled sweetly. "Then why'd you let us into your heavily warded and very nicely appointed apartment?"

"I don't like you, Detectives. I don't like your unit, and I especially don't like the way NYPD operates. Our community has been completely disrupted by your interference in our lives—we're yet another marginalized group that's been singled out by the police. But as much as I dislike you, it's nothing compared to how much I absolutely *despise* Garth Ohlmeyer."

Why am I not surprised? Ortega thought. "And why is that, Ms. Cornwell?" he asked, being deliberately obtuse in order to gauge her response.

"Magic is something that should be used to benefit humanity, not spread poison and enrich oneself."

"Lady," Fiore said, "you're livin' in a million-dollar apartment, and that's before we talk about all your stuff."

"Nice try, Detective, but I make my money legitimately, from writing, teaching, speaking engagements, and my consulting business. I file 1099s every year and pay taxes on every single bit of money I make. I also donate to plenty of charities, including ones for people who've been railroaded or mistreated by the police. I certainly don't exploit addicts for my own gain."

"And you think Mr. Ohlmeyer does?" Ortega asked in what he hoped was a good deadpan.

"I *know* he does. You don't?"

Ortega decided to drop the act. "Oh, we totally do. In fact, we've known for years, but haven't been able to do anything about it, because he's a slippery weasel with, as I said, very good lawyers. But now that we know he's a—a magus, he's an SCU case."

Cornwell hit him with a wry smile. "How is that an improvement, exactly?"

"Well, for starters, I doubt that the Narcotics detectives or the DA's investigators would ever have known that tonight's new moon, since it's right before the autumnal equinox, is a great time to perform a ritual. They also wouldn't have paired that knowledge with the fact that one of Ohlmeyer's properties is on the 125th Street ley-line."

"I imagine when you first heard the term 'ley-line,' Detective, you thought it was a place where you had sex."

Fiore rolled his eyes. "That's funny—if I was in high school."

"That is usually the level of humor I encounter in police, Detective."

Ortega was growing weary of the verbal sparring and decided to lay his cards on the table. "All right, listen. We don't just know that Ohlmeyer is a drug dealer. We know that he's enhancing the product with magic. We know that he's planning something big for tonight, something that will probably take place in the property on the hot ley-line. And we know that a day and a half ago, he kidnapped a ten-year-old kid."

It was, unsurprisingly, the last part that got Cornwell's attention. Her body language shifted from hostile to concerned; she unfolded her arms and dropped them to her side as her shoulders visibly lowered and her eyes widened. "Has there been a ransom demand?"

Hesitating, Ortega said, "Not as such."

"There won't be. On tonight's new moon, the boundaries between this and the Scythian dimension are at their weakest. This is a great time to try to bridge the gap between this dimension and that one, and the way to hold the door open, so to speak, is to sacrifice the life of an innocent."

"What the fuck's the Scythian dimension?" Fiore asked.

"Well, if you were raised in the Zoroastrian faith, it's where all the Daeva live."

Ortega swallowed, recalling that Umali and Fiore had found Zoroastrian mythology books in Ohlmeyer's penthouse apartment. "And if you weren't?"

"It's the home of some incredibly nasty creatures. Zoroastrian myth calls them Daeva, like I said, and they're basically demons. You do *not* want them to come through, believe me."

"We were afraid of something like that," Ortega said. The notion of Bobby being sacrificed hadn't in fact been mentioned or even considered, and he felt nauseous at the very thought. But there was no percentage in letting Cornwell know that.

"So what do you need me for? Besides eliminating me as a suspect? Which, by the way, my New Zealand trip has already taken care of, not just for your transmutation spell, but also for the kidnapping, if it happened on Wednesday …"

"Thursday," Fiore corrected.

Cornwell closed her eyes and shook her head. "Right, sorry—my time sense gets messed up every time I cross the International Date Line."

Ortega said, "We need something to penetrate Ohlmeyer's wards so we can get inside that abandoned supermarket and find out if he's gonna try to barge his way into the Scythian dimension."

For about ten seconds, Cornwell stood there, hands on her hips again, staring at an indeterminate point between Fiore and Ortega. Then she nodded with purpose. "I have something you can use. Wait here."

She went through the door on the right, which did appear to lead to the bedroom, given the glimpse of a four-poster, king-sized bed Ortega caught before she closed the door behind her.

Fiore regarded Ortega with amusement. "Nice job actually rememberin' the term 'ley-lines' and not callin' 'em 'magic zappy things.' "

"Kiss my ass," Ortega muttered.

Cornwell came out of the bedroom holding what looked like two metal lockboxes. She placed them side by side on the coffee table. Each was about a foot long, but only a few inches wide and five or six inches deep. The lock was in the center of the top of each box, with a crescent moon engraved over the lock and a pentagram engraved under it. On top of each box was a small metal ring, through which was threaded what looked like a silver chain.

"Is this the part where we ask, 'What's in the box?' " Ortega queried dryly.

With a smirk, Cornwell said, "Petals from a climbing hydrangea, a tomato, a vial of hydrochloric acid, and six drill bits, all of which I've used to cast a spell that will enable these boxes—and anyone wearing them—to pass harmlessly through *any* wards."

"How the hell do you wear a box?" Fiore asked.

Pointing at the chains, Cornwell said, "Around your neck. Make sure the silver chain is touching your flesh."

"You just happened to have these lying around?" Ortega asked.

"I've got a lot of things 'lying around,' Detective. I'm willing to *loan* them to your unit on two conditions. One is that you return them to me, here, in the same state they were given to you, by noon on Monday."

With a snort, Ortega said, "Assuming Ohlmeyer doesn't succeed in unleashing Zoroastrian hell on Earth, sure. What's the second condition?"

"NYPD pays me for the use of these charms."

"Fine, no problem."

Fiore shot Ortega a look but said nothing.

Cornwell, however, raised an eyebrow. "Really? No arguing, no haggling, no asking for a discount—or even asking how much?"

"There's a kid's life at stake and it's not my money, so I don't give a shit." He indicated the charms with his head. "We get the keys, too?"

"Absolutely not."

"Why not?"

Folding her arms and standing defiantly, Cornwell said, "Well, for starters, I really don't want you poking around inside my stuff. And if you unlock it, the spell expires, and then it's just a couple of metal boxes around your neck."

"Fine. Pick 'em up, Vinny."

Nodding, Fiore hefted the two charms with a grunt, stacked them, and tried to tuck them under his left arm. They proved too bulky and heavy for that, so he just cradled them in both arms in front of his chest.

"Pleasure doing business with you, Ms. Cornwell," Ortega said with a nod.

"I wish I could say the same, Detective. Oh!" Cornwell pointed a finger to the ceiling, then went to an end table, opened a drawer, pulled out a business card, and handed it to Ortega. "Keep me posted on what Garth's doing, if you can—and use that e-mail address to set up a time and place to return the items on Monday."

Ortega peered at the card and noticed that there was an e-mail address and a phone number, as well as a website address. "We can't call?"

"My phone's still set for international calling, so if you call my U.S. number, it'll go straight to voicemail. I had texting turned off while I was out of the country, and my provider hasn't turned it back on yet. E-mail's best. I check it regularly."

Nodding, Ortega put the card in his windbreaker pocket.

The two of them left the apartment, hearing Cornwell firmly close and lock the door behind them.

It wasn't until they were on the elevator and pretty much guaranteed to be out of Cornwell's hearing that Fiore asked, "I'm confused about one thing."

Ortega grinned. "Only one?"

"Fuck you, Ortega. You said we couldn't use any'a our usual—what's that word she used? Magus? Or plural, so I guess maguses?"

"Magi, probably."

"What-the-fuck-ever. Point is, we had to use Nicky 'cause we didn't wanna do the paperwork on any'a our usual hires. So why are you okay with havin' paperwork on *her*?"

"The problem wasn't the paperwork as such. We can juke that so no one'll know what we hired them for. No, the problem with our regulars is that they might talk to Hawk or the Major, and we needed to keep this on the down-low."

"But we don't gotta keep *her* on the DL?"

"This is the first, and very likely the last, time Her Royal Highness will deign to work with us. I'm not worried about her blabbing."

Once they got outside, back into the bright and sunny day, Ortega pulled out his phone and called Kiernan. He filled her in on everything that had gone down with Cornwell, including the possibility that Bobby might be a human sacrifice.

Kiernan's response was a long pause, followed by, "I'm really glad you're the kind of asshole who doesn't pull punches, Ortega. I didn't wanna know that, but I really needed to. Fuck me."

"If it makes you feel any better, Kiernan, I'm several other kinds of asshole, too."

"Already knew that—I've met most of your ex-wives." She sighed. "We need to get everyone together."

"If we don't report back to the house," Ortega said, "Hawk'll get suspicious."

"Fuck, he didn't come in today, did he?"

"No, thank God, but he's checking in."

"It'll take all of us time to get together, anyhow." Kiernan sighed again. "Can you guys take lunch at noon?"

"Don't see why not."

"Fine, it's a nice day and I'd rather meet outside, where people can't listen in on us. Let's get together at noon at the fountain in the Conservatory Garden."

Ortega nodded. "Sounds good." The Untermeyer Fountain was located in the northern part of Central Park's flower garden, which was right by the entrance to the park on 106th and Fifth Avenue, just a couple of blocks west of SCU's HQ.

"All right, I'll call Basia and Grullon." A third sigh. "I know I keep sayin' this, Ortega, but thanks."

"We'll get him back, Kiernan. Whatever it takes."

"Yeah, it's the 'whatever' part of that that's got me worried. Seeya at noon."

TWENTY-TWO

Until today, Kiernan hadn't known that the fountain where she'd called the meeting was called the Untermyer Fountain. She broke with her longstanding habit and took mass transit in to the meet, not trusting herself to operate a motor vehicle in her current mental state. En route, she looked up the Central Park Conservatory Garden on her phone, to try to distract herself.

I can't believe that fucker took Bobby.

Apparently, the fountain was a bronze cast of a statue called *Three Dancing Maidens* by Walter Schott. It amused Kiernan a bit that the statue of three dancing maidens that was the fountain's main feature had a rather boring, if self-descriptive, title.

Then she read up on Samuel Untermyer, a lawyer and civic leader from the first half of the twentieth century. He was heavily involved in creating the laws that regulated corporations and the stock market.

This had proven a useful distraction at first, until she found herself reading what was online about Garth Ohlmeyer.

She found nothing about Ohlmeyer's life as a drug kingpin. She found nothing that detailed his career as a Gandalf. All she saw was the public part of his life: that he was a real-estate magnate and corporate shark, that he was currently under investigation for a real estate deal that was connected to the disgrace of a city comptroller. There was nothing online about his magical abilities or his drug dealing—not even a rumor.

Then she began wondering if part of Samuel Untermyer's life wasn't written about. Was he a Gandalf? Was he a creature of the fae, here to help humans fix their shit? Were the three maidens portrayed in the statue actual women, transformed into bronze and imprisoned in the fountain as punishment for some affront they'd committed that was now lost to history? The statue had been in Untermyer's house for years and was donated by his kids to the park after he died ...

In the end, these thoughts did a nice job of very temporarily distracting her from the fact that Bobby had now been missing for forty-four hours with absolutely no forward movement on finding him. No ransom demand, no new anonymous e-mails—Kiernan had been obsessively checking her e-mail every five minutes or so since Thursday night. Just a bunch of useless phone calls from Detective McLain in Mamaroneck, a single text from Latzko at CCS saying they hadn't been able to trace the Hotmail address—

—and the knowledge that her son had likely been taken in order to be a human sacrifice that would unleash a mess of demons on the Earth.

I can't believe my baby has been taken.

Or that they're gonna kill him if we don't find him.

She arrived at Fifth Avenue at eleven-forty. Even though she'd had a full breakfast of cannoli, sfogliatelle, and cappuccino at the bakery that morning, she found that she was ravenous. She wandered down Fifth to a hot dog stand and got a classic dirty-water dog with mustard and sauerkraut, as well as a bottle of water. She went into the park and sat down to eat on one of the benches that faced the fountain.

The dog was tough, the mustard was mediocre, the bun was half stale, the sauerkraut was flimsy, and she loved every morsel.

Each bite reminded her of when her parents used to take her into Manhattan, which they always called, "going into the city," even though they lived in the Bronx, which was part of New York City. Ma and Dad would always buy her a hot dog from a street vendor. She'd done the same with Bobby any number of times.

And we'll do it again, dammit. For October's visit. No matter what.

By the time she finished the hot dog, Grullon had arrived. He was wearing a red polo shirt and blue jeans and had a canvas bag slung over one shoulder. "Hey, Kiernan. You've, uh, got some mustard on your shirt."

Looking down, Kiernan saw a glob of mustard on her worn, old, snow leopard T-shirt she'd gotten at the Bronx Zoo gift shop. The snow leopards were one of Bobby's favorites at the zoo, which was why she'd chosen to wear that particular shirt today. She grabbed a napkin out of her purse and wiped the yellow blob away.

Reaching into his tote bag, Grullon handed her something wrapped in tin foil. "Rachael made knishes and insisted I bring you one. I realize you just ate, but—"

"It's fine," she said, eagerly grabbing the knish and ripping away the wrapping. It was still a little warm even after an hour on the subway, and it smelled like heaven.

As she bit down on the knish, she could taste every ingredient all at once, the glorious combination exploding on her taste buds: potatoes, onions, ground beef, kasha, and sauerkraut. The latter was so much better than what had been on her hot dog.

Grullon sat next to her and asked, "This is the stupidest possible question, but how're you doing?"

After swallowing the bite of knish, Kiernan replied, "Ready to claw somebody's eyes out. Preferably Ohlmeyer's, but I'm pretty fuckin' close to doin' it to random strangers."

"Yeah, don't do that. It'd be embarrassing to have to arrest you right now."

"This knish is heavenly; you should marry that woman."

"Workin' on it," Grullon said with a grin.

"Now, tell me how the wedding planning's going. I need the distraction."

"Be happy to distract you, but amazingly things are quiet. The only recent hiccup was last week when Abuela said she wouldn't attend."

"Oh, right." Kiernan took another bite, recalling Grullon telling her about that after they'd arrested the domovoy the first time. "Did she go for it once she found out she was in the ceremony?"

"Not at first. I could tell she was close to giving in, but she insisted on holding on to her outrage. So I told her how devastated I'd be if all three of Rachael's surviving grandparents got to walk down the aisle and none of my grandparents would be with them."

Kiernan nodded. She recalled that Grullon's maternal grandparents had died before he was born, and his abuelo had died of cancer last year.

"So Abuela said they didn't need her, Rachael had three people to my one, it would be uneven, so she shouldn't go. Then Dad talked about how much he was looking forward to his own mother being part of the procession to get her only grandson married, and I pointed out that it would look better if they walked down in pairs and she could walk with Rachael's grandmother, who's also a widow. Abuela started to give in then, but said she had to meet Rachael's grandmother first."

That surprised Kiernan. "The grandparents haven't met?"

Holding up both hands, Grullon said, "*Don't* get me started. My parents and Rachael's parents get along like a house on fire, but nobody from either of our extended families has gone to the other family's events, no matter how many times we've invited them."

Kiernan found herself thinking about every excruciating holiday spent with Tim's spectacularly dull family. One of the ways she mentally got herself through the agonizing divorce proceedings was to remind herself that she'd never have to suffer through her father-in-law's droning stories about tax law or eat her mother-in-law's flavor-free cooking ever again.

Grullon continued, "Anyhow, me and Rachael took the two grandmothers to dinner at Rachael's favorite Russian restaurant in Brighton Beach Wednesday night, and they started comparing stories of the good old days and how things are so terrible now, not like when they were kids, and what it was like to come to New York, Abuela from Puerto Rico, Rachael's grandmother from Israel, and by dessert they were like sisters. It was hilarious. Rachael and I could've left the restaurant, and they wouldn't have even noticed. They had lunch together on Thursday at Abuela's favorite Cuban place in Carroll Gardens, and that's now a thing with them to have Thursday lunch. So Abuela's gonna be in the procession and the hard part's gonna be getting the two of them to talk to anyone *else* at the wedding."

"That's great, Grullon, I'm glad that worked out." Kiernan finished the knish and spotted Basia coming into the park. Unlike Kiernan and Grullon, the archivist was dressed the same as usual: a T-shirt with a Keith Haring drawing on it, ripped jeans, and Chelsea boots. She'd apparently spent the night and/or morning playing with dyes, as her hair was now fuschia, and she'd switched to a ruby nose stud.

Without preamble, Basia asked Kiernan, "Any new news?"

Kiernan shook her head. "Nope. Just what Ortega and Vinny got from Cornwell. Which ain't nothin', at least."

"I'm sorry there isn't any more than that." She put a hand on Kiernan's shoulder.

"Thanks, Basia." Her phone buzzed so she looked at it. "That's Ortega. He and Vinny are walkin' over—should be here in ten."

Sitting down on the other side of Kiernan from Grullon, Basia said, "I can't believe how hot it is after yesterday."

"Oh, come *on*, Basia," Kiernan said. "You scored major points by not asking me how I'm doing, but you just blew them by talking about the fucking *weather*."

Defensively, Basia said, "I wasn't making small talk! Honest! I really and truly can't believe how hot it is! Especially after how cold it was yesterday."

"All right, all right, I'm sorry," Kiernan said, putting a hand on Basia's thigh.

"Please, you have nothing to apologize for," Basia said, putting her hand on top of Kiernan's. "I can't imagine what you're going through right now—and I'm honestly stunned that you're this calm."

"Oh, I am *not* calm. I may *look* calm, and I may *act* calm, but I'm pretty fuckin' far from calm right now. Food helps—I've been eating like a pig for two days, I'm probably gonna gain ten pounds by the time we find Bobby. But like I just told Grullon, I'm about ready to claw out somebody's eyes."

"Food always helps," Grullon said. "Why you think I brought the knish?"

Basia pouted a bit. "You brought Rachael's knishes?"

"Just the one for Kiernan, sorry." Grullon sounded a bit defensive.

"Right, right, of course." Basia smiled. "Like I said, nothing to apologize for."

Ortega and Fiore arrived a minute or two later. Ortega was, of course, wearing his lucky tie, today over a blue, button-down shirt. Because it was the weekend, he wore jeans and sneakers instead of his usual khakis and shoes. Fiore was in the same suit he wore yesterday, which Kiernan pointedly did not mention out loud, as it meant Fiore had spent the night at some woman's place and hadn't been home yet. The last thing Kiernan wanted to hear about right now—or, indeed, ever—was Fiore's sex life.

"So this whole thing keeps getting weirder," Ortega said, "even by our standards."

"I don't like weird, Ortega," Kiernan said apprehensively. She wasn't sure how much more she could take.

"Yeah, but it kinda comes with the territory."

"No shit. What is it?"

"When we got back from talking to Cornwell, I got a call from the sergeant who was the watch commander on the overnight tour at the One-Seven last night. He said that all the usual junkie hangouts were ghost towns. So Vinny and I called a few other people today, and it's the same thing all over the east side of Manhattan, in Long Island City in Queens, and in a few spots uptown: a buncha junkies are just *gone*."

Kiernan frowned. "You're right, that is weird."

"But it makes sense," Basia said. "Remember what I was saying the other day about *qi*? A really strong magic-user can use the *qi* of other people to help power a spell."

Nodding, Kiernan said, "And who better to use than a bunch of junkies no one will miss?"

"Right."

Ortega's phone buzzed. He looked at the display. "It's Abajian from Narcotics." He accepted the call and put the phone to his ear. "This is Ortega, what's up, Abajian? … I don't like bad news on a Saturday, Sergeant … Fuck, she did what? … Dammit … All right, thanks."

Kiernan was practically vibrating. "Don't tell me those fuckers in Narcotics lost Stephanie Taylor."

"Fine, I won't tell you," Ortega said dryly. Then he quickly held up both hands and said, "All right, don't go giving me your grandmother's evil eye! I was kidding anyhow. Yes, Narcotics lost Taylor."

Kiernan hadn't even realized that she'd been warming up Nonna's look.

Grullon asked, "Wasn't the whole point of giving her that fancy lipstick mic that we *wouldn't* lose her?"

"Yeah," Kiernan said, "it's also got a GPS."

With a sigh, Ortega said, "Which is only useful if she's actually carrying it. She left it in the bathroom and slipped away. Abajian's people only found out when Jack Taylor came running out of the building, crying."

"Fuck fuck *fuck*!" Kiernan cried.

"Yeah, that sums it up," Grullon said.

"Shit," Kiernan then said, as something occurred to her. "Basia, you said Ohlmeyer could be using junkies for the ritual?"

"Possibly?"

"The magic he put into the drugs lately, I'm wondering if that same magic could be used to compel the people who take it to do his bidding."

Basia put a finger to her chin. "It's certainly possible."

"And we know that Ohlmeyer knows that we did a deal with the Taylors, so he may've specifically told her to leave her wire behind. Dammit!" She turned to Ortega. "We sure that this supermarket is where it's going down?"

"No," Ortega said, "but we've got a few hours to kill before the moon comes up, and there's a fast-food joint right across the street where you and Grullon can do surveillance."

"I can go, too," Basia said.

Ortega said, "Absolutely not" at the same time that Kiernan said, "Fuck no."

Kiernan put her hands on the archivist's shoulders. "Basia, I love you, but you're a civilian, and I don't want you anywhere fuckin' near Harlem while this is goin' on. Keep your phone charged and handy, 'cause we're for damn sure gonna need to talk to you at some point today, but you're consulting from a distance."

Basia just stared at her. "I want to help, Domenica."

"You've been a big, fuckin' help. And you'll keep bein' a help the way you always are, with that brain'a yours."

"Fine." Basia didn't sound happy, but Kiernan didn't care. She wasn't letting any more innocents get hurt if she could help it.

Turning to Ortega, she said, "So Grullon and I'll sit at the fast-food place until we confirm that Ohlmeyer's doing his thing there, and then we put on those amulet thingies you got from Cornwell—where are they, anyhow?"

"In the safe," Fiore said.

"Good." On the Gitaus' recommendation, SCU had obtained a Sorceror's Safe for storing magical items. It didn't neutralize the items, just contained them—the same way a lead container did with something radioactive. The lead doesn't make the object any less radioactive, but it does keep the effects of the radiation from spreading beyond the container.

"Also," Ortega said, "you are absolutely *not* putting one of those things Cornwell gave us on."

"Why the fuck not?" Kiernan asked angrily. "My fucking *kid*'s probably in there!

"Because your fucking kid's probably in there. And are you really gonna insult my intelligence by trying to convince me that you'll be rational and smart if you go in?"

Kiernan opened and closed her mouth several times. "Dammit."

"So who's going in with me?" Grullon asked.

"I guess me," Fiore said, "since Grandpa over here ain't gonna do it." Before Ortega could reply, he held up a hand. "I know, I know, 'Kiss my ass.' "

"I got a better idea," Grullon said. "No offense, Vinny, but you're not who I want next to me in a firefight." He smiled. "I've seen your range scores."

Shrugging, Fiore said, "I'm a lover, not a fighter."

Kiernan rolled her eyes.

"We should ask Umali," Grullon said.

"No," Kiernan said emphatically.

"I trust her," Grullon said. "She saved my ass yesterday. Hell, she saved *all* our asses. If it wasn't for her, the domovoy would've gotten away again, and he probably would've broke my neck while he was doing it."

"Hell," Fiore said, "she was the one who found out that those ESU dumbshits had loaded regular rounds instead of silver ones."

"And she's a black belt, plus she's a crack shot—I checked her range scores, too," Grullon said.

Ortega regarded Kiernan with his eyebrows raised. "What do you say?"

For several seconds, Kiernan thought about it. Umali was a good police, she wouldn't argue that, but would she go along with their rogue investigation?

"All right," she finally said, "I'll call her and ask for a meet-up. If she goes for it, I'll take her to 125th and meet up with Grullon. If she doesn't go for it, we'll have to hope like fuck she doesn't tattle to Hawk and the Major before we rescue Bobby."

Ortega was wincing. "I'm not sure you're the right one to—"

"C'mon, Ortega, you've seen her. She worships the fuckin' water I walk on. I'll be able to talk her into it."

"But—"

"And she's a mother. She'll get it."

For a second, it looked like Ortega was going to argue, but then he looked right at her and she stared, unblinking, back at him.

"You won the last one, Ortega, but I ain't lettin' you win this one. If I can't fight for Bobby, then I damn well will choose who does." She glanced at Grullon and Fiore. "And Umali really is the best bet. No offense, Vinny."

"Shit, none taken. I'd want her at my back any day'a the week and twice on Sunday."

Nodding, Ortega said, "All right, fine. Vinny and I have to get back to the house—we're supposed to be bringing pizza for all the uniforms."

Kiernan got up. "I'll let you know what Umali says."

Ortega completely surprised her by stepping close and giving her a hug. "Be strong, Domenica," he whispered.

"Trying my best, Luis," she whispered back.

"I'm here if you need to rant and rave again."

"Thanks."

They broke the embrace and Kiernan dredged up a ragged smile.

Basia also stood up. "I'll—I'll go home, I guess. Hey, Luis?"

"Yeah?"

"Can I walk you and Vinny back to HQ? I want to know what Amanda Cornwell is like. I'm a *huge* fan of her books."

"Sure, if you want," Ortega said neutrally.

Fiore smiled. "If you're a fan, you may not wanna hear it. She was an absolute bitch on wheels."

The three of them exited the park.

Grullon stood up and said, “I guess I’d better get up to 125th and hope they don’t mind me sitting at the same table for hours.”

“I’d be stunned if they even notice,” Kiernan said. And even if they do, it’s not like loitering is a thing people enforce, most’a the time.”

“Yeah.” He also hugged her. “See you soon.” He broke off the embrace and headed for Fifth Avenue.

“Hey, thank Rachael for me! The knish was fabulous!”

Grullon gave a wave in response as he continued out of the park.

Kiernan took out her phone and pulled Umali out of her contacts.

She answered on the first ring. “Kiernan? Is there news about Bobby?”

“Yes and no. We don’t got him back yet, but—” She took a breath. “I need to talk to you about something—mother to mother.”

“I just dropped off Liza for a playdate with a neighbor and I was gonna get some lunch.”

“Sounds good—I’m starving.”

TWENTY-THREE

Umali's first thought when Kiernan accepted her invitation to lunch was gratitude. She hadn't had the courage to ask Kiernan out for a one-on-one meal, though she'd wanted to do it pretty much since the Rosario case. The whole squad had shared meals in the house more than once since she'd joined the unit a little over a week ago, but that was it.

Right now, though, it wasn't nearly so much about getting to have lunch with one of her NYPD idols as it was being able to be there for her colleague during this overwhelmingly shitty time.

She'd almost canceled Liza's playdate this morning out of fear of her safety in light of Bobby's kidnapping. That fear was completely ridiculous from her perspective as a cop, and absolutely one hundred percent real from her perspective as a mother. However, the cop won, especially when Liza started carrying on about how much she was looking forward to seeing Kawtha and Kahini, the twin girls from her class who lived around the corner.

She and Kiernan agreed to meet at the vegetarian café on Dyckman Street. "I'm not vegetarian," she'd explained to Kiernan, "but the wraps are *fabulous*."

When Kiernan arrived and sat across from her, Umali was at once concerned and impressed. Kiernan looked a lot more put-together than she expected for someone whose son was missing. But she didn't look by any stretch of the imagination *good.* Wisps of her dark hair were flying out in all directions, and though Kiernan had proven to be a very neat eater in Umali's limited experience, today Umali could see food stains on the snow-leopard T-shirt she wore.

What really struck Umali was how Kiernan had walked into the restaurant. Umali had four inches on Kiernan and was in superb physical shape. Yet every time they'd walked somewhere together, Umali had had to struggle to keep up with the other woman's fast pace. She normally walked with purpose, head slightly leaned forward.

Today, though, she entered the restaurant standing straighter and stepping hesitantly, almost as if she wasn't sure where to put her feet.

It was heartbreaking.

As soon as she sat down, the server came over with menus, but Kiernan refused, having looked at it on her phone on the way up. They both ordered.

Then Kiernan told Umali what the rest of the squad had been doing for the last thirty-six hours, interrupted only by the server bringing their drinks and a basket of bread and butter, and Kiernan eating every piece of bread in the basket.

Kiernan finished just as Umali's avocado and mushroom wrap and Kiernan's eggplant parmigiano wrap arrived.

"I—" Umali found herself unable to find words.

"I get this is a lot," Kiernan said before biting into her wrap.

"That's a *huge* understatement." Umali shook her head. "I can't believe you're doing this without reading in the Major and Hawk."

"We have to," Kiernan said while chewing. "Ohlmeyer—"

"Isn't a super-villain!" Umali realized she was yelling and looked around guiltily.

After swallowing, Kiernan said, "He kinda is, actually. You saw what he did to Hertweck and Jake the Jake's corpses. That's basically him using his superpowers." She leaned forward. "And he's got my kid."

"He *might* have your kid."

"C'mon, Umali, he put a scrying stone *in our house*, he knew about the Taylors' deal, and he's got the juice—both financially *and* magically—to pull this off. Plus he's got a library full of newly purchased Zoroastrian mythology books right before the best time to perform a ritual involving summoning Zoroastrian demons, a ritual that requires sacrificing an innocent life."

Umali frowned. "It's still all supposition."

Kiernan picked her wrap back up. "Pretty damn convincing supposition. Not enough to hold up in court, maybe, but still." She took another bite, tomato sauce dripping onto her plate, and continued to talk with her mouth full, which was both gross and out of character. "You been a detective long enough. This ain't television, where the first person the cops suspect is a fuckin' red herring. The reason why the person we suspect right off the bat *is* the person we suspect right off the bat is 'cause we're fuckin' professionals. And in all our *professional* opinions, Ohlmeyer took Bobby and is using him in general as the sacrifice for his ritual and in particular as leverage against us."

"Then you investigate it."

"Which we're doing."

"In secret!" Umali had raised her voice again. *Why am* I *the one getting nuts here when it's* her *son that's been kidnapped?*

"If we do it officially," Kiernan said, "if we let Hawk and the Major in on it, Ohlmeyer'll know. Yeah, we found the scrying stone, but he golfs with the fuckin' mayor. We gotta be under the radar." She took another bite of her lunch.

Umali's head was swimming. On the one hand, this was the detective she idolized, performing a rogue investigation. Worse, doing it with the entire rest of the squad, behind her back. She felt betrayed.

On the other hand, everything Kiernan had just said made perfect sense. One of the things she'd long admired about Kiernan was that she was what the older detectives always called "natural born police." She knew the job and she did it right. And she was still doing the job right, even though she was also doing it wrong.

She shook her head. "How can you be so calm about this?"

Kiernan half-snorted, half-barked a laugh. "You think this is calm?" She popped the last of the wrap into her mouth. "Trust me, I ain't calm. This is about the nineteenth thing I've eaten just today, and if you don't start eatin' yours pretty soon, I'm gonna eat it in one bite. And I hate avocado." She shrugged as she wiped her mouth with her napkin. "Food's how I process life. It's an Italian thing."

"Not just an Italian thing." Umali picked up her wrap and took a bite, as much to claim it as anything. It was delicious as always, and the smooth texture of the mushrooms and the rougher texture of the avocado felt so very good in her mouth and did a lot to calm her down. "So fine, I've got two questions. Why'd you freeze me out, and why approach me now?"

"Honestly? You're new. You done good so far, but it ain't even been two weeks yet. I honestly didn't know if I could trust you. Especially the way you been making goo-goo eyes at me all this time."

"That's not fair."

Kiernan nodded apologetically. "You're right, it probably isn't fair. I don't do good with being put on a pedestal. A lotta the time it just makes it easier for someone to kick it out from under you."

"I get that." Umali took another bite. "You think you can trust me now?"

"I still don't know. But Grullon and Vinny vouched for you after you guys took down the domovoy yesterday, and I trust *them*. And, again, *it's my kid*. If Ohlmeyer really is doin' this at the abandoned supermarket, we can only send two people in with Cornwell's charms. Grullon's one, and much as I really really really wanna go in there to rescue Bobby, the other person can't be me."

Umali was heartened to see that Kiernan had the presence of mind to understand that.

"Ortega, God love him, would probably break a hip if he went in there, and Vinny ain't exactly Mr. Calm and Cool, plus he can't shoot worth shit. They're both great detectives, don't get me wrong, but they ain't right for this. And we can't bring in ESU 'cause we can't do this through channels as long as Ohlmeyer's got Bobby."

While Kiernan was talking, Umali finished her wrap. She was torn as to whether or not she wanted dessert. Though she had a feeling that Kiernan was going to want some.

Kiernan continued, "And then we got you. You *can* shoot worth shit, you actually showed up ESU yesterday, which was fuckin' fabulous, by the way, *and* you're a black belt."

Umali was only able to bask in Kiernan's praise for a second. "Being a black belt—"

Before she could finish, Kiernan held up a hand. "I know, I know, it don't automatically make you Bruce Lee. But I do know from Bobby's karate training that it makes you more aware of your surroundings and more confident in stressful situations. Not only that, but Grullon won't shut up about how you didn't get fazed even a little by watchin' Hertweck turn into chicken soup."

With a wry smile, Umali said, "Grullon also won't shut up about my driving."

"Yeah, well." Kiernan chuckled. "I'd say drivin' like a fuckin' lunatic on the FDR means you got guts, too."

The server came to the table. "Can I interest you ladies in dessert?"

"Absolutely," Kiernan said without hesitation. "Whaddaya got?"

"We've got gelato, tiramisu, cheesecake, a fruit cup, a chocolate mousse cake, and crème brûlée."

Umali sighed. With her lactose intolerance, she only had one option. "Fruit cup for me, please. And a coffee."

"Another coffee," Kiernan said, "and the mousse cake."

"Two coffees, one chocolate mousse cake, one fruit cup. Got it." The server left.

Shooting Kiernan a look, Umali asked, "Not the gelato? Given the pastries you're always bringing in, I figured you'd go for that or the tiramisu."

"I never get gelato or tiramisu in non-Italian restaurants. The gelato's just regular ice cream with delusions of grandeur, and the tiramisu's always too fuckin' dry." Kiernan regarded Umali with a very serious expression. Umali was grateful that it was that and not that evil eye she sometimes used when she was pissed. "So what's it gonna be?"

Umali blew out a very long breath. "On the one hand, I think it is absolutely batshit crazy to be doing this unofficially, and the number of things that can go wrong is a *very* high number. And a lot of those wrong things can ruin all our careers."

"And on the other hand?" Kiernan prompted.

She hesitated. The other hand, she knew, was the only one that mattered.

"If it was Liza, I'd be doing every single thing you're doing, and I'd probably be hyperventilating into a bag on top of that. So yeah, I'm in."

TWENTY-FOUR

By the time Ortega arrived at the fast-food place at four forty-five p.m. on Saturday evening, Grullon was getting well and truly frustrated.

He was sitting in the restaurant on the north side of 125th Street, at a table by the big picture window, looking out onto the thoroughfare. As promised, it was directly across the street from the abandoned supermarket. Grullon had arrived at around twelve-fifty and had had a meal of soggy fried chicken and limp French fries, accompanied by a large soda in a refillable cup.

The supermarket across the street certainly *looked* abandoned. The windows were all opaque, a metal grate had been lowered to cover the front door and was padlocked shut, and there was no sign of life or light from inside.

For hours, he'd sat there, watching people go by, watching cars jockey for position, watching buses have to go around the cars that were illegally parked in the bus lane, watching delivery bikers weave around cars, buses, and pedestrians. At one point, he'd been worried that he'd have to break up a fight, as a delivery biker nearly ran over someone on a rented scooter, but the two moved on without confrontation, thankfully.

Kiernan had texted him at around one-fifteen:

> Umali's in. We'll head down soon.

They hadn't shown up until almost three. Their arrival had prompted Grullon to get up, say, "Thank *God*, I've had to pee for an hour," and dash to the restroom.

Once he'd relieved himself, they'd explained their tardiness: Umali had had to arrange childcare for Liza, the A train was running slow due to weekend track work, and then they'd checked 124th Street to make sure there wasn't a back way into the supermarket. There wasn't; the rear of the supermarket was completely occluded by a huge apartment building for senior citizens, which had its own security. That building had gone up a year earlier, replacing a parking lot, and completely blocked the supermarket's loading dock and basement access.

For the next two hours, the three of them watched the place. Nothing happened. Grullon was grateful that he could take regular bathroom breaks, since he'd been making full use of the refillable soda cup.

"I think," he said at one point, "I've had more Cherry Coke in the last three hours than I've had in the last three years."

Having Umali and Kiernan present also had meant he could take a break to call Rachael.

Kiernan had spent the entire time practically vibrating in her seat. After a while, she had ordered what the menu advertised as a family meal and devoured it all by herself.

The tension was relieved a bit when Ortega showed up, carrying the two charms in a canvas bag with the NYPD logo on it, which he dropped on the linoleum floor with a heavy thud. "Vinny's running an errand," he said as he took a seat next to Grullon.

"The Taotie?" Umali asked.

Shaking his head, Ortega replied, "No, something for this. He didn't say what. Any movement here?"

"Nothing," Grullon said. "I'm about ready to jump out of my skin."

"Me, too," Kiernan said with a snort, "but that's been my natural state for two days."

Grullon nodded. "Yeah. Well, anyhow, I've been sitting here all afternoon, mainlining Cherry Coke, and I can safely say that nothing's going on there."

"Not nothing," Kiernan said. "People walk by all the time, but when they go past the supermarket, they're on the far side of the sidewalk, right on the edge of walkin' in the street. And that's *only* in front of the supermarket that people are doing that, not in front of the nail salon on the left or the cell phone store on the right. Not only that but look at the wall."

"What about it?" Grullon asked.

"It's a long, empty wall," Umali said. "So what?"

"Yeah, empty." Kiernan pointed at the wall. "Not just empty, but clean, with no sign that anyone's ever been up against it. And no graffiti. Place has been abandoned for five years and you're tellin' me nobody's tagged it? And not a single homeless person has set up there?"

Ortega whistled appreciatively. "Those really *are* powerful wards."

Shaking his head, Grullon said, "Damn. Been sitting here for *hours* and I didn't pick that up."

Umali chuckled. "All that Cherry Coke has affected your brain, obviously."

"Yeah, what's your excuse?" Grullon asked with a chuckle.

Shrugging, Umali said, "Insufficient lactose?"

"By the way, I checked in with the One-Seven, the One-Nine, the Two-Three, and the One-One-Four," Ortega said, referring to the three precincts that covered the east side of Manhattan between 30th and 116th Streets and to the precinct that included Long Island City in Queens. "Nobody's seen any of the usual junkie crowd around today. According to Sergeant Woodward in LIC, there's a homeless encampment in Queensboro Plaza that's missing a mess of its usuals."

"That's where Ohlmeyer's dealers work?" Umali said.

Ortega nodded. "A good chunk of 'em, yeah."

Finally Fiore showed up. Grullon knew that when this was all over, Fiore was going to invite him out for drinks and tell him *all about* last night. He'd been forbidden from discussing his off-duty sexual exploits in the squad room by every woman who worked there, and the other men weren't interested, either. So Fiore had latched onto Grullon when he'd arrived in the unit six months ago. Grullon allowed Fiore to carry on about his sexual encounters, mostly as a way of reminding himself that he was grateful to soon be married and not have to do crazy shit like Fiore.

"Got a present," Fiore said, holding up something that looked like the love child of a car vac and a flashlight.

Umali's eyes went wide. "Is that an IR thermal imager?"

Ortega stared at her. "A who of the what now?"

"Infrared scanner," Grullon said. "You use it the same way you use an infrared thermometer. It can detect heat signatures. ESU uses it to see if there are people inside a structure before breaching." He looked at Fiore. "Where'd you get it?"

Fiore grabbed a chair from another table—theirs only had four chairs—and squeezed in between Grullon and Ortega. "Herrera in ESU."

"How'd you swing that?" Kiernan asked.

Grullon answered. "We were with Herrera's team on the domovoy takedown yesterday."

Grinning, Fiore added, "And he's *real* grateful to SCU, since if we hadn't'a saved his ass and caught the domovoy—"

Raising an eyebrow, Umali said, "'We'?"

"Yeah, 'we,' you saw him and kicked him, I shot him. We."

Umali snorted. "You *barely* shot him—but fine, whatever."

"Anyhow, *we* kept his squad from havin' egg on their faces, so he was totally happy to lend us this, no questions asked."

"Good," Kiernan said, "'cause I don't wanna answer those questions yet."

Fiore offered the IR imager to Kiernan. "You wanna do the honors, Dom?"

Grullon tensed a bit. If she saw people in there, she might try to do something stupid. But then he reminded himself that, as long as she wasn't wearing one of Cornwell's charms, she wouldn't be *able* to do anything stupid.

However, Kiernan, after almost snatching the scanner out of Fiore's hands, let her shoulders slump. "Best not."

"I got it," Grullon said, taking the scanner and standing up. "I need to stretch my legs anyhow."

He exited the restaurant and stood for a moment on the edge of the sidewalk, waiting for the traffic to clear enough for him to cross. Once it did, he jogged across the two-way street. Upon reaching the sidewalk, he took a step up onto it—

—and found himself changing his mind about walking any further forward.

Dammit, those wards are tough. It wasn't just that Grullon had stopped, it was that he felt like he'd stopped of his own volition, even though he intellectually knew he wanted to walk up to the wall.

Psyching himself up, he tried to walk straight for the wall—

—but only made it about three-quarters of the way across the width of the sidewalk before he once again found himself changing his mind.

Sonofabitch.

Rather than risk moving any closer, he tried the IR scanner, pointing it at the supermarket wall and activating it.

Luckily, ESU had the best toys. Even from this far out, he could see deep into the supermarket. Most of the space was cold, a bit below room temperature, showing on the scanner's display in dark blues.

Then he saw a blob of yellows and reds. Focusing the scanner, he saw heads and arms protruding from parts of the blob. Overall, it looked like dozens of human-sized shapes that gave off body heat, all bunched close together.

Grullon turned and jogged back across the street, dodging one oncoming car that was coming faster down the thoroughfare than expected. He reentered the restaurant and filled the others in.

"For what it's worth," Grullon finished with a look at Kiernan, "I didn't see anybody in there who was kid-sized. I didn't have a detailed look at everyone, so I can't say for sure Bobby *isn't* there, but there wasn't any sign that he *was* there."

"We should go in," Kiernan said.

Ortega shook his head. "No. Five'll get you ten that's just a gaggle of junkies gathered from the east side and LIC. We've had eyes on the place since lunchtime and nobody's gone in. We'll keep checking that scanner thingie every ten minutes or so to see if there's a change, but *until* there's a change, we should wait."

With a small snarl, Kiernan said, "I wish you'd stop doing that."

"What, being right?" Ortega asked with a smirk.

"Yes. It's annoying."

Ortega shrugged. "So many of my wives have told me."

Fiore and Ortega went to get some food while Grullon took another bathroom break.

As the sun started to set, around six-thirty, Grullon went out to use the IR scanner again. But before he even started to cross the street, a Lexus pulled up in front of the supermarket and Garth Ohlmeyer himself got out of the passenger side, wearing a light blue, button-down shirt, dark gray slacks, and leather shoes. The Lexus drove off and Ohlmeyer walked calmly up to the metal grate, unlocked the padlock with a key, then pushed a button on a remote on the same keychain, which slowly and loudly raised the grate. Once the grate finished its climb, he went inside. To Grullon's relief, he didn't lower the metal barrier, probably expecting the wards to be sufficient.

Grullon dashed back inside the restaurant.

Kiernan immediately asked, "Why didn't you check the scanner?"

"Didn't want to risk Ohlmeyer making me."

"Good idea," Ortega said before Kiernan could object. "Besides, this is what we were waiting for." Heaving the canvas bag up from the floor onto the table, he pulled out, not just the two charms, but also a radio and several earpieces. He handed two of the latter to Umali and Grullon. "Put those in."

"I'm guessing," Umali said, "that this isn't on NYPD frequencies?"

"You guess correctly," Ortega said.

Kiernan was shaking her head. "Didn't Basia say wards this strong are like a Faraday cage? The radio probably won't work."

Ortega shrugged. "'Probably' ain't 'won't.' It's worth a shot to be able to stay in contact."

"I guess."

Grullon grabbed one of the charms. The chain was attached to one of the short ends of the box. He hung it around his neck and when he let go, felt the chain dig into the back of his neck. "This thing ain't light."

Fiore said, "Make sure the chain's touchin' your skin, otherwise it won't work."

Nodding, Grullon adjusted the chain so it was under the collar of his polo shirt.

Umali was making sure the chain was under the neckline of her plain blue T-shirt. "I think I'm gonna recommend to Sensei that he make people wear these during their belt promotions."

Everyone also put in an earpiece, then tested them. Once they confirmed that everyone could hear everyone else, Grullon and Umali hit the street.

After they crossed, Grullon took a breath. "Moment of truth," he said as he stepped onto the sidewalk—

—and had no trouble walking forward to the door.

"Wow, I didn't even feel anything."

Umali glanced at him. "You expected to?"

"When I hit the wards before, I kept finding myself just deciding not to move forward or go toward the supermarket. But this time I didn't feel anything, and my decision stayed the same."

"Let's hope the rest of this is just as easy," Umali said. "Making entry." She opened the glass door, which was covered in dust and grime. "Ortega, you copy?"

There was complete silence over the earpiece, save for a bit of low-level crackling static.

Grullon shook his head. "We knew they probably wouldn't work through the wards."

Once they were inside the darkened space and out of sight of the sidewalk, they each took out their department-issue Glocks. The front of the store was a series of register stations, with conveyer belts and barcode scanners, like pretty much every supermarket everywhere, all covered in a thin layer of dust. Past the registers were aisles divided by shelves, which were covered with tarpaulins. Off to the side was a row of nested metal shopping carts.

There was a light source at the back, in the far corner. Grullon whispered, "That's where I saw the heat signatures."

He and Umali moved slowly and carefully through the supermarket. As they got closer to the light, it was clear that while most of the place hadn't been maintained in the five years since the store had shut down, the back corner had had some attention paid to it. A bunch of shelves had been removed and there was wiring visible along the back wall that indicated that a refrigerator or freezer unit had once stood there.

Taking up a position behind one of the tarp-covered shelves, Grullon surveyed the cleared-out area. Umali did the same behind a different shelf.

Sitting against the back and side walls were around forty or fifty people of varying enthnicities, all sitting cross-legged in the exact same manner, all staring straight ahead with their mouths hanging open. Some were well dressed, while others wore raggedy, unlaundered clothes. Even from this distance, Grullon could tell that a few hadn't had a shower in recent memory.

They were all in the exact same position, all staring blankly ahead in the same direction. It was creepy as hell.

Grullon spotted Stephanie Taylor among those seated on the floor, which, at the very least, confirmed their theory about what had happened to her.

In the center of the open space was a waist-high platform that had a maroon sheet decorated with weird symbols draped over it. The supine and sleeping form of Bobby Kiernan lay atop it. From where Grullon had been standing earlier with the IR scanner, the dais had been concealed by the cluster of people, which was why he hadn't been able to make it out.

Grullon felt both elation and anger, the former at finally finding the missing child, the latter at the fact that the poor kid was probably drugged to the gills and about to be part of a nasty-ass ritual that was not going to end well for him.

He noticed a set of swinging double doors that probably led to the now-blocked loading dock. Grullon could see movement back there. He pointed at the door, Umali nodded, and they started to work their way toward it.

As soon as they stepped out from behind the shelves, however, Grullon found himself unable to move.

He couldn't turn his head or even shift his eyes, so he couldn't tell if the same was happening to Umali. But she didn't make a sound or move into his line of sight, so he had to assume she was frozen in place as well.

Amazingly, he could still breathe, but only short breaths in or out.

This is not good.

One of the two doors swung open slowly, with a figure backing into it to open it. The figure turned around to reveal that it was Garth Ohlmeyer, dressed as he had been outside, carrying a brass bowl. Grullon noticed a dagger in a small scabbard, looped around Ohlmeyer's belt. The dagger's handle was either gold or brass and had a large ruby embedded in it.

Placing the bowl on the platform near Bobby's feet, Ohlmeyer looked directly at Grullon. "Well well well. I'm impressed. You two are, presumably, with the Supernatural Crimes Unit? Don't bother trying to respond, you can neither speak nor move. I'm guessing those things around your neck are what enabled you to get through my wards without my even noticing. A pity for you about my other little security measure. I put it there to keep my customers here from leaving, but of course it works just as well to keep nosy detectives out." He let out a very dramatic sigh. "I kept telling both the mayor and the commissioner that forming this unit was a *terrible* idea. For your sake, it's a pity they didn't listen."

Grullon summoned up all his willpower, trying to push past the spell or whatever it was that Ohlmeyer had done to them.

He didn't budge. He couldn't even blink and his eyes were starting to feel dry and gunky.

Ohlmeyer approached the pair of detectives. "Fascinating. You're a lycanthrope."

Now panic—or, rather, *more* panic—suffused Grullon's unmoving person. *How the hell did he know that?*

He answered his own question: *If a vampire can smell it on me, surely one of the five most powerful Gandalfs in the world can, too.*

"A young one, by the looks of it," Ohlmeyer continued. "I still have a few minutes before moonrise and the summoning may commence. I'll be right back." He smiled wryly. "Don't go anywhere." He turned and walked back through the swinging double doors.

Eyes and mouth getting progressively drier, several thoughts barreled through Grullon's head at the same time:

What did he mean by "a young one"?

I hope Umali's okay.

I wish I could see anything besides what's right in front of me.

I wish I could contact the others and call in a 10-13. At this point, rogue investigation be damned, they had to call in as officers in distress. Not only had they been effectively kidnapped, they'd also found a missing child. Said child was the leverage forcing them into a rogue investigation, so that cat was out of the proverbial bag anyhow. They needed backup.

Ohlmeyer returned, holding a Durian fruit, a purple-leafed flower, some black powder, a mortar, a kitchen knife, and a lighter.

Well, this can't be good, Grullon thought, and not just because Durian fruit smelled *horrible*.

"I've been preparing for this evening for a long time, you know. I'm certainly not going to let you silly detectives interfere. And you've been kind enough to give me an advantage." As he spoke, he cut a few slices of the Durian fruit—which just made it smell worse—then sliced off three petals of the purple flower. He tossed those items into the mortar, added the powder, lit it with the lighter, and started whispering.

Grullon couldn't hear exactly what Ohlmeyer was saying; the few words he caught didn't sound like English—or, for that matter, Spanish or Gaelic, the other two languages he had any facility for.

The flames had licked very high at first but were already starting to die down.

Ohlmeyer was smiling. "Alas, this won't work as long as you're immobilized."

Grullon wasn't sure what to make of that.

None of the junkies had budged. They all continued to sit cross-legged, continued to stare straight ahead, open-mouthed.

Once the flames in the mortar were almost completely out, Ohlmeyer put two fingers to his temple.

Suddenly Grullon could move. The first thing he did was take a deep breath and blink several times. The second thing was glance to the side to see that Umali was indeed just as frozen as he'd been a moment before.

The third was to raise his weapon. "Don't move, Ohlmeyer!"

"Was that supposed to be funny?" Ohlmeyer asked as the fire completely died.

A familiar pain started to cascade through Grullon's body, starting from his core and working its way outward.

He'd experienced this pain twice since Van Cortlandt Park, and he was due to feel it again in two weeks' time when there was another full moon.

Which made experiencing it now something of a surprise. He could feel hair all over his body start to grow, his fingers twist and get both thinner and longer, his fingernails and toenails sharpening into claws, his jaw and nose shifting.

Grullon tried to fight it, the same way he had the first time it had happened. But unlike the night of the full moon three months ago, this time he felt his efforts bear fruit. His jaw stopped shifting and his fingers reverted to their usual shape.

Then they changed again and Grullon fought again.

"Fascinating. I wouldn't have expected you to be able to resist the change, especially since you're probably still tiresomely beholden to the moon's waxing and waning, like most young lycanthropes."

Somehow, Grullon had the presence of mind to holster his weapon. He fell to the floor as he struggled to keep his body from rearranging its mass to accommodate his wolfen form.

It was always bizarre, observing the transformation as he underwent it. The first time it had happened, it had been a Sunday, He and Kiernan had been at SCU, working, and she had had the presence of mind to get him into one of the special cells. The next time was in the dungeon that he and Rachael had had constructed in the basement of their house in Brooklyn. Grullon had been pissed at the contractors who made lewd remarks as they worked, thinking that the dungeon was for sexual purposes. Now, mid-change, he wondered if that was why he'd responded so viscerally to Valapart's club.

He stared at his hands, watching his fingers elongate and grow narrow, then thicken and shrink, back and forth. Hair grew and then fell out, like a dog shedding in the summer.

"As entertaining as it might be to see if your willpower can outlast the duration of my spell, the moonrise is upon us and the Daeva are waiting."

Again, Ohlmeyer put two fingers to his temple, and again, Grullon found himself frozen in place.

He was on his hands and knees when Ohlmeyer re-froze him, his fingers in a weird halfway point between human and wolfen. The back of his hands and his wrists were covered in hair, but his jaw felt normal. Unfortunately, he was stuck looking down at the floor, so he had no idea what Ohlmeyer was doing.

At various points over the next thirty seconds or so—though it seemed significantly longer—Grullon felt Ohlmeyer's footfalls through the old linoleum floor, heard the lighter being lit once again, and smelled something burning. He also tasted—well, *something* in the air, but couldn't place it.

And then, out of nowhere, his hands reverted to normal, the hair on his body shed, and he could move again. He was itchy as hell from all the stray hairs stuck between his clothes and his skin, but there was nothing to be done about that.

Umali was mobile also. She took a deep breath and blinked several times, but she recovered much more quickly than Grullon had, raising her Glock and saying, "Do *not* move, asshole!"

Getting to his feet, Grullon saw that the fire he'd smelled was a circle of flame that surrounded the platform where Bobby was. Ohlmeyer was standing at the base of the platform, in front of the brass bowl, arms raised, chanting something in a foreign language that was not the one he'd been speaking when he'd tried to force Grullon's transformation.

Ohlmeyer was ignoring Umali, who now said, "Put your hands down and stop talking!"

He continued to chant.

The flames were about waist height. There was no way they could get through to Ohlmeyer.

"Fuck," Umali muttered, and squeezed the trigger twice.

The rounds ricocheted off to the side as if they'd hit something in midair, right above the ring of fire.

"Um, Umali?" Grullon pointed at the immobile junkies, who remained seated, staring into space. Except now, they were staring with eyes that glowed a bright blue. The glow completely obscured their pupils and irises.

A ball of light of the same blue was forming over the bowl.

Looking back and forth, Grullon saw that the light over the bowl was expanding and brightening while the glowing eyes of the junkies got brighter and wider.

After a few seconds, he had to raise his arm to shield his eyes from the worst of the incandescence. At this point, the glow was covering the junkies' entire faces, while the ball of blue light was now twice as wide as the bowl it hovered over.

Ohlmeyer had finished his chant and was regarding the detectives with a smug smile. The brightness of the blue ball in front of him cast sinister shadows on his face.

"There's nothing you can do, Detectives. I'm protected from your persons by the ring of fire and from your bullets by the very same wards that surround this structure. Very shortly, the portal will open, and the Daeva will be released upon the world to do my bidding."

Even as Ohlmeyer spoke, Grullon watched in horror as something he could only describe as a hole opened in the space above the platform. The hole kept changing size and shape.

In the middle of the hole was a turbulent vista. Grullon could make out six figures working their way toward the portal. The figures were all roughly human shaped, but he couldn't make anything out beyond that.

"Alas, it is unstable," Ohlmeyer said as he unsheathed the dagger. The ruby twinkled in the firelight. "More power than even this collection of addicts can muster is required to stabilize it."

He walked over to Bobby.

Grullon watched helplessly as Ohlmeyer raised the dagger.

Beside him, Umali lifted the chain holding the charm around her neck over her head.

What the hell is she doing? he wondered as she took the charm in her right hand and hefted it.

She reared back and threw the charm as hard as she could toward the platform.

The metal box flew through the air, over the ring of fire, and right through the wards—as it was made to do—and struck Ohlmeyer directly on the skull.

Blood spattered as the man collapsed like a sack of potatoes.

The ring of fire died down.

The large blue light at the foot of the platform winked out.

The glow in front of the junkies' faces dimmed. The people sagged and fell over, moaning.

Grullon suddenly heard Kiernan's voice in his ear, saying, "We should try again."

Then Ortega's voice: "It hasn't even been a minute, Kiernan."

"Ortega, it's Grullon," he said, interrupting. "Ohlmeyer's down, we've got Bobby, and we stopped the ritual."

Kiernan said, "*Madonna mia*—really?"

"Really. Your son seems to be asleep or in a coma or something, but he looks okay. He's breathing normal. Umali stopped Ohlmeyer before he could do anything. We'll need multiple 10-54s," Grullon said, calling for an ambulance.

"We already radioed for backup," Ortega said, "once the lightshow started. Are we 10-80?"

Before Grullon could confirm cancellation of the backup, Umali spoke in a very shaky tone. "Um, maybe not."

Looking at her, Grullon saw that she was pointing at the platform.

Following her gesture, Grullon saw that the hole in the air was still there. It was starting to close, but not nearly as quickly as everything else had collapsed.

Several of the figures on the other side were still moving toward it.

"What's going on, Grullon?" Ortega asked over the radio.

"Not sure," Grullon said, "but we need to get everyone out of here."

"I got Bobby," Umali said.

Nodding, Grullon said, "I'll evac everyone else."

Grullon started rousing and gathering up the assorted addicts as Umali gently picked Bobby up and put his sleeping form over her shoulder in a firefighter's carry.

"I'm getting him outta here," Umali said as she ran for the exit.

"Right behind you," Grullon said as he helped one of the addicts to her feet, then added a muttered, "I hope."

The portal continued to close, but two of the figures were *very* close to the threshold.

Grullon started guiding the addicts toward the front door, but many of them were moving sluggishly, if they were moving at all.

A four-armed figure started to cross the threshold of the portal.

The building started to shake.

"C'mon, move, *move*!" Grullon said, herding the addicts toward the exit.

Plaster started to fall from the ceiling and suddenly everyone was awake and running down the empty aisles toward the front. When they got there, Grullon was relieved to see Ortega and Fiore helping guide people out the door.

A long fluorescent bulb came crashing down right in front of Grullon—followed quickly by the entire light fixture. He pushed one of the addicts out of the way just before it fell on him.

"Move your asses!" Fiore yelled.

Glancing back, Grullon saw three figures standing near the platform: the four-armed one, another with ram-like horns and huge bat wings, and a third with what looked like twelve arms.

They got everyone across the street just as the building collapsed, kicking up a ton of dust and smoke. Glowing red, white, and blue lights from NYPD and FDNY vehicles and ambulances strobed across the entire area, flickering weirdly through the haze of dust created by the implosion.

Grullon noted that four patrol cars from the 28th Precinct were blocking traffic on 125th, two each on either side of the supermarket. The addicts were being herded to the other side of the blue-and-whites. Grullon nodded in approval even though nobody was really paying attention to him.

Then he spotted Stephanie Taylor near one of the patrol officers. Squinting at the uniform's nameplate, he cried out, "Jenkins! Hold her!"

Jenkins looked at him, then pointed at Stephanie. Grullon nodded and Jenkins grabbed her. She struggled a bit, but futilely.

Three ESU trucks were heading toward their location, one from the west, two from the east.

Grullon joined the rest of the squad in front of the fast-food joint. Bobby was sitting on the restaurant's stoop, blinking heavily. Kiernan was sitting next to him, with both arms around her son. Fiore, Umali, and Ortega were standing in a semicircle around the stoop. Grullon was trying and failing not to scratch where all the wolf hairs that had grown and fallen out were sitting between his clothes and skin.

"You okay?" Fiore asked.

"Been better," was his neutral answer.

Umali stared at him. "What the *hell* did he do to you? And how the fuck are you a lycanthrope?"

Before Grullon could even start to figure out how to answer that question, Ortega said, "We don't have time to get into that. Kiernan needs to get Bobby out of here now that the cavalry has shown up. I can bullshit a reason why the four of us were here, but not her."

Nodding, Kiernan looked at her son. "Kidso, you okay to stand up?"

Sounding *incredibly* bleary, Bobby said, "I—I think so. Wha' happened?"

"I'll tell you about it on the subway."

Fiore looked around, then called out, "Hey! Amalfitano! Omondi!"

Two patrol officers came over, one Caucasian, one Black. "What's up, Vinny?" the former asked.

"Get Detective Kiernan and her son here over to the D train."

"You bet," Amalfitano said. "Let's go, Detective."

Kiernan gave Fiore a grateful look, then looked back at the rest of the squad. "Thank you, guys."

"Get your ass home, Dom," Fiore said.

Ortega shot Fiore a nasty glance. "You trust those two?"

"Amalfitano went to school with one'a my cousins and my niece. He'll do whatever I ask, trust me."

"What about his partner?"

"Omondi's a rookie, he'll follow Amalfitano's lead."

"Hope so." Ortega shook his head. "All right, we've just gotta clean up here."

Grullon shook his head. "I'm not so sure about that."

Ortega looked at him quizzically. "What do you mean?"

Umali said, "He means that Ohlmeyer got the portal open, at least for a little bit, and some of the Daeva were starting to come through when the building went down."

"You're sure it was that spell? The one Cornwell warned us about?" Ortega asked.

Nodding, Umali said, "The spell was in Arabic and mentioned all six of the Daeva: Akoman, Indra, Nanghait, Sawar, Zaris, and Tauriz."

Herrera and two other ESU sergeants, Attico and O'Malley, approached them. Behind them, the twenty-one officers under their respective commands were gathering, looking ready to do whatever needed to be done. Grullon recognized Simms, Okonta, Mota, Dominguez, and Jessup. He didn't see Annichiarico or Soo anywhere, which meant that Herrera's displeasure with Fiore's cousin and his spotter not following orders had, at the very least, benched the pair of them from field work, if not removed them from ESU altogether.

"What's the situation?" Attico, a short, broad-shouldered Black man, asked.

Before anyone could answer, what sounded like an explosion came from the rubble of the supermarket.

Grullon looked over to see a bunch of debris from the back left—where the ritual had been taking place, and where Ohlmeyer, unconscious or dead, was buried under broken plaster, sheetrock, and metal—fly straight up and outward, as if thrown by great force.

Standing in the clearing made by the violent relocation of that debris were four figures. The four-armed one, who had bright red skin. The one with the ram horns and large bat wings, who had scaly green skin. A gray-skinned giant of a man with faces on both the front and the rear of his head and horns on his back. And finally, the pale, twelve-armed figure, who was actually a ten-armed figure. The final two "arms" were actually serpents growing out of his neck.

Grullon swallowed. "Maybe they're not really arch-demons, just refugees from another dimension?"

"That," Ortega said, "would be a very welcome, if extremely unlikely, scenario."

The red-skinned one raised all four arms and cried out something.

Umali shuddered. "He just said, 'Kill them all!' in Arabic."

"Maybe don't call the Red Cross just yet," Ortega said, just as the one with the bat wings raised an arm and pointed at one of the blue-and-whites.

The car exploded a second later.

TWENTY-FIVE

Umali was learning, to her great chagrin, that the line drawings of Zoroastrian demons she'd seen in books and on the Internet when she was in college—and had also seen, more recently, in Ohlmeyer's book collection—did absolutely nothing to prepare her for how *incredibly* scary they were in person.

The three ESU squads were moving toward the rubble of the supermarket, hoping to take on the demons.

A fire truck was driving slowly down 125th toward them, even as uniformed officers surrounded the blue-and-white that was on fire, trying to put it out with extinguishers taken from other cars.

The air tasted like dust and smoke and Umali's mouth was getting dry.

Ortega looked at her. "I don't suppose any of those classes you took told you how to get rid of these four assholes?"

"Uh, no."

"Didn't think so. Get Basia on the phone, see what she can tell us."

Nodding, Umali pulled out her phone.

As she found Basia in her contacts, she saw Indra—the four-armed, red-skinned one—gesture, and suddenly Attico and three of his squad just stopped moving. Two-faced Nanghait pointed directly at Mota and Jessup and to Umali's horror, the men turned their weapons on each other. "Drop it!" each shouted.

As Basia answered the call, the two ESU officers shot each other in the chest, both falling onto their backs. Their tac gear included Kevlar vests that would blunt the damage, but at that close range, they probably both had some bruised and broken ribs at the very least.

"What's happening, Sofia?" Basia asked as Umali watched Tauriz spread his massive wings and take to the air.

"We stopped Ohlmeyer and rescued Bobby, but not before Ohlmeyer opened the portal to summon the Daeva."

"Oh no!"

"The sort-of good news is that only four of the six made it through: Indra, Tauriz, Sawar, and Nanghait."

Even as she spoke, the two serpents jutting from Sawar's neck separated and flew toward Herrera and O'Malley. At the same time, Simms and Okonta shot Sawar, and he fell to the ground, bleeding a yellowish ichor.

"More good news—they're vulnerable to gunfire. But we need a way to send them back."

"Um—I'll dig around, but off the top of my head, I haven't the first clue how to do that."

"Right now, we'll settle for a way to hold them."

"The pentagrams in the holding cells *should* do it, but I'll check."

At this point, FDNY had arrived on scene and was putting out the car fire. Tauriz pointed at the fire truck, and *it* exploded, and then Herrera and O'Malley turned on their officers and started firing.

"Shit, Sawar used his serpents to control Herrera and O'Malley—and they're still under his control, even though Sawar's down."

"Can you see the serpents?" Basia asked.

Looking around, Umali saw that the two serpents were, weirdly, swimming in the air. "Yeah."

"You have to take the serpents out."

"Hang on." She shoved her phone into her pocket and pulled out her Glock. Controlling her breathing, she took aim and shot.

One serpent spiraled toward the ground like a popped balloon. The other started flying around faster, and she was having a harder time getting a bead on it.

O'Malley, who was shooting at the ESU personnel Indra had frozen in place, suddenly lowered his M4. "What the *fuck*?" He immediately ran to the aid of the people he'd shot.

Simms and Okonta were trying to take down Tauriz, but he flew around too fast.

"Hey, Simms!" Umali shouted. "Shoot that snake in the air! That'll get Herrera back on our side!"

Simms nodded, took sight of the snake, and with well-practiced ease, shot it.

Herrera lowered his weapon, looking befuddled.

Nanghait then pointed at Simms and Okonta.

Shit, Umali thought as she watched the pair turn on each other.

She aimed her Glock at Nanghait and fired.

The bullets bounced off him.

Again, she thought, *Shit*.

Simms and Okonta had fired at each other, but while Okonta went down onto the ground, Simms had only fallen to his knees.

Pulling her phone out, Umali said, "Basia, Nanghait is bulletproof! What can we do?"

Simms was slowly getting to his feet, a snarl on his face, heading toward Okonta's prone form.

Basia answered Umali's question with a question of her own: "Regular rounds or silver ones?"

That hadn't even occurred to her. "Basia, I could kiss you." She pocketed her phone and ejected the magazine from her Glock. Letting it fall to the ground with a clatter, she reached into her back pocket, where she kept both her spare supply of regular ammo and the silver ammo that ESU had gifted her, Fiore, and Grullon.

Herrera tried to stop Simms, but the latter turned and fired his weapon at the former's chest. Herrera dropped to the pavement, wincing in pain.

Once Umali had loaded and locked her weapon, she once again took aim at Nanghait. Simms was starting to take aim at Okonta's face.

Ignoring the sandpaper that her throat had turned into, Umali swallowed, then squeezed the trigger three times, keeping herself steady from the recoil.

All three shots struck Nanghait in center mass and immediately started smoking and burning.

The demon screamed out of both mouths, his wails echoing off the buildings on 125th.

She took another shot, this time hitting it in the open mouth that faced her. The bullet went flying through and out the other mouth in a spray of ichor.

Nanghait collapsed to the ground, all five wounds smoldering.

Simms's eyes went wide, and he quickly raised his M4 upright and away from Okonta's head. "Fuck me!"

Umali looked around. Only a small handful of the two dozen ESU personnel were still standing.

Tauriz was still pointing at things and blowing them up, having now taken out two cars parked on 125th and a fire hydrant, which was sending a massive waterspout straight up into the air. Every attempt to shoot him missed.

A wolf-like creature wearing blue jeans and the tattered remains of a red polo shirt leapt into the air and bodyslammed Tauriz.

"Grullon?"

Umali was still gobsmacked by Ohlmeyer's comment that Grullon was a lycanthrope, followed by his attempt to force the transformation. Ortega had been right to shut down Umali's questions then as they had bigger fish to fry.

Now, though, the subject was on her mind again. What was especially confusing was that Ohlmeyer had said that Grullon was reliant upon the phases of the moon.

So how had he transformed just now?

An ambulance was coming down 125th toward the scene. Herrera was screaming into his radio, "2E30, tell that ambo to *stay the fuck back.* We got a monster blowing up vehicles!"

A distant, tinny voice said, "Sofia, you there?"

Having completely forgotten about Basia, Umali abashedly put the phone back to her ear. "Sorry, Basia. Nanghait's down now, too, and—uh, well, did you know Grullon was a werewolf?"

"I'm sorry?"

"Grullon is apparently a werewolf. And he's fighting Tauriz right now. As a wolf."

"O—okay. That's—that's not what I expected to hear. Um, I checked into what the pentagram in the cells can hold."

"Can it hold the Daeva?"

Basia hesitated. "Best I can do is a maybe."

Umali bit her lip. Grullon was struggling with Tauriz, who was continuing to fly around, trying and failling to shake the wolfen detective off. But at least Tauriz wasn't able to blow anything else up while he was fighting Grullon.

"I don't have a shot," one of the ESU officers said.

"No shit," Herrera said.

With a sigh, Umali asked Basia, "Just a maybe?"

"Afraid so. Extradimensional creatures are tricky. The pentagram might hold them, or we might get a rerun of the Bulgasari disaster."

"Do I want to know what the Bulgasari disaster was?" Umali asked hesitantly.

Basia said firmly, "You absolutely do not."

"Okay, then." Umali made a mental note to ask Ortega about it later.

Assuming they survived.

TWENTY-SIX

Minutes earlier, Grullon had watched in horror as the Daeva made the ESU officers turn on each other in various ways.

Even so, the cops were able to take down three of the demons. Umali herself administered the coup de grace by shooting the two-faced one with her silver rounds.

The fourth, though, was still flying around and destroying things. The firefighters and cops present were trying to contain the fires it caused while it swooped around in the air, constantly being missed by every shot thrown at it.

I need to do something. The urge was palpable, but what could he do? He was just standing on the 125th Street sidewalk, helpless, and still itching like a sonofabitch.

Then a voice in his head said, *Unleash the beast.*

Even as he thought those three words, he felt his fingers elongate, his nails sharpen.

What the hell?

He concentrated and his hands continued to change. Grullon could feel his nose recede, his jaw elongate.

Amazingly, it was happening because he wanted it to.

Did Ohlmeyer's spell unlock something?

"I know it is far too soon for you to have control of the beast."

"I said you'd have to accept the consequences of that choice. Welcome to the consequences of that choice."

"I wouldn't have expected you to be able to resist the change, especially since you're probably still tiresomely beholden to the moon's waxing and waning, like most young lycanthropes."

The few ESU officers and patrol officers who remained standing, along with the SCU detectives, were continuing to fire at the monster and continuing to miss.

Guess it's up to me.

He lifted the chain holding Cornwell's charm over his head and handed it to Ortega. "Ain't gonna need this."

Ortega nearly stumbled from the sudden weight of it. "What the hell, Grullon?" he said, his eyes wide. Grullon wondered what he looked like to Ortega.

He took a deep breath and completely let go, becoming the wolf.

It wasn't until that moment that he realized that just because he could control the change didn't mean he could control *himself.* He had hoped that a willing metamorphosis would also mean he would retain control. He was wrong.

The last thought Liam Grullon had before his body completely transformed was that he needed to stop the winged creature.

Then he was lost to a red haze of anger, fear, and a desire for vengeance.

But unlike the two times he'd changed on the night of the full moon, this time Grullon was aware of what was happening!

However, while he had awareness, he had no control.

He leapt into the air like the incredible Hulk and bodyslammed the creature.

Wind rushed through his fur and only then did Grullon realize that the transformation had trashed most of his clothes. His torso had shifted during the re-distribution of mass so that his shoulders were broader and his belly much narrower, which had destroyed his polo shirt, and the alteration in the shape of his feet had shredded his socks and shoes. His pants and underwear seemed intact, at least.

And he wasn't itching anymore.

The demon was flying around like a kite in high winds. Grullon was starting to fear for his life, but the beast that controlled him had a firm grip on the thing's arms. Which was good, as the creature bucked and flipped and spun—it seemed to be pretty strong, and though it couldn't break the beast's grip, it wasn't remotely immobilized.

The good news was that, as long as the beast had the creature's arms in its grip, the Daeva wasn't blowing up vehicles.

Then the demon flew straight up.

Oh, shit.

Wind streamed through his fur and his eyes were getting watery. The creature kept going up.

The beast looked down and Grullon was stunned to see the entirety of Manhattan, as well as large chunks of Queens, Brooklyn, the Bronx, and northeastern New Jersey laid out below him like a map.

It was getting very cold, which Grullon could feel even through the fur he was now covered in. But the wolf did not relinquish its grip—for which Grullon was grateful, as it was a *very* long way down.

The creature began to look frightened. It shook its head back and forth, trying to stab the beast with its ram horns, but the hairy thing dodged each strike.

Then the beast leaned in and tore the demon's throat out. *Are you fucking kidding me?* Green ichor splurted all over the place, getting in Grullon's eyes, snout, and mouth.

They were hovering in the air, the creature's massive wings flapping steadily, but Grullon knew that was unlikely to last much longer.

Why the hell couldn't we have done that while we were still only a few feet off the ground?

Daeva and wolf started plummetting, though not as fast as Grullon feared they would. The demon's wings were still flapping, so it was a controlled descent, sort of.

For now.

Grullon felt the beast gasping for breath. The speed of their descent was increasing and what felt like a cold wind straight out of hell slammed into his body.

Still, the wolf-thing didn't relinquish its grip. At this point, Grullon had no idea if that was good or bad.

They were diving right toward 125th Street and the crowd of police, firefighters, EMTs, and burning vehicles around what used to be an abandoned supermarket.

I love you, Rachael.

When he was a kid, Grullon had been in a car accident. He was in the back seat, not wearing a seat belt—his parents had, until that point, never enforced the rule of wearing seat belts in the back seat, even though the law in New York said that kids under sixteen had to wear them. The family car had slammed into a minivan that had stopped suddenly on the highway. Grullon had smashed face-first into the back of the driver's seat, resulting in a broken nose, two black eyes, and bruises all over his shoulders, chest, and arms.

Prior to today, he would have said that was the worst pain he'd ever experienced.

Hitting the rubble of the supermarket on 125th Street felt very much like that car accident—going very fast, then coming to a sudden, bone-jarring stop—ramped up by about a thousand percent.

Grullon and the winged demon were a tangle of limbs on top of a pile of broken sheetrock, shattered plaster, twisted metal, and cracked linoleum. Every single part of Grullon's wolfen body hurt and his primary feeling was annoyance that all five senses worked perfectly but he had no control.

He smelled the metallic odor of the green blood that was still pouring from the Daeva's ravaged throat.

He heard the blast of hoses as FDNY worked to put the fires out.

He tasted the bits of monster flesh in his mouth, which oddly had the texture of cardboard.

He felt the pain of his impact with the debris-covered ground.

And he saw several ESU officers moving toward him.

Whirling his head around, the beast looked behind him and saw the broken dais and the bleeding, bruised, and unconscious form of Garth Ohlmeyer. Grullon really thought the man needed an ambulance.

When the beast looked forward again, the ESU officers were closer. Grullon recognized only Herrera—the others were from O'Malley or Attico's squads, and he didn't know any of them.

"Don't shoot!"

While Grullon wished he'd been able to say that it was, in fact, Umali who'd spoken as she and Fiore ran up to join the ESU personnel.

"That's Grullon," she continued, "you can't shoot him."

One of the ESU guys said, "Are you shittin' me, Detective?"

"She's not," Herrera said.

Despite the pain, the wolf started to growl. Grullon concentrated and tried to will the change back, but absolutely nothing happened.

Herrera added, "But we may not have a choice, here."

"It ain't just that you can't shoot him 'cause he's a member," Fiore said. "Regular rounds won't work on him when he's all wolfy."

"We need silver rounds," Umali said. "I'll do it."

Grullon felt fear grip his heart as his fellow detective raised her Glock.

Herrera said, "Fuck that," as he lifted his taser and fired. Grullon felt the two prongs attach to his furry chest, followed immediately by the sensation that every single nerve in his body was on fire.

Then he didn't feel anything, as the world went black.

TWENTY-SEVEN

Four months ago, Ortega had been present when the werewolf had bitten Grullon. He hadn't been there when the next full moon arrived and he transformed, but Kiernan had called him to inform him that their worst fears were realized.

But Ortega had never seen the transformation—in either direction—before. The other time, Grullon had changed at home in Brooklyn, with only his fiancée to see it.

Ortega had, more than once, wondered if any of his wives would have put up with him changing into a slavering hairy beast once a month the way Rachael did. He'd come to the conclusion that Maria might have, Estella and Mayli definitely would have, and Renata and Yzabella never would have in a million years.

Seeing it now creeped him the hell out. He'd seen a lot of crazy things in his time in SCU, but all the really bizarre-ass stuff happened to civilians or perps. The only times his fellow police had been affected had been straight-up injuries, like what happened to Jiminez.

This was different. To see Grullon's entire body reorient itself into that of a six-foot-tall ambulatory wolf was—well, gross.

Once Herrera hit Grullon with the taser, the lycanthrope had collapsed onto the pile of debris that he and the bat-winged thing—Umali had called it Tauriz—had landed on.

Right before Ortega's eyes, the wolf's snout shrunk, his nose grew, his fingers shortened and fattened, his shoulders contracted, and his belly expanded. And then all the beast's hair fell out. Most of the metamorphosis was really disturbing to look at, but *that* part was hilarious. Now he lay shirtless and shoeless, surrounded by piles of reddish-brownish hair.

Ortega turned and yelled toward the ambulances that were just down the street. "Get the EMTs over here!" he shouted to both no one in particular and to everyone in the vicinity in the hopes that someone would follow the directive.

Seconds later, a bunch of EMTs arrived, checking over the various ESU officers and Grullon.

Umali said, "Someone should check on Ohlmeyer, too."

"Yeah." Ortega grabbed one of the EMTs—a dirty blonde with a round face, whose jacket had BRUNINGS stitched on the right-hand side. Beside her worked a woman with coffee-colored skin and long hair in box braids, whose name was FORDE. Pointing at Ohlmeyer's prone and bleeding form, Ortega said, "Better check him out—he's our suspect." He unslung the canvas bag from his shoulder and pulled the charm Grullon had handed him out of it. "And look for the twin to this."

Forde nodded, her braids bouncing. "You got it."

"Well, this is a mess," came a voice from behind Ortega.

He turned to see that the sergeant had arrived. "Hawk."

"I, uh—I have a few questions. Starting with, why is Grullon laying on the ground with no shirt and bare feet?"

"Short answer: he turned into a wolf."

"Full moon's not for two weeks."

"I don't get it, either."

Umali said, "Ohlmeyer did something to him, Sergeant. Tried to force the transformation. But Grullon resisted it, so Ohlmeyer gave up and went back to his crazy-ass ritual."

"So Cornwell was right?" Hawk asked.

Nodding, Umali pointed at the four demons on the ground. "He opened a portal to let the six Zoroastrian arch-demons loose, but only four got through. Grullon and I knocked him out before the other two could make it."

"And then Grullon got turned into a werewolf?" Hawkins asked.

"No, he did that on his own. We had taken down Sawar, Indra, and Nanghait, but Tauriz was still going around blowing things up—that's why we've got all these car fires and broken hydrants. Grullon turned into a wolf and attacked. Ripped Tauriz's throat out. Then Herrera had to tase him."

"Since when does he have control of it?"

"Well," Umali said, "since I didn't know he was a lycanthrope until twenty minutes ago ..."

"Yeah, me either," Fiore said.

"We can talk about that later," Ortega said quickly. He pointed at the gathering of drug addicts all herded on the sidewalk. "We got a whole mess of addicts that were being used to power the spell. Pretty sure they're all victims—and witnesses."

"They'll have to be processed, but we can let the Two-Eight do that," Hawkins said, to Ortega's relief, as they did *not* have the staff to handle that many witnesses.

"One exception," Ortega said, pointing at Jenkins, who was standing outside his still-intact blue-and-white. "Jenkins over there has Stephanie Taylor in custody. We need to handle her."

"I thought Narcotics lost her."

Somehow, Ortega wasn't surprised that Abajian had informed Hawkins. "They did."

"And why are you here? All four of you should be off-duty. Even you, Ortega, and Fiore—you're off the clock."

"The four of us were having dinner at Julia's," Ortega said, having prepared this story ahead of time. "I got a text from one of my CIs about some weirdness at this old supermarket, so we checked it out. We were just finishing dinner anyhow, and the supermarket was on the list of Ohlmeyer's properties."

"And you didn't call it in?"

"It was Dunlop," Ortega said, referring to a drunk, homeless guy who was not always reliable and who had trouble remembering what day it was most of the time. "I didn't want to call it in until I knew it was legit." He pointed at the rubble. "Then we saw the light show and called in backup. We had a couple of charms with us from Cornwell, so we thought we'd be okay."

"What charms?"

Ortega held up the charm that he'd shown to the two EMTs. "When Vinny and I met Cornwell this morning, she suggested we use these charms she had to penetrate any wards Ohlmeyer might use to protect himself."

"Two charms? Where's the other one?" Hawkins asked.

Umali said, "I, uh—I threw it at Ohlmeyer. That's, ah—that's how I knocked him out." At Hawkins's look, she quickly added, "He had a ring of fire around him, so we couldn't approach, and he put up wards that kept us from shooting him. So—so I threw the charm. I knew it would go through the wards, and it was heavy enough to do damage."

"That's—" Hawkins blinked a few times. "That's actually very clever, Sofia. Well done."

"I did fire my weapon, though," Umali said, unholstering her Glock.

"IAB will definitely need to speak to you—especially since you were off the clock." Hawkins reached into his coat pocket and pulled out a couple of evidence bags. Somehow, Ortega was not surprised that the sergeant kept evidence bags in his coat. Hawkins looked at Fiore. "Please tell me you didn't fire your weapon, too."

"I didn't fire my weapon," Fiore said. "Why?"

"I got a text from IAB wondering why you were on duty today after throwing a shot yesterday. I admit, I lost track of that in all the mess with Ohlmeyer and Domenica's son. I need your weapon, too, and you're off tomorrow."

Umali picked up a shoulder holster that Ortega hadn't even noticed off the ground. "Better take this, too—it's Grullon's."

Brunings and Forde passed nearby, wheeling a stretcher containing Ohlmeyer's unconscious form. He had an oxygen mask affixed to his face and a neck brace.

"How is he?" Ortega asked.

"In a coma," Brunings said. "Maybe subdural hematoma. We gotta get him to the hospital, stat."

Forde reached over to grab something next to Ohlmeyer—the other charm. Unlike the one Grullon had handed to Ortega, this had a blood-covered dent on it. "This what you wanted, Detective?"

"Thank you." Ortega took it and put it in his tote bag. "We also need someone to go with you, so hold on a second while—"

"We can't wait, Detective," Forde said. "We gotta get him treatment *now*."

Hawkins said, "It's okay, go ahead."

Ortega turned angrily to Hawkins. "We gotta keep him under guard and under arrest."

"No, we don't."

"What? Why the fuck not?" Ortega asked angrily as the two EMTs continued rolling Ohlmeyer to their ambulance.

Hawkins put his hands on his hips. "Because if we arrest him while he's in the hospital, then NYPD is on the hook for his medical bills. When he regains consciousness—*if* he regains consciousness—*then* we'll arrest him. Hell, Luis, right now he can't even understand Miranda."

"So, wait—we're not arresting him because it isn't in the budget?"

"*Overtime* isn't in the budget right now. What makes you think paying for that guy's hospital stay is? Besides, he's Garth Ohlmeyer, he can afford it. When he wakes up, we can arrest him for kidnapping all these people and we can probably pin the property damage made by our Zoroastrian friends here on him, too."

Ortega sighed. Intellectually, he knew Hawkins was right. Budget considerations always won out over every other argument and dictated policy most of the time. Ortega had seen that firsthand for four decades now.

But dammit, he really wanted to finally arrest that motherfucker.

Grullon came by in another stretcher, but he was conscious.

Umali and Fiore went to check on him, as did Hawkins and Ortega a second later.

"How you feeling, Liam?" Hawkins asked.

In a ragged whisper, Grullon said, "Like a giant bruise."

"You saved the day, there, Detective," Ortega said with a smile. "Nice work."

"Thanks, Ortega. Can someone call Rachael?"

Hawkins nodded. "I'll take care of it."

The EMT, a very tall man with a thick beard, and whose name was Mazur, said in a gentle voice, "I gotta get moving, Detectives."

"Go," Ortega said.

As Mazur wheeled Grullon toward an ambulance, Ortega turned to look at the tableau.

Several ESU personnel were also being wheeled off in stretchers. Others were being treated for more minor injuries. Herrera, O'Malley, and Attico were physically okay, but all three looked completely devastated.

O'Malley was shaking his head. "Can't believe I shot my own people."

"It's not your fault," Umali said. "These are powerful demons."

"And," Fiore added, "you took the fuckers down."

"Well, two of them." Attico looked at Umali. "Nice shooting on Two-Face, Detective."

"Thanks," Umali said with a nod.

O'Malley looked at Grullon, who was being loaded into an ambulance. "Didn't know you guys had a werewolf in the squad."

Fiore looked at Ortega. "We didn't, either."

Hawkins held up a hand. "We'll talk about that later. Right now, we need to get these four creatures to our house. Can we borrow one of you guys to drive them in your truck?"

The three sergeants exchanged glances. Herrera said, "All my guys are going to the hospital."

"Same here," O'Malley said.

Attico said, "My driver didn't get shot at. She'll take you." He turned around. "Hey! Fitzpatrick!"

A very tall brunette came over. "Yeah, boss?"

Pointing at the four demons, Attico said, "We gotta load these four into the Blue Meanie and get 'em over to SCU."

Nodding, Fitzpatrick said, "I'll get Imhoff and Kravchuk to help."

Ortega said, "Umali, you ride with them."

"No," Hawkins said. "You guys aren't even clocked in, and I can't authorize the OT." Ortega was about to object, but Hawkins cut him off. "I'll follow the sergeant's people to HQ and supervise putting the demons in the cells. Then I'll call the Major and we'll see about authorizing Sofia to come in tomorrow with you two, but not until the day tour starts, all right? And even if you do come in, Sofia, both you and Vinny are chained to your desks, period."

Again, Ortega was about to object, but this time it was Fiore who interrupted. "That's fine, Hawk. We should head over to Harlem Hospital and keep an eye on Grullon anyhow."

Ortega deflated. Fiore was certainly right about that.

"That's a good idea," Umali said. "On the way, Ortega can tell us when, exactly, Grullon became a werewolf."

Sighing, Ortega said, "It's not that big a deal. Him, me, and Kiernan were pursuing a werewolf in Van Cortlandt Park four months ago. The werewolf bit Grullon. He told the Major and Hawk here, then asked the four of us to keep it on the DL, which is why you two didn't know about it. So if your noses are out of joint, take it up with him." Ortega sighed. "Until tonight, it was only an issue on the night of the full moon. Now—I don't know what the hell to think."

Hawkins was looking at his phone. "Well, here's a bit of good news. Domenica just texted me—Bobby's been found!"

Ortega smiled. "How about that?"

TWENTY-EIGHT

The two officers Fiore had asked to escort Kiernan and Bobby to the 125th Street subway station on St. Nicholas Avenue stayed with them all the way to the platform, not leaving until mother and son were seated on an uptown D train.

Once the train was rattling up the tracks toward the Bronx, Kiernan started texting people to tell them that Bobby had been found, that he was all right, and was with her. She didn't provide specifics, used the passive voice, and hoped that everyone would be too busy being relieved to ask further questions.

Her first text was to Detective McLain. The next two were to the Major and Hawkins. Then Ma and Dad. Then Nonna.

Finally, she texted Tim, though not until she'd texted Roseline—the nanny had gotten a new phone with the same number after reporting the old one stolen.

Kiernan composed all those texts with her right thumb, holding the phone with the other fingers of her right hand. Her left arm was wrapped around Bobby's shoulders, holding him close. The boy was dozing, drifting in and out of sleep.

McLain texted back:

Good newss! I left msg with wknd watch cmdr to take down amber alert. Can finish papwk Mon.

The Major replied:

Thank God. Do you need more time off or you coming in Monday?

To which Kiernan typed:

Hell yes, I'm coming to work Monday. I'll come in tomorrow if you want, I'm sick to ducking death of my apartment.

With a sigh, she once again uncorrected her phone's autocorrect of "fucking." You'd think her phone would know how she spoke by now.

First the Major sent a smile emoji, then:

Understood. Hanna sends her love. See you Monday.

Ma texted seventeen heart emojis. Nonna tried calling—she hated sending texts—but Kiernan declined the call. She texted Nonna:

I'm on the D train. I'll call later, okay?

Hawkins texted:

SO glad to hear it. I'll tell Squad. I'm here with them. Looks like we finally got Ohlmeyer.

Kiernan blew out a relieved breath, grateful that she'd left the scene. If Hawkins had seen her there when he'd shown up, there'd have been hell to pay.

She looked at Bobby. "How you feeling, kidso?"

"Tired. And hungry, I feel like I haven't eaten in forever."

"How much do you remember of what happened?"

"I—" Bobby made a face. "I don't know? I mean, I remember Monique—the security guard?"

"I know Monique," Kiernan said.

Rolling his eyes, Bobby said, "Dad always forgets who she is. Anyhow, Monique called the band room. She said my pickup was here, which was weird. But sometimes Dad and Julia change things and don't tell me? So I got my stuff, and I went up front, and there was this guy I didn't know. He had a glowy thing in his hand."

"Then what?" Kiernan asked.

Bobby shrugged. "Next thing I remember is waking up on those restaurant steps next to you with all the flashing lights around. Is it really Saturday?"

"Yeah, kidso, it is." His lack of memory was actually a relief. As a cop, Kiernan was disappointed that Bobby couldn't provide many details about his kidnappers. As a mother, she was grateful that his statement would be brief and include very few traumatic recollections.

Flipping through her phone, she called up a picture of Ohlmeyer. "Was this the one who picked you up?"

Bobby stared at the picture. "No, it was a Black guy."

Figures. Since Bobby was apparently magically whammied before he could tell Monique that he didn't know the person picking him up, Kiernan had hoped that Ohlmeyer himself had done the deed. She knew the odds were slim, though, and recalled something Ortega had said back when they first started working together: *"Bosses don't do grunt work. It's why the lieutenant doesn't pick up perps and it's why the big-shot drug lords don't sling on the corner."*

Ohlmeyer probably gave a charm he magicked up to a flunky.

Her phone buzzed with a text from Roseline:

Gracias dios

This was followed by several hands-together emojis.

After sending a heart emoji to Roseline, she checked her text to Tim, which showed as having been delivered but not read yet.

She texted Roseline:

Where the fuck are Tim + Julia?

Mr. Tim fired me, so I don't know. I'm sorry.

"Fuck," Kiernan muttered.

"What is it?" Bobby asked.

For a second, Kiernan considered not telling him, then decided he was going to find out anyhow, and besides, she didn't want to lie to him. "Your father fired Roseline."

"Why?"

She quickly explained that Roseline's stolen phone had been used to set up the abduction.

"That's not fair," Bobby said when she was done. "I love Roseline. She's the best!"

"I'll talk to your father."

"Well, *that* won't help. Dad *never* listens to you. You should talk to Julia."

On the list of things Kiernan wanted to do, talking to her asshole ex's new wife was somewhere between walking barefoot on broken glass and being hit over the head repeatedly with plates.

But she loved her son, so she said, "Maybe."

When they were two stops from where they would get off, she opened a rideshare app, looking for a driver who would take them to St. Barnabas Hospital, which was only a few blocks from Kiernan's apartment. No way she was waiting for a bus, and there had been a rash of assaults and thefts in the cabs that picked people up at the train stations up and down the D and 4 lines in the Bronx, so she wasn't risking that.

Now that they were far from the scene, she needed to have Bobby checked out. She texted to a physician's assistant friend of hers, Ruth Pawlowski, hoping that the woman was on-shift at Barnabas tonight. Back when she was a patrol officer in the 48th Precinct, Kiernan had first encountered Ruth on one of her many visits to the St. Barnabas ER. On one occasion, Kiernan had saved Ruth from a perp who was high and trying to beat her to death. They'd become friends—Ruth had come to Kiernan's wedding—and since Kiernan had moved to Belmont after the divorce, they'd regularly gotten together for coffee or lunch.

The black Nissan Sentra driven by a woman named Kaela was waiting for them as they came up to street level from the subway platform. The driver was a redhead, who put down the passenger-side front window and called out, "One'a you Dominic?"

"Domenica," Kiernan said, rolling her eyes. "You're Kaela?"

"Yeah. I musta misread your name, sorry."

Once they both got into the back seat, Kiernan checked her texts. Tim *still* hadn't read hers—but Ruth had, and, thank goodness, she was working the ER tonight. She said to text her when they arrived, and she'd give Bobby a once-over as soon as she could.

Kiernan tried calling Tim. It rang four times before going to voicemail.

"You've reached the voicemail of Timothy Kiernan, Attorney-at-Law, partner at Johnson & Hauxhurst Associates. You can leave a message after the beep, text me at this number, or e-mail me at tkiernan@jha.biz. Thank you."

After the beep, Kiernan said, "I don't know where the fuck you are, Tim, but I found our kid. I'm bringin' him to St. Barnabas, then to my place. Let me know when you deign to check your fuckin' phone so I can bring him to your place." She ended the call, then let out a long breath. "Wish I knew where the hell he was."

"It's okay, Mom," Bobby said. "I'd rather sleep at your place tonight anyhow."

Part of her desperately wanted to just keep her son at her place from now on, but that was never going to happen and trying it would severely damage her case when she sued for more custody. Until she formally brought Tim back into family court, she had to play by the rules, and that meant taking Bobby back to his custodial parent ASAP.

But that wouldn't be till morning, especially with Tim not reading his texts or answering his phone.

The ride to St. Barnabas went quickly and Kaela soon dropped them at the emergency room entrance. To Kiernan's relief, Ruth was free when they arrived and took Bobby directly into the back to check him over, bypassing triage, the front desk, and the paperwork. It was a fairly quiet night in the ER, Ruth said, so Kiernan didn't feel too guilty about taking advantage of their friendship this way.

Had Ruth found anything amiss, she would have initiated the formal process of ER admission, but the boy's vitals were all strong and he showed no physical signs of trauma. She took some blood and promised to call as soon as the labs came back, but otherwise, he was free to go. Kiernan was profuse in her thanks.

As soon as they got back out onto the street, Bobby looked at her and asked, "Pizza?"

"You bet. Sauseronismush?"

"Sauseronimush!" Bobby repeated with the first smile he'd managed since being rescued.

As they walked toward Kiernan's apartment, she called their favorite pizza place, which was over on 191st Street, right by the university.

"Pugliese's," said the voice on the other end of the call.

"Hey, Joey, it's Domenica."

"Hey, good to hear from you. What's up?"

"Can you deliver a large pie with sausage, pepperoni, and mushrooms?"

"Got your kid this weekend, huh?" Joey said with a laugh. "You got it. Vito'll ring your bell in about half an hour."

"Great. Charge it to my card."

"Roger that. Take care, Domenica, and give Bobby a high-five from Joey."

She ended the call and said, "Joey said to give you a high-five."

Bobby nodded and held up his hand, which Kiernan dutifully high-fived.

The front door to her building, as usual, refused to open properly the first time, but finally they got upstairs and into her apartment.

"Can I change?" Bobby asked. "These clothes are all stinky."

"Of course."

As Bobby went back to the bedroom, she checked her phone again. Tim still hadn't seen the text. She sent him another one, this time saying that Ruth had given him a once-over at the hospital and that he was fine, pending lab results.

Bobby came out a few minutes later, now wearing a Naruto T-shirt and a fresh pair of jeans. Just the act of putting on clean clothes had seemed to brighten him, and he looked less like an exhausted kid and more like himself.

Suddenly, Kiernan found that she was completely wiped out. The adrenaline that had been pumping pretty much nonstop since the phone call from McLain Thursday night was finally wearing off, and she fell more than sat on the couch, barely able to summon the energy to grab the TV remote.

Luckily, the Yankees game was on. Bobby sat next to her, and they watched the game in comfortable silence until the pizza came.

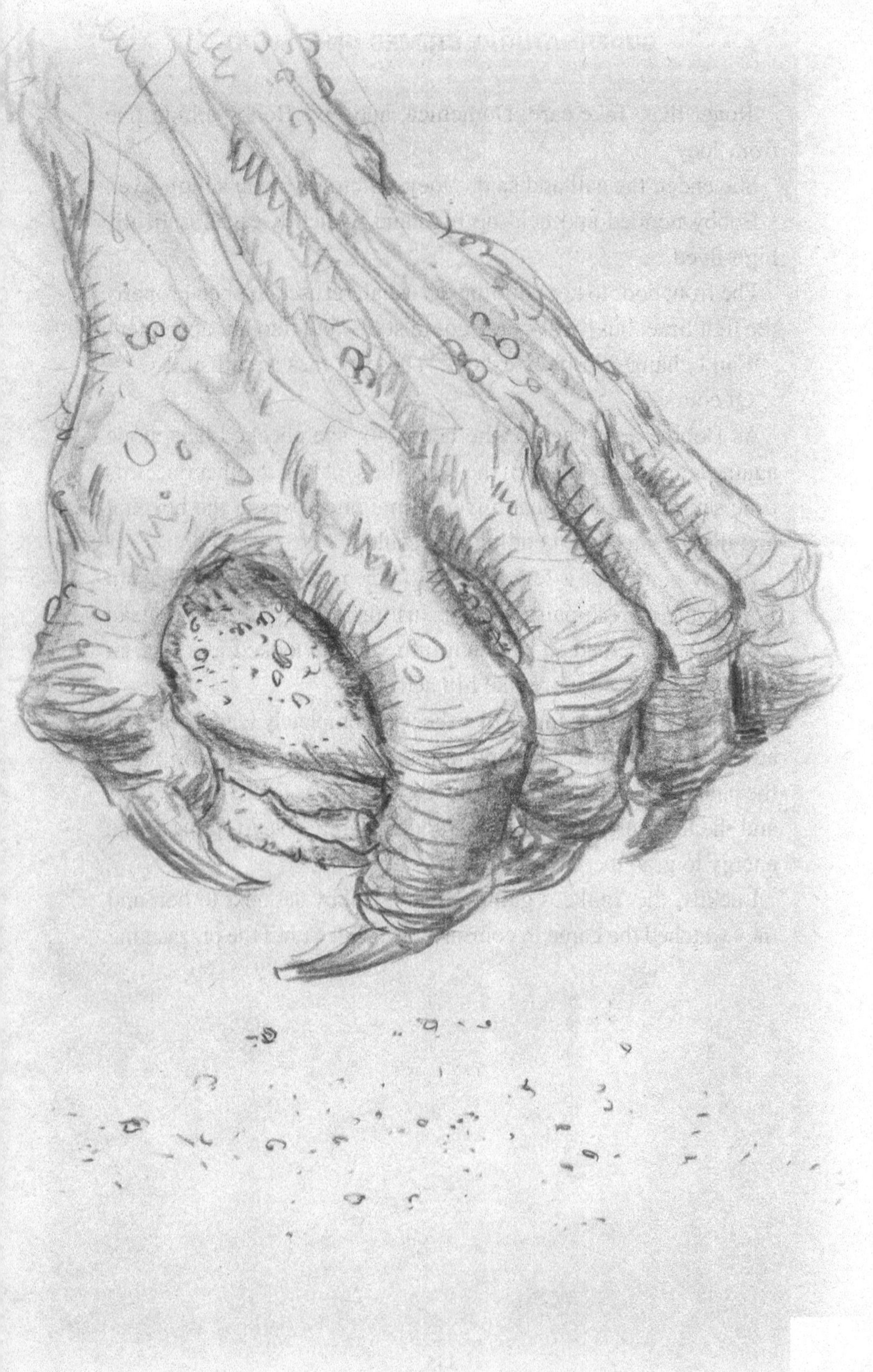

TWENTY-NINE

It was cold and raining as Umali approached SCU headquarters on Sunday morning. Her gratitude when Hawkins had texted her last night confirming she was approved to work had modulated to annoyance when she woke up and saw that it was pouring out.

Liza was still with Umali's lola, as the seven-year-old had already been asleep in her great-grandmother's guest bed by the time Umali got back from visiting Grullon in the hospital last night. Umali had woken up early, knowing that the buses would be running on the usual, too-damn-slow, Sunday schedule, and there was no train that went directly from Inwood to East Harlem.

By the time she walked the last couple of blocks from the bus stop to the house, her shoes, socks, and feet were soaked, the wind had nearly taken her umbrella away, and she was seriously regretting pushing Hawk to let her come in today.

She entered the five-digit code that unlocked the front door, opened it, then closed her umbrella, shaking out the water as she did so, and placed it in the bucket left by the door.

She was unable to properly appreciate being out of the rain, as a familiar face was bitching at the desk officer—today, that was Guillaume Laguerre, one of the uniforms assigned to SCU.

Normally, he guarded the cells, alongside two other uniforms, but all three were supposed to be off today. Umali assumed that Laguerre had probably traded tours with someone.

"I just want to see my wife!" Jack Taylor was dripping wet and looked like he'd been in the rain for ages. Umali wondered if he'd walked all the way from Williamsburg.

As Umali approached, Laguerre looked massively relieved to see her.

"What's the problem, Mr. Taylor?" she asked.

When Jack turned to look at her, she saw that his eyes were horribly bloodshot. She wondered when he'd last slept. "Detective, I understand you have Stephanie in custody. I want to see her. I also want to know why she was arrested."

"Your wife violated the terms of her plea agreement, Mr. Taylor. That means she's back on the hook for all the charges."

"That's nonsense! Ohlmeyer *did* something to her! She never would've left the mic behind if she was in her right mind!"

Slowly, Umali said, "Your—your lawyer's entitled to argue that in court. But from our point of view, she violated the agreement, and we *had* to arrest her."

Jack's shoulders slumped. "All right, fine. Dan's not working today, he said he'd meet us here tomorrow morning, before we go to court. I can't believe she just has to *sit* here all weekend." He looked at her, those bloodshot eyes pathetically pleading. "Can I *please* go up and see her?"

"Sure." Umali looked at Laguerre. "I'll take care of it."

"Thank you," Laguerre said emphatically.

She led Jack all the way up to the fourth floor, where the regular holding cells were. All were empty, except for the one where Stephanie Taylor lay on a bunk. Another uniformed officer, Gary Crowe, was sitting in a chair outside the cell, reading the same coffee-table book about 1970s and 1980s television shows and movies featuring superheroes that he'd been reading for the entire ten days that Umali had been with the unit.

When Umali and Jack Taylor arrived, Crowe put the book down on the floor, with a rather large thud, while Stephanie sat up very slowly.

"Jack?" Stephanie said. "Sweetie, is that you?"

Running up to the bars of the cell, Jack said, "It's me. How are you doing?"

Stephanie winced. "It hurts, Jack."

"What does?"

"*Everything*," she said in a very loud whisper.

Jack turned to Umali. "She needs something for the pain."

Crowe said, "We gave her ibuprofen an hour ago."

"I need something stronger," Stephanie said.

Umali shook her head. "Sorry, over-the-counter is the best we can do."

Jack's pleading look came back. "Can I sit with her, please?"

"Not in the cell," Crowe said.

"Can you get him a chair so he can sit outside the cell?" Umali asked.

Nodding, Crowe got up and moved his chair over to Jack. "Here, take this one. My butt was falling asleep anyhow."

Leaving the Taylors some privacy, knowing that Crowe would let the squad know if anything untoward happened, Umali went back downstairs.

As she reached the second floor, she met a very tall woman, with dark brown hair tied back in a ponytail, who was coming up from the ground floor. The woman was wearing a cable-knit purple sweater that matched the highlights in her hair, leggings, and cowboy boots.

Hawkins was walking toward the staircase, one hand extended. Umali wasn't surprised to see that he was the only one in the squad room, and that she'd gotten in before both Fiore and Ortega. The sergeant was dressed the same as always: perfectly fitting dress shirt with cufflinks, thin tie, neatly pressed slacks, polished shoes.

Greeting the stranger, Hawk said, "You must be Ms. Cornwell. I'm Sergeant Simeon Hawkins."

So this is Amanda Cornwell. Umali had to admit to not expecting someone so intimidatingly tall.

Cornwell looked at Hawkins's hand like it was a diseased rat, then shook it anyhow. "Sergeant."

Indicating Umali, who was shrugging out of her coat to reveal her plain red T-shirt and blue jeans, Hawkins said, "This is Detective Sofia Umali. If you'll accompany me and the detective upstairs to our conference room, Lieutenant Majorowicz is waiting for us."

Umali hadn't realized that the Major was in today, too.

Hawkins and the two women went up to the third floor and entered the nearer of the two conference rooms. Both Majorowicz and Basia were already seated at the large table. The Major was wearing his usual white, button-down shirt and rainbow suspenders over khakis, but in deference to the day of the week, had foregone his tie. Basia looked the same as always, wearing a T-shirt bearing a portrait of a man and the word REMBRANDT, ripped jeans, and Chelsea boots.

"Ms. Cornwell," the Major said, getting to his feet, "thank you for coming. I'm Lieutenant Stan Majorowicz. I'm the commander of SCU. This is our archivist, Basia Pietri."

Basia said quietly, "It's an honor, ma'am."

Cornwell barely acknowledged Basia. "I was surprised to get your summons, Lieutenant. My agreement with Detectives Ortega and Fiore was that my items would be returned to me tomorrow. I resent being forced to come here to claim my property."

"My apologies if you feel you were coerced in any way, Ms. Cornwell," the Major said. "That wasn't my intention when I asked Sergeant Hawkins to e-mail you and request your presence. Please, have a seat."

Her nostrils flaring, Cornwell waited until Hawkins sat next to the Major and Umali sat next to Basia. Then she sat at the far end of the table, as far away from the cops as possible. That, Umali recognized, was consistent with how Ortega and Fiore had described their own encounter with Cornwell.

Majorowicz also sat back down. "We'll return your items to you, though I must warn you that one is slightly damaged."

Scowling, Cornwell asked, "Oh?"

Umali raised a slightly guilty hand. "I'm afraid that's my fault, ma'am. I, uh—I threw the charm at Garth Ohlmeyer. It was the only way to stop him—he'd put a ring of fire around himself so we couldn't approach, and he surrounded himself with wards, so we couldn't shoot him. I hit him, which stopped the ritual, thankfully, and he's still in a coma, but, well, his skull dented your charm. I'm sorry."

For a few seconds, Cornwell stared at Umali.

Then she burst out laughing. "Oh, Hel's teeth, that is *perfect*! Detective Umali, I must commend you, that is both brilliant and absolutely hilarious. I was going to charge you extra for the damage, but honestly, knowing my charm was dented when it conked Garth on the head? Priceless. Brava, Detective."

"Th-thanks. I guess." In truth, while Umali was somewhat proud of getting through Ohlmeyer's wards, she wasn't happy about the outcome. Ohlmeyer was still in a coma, and he wasn't going to pay for his crimes—or even be arrested—until he woke up, and the doctors weren't sure that he ever would. She suspected that there'd be hell to pay from the DA's office, too, since Ohlmeyer's condition put a crimp in the Hudson Yards investigation.

Cornwell was now looking at Basia. "Wait—you're Basia Pietri?"

Looking suddenly *very* self-conscious, Basia said, "Um—yes?"

"You do the *Basia's Bits* podcast?"

Basia blinked three or four times. "You—you've heard my podcast?"

Umali was equally surprised, mostly because she had no idea that Basia even had a podcast.

"Absolutely!" Cornwell's face completely brightened; it was, Umali thought, a marked difference. "It's got some of the better discourse on magic and the supernatural I've heard. In fact, it's one of the few that's even tolerable. What are you doing working for *these* people?"

"I'm their archivist. I help them with the lore and make sure they know what they're facing. I'm also tech support, so I, um, fix the computers and stuff."

"Basia's a very important part of the team, Ms. Cornwell," the Major said. "That's why I asked her to come in on her day off to be part of this meeting."

"And what is this meeting about?"

Majorowicz nodded to Hawkins, who said, "Yesterday, Garth Ohlmeyer did exactly as you warned us he would do: used the power of the ley-lines charged up by the new moon and the life-force of a bunch of addicts high on his magically altered narcotics to cast a spell that opened a portal to another dimension in order to let the Daeva through."

"Hel's teeth," Cornwell muttered. "Every time I think Garth can't be a bigger jackass, he goes and raises the bar. Those six would've killed him along with everything else if they got out." She looked at Umali. "I take it you stopped him in time?"

Wincing, Umali said, "Not *quite*. Four of them got through: Nanghait, Indra, Sawar, and Tauriz."

Now Cornwell went ashen. "They were freed?"

"And stopped," Majorowicz said. "We had a lot of *very* bad injuries among our ESU personnel and among the firefighters who were too close to a fire truck that got blown up, but thank God no one was killed."

"I imagine that Sawar and Nanghait were able to make your people fire upon each other?"

The Major nodded. "But they were in full tac gear, so no fatalities, as I said."

"I'm impressed that your ESU thugs were able to take down all four of them," she said, shaking her head.

"Two of them," Hawkins said.

Shooting him a surprised look, Cornwell asked, "Who subdued the other two?"

The Major spoke in a tone that made it clear no further information would be provided. "My detectives."

Getting the hint, but not looking especially happy about it, Cornwell asked, "Where are the demons now?"

"Downstairs in our holding cells—which is where you come in."

Cornwell raised an eyebrow. "Oh?" Whatever good will had been engendered by her amusement at Umali's cleverness and her respect for Basia was gone, and she was back to being the arch, cranky person she'd been when she first walked in.

"The demons don't have any legal standing in New York. Or, frankly, on Earth. We don't have any mechanism for prosecuting them. And while we were able to subdue them, they're healing themselves, even the one who was shot in the head with a silver bullet. I'm betting that eventually they'll be back to full strength."

Looking at Basia, Cornwell said, "I assume they're in a cell with iron bars and shackles?"

"And a pentagram," Basia said.

Rolling her eyes, Cornwell said, "Please tell me that you didn't just draw a star and a circle on the floor and hope for the best?"

"No," Hawkins said, "it was inscribed by a magic-user."

"Who?"

"Judith Stein."

Cornwell's mouth twisted a bit. "You could've done a lot worse, I suppose. In any case, demons as powerful as this will be limited by the iron and the pentagram for only so long. The iron will also help retard their healing, but the effect won't last forever."

"We know that," the Major said, folding his short arms over his big chest. "That's why we asked you to come here."

"Oh? Why, exactly?"

The Major leaned back in the chair. "When someone from a foreign country commits a crime, one of the methods of dealing with it is to deport them back to their place of origin."

Once again, Cornwell started laughing, but this was a more bitter, derisive chortle compared to the pleased guffaw of earlier. "You want me to send them back to the Scythian dimension?"

"You're our only option," Hawkins said. "The magic-user who summoned them is in a coma and you're the only person as strong as him who's also local. And, honestly, there's not much else we *can* do. We have no means of providing them even the most basic care while they're incarcerated. We can't feed them, and we can't heal them, though they seem to be doing that on their own. But they need to go home."

"SCU will pay you for your time and for the spell components," the Major said with a smile. "And feel free to overcharge us. We have a pretty big budget and the bean-counters at 1PP don't understand *any* of our expense invoices, so they tend to just rubber-stamp them."

Cornwell raised an eyebrow again. "Fascinating."

"What is?" the Major asked. "Or are you just doing a Mr. Spock impersonation?"

"You, Lieutenant, are not what I expected."

"I get that a lot. So—are you willing?"

Getting to her feet, Cornwell said, "I am willing to go to your cells and observe the demons for myself before making a decision."

Majorowicz nodded. "That's completely reasonable. Detective Umali will escort you."

Umali stood up and indicated the conference room door. "Ms. Cornwell?"

Basia also got up, and the three of them walked out and to the staircase.

"Ms. Cornwell," Basia said shyly, "I don't suppose you'd be interested in being interviewed on my podcast?"

"We might be able to arrange something," Cornwell said with a nod. "My schedule is still in disarray after my trip, but your coworkers have my contact info. Send me an e-mail and we'll figure something out."

Breaking into a huge grin, Basia said, "Great! Thank you *so* much!"

The archivist turned and headed to her office.

Ortega was coming up the stairs as Umali led Cornwell down them.

"Detective Ortega," Cornwell said.

"Ms. Cornwell. Glad you could make it. We've got your charms, but I'm afraid—"

Cornwell held up a hand and gave Ortega a half-smile. "I've already been told that one of my charms was wounded in battle against Garth Ohlmeyer." Then she frowned and peered at Ortega's chest. "Is that the same tie you wore to my apartment yesterday morning?"

"It's my lucky tie."

"It would have to be, as you obviously are *not* wearing it for aesthetics."

Umali somehow held in a laugh, though she did snort a bit.

Ortega looked at Umali. "You're taking her downstairs?" After Umali nodded, Ortega sighed and said, "I don't suppose you brought any of those cookies from your grandmother?"

"Afraid not."

"I hate weekends Kiernan isn't working. There's no pastries." Another sigh, and he continued into the squad room.

As Umali led Cornwell into the basement, the latter asked, "Pastries?"

"Detective Kiernan lives in Little Italy in the Bronx and usually brings pastries to work. When I visit my lola, I usually come home with a box of ube crinkle cookies, and I bring those in sometimes, too."

"At least it's more original than a box of donuts."

The staircase down to the basement led to a very small landing. The lockup was sealed with a giant iron door, etched on the surface with runes. A video intercom and keypad were mounted next to the door. Umali pressed the red button next to the keypad, and a second later the pale, freckled face and bald head of Kevin Michaels appeared on the screen. Michaels and another uniformed officer, Joe Mitchel, were on duty in the cells.

"It's Umali," she said, "I'm coming in with a visitor."

"Cornwell agreed to it, huh?" Michaels said over the speaker. "C'mon in."

Umali entered a five-digit code—which was different from the one on the front door, and which Basia changed periodically, though never on any kind of set schedule.

There was a hissing noise, then the iron door opened inward.

"Decent security," Cornwell said, sounding begrudging, "though the door is protected only by the simplest of wards."

"Yeah, but they're what we can afford," Umali said. "The Major was right; we do have a good-sized budget. But it's not infinite, and it's hard to justify some of the ongoing ones, like renewing a set of wards."

"I hope for your sake," Cornwell said as they entered, "that no one of significant power tries to break in—or out."

"That's kinda why we want you to send the Daeva home."

The door opened onto a very narrow hallway, which contained two chairs, on which Michaels and Mitchel were sitting.

Each side of the hallway had two large iron doors, each marked with the same runes as the main door. A monitor screen beside each door showed the entirety of the inside of the specific cell.

"No windows in the doors?"

"Too risky," Umali said, which was what Hawkins had told her when she'd asked the same question on her first day. "Each of those screens can be adjusted to show a more detailed view of a particular part of the cell—every cell has a dozen cameras in it, but we mostly default to the full view. And, no, there are no blind spots, and the prisoners can't see out." She chuckled. "Apparently, Albescu hypnotized the officers who guarded him when he was first arrested, and they learned their lesson about allowing prisoners eye contact."

The two cells on the right contained the kappa who'd murdered his slime-monster roommate on City Island and the domovoy they'd subdued in Central Park two days ago. Cornwell glanced at each, dismissively, then focused on the two screens on the left.

In those two cells, the overfloor had been rolled back to reveal the large pentagrams etched into the underfloor. One screen showed Indra and Nanghait, both laying down inside the pentagram and both also shackled to the floor. Nanghait was on his stomach, likely the more comfortable position given his horned back, and the face on the back of his head could see anyhow. Indra lay on his back, his skin a lighter shade of red than usual. He had visible bullet wounds, though they were all healed over to a degree that would have taken weeks in a human. Nanghait's wounds weren't visible in the position he was in, but Umali assumed they also had probably healed some.

Cornwell stared more intently at the other screen. Tauriz also lay inside the pentagram, also on his back. His wounds were far more severe and showed very little sign of healing. By contrast, Sawar was sitting up; though he had no visible wounds, the two snakes on his neck hung limply. These two Daeva were also tethered to the floor by iron shackles.

"Fascinating," Cornwell said. "Sawar's snakes have not revived. I assume they were shot when separated from Sawar's body?"

Umali nodded.

Again Cornwell said, "Fascinating." Then she turned to Umali. "Please explain what happened to Tauriz."

Evasively, Umali asked, "What do you mean?"

"Sawar, Indra, and Nanghait were very obviously defeated by, shall we say, traditional police means? Tauriz, though, looks as if he was attacked by a wild animal. I was not aware that the NYPD employed attack wolverines." She gazed nastily at Umali. "But you may employ a lycanthrope."

"It's not my place to say—" Umali started.

Cornwell was having none of it. "If you wish me to send the Daeva back to their home dimension, you will tell me what happened to Tauriz."

Umali tried one more out. "I really should check with Lieutenant Majorowicz bef—"

Michaels interrupted. "For fuck's sake, Umali, just tell her that Grullon's a goddamn werewolf!"

Again Cornwell raised an eyebrow. "I assume Grullon is another officer assigned to this unit."

Sparing a glower at Michaels, Umali paused a moment to compose her thoughts. "Four months ago, Detective Grullon was bitten by a werewolf up in the Bronx."

"Four *months*?"

Umali nodded. "Up until yesterday, that meant he had to lock himself away every full moon. But Ohlmeyer tried to force the transformation when Grullon and I confronted him in the supermarket yesterday. Grullon resisted the change and Ohlmeyer gave up. Then later, when Tauriz was blowing up patrol cars and fire hydrants and nobody in ESU could throw a shot at him, Grullon changed on his own and took him out."

"Huh. Looks like Garth did your friend a favor. It's very rare for a werewolf to be able to effect the change inside of five or six years. Can he control the wolf?"

Shaking her head, Umali said, "I doubt it. After Tauriz went down, he was all set to go after the rest of us until Sergeant Herrera tased him."

"Hm." Cornwell seemed to stare at an indeterminate point between Umali and the two seated uniforms before saying, "Very well. Let us return upstairs and I will provide you with a list of what I will require to send the Daeva home."

Breathing a sigh of relief, Umali nodded to Michaels and Mitchel, then led Cornwell back out, using a different code to open the door from the inside.

THIRTY

Ortega spent the first hour of his Sunday in the office on the phone.

He left a message for Yvette Wood at the DA's office, informing her that Stephanie Taylor had violated the terms of her plea deal.

Then he checked in with Herrera, getting updates on the various injured personnel at Harlem Hospital. Most of the ESU folks were okay but would be out of action for a while, with broken bones—mostly ribs—and various bruises; one had a concussion. Two others, unfortunately, were in critical condition. Mota had internal injuries near his heart, and another had had a hot appendix he hadn't been aware of until it ruptured during the donnybrook. Two of the firefighters were also in comas, though the others who'd been injured were in better shape.

Best of all, Grullon was being released this morning with a completely clean bill of health. That had surprised both Ortega and Herrera—he had been pretty badly injured, and the doctors had been making noises about admitting him the previous night.

Then he called Vondelikos.

First, Ortega answered several questions the lieutenant had about the injuries sustained by the various ESU personnel. Ortega was grateful that he'd talked to Herrera first, since he could put the injuries in some kind of context.

Once he'd answered all those questions, Ortega said, "And by the way, we've got a bone to pick with you."

"Look," Vondelikos said quickly, "Soo and Annichiarico are off ESU. Soo's transferring to evidence control, and Annichiarico's putting in his papers. You don't have to worry—"

"That's not the bone—though I gotta tell you, I ain't sorry to hear that, either. No, it's that you found a vendor to supply silver ammo and didn't *tell* us about it. What the hell, Elias?"

"You're *detectives*, Luis."

"Yeah, I know that, Elias, but—"

"But nothing. The average detectives never discharge their weapons outside the range. You get some backup ammo from Moore Hill, that's great, that's all you need. ESU's entire *function* is to provide muscle for the detectives. They need quick delivery of ammo. You guys don't."

"Y'know, Elias, when the Major bitches about you, I try to defend you 'cause we've known each other so long, but I gotta tell you, right now? You're a fucking *moron*."

"Hey!"

"We are *not* average detectives! IAB's thinking about giving someone a desk here 'cause they have to come up so often to deal with police-involved shootings. Kiernan, Fiore, Grullon, and Umali *all* had to discharge their weapons in the last two weeks alone. Kiernan's gone through all six of her silvers and the new ones haven't shown up yet."

"Oh hey, I heard about her kid. He okay?"

"Yeah, he's home safe. And don't change the subject."

Vondelikos sighed. "What *is* the subject, Luis?"

"Will you please give Jurienny the information on Striker so we can requisition our ammo from them instead of Moore Hill?"

There was a lengthy pause before Vondelikos said, "My job is to facilitate between the units. I'll have Meg take care of it."

"*Thank* you."

"Take care of yourself, Luis. Hey, you finally divorced from Yzabella?"

"Not yet."

"Get a move on, willya? I got fifty bucks on you being single again by Hallowe'en."

Ortega chuckled. "Fuck you too, Elias."

With that, Ortega was finally done with the calls he needed to make from the office phone. Pulling out his cell, he found five texts. One was from Kiernan, saying she was on her way to Mamaroneck, taking Bobby back to his father's place.

The other four were from his son Ezequiel, his first two wives, Maria and Estella, and, surprisingly, his fourth wife Renata, all asking if he was okay after yesterday's events. Apparently, it had made the news, though Ortega and the others had left the scene before any press had arrived. However, his ex-wives and son all assumed, based on the look of the Daeva, that it was an SCU case.

Just because of the sheer novelty of the occurrence, he replied to Renata first:

Glad to hear from you, Rennie. I'm fine. None of our people got too badly hurt.

He replied to the others with variations on that theme. To Estella and Ezequiel he specified that Grullon had been hurt but was being let out of the hospital this morning, since they'd both met him.

Renata's reply:

You know I hate being called Rennie, right?

Ortega blinked in surprise. That had been his pet name for her. He'd had no idea that she hated it.

She continued in another text:

> But I'm glad you're okay, you stupid old man. Retire, already, will you please? You're too old for this shit.

He texted in response:

> Thank you, Danny Glover

Her reply:

> Ay ay, I'd rather you called me "Rennie."
> Take care, Luis.

Estella texted:

> Come to dinner tonight.
> I'll make pernil for you. You deserve it.

Ortega sighed and debated how to reply. He loved Estella's pernil. But he didn't want her fussing over him, which she most definitely would, probably also urging him to retire.

But he really loved her pernil.

At some point during Ortega's various phone calls, Fiore had made it in, *finally* wearing a different suit. But still a suit. He was late because he'd gone to mass first thing, and he didn't want to be haunted by all his dead female relatives by not dressing for church.

Now Fiore called out, "Hey, look who's here!"

Turning, Ortega saw Grullon and his fiancée walking up the stairs. Grullon was wearing a sweatshirt from Rachael's alma mater, Yeshiva University, jeans, and sneakers. Ortega assumed that Rachael had brought him fresh clothes when she'd picked him up from the hospital.

The Major came out of his office, and he, Hawkins, Ortega, and Fiore all went to the front to greet the returning detective.

"How you feeling, Liam?" Hawkins asked.

"Exhausted. But I'm not hurt anymore, which is *really* weird, given that I fell to the Earth like fucking Icarus. I'm not gonna stay too long, but I wanted to apologize to Vinny and to Umali. Where is she?"

"She's down at Persaud's," Ortega said. "Cornwell agreed to send the Daeva home, but she needs some spell components, so Umali went downtown to buy them."

Grullon chuckled. "She was like a kid in a candy shop when we went there Thursday."

"Yeah, she's gonna love browsing."

"Well, I'll talk to her tomorrow."

The Major asked, "Are you sure?"

Rachael said, "No," at the same time that Grullon said, "Absolutely."

With a half-smile, the Major said, "There seems to be some domestic strife on the subject."

Staring intently at her fiancé, Rachael said, "Even your boss thinks you should take tomorrow off, my love."

"Kiernan will be back on the clock tomorrow," the Major added, "so we can fade having you stay home for a day."

Rachael's stare got more intense. "Let me take care of you, please? I already defrosted the big Tupperware of chicken soup."

Grullon smiled at her. "Well, sweetness, if you feed me your magical chicken soup today, I'll be a hundred percent tomorrow, and I can come to work for sure!"

At Rachael's aggravated look in response to that comment, Ortega quickly said, "Take it from an old, divorced man, Grullon—do what she says."

"And," Majorowicz added, "if you don't want to take relationship advice from someone going through his fourth divorce, take it from a happily married man: he's right. Let her pamper you for a couple days. You've earned it."

"Fine." Grullon turned to Fiore. "Vinny, I'm really sorry. When I realized I'd been changed into a werewolf, I got all freaked out. I didn't want anyone to know. I mean, Ortega and Kiernan were there, and I had to tell Hawk and the Major, 'cause they're my supervisors, and I obviously had to tell Rachael. But they all *had* to know. Nobody else did, and I didn't want 'em to."

Fiore asked, "Even Jiminez?"

Nodding, Grullon said, "Yeah."

"Well, that's fuckin' stupid," Fiore said. "He's your best man—and your best friend. Best friends are there for shit like this."

"I know," Grullon said quietly.

Fiore went on, "But hey, I get it. We all got us some skeletons in the closet."

Ortega said vehemently, "We do *not* want to know yours, Vinny."

Everyone laughed at that, including Fiore, who then said, "Apology accepted." Then he grabbed Grullon and pulled him into a bear hug.

"Thanks, Vinny," Grullon said in a whisper.

Once the embrace broke, Grullon looked at the Major. "Valapart said something to me when I visited him the other day. He said he could teach me how to deal with this."

Fiore's eyes widened. "Wait a minute—fuckin' *Valapart* knew?"

Holding up both hands, Grullon said, "I didn't tell him! He smelled it on me!"

"Which," Rachael put in, "freaked me the hell out when Liam told me."

Shaking his head, Fiore said, "Fuckin' vampires, man."

"Anyhow," Grullon said, "while I don't trust Valapart as far as I can throw him, the idea's a good one. There's gotta be somebody actually trustworthy who can help me with this."

"Talk to the Gitaus," Hawkins said. "They'll know who to refer you to."

The Major nodded. "Good idea."

"Great. I'll send them an e-mail when I get home." Grullon took a deep breath. "All right, there's a Tupperware full of the best chicken soup in the world with my name on it in Crown Heights. Let's go, sweetness."

As the happy couple went down the stairs, Hawkins and Fiore started toward their desks.

Jerking a thumb toward his door, Majorowicz said, "Ortega? My office."

Oh, great. Ortega had gotten pretty good at reading the lieutenant's tone over the time the unit had been in existence, and the inflection of this particular "my office" did not bode well.

They entered, and the Major closed both the door and the blinds, which were more ill omens.

With a due sense of apprehension and dread, Ortega sat in one of the guest chairs.

As the Major sat down behind his desk, he asked, "So, how's your stomach?"

That was not what Ortega was expecting. "Um—my stomach's fine."

"Really? That's a surprise."

"Why?"

"Because every single time you eat at Julia's, you spend the next two days popping antacids like Tic-Tacs."

Shit.

"Plus," the Major continued, "I know that the maître d' at Julia's owes you a favor, and I expect she'd gladly commit a misdemeanor on your behalf and lie and say you were there when you weren't. Furthermore," he said loudly, before Ortega could even attempt to reply, "I've been reading the witness statements from the addicts Ohlmeyer was using to power his spell. The Two-Eight sent them over. They're pretty hilarious for the most part—one person said a giant goat kidnapped them, a couple said they were tormented by Satan himself, and three said they were put under a spell by the King of England."

"Did they say which king?"

"No, unfortunately. I was curious, too. Anyhow, lots of fun delusions from our friendly neighborhood drug addicts, but about half a dozen folks mentioned that they saw a brown-haired little boy on an altar. Yet there was not a single sign of a brown-haired little boy at the scene. And then, by a *startling* coincidence, shortly after shit went down on 125th Street, Kiernan sent out a text saying that *her* brown-haired little boy was safe with her—with no details as to *how* exactly Bobby was found."

Once he was sure that the Major was done with his rant, Ortega said, "You're absolutely right, Lieutenant. It is a *startling* coincidence."

"Mhm." Majorowicz folded his hands on his desk and leaned forward. "Anything else you want to say, Detective Ortega?"

"Is there anything else I *need* to say?" Ortega threw up his hands. "I don't know what I can add. Except this: because of the hard work of the detectives of this unit, Garth Ohlmeyer is on the hook for multiple kidnappings and opening a portal to a demon dimension. And yeah, okay, that last one isn't a formal crime on the books, at least not yet, but I'm thinking the DA's office can make a case for reckless endangerment, maybe even attempted murder. Either he stays in a coma forever, in which case good riddance, or he wakes up and we arrest him and have a party. After all the years that he's been NYPD's white whale, Ohlmeyer is *done*. And *we* did that, even though the sonofabitch put a scrying stone in our house." Ortega put significant emphasis on the scrying stone, hoping the Major would understand its importance to their rationale for a rogue investigation.

The Major was now leaning back in the chair. "Don't go taking *all* the credit, Ortega. The main reason why we nailed Ohlmeyer is the same reason why we nail most perps: he was stupid. Even the smart ones like Ohlmeyer do stupid shit sometimes, and Ohlmeyer was *incredibly* stupid this time. If he hadn't cast that spell to turn two dead bodies into goo, we wouldn't have even had a case. They just would've been two homicides that probably never would've been linked, at least not right away."

Ortega nodded. "Yeah, and by the time they did get linked, Ohlmeyer would've let the Daeva loose. But he didn't, and that really was us, no matter why we were on it in the first place."

"True." Majorowicz rested his large hands on the desk and leaned forward. "On top of that, Bobby Kiernan is home, and that's definitely something we should be celebrating. So this is the last time I'm gonna mention any issue with how you write this up."

"Thank you," Ortega said, starting to get up.

"*This* time," the Major added.

Ortega stopped halfway up and wondered if he should sit back down.

"I never want to have a conversation like this ever again, Ortega, understood? Chain of command is here for a goddamn *reason*, and if you forget that again, it's the chain I'm gonna beat you with. Now get the hell out of my office."

Nodding, Ortega rose all the way and departed the Major's office with all due haste.

Damn rookie mistake, he thought as he went to sit down at his desk. He was so busy pulling the wool over Hawk's eyes—which was about as difficult as putting on a hat—that he forgot to adjust for the fact that he also had to pull the wool over the Major's eyes. Hawkins may have been a desk jockey his whole career, but Stan Majorowicz had been a damn fine detective back in the day, and Ortega forgetting that nearly got them all in serious trouble.

Luckily, the Major was willing to forgive, *this time*, given that it had all come out okay. But if it hadn't …

If it hadn't, the Daeva would've killed everyone, probably.

He pulled out his phone and called up Estella's text.

The hell with it. After the last few days, I deserve some pernil. And after pissing off the Major, I deserve Estella bitching me out about retiring.

He sent her a text asking what time he should be there.

WE ARE HAPPY
TO SERVE YOU

THIRTY-ONE

Tim *finally* texted back some time after both mother and son had fallen asleep on the couch while watching the Yankees game. Kiernan had awakened around one a.m., having to pee. First, she'd carried Bobby to the bedroom and tucked him in, still in his clothes. He had rolled over, made a moaning noise, and wrapped his arms around Usa-chan.

While in the bathroom, she'd checked her phone, to find that Tim had texted several times after they'd fallen asleep. She'd also apparently slept through three attempts to call her.

The first text message:

> Oh, thank God. Sorry I didn't answer before, but they told us not to take any calls except ones we don't recognize, in case of a ransom. Glad he's okay and that Ruth could look him over. Can you bring him up tonight?

That was followed by:

> Hello? Domenica?
> Jesus, answer your damn phone, will you, please?
> ANSWER THE F***ING PHONE, DOMENICA!

Somehow, Kiernan had not been surprised that her ex-husband's phone censored his texts. It was probably necessary for his job, but it had amused her that he was *still* a tight-assed prude.

Julia just pointed out that you said you were going to your place, and you're probably both asleep. I hope to God she's right. We'll talk in the morning.

Her desire to let Tim twist in the wind had warred with her desire to possibly wake Tim up, and the latter won. It had been the more compassionate notion in any case: he'd likely be okay with being awakened by the reassurance that Bobby was safe.

Yeah, we fell asleep over pizza and the Yankees game. We'll come up in the morning after we both get some real rest.

She'd undressed and climbed into her futon, and had just plugged the phone in when he'd texted back:

Good. See you soon.

Bobby had insisted on taking a very long, very hot shower in the morning, and then they'd stopped at the bakery to get cappuccino for her and pastries for both of them, which they ate during the drive. Kiernan also texted everyone in the squad to let them know that she was taking Bobby back to his father.

She had taken a more circuitous route than usual on this rainy Sunday morning, as the Hutchison River Parkway was likely to be flooded in, given the weather, and finally arrived at the large house on Clafin Avenue that used to be half hers at nine-thirty.

Mother and son ran from the end of the driveway to the front door in the rain. Bobby rang the doorbell once they reached the protection of the front porch.

Tim opened the door and immediately grabbed Bobby into a hug. "Oh, thank God." After a few seconds, he broke the embrace. "You're all wet."

"You know how Mom is about umbrellas," the boy said.

Kiernan rolled her eyes. "I'm five-two, every time I use an umbrella I poke people in the eye."

Tim chuckled at that, and so did Bobby, and Kiernan found herself laughing, too. It was a stupid old argument, but it was a familiar one, and they all needed that right present.

"C'mon in," Tim said, opening the door the whole way so they could both step into the big foyer. There was a large doorway to the living room on the left, a much smaller doorway to the dining room on the right, a winding staircase that led up to the second floor, and a small hallway that went past the staircase to the kitchen. A chandelier hung from the high ceiling.

Kiernan had never liked this house, as it felt three-quarters of the way to a cheesy McMansion. But Tim loved it and had insisted on buying it when Kiernan was pregnant with Bobby. He said it was important for status in his job, plus it was in a good school district. The second argument had carried a lot more weight with Kiernan than the first one.

Whatever the problems with her shitty apartment, at least it was a *home*. This place was a trophy.

Julia was coming downstairs. "Oh, thank God you're home, baby doll."

Bobby winced at the nickname, and so did Kiernan. He'd told her he hated being called *baby doll* for years now.

But this wasn't the time to correct his stepmother. Julia gave him a big hug, which Bobby returned.

She pulled out of the embrace and put her hands on his shoulders. "Oh, let me look at you. Are you all right? What are these clothes?"

"They're what he had at my place," Kiernan said. "The kidnappers didn't give him a change of clothes, so he was still wearing what he wore to school on Thursday. I'll put 'em through the laundry and get 'em back to you."

"Maybe now," Julia said, "they'll finally release his stuff. VMPD has been holding his phone, backpack, and clarinet."

Kiernan looked at her like she was nuts. "It's evidence, Julia, of course they're holding it."

Tim said, "Go upstairs and change into something dry."

"Dad, I—"

"Just do it."

With a dramatic sigh, Bobby went upstairs.

Turning to look at Kiernan, Tim said, "I don't know why you let him wear those silly cartoon shirts."

"I don't know why you *don't*. He *likes* anime."

Tim started to say something and then stopped himself. "Never mind. Tell me—how did you find him, anyhow?"

"It's a long story, and it's part of an active investigation, so I can't really talk about it."

Putting his hands on his hips, Tim said, "You're really hiding behind *that*?"

"You really think I'm lying to you, Tim?"

Shrugging, Tim said, "It wouldn't be the first time. Like when you said you'd quit your job when Bobby was born."

Kiernan stared at him incredulously. "For the nine *thousandth* time, I never fuckin' said that! Ever! And do you *really* wanna compare lies?"

"Oh come on, when did I ever lie to you, Domenica?"

"Well, we can start with when you were fucking *her* while we were still married." She pointed at Julia.

Julia had the good grace to look embarrassed.

Tim did not. "I never lied about that. I just—never told you about it."

Clapping her hands, Kiernan said, "Well, bravo for splitting *that* hair, counselor! I—" She took a breath. "Fuck it."

"Leave it to you to ruin what should've been a happy occasion, Domenica. We should be celebrating Bobby being home."

"I didn't ruin a fuckin' thing."

"And you should've brought him home last night."

"We were both exhausted and we fell asleep on the couch. If you'd answered your fuckin' *phone* when I called or *looked* at a text …" She took another deep breath and then held up a hand. "Forget it. I'll stop ruining your fuckin' day."

She turned and went out into the rain without another word. The downpour had intensified in the few minutes since she'd arrived, and she was soaked to the skin by the time she went the twenty feet from the porch to her car.

As soon as she closed the door and settled into the driver's seat, Kiernan pounded the steering wheel and screamed incoherently for about ten seconds.

Fuck, she thought, *I didn't even get to yell at him about firing Roseline.* On thinking about it, however, she had to admit that it just would've made the nastiness nastier, because Tim was, of course, never wrong about *anything*. Bringing up Roseline would have made a brutal situation unbearable.

She started the car and headed home, driving cautiously. She was so out of sorts that she was driving on autopilot and therefore went to the Hutchison River Parkway, which was indeed flooded. The twenty-minute drive home instead took over an hour.

Once she finally made it back to Belmont, she found parking relatively easily—parking on Sunday was always a snap, as most parking restrictions didn't apply—and ran down Hughes Avenue to her building, where Sabri was struggling to open the front door.

Sabri, of course, had an umbrella.

He got the door open and held it for her. "How are you doing, Domenica?" he asked.

"I been better." Then remembering that Sabri didn't know the good news, she added, "But I also been *way* worse. I just drove Bobby back to Mamaroneck."

His entire face brightening as they approached the staircase, Sabri cried out, "They found him?"

She nodded. "Yup."

"That's fantastic, Domenica!" Sabri threw his arms up in the air like he was calling a touchdown. "Oh my goodness, that's so wonderful! We should celebrate!"

Kiernan had planned to go upstairs and sulk and maybe get an early Sunday drunk on, but Sabri's enthusiasm reminded her that she should be *happy*, dammit. She smiled as they started up the stairs. "I like that idea."

"As it happens, I'm a free agent today. Violeta is away with the basketball team—they're playing a school in Suffolk County somewhere this afternoon—and I just dropped Mimoza off at her friend Peralee's house for a playdate that should last all day."

They got to the second floor. Kiernan said, "Normally I'd say let's go somewhere, but I already been out in the rain, and I'd like to stay dry." They started up the stairs to the third floor. "How you feel about drinkin' *really* good wine before noon?"

"Depends on the wine."

"A 2010 Brunello that my uncle brought back from Italy. He told me to save it for a special occasion, and I think my kid being home safe is damn special."

"I agree. Let me just take care of a few things in my apartment—give me ten minutes?"

She nodded as they got to the third-floor landing. "That'll give me a chance to change into dry clothes."

Unlocking and entering the apartment, she went to the wine rack in the living room, grabbed Uncle Hermenegildo's Brunello and applied a corkscrew, this time without bits of cork invading the wine. Standing on her tiptoes, Kiernan got the decanter down from the cabinet over the sink and poured the wine into it. Strictly speaking, it should breathe for an hour or so, but she didn't want to take that kind of time before the celebratory drinking.

She went into the bedroom and changed. She debated what to wear, finally deciding on a tight tank top in lieu of a bra, with one of her nice, red, cable-knit sweaters over it, as well as her yoga pants. She left her feet bare.

There was a knock on the apartment door, which she was grateful for. Last time, she'd told Sabri to just come right in, but she hadn't said that this time, and he obviously didn't assume the prior consent still applied. She appreciated that.

Opening the door, she saw that Sabri had removed his ankle-length raincoat and was wearing a black turtleneck and black jeans. In one hand, he held something that looked like an oversized thimble.

"Thought you might want this," he said, offering her the object. "It's an infuser. Pour the wine through it and it has the same effect as letting it breathe for an hour or two."

"Oh, you're brilliant."

Kiernan led Sabri into the kitchen, where the decanted wine was sitting on the counter. Pulling out two large wine glasses, she took the infuser and turned it over. "How's it work?"

"Put it over the glass, wide end up, and pour. The wine comes out through the skinny end."

"Nice."

As she poured, he said, "I've become something of an oenophile since Ambra died. She was a devout Muslim, so we never had alcohol in the house."

"I take it," she said, now pouring the second glass, "that you're not so devout, since you were swozzled when I saw you Thursday night?"

Sabri nodded. "I was a teetotaler out of respect for Ambra, not respect for Islam. I saw no reason to continue to follow the teachings of a religion I don't believe in—and," he added with an infectious grin, "I really do love wine. I've focused mostly on French wines thus far, but what little I know of Italian reds is that Brunellos are superb."

"Definitely," she said, handing him a glass and holding up the other one. "To Bobby being safe."

"To Bobby," he said, and they clinked their glasses together.

Kiernan sipped the wine, which was magnificent. It was soft and lovely and coated her entire mouth like a flannel blanket that tasted like fruit.

"This is glorious," Sabri said, taking another sip. "Mmmm. Magnificent. So Bobby's home?"

"Well, he's with my asshole ex and his bitch of a second wife, yeah."

He winced. "I'm sorry, I shouldn't have brought up a sore subject."

"No, no, it's fine," she said, holding up her free hand. "Honestly, it's impossible *not* to bring it up if we're gonna talk about Bobby. Tim *is* Bobby's dad. Well, okay, he's his *father*, I don't think he's any kinda fuckin' *dad*. You know he won't let Bobby wear anime shirts?"

That visibly took Sabri aback. "Really? That's amazing."

"Right?"

"I mean, if I tried to do that with my girls, they'd just laugh in my face and continue wearing *Legend of Korra* shirts."

Unable to help herself, Kiernan chuckled. "Yeah, but you wouldn't, right?"

"Goodness, no. All it would do is foster resentment, and children resent their parents often enough on their own without our giving them help in doing so."

Kiernan took another sip of the lovely wine. "Can I ask you something?"

"Of course."

"Why do you live in this shithole? I mean, I'm here 'cause I'm tryin' to save up to pay for a really good lawyer so I can get a better custody agreement. What's your excuse?"

"Are you familiar with how much college professors are *not* paid?" Sabri said with his musical laugh. "Ambra was the true breadwinner in our house, and we hadn't gotten around to taking out life insurance policies on each other. We—" He sighed. "We thought we had more time. And once we realized we *didn't* have more time, no insurance company would touch us. So the girls and I moved to a place we can afford on the salary of an associate professor without tenure."

"I'm sorry."

"I'm not." He grinned, brightening his face. "It's a lovely neighborhood, even if the apartment itself leaves much to be desired. It's close to work, the food options are phenomenal—and I got to meet you."

Kiernan looked away, feeling herself flush a bit, though she thought it might be from the wine. "You say that now, but once you realize I'm a loudmouthed bitch, you'll probably run screaming."

Again, that musical laugh. "My dear Domenica, I've been aware that you're a loudmouthed bitch since you scared the life out of me by yelling 'fuck!' at the top of your lungs Thursday night. Note that I am neither running nor screaming."

"Well, thanks for that." She raised her glass and clinked it against his, then took another sip, which finished it off.

"You're very welcome." He still had about a third of his wine left.

After she refilled her glass, she asked, "Hey, have you ever seen *My Neighbor Totoro*?"

"I don't recognize the name."

"Really? It's a Hayao Miyazaki film—I thought your girls were into anime?"

"They are, but—when was this film released?"

"Um, late 1980s, early 1990s, 'round then."

"Ah, that explains it. My daughters do not watch anything that was made in the prior millennium."

Kiernan laughed. "Well, I don't listen to any music made in *this* millennium, so I guess it all balances out. Anyhow, *Totoro* is Bobby's favorite movie, and I *really* wanna see it right now. Will you watch it with me?"

"I would be honored."

They went into the living room and sat on the couch. She grabbed the remote and soon had the movie playing.

When the two of them sat on the couch together on Thursday, they had been at opposite ends, facing each other.

This time, they sat in the middle of the couch, both facing the television.

She wasn't sure when her hand wound up in his. But it felt warm and comforting.

They watched the movie and finished the bottle of wine, holding hands the whole time.

ACKNOWLEDGMENTS

Primary thanks go to John Harlacher and Jonathan Maberry at *Weird Tales* Presents and Blackstone Publishing, who thought this book was worth a shot; to my amazing editor Melissa Ann Singer, whose insights and edits and suggestions were brilliant; to my excellent copy editor Windy Goodloe, who made it all hold together; and to my agent, Lucienne Diver, who keeps the paperwork wheels turning expertly.

Of course, I have to thank my ever-valuable in-house editors, Wrenn Simms and GraceAnne Andreassi DeCandido. Yes, they are, respectively, my wife and my mother, but they're also professional editors with a combined fifty years' experience. Trust me, this book is way better than it would've been without their sage wisdom and red pens of doom.

Huge thanks to my five expert beta readers: Kate Brooker, a detective with the San Diego Police Department; Stephen Kerekes, a former detective with the New York Police Department; Francisco Cardona, a current NYPD officer; Jack Cullen, a retired New England police captain; and John L. French, a retired crime-scene investigator for the City of Baltimore. Any errors regarding procedure that remain in the manuscript are entirely the fault of your humble author and not these five noble, and immensely helpful, folks.

My interest in both police procedure and fantasy literature germinated at a young age. The former was sparked initially by watching *Barney Miller* and *Hill Street Blues* as a kid and fanned into a flame by David Simon's book *Homicide: A Year on the Killing Streets*, and the two fantastic TV shows that grew out of that great tome: *Homicide: Life on the Street* and *The Wire*. The latter is due to early reads of the works of Ursula K. Le Guin (the Earthsea trilogy) and J.R.R. Tolkien (*The Hobbit*), which started me down the path that led me to becoming the genre fan and genre writer I am today.

Great thanks to Shuseki Shihan Paul and everyone else at the dojo, who help keep me centered, and especially to all the kids I teach in my weekly afterschool karate class, who are always a delight.

The usual thanks to my family, both blood and chosen—not just the aforementioned wife and mom, but also the rest of the Forebearance, as well as Livia, ToniAnn, Kyle, Drew, Meredith, Sas, Anneliese, Matthew, and all the various fuzzballs: Kaylee, Louie, Professor Zoom, Loki, Jazz, and the dear departed Thor, Tempura, and Adrien.

And finally, thanks to New York City, the greatest metropolis in the world, for giving me such a great canvas on which to paint my story.

ABOUT THE AUTHOR

Keith R.A. DeCandido is a white male in his 50s, who has most recently been spotted in New York City. Armed with a laptop, he has inflicted more than sixty novels upon an unsuspecting public in addition to the one you hold in your hand. Some of these include: another series that mixes fantasy (in that case, sword-and-sorcery) with police procedure, which began with *Dragon Precinct* and has continued through five more novels (and dozens of short stories) to date; another urban fantasy series taking place in New York City, the Bram Gold Adventures, which so far includes *A Furnace Sealed* and *Feat of Clay*; and also a novel and several novellas and short stories featuring the Super City Police Department, about cops in a city filled with superheroes.

DeCandido has also perpetrated two collections of fantasy short stories set in Key West, Florida, and featuring a weirdness magnet named Cassie Zukav, entitled *Ragnarok and Roll* and *Ragnarok and a Hard Place*. He is also working on a new series about a team of superheroes in 1970s New York City, *The Inflictors*.

In addition to worlds of his own creation, DeCandido has associated with more than thirty different licensed universes, from *Alien* to *Zorro*, including works in the milieus of TV shows (*Star Trek, Supernatural, Farscape*), movies (*Cars, Kung Fu Panda, Serenity*), games (*Resident Evil, World of Warcraft, Dungeons & Dragons*), comic books (Spider-Man, Thor, the X-Men), and literary characters (Sherlock Holmes, Professor Challenger, Joe Ledger). DeCandido was granted a Lifetime Achievement Award by the International Association of Media Tie-in Writers in 2009 for his nefarious activities in this regard.

Reports indicate that DeCandido has also worked in short fiction as both author and editor. Among the recent such incidents are stories in the anthology series *Sherlock Holmes: Cases by Candlelight, Phenomenons, Forgotten Lore*, *Sherlock Holmes: Eliminate the Impossible*, and *Thrilling Adventure Yarns*, as well as in the anthologies *Weird Tales: 100 Years of Weird*, *Joe Ledger: Unbreakable*, and *The Good, the Bad, and the Uncanny*, in addition to several stories in the magazines *Weird Tales* and *Star Trek Explorer*. He has also been known to collaborate on such endeavors, having committed *Double Trouble: An Anthology of Two-Fisted Team-Ups* with Jonathan Maberry, and *The Four ???? of the Apocalypse* with Wrenn Simms.

Other known associates are the artists with whom he did comic book work, including the *Resident Evil* graphic novel *Infinite Darkness: The Beginning*, a story for the *Farscape 25th Anniversary Special*, and *Animal*, the comic book adaptation of the serial-killer novel he co-authored with Dr. Munish K. Batra.

DeCandido's other alleged crimes include nonfiction for a variety of sources, most commonly the award-winning web site Reactor Magazine (formerly Tor.com), as well as for his own Patreon (patreon.com/krad) and various essay collections published by Becky Books, Crazy 8 Press, Sequart, and ATB Publishing; being a fourth-degree black belt in karate, which he also teaches to adults and children; a musician, currently percussionist for the parody band Boogie Knights; and possibly some other questionable activity.

If you see DeCandido, do not approach him, but call for backup immediately. Among his associates are a spouse, as well as two black cats, who have the street names of "Louie" and "Kaylee." More information can be found in the casefile at www.DeCandido.net.